CROWNING DESTINY

THE FAE CHRONICLES PART TWO

AMELIA HUTCHINS

Authored By: Amelia Hutchins

Cover Art Design: Eerily Design

Copy edited by: Melissa Burg

Edited by: Melissa Burg

Published by: Amelia Hutchins

Published in (United States of America)

10 9 8 7 6 5 4 3 2 1

AMELIA HUTCHINS BOOKS

LEGACY OF THE NINE REALMS

Flames of Chaos

Ashes of Chaos

Ruins of Chaos

Crown of Chaos

Coming Soon

Queen of Chaos 2023

King of Chaos

Reign of Chaos

THE FAE CHRONICLES

Fighting Destiny

Taunting Destiny

Escaping Destiny

Seducing Destiny
Unraveling Destiny
Embracing Destiny
Crowning Destiny
Finished Series

THE ELITE GUARDS

A Demon's Dark Embrace
Claiming the Dragon King
The Winter Court
A Demon's Plaything
A Touch of Fae coming soon
Wickedly Fae coming soon.

A GUARDIAN'S DIARY

Darkest Before Dawn
Death before Dawn
Midnight Rising -TBA

MONSTERS SERIES

Playing with Monsters
Sleeping with Monsters

Becoming his Monster
Revealing the Monster
Finished Series

WICKED KNIGHTS

Oh, Holy Knight
If She's Wicked
If He's Wicked TBA

MIDNIGHT COVEN BOOKS
Forever Immortal
Immortal Hexes
Midnight Coven
Finished Series

BULLETPROOF DAMSEL SERIES
Bulletproof Damsel
Coming Soon
Silverproof Damsel
Fireproof Damsel

Alpha's Claim Standalone

WITHIN THE DARKNESS

Moon-Kissed

Night-Kissed TBA

THE DARKEST FAE

King of the Shadow Fae

Coming Soon

King of the Night Fae

Queen of the Stars

Fate Series

Whispers of Fate (Intro to Kahleena's book)

RED FLAGS SERIES

The Devil of London

The Devil's Queen

If you are following the Fae Chronicles, Elite Guards, and Monsters series, the reading order is as follows.

Fighting Destiny

Taunting Destiny

Escaping Destiny

Seducing Destiny

A Demon's Dark Embrace

Playing with Monsters

Unraveling Destiny

Sleeping with Monsters

Claiming the Dragon King

Oh, Holy Knight

Becoming his Monster

A Demon's Plaything

The Winter Court

If She's Wicked

Embracing Destiny

Crowning Destiny

Revealing the Monster

Whispers of Fate

WARNING

Warning: This book is **dark**. It's **sexy**, hot, and **intense**. The author is human, as you are. Is the book perfect? It's as perfect as I could make it. Are there mistakes? Probably, then again, even **New York Times top published** books have minimal mistakes because, like me, they have **human editors**. There are words in this book that won't be found in the standard dictionary because they were created to set the stage for a paranormal-urban fantasy world. Words in this novel are common in paranormal books and give better descriptions to the action in the story than can be found in standard dictionaries. They are intentional and not mistakes.

About the hero: chances are you may **not** fall instantly in **love** with him, that's because **I don't write men you instantly love**; you grow to love them. I don't believe in **instant love**. I write flawed, raw, caveman-like **assholes**

that eventually let you see their redeeming qualities. They are **aggressive assholes**, one step above a caveman when we meet them. You may ***not*** even like him by the time you finish this book, but I promise you will **love** him by the end of this **series**.

About the heroine: There is a chance that you might think she's naïve or weak, but then again, who starts out as a badass? Badass women are a product of growth, and I am going to put her through **hell**, and you get to watch **her** come up **swinging** every time I knock her on her ass. That's just how I do things. How she reacts to the set of circumstances she is put through may not be how you, as the reader, or I, as the author, would react to that same situation. Everyone reacts differently to circumstances and how Synthia responds to her challenges is how I see her as a character and as a person.

I don't write love stories: I write fast-paced, knock you on your ass, *make you sit on the edge of your seat wondering what is going to happen next* books. If you're looking for cookie-cutter romance, this isn't for you. If you can't handle the ride, ***unbuckle your seatbelt and get out of the roller-coaster car now***. **If not, you've been warned.** If nothing outlined above bothers you, carry on and **enjoy the ride!**

For everyone just trying to get through this crazy world, you got this. This world is a scary place, and it's my pleasure and honor to allow you to escape into the world I created on a whim. I hope you stick around for the other series coming, and to see old friends as we me need new ones. Some endings are only the beginning to new adventures. Thank you for your support, and your unwavering loyalty. My tribe, my people, and my world.

CHAPTER ONE

SYNTHIA

THIS WAS ALL WRONG. Everything seemed off and backward, and nothing made any sense. I had no memory of ever entering this flipping farting world of fairies, but there was no denying that we were in Faery.

A group of fae men stood on the far side of the room, speaking quietly amongst themselves, glancing at me every so often, while Adam and I sat alone at a table in the corner. He'd spent the last two hours trying to explain things for the third time, but he was talking a bunch of nonsense that couldn't possibly be true.

It was evident to me that he had been mind-fucked by the fae, and they were using him to turn me. That was the only explanation I could come up with to justify the batshit crazy story he was expecting me to believe.

I began to tune Adam out as my gaze slid to the largest fae male, who seemed to be watching every single thing I did with interest. It both bothered me and made my body heat in ways it never had before. I'd felt excited with Adrian, and still did, but this male? He dripped pheromones that made me ache with merely the heated gazes that he slid over my body.

If I moved, those onyx and gold-sparkled depths followed as if I was the prey he was hunting. Worse than that, my body responded as if it wanted him to pursue me, and that pissed me off. Like that fairy-farting ogre had tied an invisible string to my vagina, and as he pulled it, I quivered with the need for him to pull harder. It was disgusting. I felt my cheeks flush, and I frowned as a deadly smile graced his mouth. My eyes widened, and my nipples perked up as if they needed to be sure he'd noticed they existed. Bodies were dumb, treacherous things that took joy in betraying us. Dismissing the fae, I turned my attention back to Adam.

"We need to find Larissa and Adrian and get out of here now," I whispered. "Nothing you've said makes sense, Adam. We're in danger, big danger. Like, if we don't leave right now, we're going to be Happy Meals for these assholes." Adam leaned back in his chair and sighed. "Why aren't you panicking? Help me get us out of here, and stop lying," I muttered, glancing at the golden-eyed fae who watched me with his intense stare. I hated his sexy face and the power that rolled off him in turbulent waves. It was rolling through me, creating a deep, unsated ache that pulsed until I was afraid I would burst into spontaneous orgasms and make a total ass out of myself.

The prick had yet to take his eyes off me, and it felt like he knew me in a really intimate way. If that was the case, it meant I might also be compromised. I'd woken up in a field clothed in a flimsy-ass dress with Adam holding me in the middle of a fantasy meadow, complete with a castle in the backdrop, and no memory of how I had gotten there.

My boobs had been pushed up so high while being held in place by the bodice I was wearing that they waved hello to the asshole that wouldn't stop staring at me. It was very possible I had been in a balls-deep kind of compromised situation so horrible, that I'd blocked it out.

I had never worn shit like this. I had standards, and an outfit that exposed my body parts wasn't on the list of things I'd ever allow myself to wear, no matter what mission the guild had planned for us. I didn't care if they wanted me to strip down naked. They could suck my butt before I'd knowingly do anything of the sort.

Unless it was life or death, my moral compass directed my decisions. Considering that this was actually a life or death situation... If stripping down to my birthday suit meant getting my team out of here, I'd damn well do it. I just hoped that wasn't what it would take, but considering the hungry gaze that remained locked with mine, I was sweating bullets, because it may come down to that, or worse.

"Syn, a lot has happened." Adam fidgeted uncomfortably as he rubbed the back of his neck, studying me.

"Like what?" I leaned back in my chair, mirroring Adam's posture as I examined his body language, noting how nervous and uneasy he was at the moment. "Why do you look like someone died?"

"Someone did die, Syn," he whispered through thick emotions that caused his Adam's apple to bob up and down as he swallowed hard. "It was Lari."

Tears pricked the back of my eyes, burning to be released, and I shook my head. I cleared my throat, ignoring the vise-grip that clenched around my heart, squeezing it painfully. Adam shook his head, scrubbing his hand down his face while he adjusted in the chair.

"That's not funny at all, Adam," I hissed as tears ran down my cheeks.

"Syn, we took a mission to help the fae, and things happened. Some bad and good things have occurred in the last year. Good things like you're a mother. You have three children." He'd lost his mind. My brows shot up as I gave him a deadpan stare, and his eyes narrowed.

"I think I would know if I'd had babies, especially three. Does this body look like it's given birth to anything?" I frowned deeply, pulling the gaudy dress I wore out and looking down at my flat stomach, with not even one single stretch mark marring it.

Yup, Adam was compromised. I let the bodice snap back into place, studying him carefully, noting the way he had spoken with conviction. He believed what he was saying to be true, which meant he was feeding me whatever story the fae had wanted him to sell. Great, why was it always when I needed my team to be on-point that they got distracted and acted like a bunch of cats rolling around in a field of catnip?

"You have been brainwashed, Adam. You can shut your fat mouth because I believe nothing that rolls off your tongue. Stop feeding me whatever it is that they want you to say. Lari isn't dead; she can't be," I hissed angrily, glaring at him as his mouth opened and closed repeatedly before he sat up and shook his head.

Heavy footfalls sounded on the stone floor outside in the hallway, and I turned slowly, watching as a new male entered the room and then paused. "Oh, thank God," I whispered breathlessly, standing and rushing to Adrian.

Throwing myself at him, I wrapped my arms around him and claimed his mouth with urgency. He spun his head in the direction of the golden-eyed fae and chuckled against my lips. He pulled me closer, kissing me deeply, groaning as my tongue pushed into his mouth, and a moan slipped from my throat.

His arms lowered to rest on my waist, and his mouth drew away from mine as he studied me curiously. I stepped back, holding his hands in mine, and smiled into his pretty turquoise eyes, taking in the roguish charm that had drawn me to him. I took a step forward and leaned against his ear, whispering softly so as not to be heard.

"We need to get out of here now." My cheek brushed against his 5 o'clock shadow, and my nipples hardened with the memory of how it felt between my thighs as he'd taken me to heaven.

Adrian pulled back slightly and looked at me, confused. "Adam has been brainwashed, and I think the fae are using mind control to make him tell me things that can't possibly be true, Adrian. I need your help to get Adam and me out of here before they eat us."

I nodded my head in the fae's direction as I slid down his body, peering into the turquoise depths that studied me like I'd lost my mind. He narrowed his eyes, glanced at Adam, then the fae, and I frowned. His expression was filled with pain as my body rested flush against his.

"You broke her fucking brain, asshole?" he asked angrily, spinning toward the golden-eyed fae, the one the others had called Ryder. "What the fuck did you do to her?"

"Balls! You're compromised too?" I frowned worriedly, moving back further, turning to glare murderously at the male named Ryder, who crossed his arms. He glared at Adrian like he wanted to kill him. Adrian met his glare head-on, and I shook my head vigorously.

"A lot has happened, Adrian," Ryder snorted. "None of it good, I'm afraid."

"No. Don't look into his eyes. Look at me, baby," I whispered, pulling his face back to mine. My lips brushed against his, and I winced, stepping back as I tasted coppery blood on my lip. My hand lifted to his mouth, holding it open, and I stared at twin incisors. I pulled my hand back and slapped him hard, the noise echoing through the room as my heart thundered against my ribcage. "You have a major dental issue!" A smile curved his generous lips as his head tilted, watching me, so I slapped him again, harder this time.

"Yeah, I'm a vampire, Synthia." Adrian watched me with wide eyes as tears filled mine, and denial ripped from my lips as a sob. "No. No, angel eyes. Don't do that. Don't cry." He reached for me, and I flinched, recoiling from his touch. "Fuck, a little help here?" Everyone in the room just stared at him as if no one wanted to intervene.

"Did the entire world go crazy? What is happening?" I demanded, slowly stepping back from him, with tears rolling down my cheeks. My heartbeat echoed in my ears, my heart clenched in pain with the meaning of those fangs. Adrian was dead, as in the undead. I had to end his suffering. "What did you do to us?" I asked through trembling lips, turning my attention to Ryder.

His eyes narrowed on me, a flash of something like regret entering his beautiful depths, before he shook his head and opened his mouth to respond. I beat him to it as anger replaced sorrow, and my spine snapped into place.

"I didn't do what you think I did," Ryder snorted, pinching the bridge of his nose as Adrian looked between us in confusion.

"If you don't let us go, the entire fucking Spokane Guild is going to come down on your ass! Do you hear me? I will bring you to your fucking knees and take your pretty head from your shoulders, you fairy-farting-fuck-face fucker."

"Somehow, I doubt the guild is coming, Pet."

Anger boiled within me, and I pointed my finger at Ryder as I over-enunciated every word through gritted teeth. "I'm. Not. A. Fucking. *Pet!* My name is Synthia Raine

McKenna, and you would do well to remember it, as I will be the one to murder you, bastard."

Sighing, Ryder turned to look at the men beside him, none of which offered him any support. Turning back to me, he smiled slightly. "You'll try, I'm sure. Not today, though. Today you're just an enforcer who is in my world now, and you're not leaving until I decide otherwise." His grin increased as he walked to the front of the table and leaned against it. "Besides, can't let my girl slip away now, not when she's plotting to murder me, which is hot as hell. I look forward to playing with you, sweet wife."

My head tilted, and I snorted loudly. I crossed my arms over the gaudy white dress to glare at him, raising one delicate brow to my hairline with ire. "You think I'm buying the shit Adam is selling today? I'm smart enough to figure out they have compromised him, and that you're feeding him lies to tell me, asshole. I'm also not your *anything*. You don't own me. You're *nothing* to me. I sure in the fuck wouldn't have tripped and landed on your dick and got knocked up. You're not even pretty enough to lure me on to that pathetic little thing in your pants." I said, waving my finger in a circle, indicating his crotch. "I'm smarter than most women, and I sure as hell don't fall onto a dick just because it's attached to a pretty face, fairy boy. I mean, seriously! Adam said I died. Do I look dead? I assure you, I'm very much alive."

Taking a step forward, I ran my hands down the sides of my body and glared at Ryder. "Does this body look like it created triplets? And if it had, why the fuck would I want to come back to you? You're just some pathetic fuck that needs me to buy the lies you're selling because you can't keep me in this world without them. Fairies have laws, and they have to abide by them. I assure you, I follow no rules, and I sure as hell have not broken a single one that would allow you to hold me here. You *will* let me leave this place, and you'll watch me walk out your front door one way or another. How I do, well, that is up to you. With your head, or without it, but either way, I *will* go home."

"I think I like you better when you just wanted to get fucked by random dick."

"Excuse me? I wouldn't fuck a random dick, and I sure in the fairy-farting-blue-balls wouldn't fuck you. I'd rather play dead than touch you. You want to fuck a corpse, bring it, Fairy."

"Clearly," he chuckled huskily, watching me as if he wasn't afraid in the least of my threats—idiot.

I'd brought down monsters larger than this prick before I'd even cut teeth. I turned on my heel, flipping my hair and dismissing Ryder. I walked back to Adam, glaring over my shoulder at Adrian, who watched me with his mouth still wide open, his *fangs* on display.

"Adrian's a dead stick. I need to find an actual stake and release him from that shell he's stuck in." My throat tightened, and I fought tears that burned my eyes as my heart shattered at the reality of what that meant. I'd lose Adrian forever once I freed him. "We can't leave him like that. Adrian would hate being a vampire for all eternity, watching us age while he remained eternally cursed." Emotion clenched in my throat as pain echoed through my chest, the familiar sensation of losing more people struck me hard, threatening to swallow me whole again.

"Actually, Adrian chose this life, Synthia." Adam shrugged as if it wasn't a big deal. My gaze zeroed in on the frown tugging the corners of his mouth while he continued looking to the fae as if they held the answers he was seeking. "Let's not go pushing any stakes through his chest just yet, okay? At least wait until he pisses you off first, then you can free him."

"This is all wrong. We are inside Faery." I closed the distance between us and grabbed his hand, preventing him from leaving me. "You have to fight this hold they have on you. Do you hear me? Whatever the fae did to you, you are strong enough to fight against them, Adam. You have to. I need you to help me figure out what they have done with Lari. Do you think they are holding her upstairs? If they are, I can try seducing the big, sexy fae that wants me to believe we're married. I can use him to get up there and check it out."

Adam put his hand over his forehead as his fingers pinched his eyes like he was suffering from an extreme headache. We didn't have time for this. I turned to look at the fae, and they were all trying to act busy, but I could tell they were watching our every move. "We have to do this now, Adam, before we all end up being turned into mindless beings. I mean, what if they turn Lari into a vampire, just like they did to Adrian?"

He smiled tightly. Pain filled his gaze as he stood. "I'll be right back, okay?"

I grabbed hold of his hand before he walked away and whispered low. "Don't look into their eyes. We don't know enough about this type of fae, and they could be the nasty ones. They're obviously not Dark Fae, nor Blood. Light Fae would have already tried to seduce me into submission, and I hate to say it, but looking around, I think we may be in the Horde Kingdom, which means we have to escape like now, for reals." He tried to pull away from me, but I squeezed his hand hard as I pulled him down, forcing him to make eye contact. "Our lives are in danger, so you need to snap out of whatever the hell is going on inside your head. We need to find a way back home, regroup, and come back for the others. Understand?"

"I think we need to get Alden here," he stated, and my eyes widened, and then a frown creased my brow. My heart pounded in my ears at the idea of bringing an elder this close to the fae. Let alone that particular elder, who I thought of as family. If we were going to die, it would be better for Alden to remain where he was: safe from these monsters. There were rules, and if we went down in this shithole castle, we did it on our terms, and we didn't take anyone else down with us.

"We can't bring an elder into Faery. Are you crazy? If it comes to it, I'll take down Ryder, the big one with the golden eyes; he looks to be in charge here. They won't chance losing him with the Horde King gone. They have to be able to follow someone while he's out on his walk-about, or whatever it is he's doing. The guild thinks that power fuels the horde, and that creature is powerful. I can feel it caressing me even now."

"Take him out, how, Synthia?" Adam smirked. He spoke barely above a whisper as his eyes sparkled with mis-chief.

"I don't know, my weapons are gone," I shrugged, as if that knowledge should have been easy to figure out. "I could wield a spell and make him drown on saliva, which may cause enough confusion that we could escape as they try to save him." I turned to peek over my shoulder as Ryder's dark brows lowered while he locked gazes with me. "I think he can hear us. Let's try this," I said, clapping my hands over Adam's ears as I peered directly into his emerald-green eyes.

I focused on the spell that would deliver the telepathic channel where we could talk, but it wasn't Adam's voice that I heard in my head.

"You are so fucking delicious when you're plotting to murder me, sweet girl. My dick is hard with anticipation for you to fucking try me." A deep, rich baritone voice entered my mind, and I pulled my hands back from Adam, turning to stare at Ryder. A smile curved his lips, and I opened my mouth to tell him off, but my body ached, pulsing with need as his gaze swallowed me whole. *"Your pussy remembers me. Doesn't it? I can smell it begging me to fill it until you ache from the fullness."*

"Stay the fuck out of my head, asshole. My body's only response to you is repulsion." I narrowed my eyes at him and glared.

"Or you'll do what? Drown me with water? My saliva? Which is it, witch?"

I stood, calling my magic to me, and repeatedly blinked when nothing happened. I stared down at my hands in disbelief because my magic had never failed to come when called. I was powerless here! I huffed. My mouth opened and closed, and I crossed my arms, staring daggers at Ryder, where, no doubt, the blame should be placed. I lifted a brow, daring him to make a move against me. Fuck it. Plan B. I would rip his throat out if he tried to touch me, and I'd make him scream.

"Even without my magic, I'll still kick your ass," I warned him pointedly, studying the way the people around the room laughed.

Dark eyes smiled into mine. His sinful lips curled into a wicked grin that I wanted to slap from his too beautiful face. Numerous brands of gold and obsidian danced over his arms, pulling my focus to them. They held me enthralled for a moment, and I was hypnotized by them.

I could not look away from the way they pulled, calling me into his sinfully carnal web that would consume me whole. My hands slapped over my eyes as I spun back around, sitting down by Adam.

"This is terrible. We have to escape soon. That fae is oozing sex from his freaking pores, and my body *is* responding in ways I'm embarrassed to admit to myself, let alone you. The sooner we break out of this place, the better. I'm guessing he is just letting those powers work their way over here until I cannot deny how they're affecting me. If they turn me FIZ, you have to get out of here; promise me you will escape. Do you understand what I am saying to you?" I was telling Adam to abandon me and live. Leave me here to this hellish fate where I would be turned mindless and forced to lay in a bed awaiting this monster's lust, unknowingly.

"I do," Adam replied carefully. Standing, he glanced over at me before lifting his eyes heavenward as if he were trying to figure out how to handle the situation. "I'll be right back. Don't stake Adrian while I'm away, okay? You actually are fine with Adrian being a vampire, Synthia."

"Whatever, I'll wait, but we cannot leave him like that."

I watched Adam as he crossed the room, narrowing my eyes, when he stopped in front of the male named Ryder. He wasn't just drop-dead gorgeous. Ryder's gaze burned with an intensity that ate away at my soul, consuming my will as it chipped away at my resolve until nothing was left.

Those eyes held mine, and I repeatedly swallowed, trying to ignore the desire that rushed through me, wrapping around me, causing my sex to clench with need. I wanted to scream in frustration because Adrian never had this effect on me. He had never made my panties need to be changed. I was sure if I snuck into the bathroom, I could actually wring them out. I surveyed Ryder carefully as Adam whispered into his ear.

"Balls," I muttered as I rubbed the tension in my temples from being wound tighter than a bowstring.

A commotion started in the hall and continued to the doors. Turning, I watched in horror as Alden entered, staring across the room before he moved to Ryder. I was up, running before I could talk myself out of it.

I leaped into the air, landing high on Ryder's back, and then I wrapped my arms around his neck, holding on. He made a strangled sound of surprise as everyone else observed, but didn't move from where they stood.

"Run, Alden!" I screamed, offering myself as a sacrifice for him to survive.

"Why would I run, kid?" Confused, he looked from me to Ryder, then back as he frowned. "What the hell is happening?"

"You have to escape. Now!"

"Did you change sides in the war? Ryder, what the hell is wrong with her?"

I huffed, noting Ryder wasn't even fighting against me, just huffing as well. I slid down his back and scrutinized him, *laughing* at me.

I growled and kneed him in the nuts, watching him drop before I knelt in front of him. My finger tilted his chin up as I peered into his pretty eyes and smiled coldly. His lips lifted in a sneer, the first sign of anger he'd exhibited since I'd awakened on the field.

"You may have compromised my team, but you will never compromise me, dick-face fairy-fuck," I hissed.

"Pet, I knocked you up and tore that pretty pussy up until it *viscerally* knew who owned it. I wrote my fucking name on your soul, and I assure you, I will do it again until you remember that you're my wife. You already feel me. You may hate it, but you feel me inside of you, but that's okay. I can wait you out. I damn sure plan to remind you why you're mine, vividly, in every sexual way you're imagining us together in that pretty head of yours." His golden eyes stared challengingly at me.

"Fuck you, Fairy."

"Nah, little girl," he whispered huskily, licking his lips, which held me mesmerized as I imagined how they'd feel against my girly parts. His finger lifted my chin until I was forced to peer into his star-banked depths, lost in the galaxies of constellations that sparkled and burned for me and me alone.

"I'm not little."

"I'm going to fuck you so hard that every time you sit down tomorrow, that pussy aches deliciously while you're reminded of who the fuck made it throb as it clenches with the need to be fucked again. You'll remember me tearing you up as you screamed for more, coming undone around me until you're a quivering, shaking mess that pleads to be fucked repeatedly because you always fucking do, Pet. You're insatiable, just like me, Synthia. If you're a good girl, I may even give it to you a few times without making you beg for it."

I laughed outright in his face at the absurdity of his words. "Oh, you're hysterical if you think that is happening. Dream on! As if I'd ever beg for your dick. I'd rather ring the devil's doorbell alone than ever let you touch it," I snorted, turning to stare at Alden. "I can't believe he got to you, too! Of all the stupid shit you have taught us! You should have been the one freaking person he couldn't reach, old man! What the hell were you thinking coming here? And why the hell would you even step foot into Faery? You taught us that if they pulled a coven into Faery, they were a lost cause. But no, here you are! Inside. Faery. Old. Man!" I threw my hands up, stomping back to the other side of the room with hopelessness that ate at me as my mind ran scenarios around how we could have ended up here, and none of them were good.

"Are you seriously giving me the *what-for* right now?" Alden's eyebrows shot to his hairline as he looked around the room. "What the hell is happening? Syn? Ryder?" he asked, turning his steel-colored eyes between us in confusion. "Why do you sound like the *old* Syn?"

"I'm not old! Balls!" I stomped further away from Alden, huffing as I sat in the chair, glaring daggers at the huge Neanderthal who was now speaking to Alden. I watched as Alden threw back his head, laughing at whatever the jerk was saying. I glowered, growing angrier by the moment.

"Well, now you know how it feels to lose every memory of who you were and who they expect you to become again. It's not a pleasant feeling being fractured. Now you've gotten a taste of what I've been dealing with these past few months." A beautiful redhead slid next to me into the empty chair. Her power slithered over me, and I studied her blue gaze. She was more powerful than anyone else in the room, even though she'd dimmed her energy.

"You're not fae. What are you?" I asked bluntly.

"What am I?" She laughed, tapping her fingers on the table. "A little bit of everything, but right now? I'm a friend. You may not remember it, but when I needed a friend, you were there for me, Synthia. My memories are also scattered, so out of everyone here, I understand what you're going through the most. No matter how much I pretend otherwise, I can still only access a tiny percentage of my memories. Besides that, I'm also the Goddess of War, and good to have on your side." She wiggled her brows, handing me a bottle.

"I am not accepting food or drink from any fae."

"I'm not fae, now am I? You need a drink, and I don't need to be told that you don't drink alcohol at whatever age your brain is saying you are. You weren't the good girl at the guild. I know. Alden's told me horror stories about you that personally make me like you even more."

"Great. Since when did the fae become able to compromise the gods? No wonder everything is so fucked." Picking up the bottle, I tipped it back, drinking deeply to ease the ache in my chest. I watched the man who had raised me, studying me alongside that frustrating fae, who nodded, smiling smugly. "I'm going to kill him."

"Well, at the very least, you should definitely kick his ass."

"I think I'm going to like you," I announced, handing her the bottle of scotch.

"Hey, we're already friends. Not that I'm opposed to starting over, but I am hoping my friend comes back soon, Synthia. She's a badass, and we need her to fight this war."

"What war?" I demanded.

"The one we're balls-deep in the middle of, and unable to stop without her," she admitted, passing me the scotch again.

"Awesome, just fucking awesome," I groaned, uncertain who to believe anymore.

My team had been brainwashed, as was Alden himself. Hell, I wasn't certain that at this point that I wasn't compromised as well. My body ached with a need to be touched, and I was never needy. I had never craved sex, but here I was, wet with anticipation for the asshole that held some invisible control over my body. Everything inside of me lit up like a Christmas tree in December every single time those golden-flecked eyes landed on me.

Ryder chuckled huskily, pulling my attention to where he stood, watching me with a wicked smile on his lips. My nipples pebbled with anticipation, beckoning him to taste them. My pussy clenched, weeping to be filled. I'd fallen down a rabbit hole, and in that rabbit hole, I was a hussy who wanted that monster to spread me wide and fuck me until I no longer cared to escape this alternate universe in which I'd woken. Ryder's nostrils flared, and I shrank away from his gaze, praying to Hecate that he couldn't smell the arousal that soaked my core. The hungry look in his eyes told me he could, and I blushed like some stupid school girl crushing on the bully who pushed her around. I was such an idiot.

CHAPTER TWO

ALDEN ATTEMPTED TO EXPLAIN everything to me slowly. The problem was, it was precisely the same story that Adam tried to convince me was true. My eyes literally could not roll back any further because they actually hurt. I shook my head, scowling through a growl of frustration as I glared at the elder who had been like a parent to me.

Alden and Adam had spent the last couple of hours telling me lies, and I'd started to block them out as I stared murderously at the male who now sat beside other fae men, glaring back at me as if we were in some kind of fae fucking standoff. He sat slightly forward, with his fingers steepled in front of him, oozing confidence he had no business leaking.

"Why would I marry that *thing*?" I demanded, throwing my hand in the direction of the asshole they were expecting me to believe I'd wanted to marry. As if! I wasn't even old enough to want to get married, let alone the fact that I would never marry a creature like Ryder. He was fae, and I loathed every single detail about his breed. I had high standards, or at least higher than that!

"Because you love him," Alden shrugged and sighed as he observed me rolling my eyes for the hundredth time in annoyance and disbelief. His hand scrubbed down his face, and he peered toward Adam, who grunted as he shook his dark head.

"No, I don't even know him. If I did, I sure as fuck wouldn't marry him. You also said I died, and clearly, I'm not dead. Not to mention that if I were actually some kind of goddess, wouldn't I have powers? And if I had powers, wouldn't I use them to get out of this place and back to the guild?"

"What's the last thing you remember?" Adrian asked from a safe distance away from me. I'd unsuccessfully tried to free him from the meat suit he wore three times already. They finally removed all the stakes—or items that could be made into stakes—out of my reach, unfortunately.

"You and me, in the catacombs," I snapped, blushing as a smile lifted over Adrian's sinfully hot lips.

"The last thing you remember is me taking your virginity?" He lifted his brows and slid his gaze down my body as he swallowed hard.

"Yeah, but you had a pulse when I let you touch me, dick." I dismissed him and looked away.

"Holy fuck! She's seventeen." Adrian's eyes widened, and then he turned to look at Adam, who had suddenly gone still.

"We're fucked," Adam groaned, rubbing his eyes with his fingers. "Do you remember her at seventeen?"

"I do, unfortunately," Alden groaned, running his hand through his hair. "I've never written that many accident reports in my entire life." Someone walked across the room, handing Alden pictures, and he set them on the table in front of me.

I studied the one with Ryder, kissing me in a dress I'd never wear in a million years. We looked happy together in the Photoshopped wedding pictures. Whoever had worked to make it look real had done an amazing job. His hands cradled my cheeks as we stared into one another's eyes, happiness basking in them. I picked up another photo from the pile, staring at the children that stood around Ryder and me, causing pain to throb between my eyes.

I quickly hid it beneath the other, ignoring the tightening in my chest their little faces created. The next photo was of the guild, and yet again, Ryder was in the picture with several other men, but he didn't fit into the photo. He and his men, who obviously had been edited into the image, weren't smiling. The next was of us older, and I frowned, turning to look at Alden.

"Where is Adrian in these? We were never separated."

"He, uh... he died, Syn. Adam, you may want to step back for these next images."

"I can handle it," Adam said, resting his hand on his knee that bounced nervously.

Alden handed me a folder, and I pulled out the pictures and dropped them to scatter over the floor as I stood, shaking my head. Nausea churned in my belly while I repeatedly moved my head from side to side.

Tears burned and pricked in my eyes. A sob broke from my lips as it rocked through me. I slammed my hands down on the table, and I stared into Alden's shocked expression. Rage bubbled up through my chest, and I screamed at him, growling until my entire body trembled in horror from the grotesque images contained in the file.

"Why would you show these to me? Where is she?" I demanded, pacing as denial and fear pulsed through me, tightening in my belly until I was confident I was going to throw up everywhere.

"Calm down, Synthia," Alden muttered, pinching his nose in frustration.

"Where is Lari? That's not her!" I pointed at the pictures as a sob exploded from my lips. "It can't be! I'd remember that!" My hands went to my hair before I moved to the table, shredding the photos before I threw them at the men sitting there. "You're lying! She isn't dead! She can't be! You're all horrible people."

"Lari died, Syn. You went to the apartment, and she was being tortured. You were tortured too, and she was killed while you watched." Adam stood as if he would comfort me. I clamped my hands over my ears and shook my head as tears ran down my cheeks. "She's gone."

"No! You're sick! You are all sick! This isn't a game, where *is* she?! What did you do to her?" I demanded, staring at Ryder, who studied me without the cockiness he'd shown before.

His eyes held regret, and his hands clenched as if he wanted to comfort me through the pain, and worse, I craved it from him. Unlike my coven, he wasn't trying to show me horrendous pictures that depicted my best friend cut up and missing parts of her body.

"Synthia, a lot has happened. You need to recall who you are now," Alden said as he stood. "We're trying to help you remember, but you have to want to come back from this. Let us help you."

"No, you're compromised and under their control. You all are! *You* need to wake the fuck up and fight it! Your tattoos should be working. Mine is! Titus's tattoos suck. I warned you to replace that loser weeks ago."

"This isn't working," Adam said with a disgruntled sigh, watching me through watery eyes, unwilling to look down at the table where Alden had returned the torn pieces of the pictures.

His unwillingness to look at them made my stomach flip. He'd always had a thing for Larissa, and if they were affecting me this much, even turned against me, he was having a hard time looking at the fake photos.

"What did you expect? She's fucking seventeen! The last thing she remembers is my dick and the catacombs, which I'm sure won't impress her husband," Adrian sneered.

"What did you just fucking say?" Ryder asked, and I blinked, watching him.

"She's seventeen years old, and that is when I deflowered her. I fucked her. I took her down to the catacombs, and I popped that succulent cherry, asshole." Adrian looked like he was taking great pleasure in repeating the details of our first sexual experience as he smiled smugly at Ryder.

I repeatedly blinked, watching the anger that formed on Ryder's features as he closed the distance between himself and Adrian in one fluid motion. He reached for Adrian, and the room exploded into action as everyone pulled them apart.

I turned, staring at the wooden chair I sat in while everyone struggled to protect Adrian from Ryder as they fought. I snapped the leg off it and swallowed down the agony of my decision.

Turning back to the tangled bodies as they rolled over the floor, assaulting each other, I closed my eyes, fighting for strength before sending a silent prayer to Hecate. I started forward toward the boy I loved, intending to end his suffering.

"That's my wife. If you fucking kiss her again, I'll pull out your fucking fangs."

"She was mine first, and then you took her from me, fucker. I can't change that I had her first, nor would I," Adrian snapped, turning red eyes toward me as I held up the stake and rushed at him.

Ryder's hand shot out, slapping the stake from mine before he smiled, throwing his head back and laughing. His gaze burned with naked heat as it settled on me, a roguishly handsome smile tugging against his lips as he exhaled the tension.

"I don't have to kill you. Synthia is going to do it for me."

"Syn, do not stake me! You like me like this, remember? I'm your boyfriend," Adrian said, holding his arms out as a deep growl rose from Ryder's lungs.

All around us, people were laughing, and my heart was breaking. My eyes filled with angry tears as my stomach churned, clenching while my pulse echoed in my ears until I felt it in the vein above my eye. Everything and everyone was wrong here.

It was as if I'd stepped into the worst episode of the *Twilight Zone*, and I couldn't escape. Tears rolled down my cheek, which Ryder seemed to note first. His hand lifted, and his thumb wiped the tears away.

His hand against my cheek sent a shock wave of heat coursing through me to pool between my thighs. His scent slammed against me, heady and intoxicating, as my body clenched, heating in a way that terrified me. I stepped away from his touch. His eyes widened and then narrowed while remaining locked with my own.

"If you really want to, I'll hold Adrian down so you can kill him, Pet."

"I want to go home," I whispered through trembling lips. "I just want to leave here with my friends. Let us go, and I'll do anything you want me to do."

"How about this? You give me a few nights to show you who I am? After that, if you still want to go home, I'll let you leave."

"What game are you playing?" I asked, watching him carefully while I replayed his words, ensuring he wasn't trying to manipulate or trick me.

"I will take you and your friends to the portal. I'll let you walk away from me if you still wish to do so after I've reminded you of who you are and what I am to you. Give me a few nights. My rules, though."

"Are you going to rape me if I agree to your terms?"

"I have never raped you or forced you to fuck me. I love you, woman."

"I thought the fae couldn't tell lies?" I asked, tilting my head while I sucked my bottom lip between my teeth, which made his eyes lower to my mouth.

Ryder's smile tightened. His intense gaze watched me as I became lost within their depths, unable to look away. He didn't reply, and I mentally shook myself from the daze his perfection had locked me in.

I studied my team that was depending on me to get them out of here. Well, what was left of it, that was. They all nodded at me encouragingly, and I glared at them.

Bastards.

Of course, they'd agree to use me as bait to set them free. They had no idea of the sex-induced stupidity this prick was creating within me. My vagina was all amped up and calling him to play peekaboo with his cock.

Releasing my breath, I reluctantly held up two fingers. "Two days."

"I'm not negotiating days, Synthia. Not with how fucking stubborn you are."

"How many days do I have to stay here with you, then?"

"One week. At the end of the week, if you don't love me again, or remember who I am, you can walk away. Hell, when you remember who I am, you may still want to leave."

"Why? If I truly loved you, why would I want to leave you, Ryder?" I placed my hand on my hip, tilted my head, and studied him cautiously.

His pupils constricted as his name rolled off my tongue. His words were thick, filled with emotion. "Because I fucked up big time with you." He lifted his hand to touch my face, only to pull away when I flinched. "I left my greatest love in a pit full of monsters, and she came out of it as someone who doesn't even remember who I am. I'm not so sure I deserve her love anymore."

"Why the hell would you do that to someone you're supposed to love? You're a fucking dick."

"Yeah, but that dick is the thing that made you mine." He wiggled his eyebrows, no doubt trying to lighten my mood.

"Are we talking metaphors here?"

"No, you love my dick." The look of smug satisfaction was enough to make me puke.

"Oh, this is awkward, but I wouldn't touch your dick with Adrian's dick, and I actually liked his dick."

Ryder bent down and held out the stake. "Try it again. I promise not to interfere and save Adrian this time."

"Really?" I took the stake, and he held his hands up and stepped back.

"Really, fucker? You know, she was a total badass at seventeen. Right?" Adrian groaned as I turned, smiling sadly as I took a step toward him. "Come on, this is so wrong on so many levels, Ryder!"

"You kissed my wife, so I'm willing to help her out," Ryder chuckled, sitting down and placing his arms behind his head, watching as Adrian started forward.

"Oh, that's sweet," I said, tilting my head, studying Adrian. He observed me, noting every subtle move I made. He was so handsome, even without a pulse. "Baby, you wouldn't want to live like this."

"Oh, no, I'm totally good with it. Fangs are a chick magnet." He shrugged before his hands rose in mock surrender when my brows lifted, and I pierced him with a look of anger.

"Really, asshole? You are supposed to be my boyfriend. You know that, right?"

"Adrian, run!" Adam doubled over in laughter, watching as I launched myself at Adrian. Adrian caught my arm and snorted, grasping my hand that held the stake over my head. Eyes the color of the Caribbean seas crinkled as he chuckled. He knew every move I could make since we'd trained together growing up.

"Help me, asshole!" Adrian shouted at Adam. "I don't want to hurt her. She's only seventeen."

"She's not seventeen, you idiot, she's a fucking goddess," Adam laughed, holding his stomach as he hooted while tears ran from his eyes. "Either fight back, or you're about to end up ashes, vampire."

Adrian took me to the floor, rolling me until the stake was beside me, then one last roll ended with me on top of him, his hands holding my wrist against my chest as he smirked. He lifted his hips, and my lips parted as he watched me.

"You guys are stupid," I said, pulling back to stare at Adrian, who tossed the stake away and placed his hands on my hips.

"You want to ride it?" he asked before he was picked up and tossed aside by Ryder. "Sorry, but she's mine at the moment. I'm her *boyfriend*." Adrian grinned, then looked at me seriously. "God, woman, what I wouldn't give for a redo to go back in time with you and make you see you were worth so much more than I could ever give you."

"Yeah? How well did that work out for you last time?" Ryder asked, noting the way my heated gaze slid to him. Even with Adrian present, I was drawn to the flipping fairy. That's annoying.

"Don't threaten my boyfriend!" I said, standing up to glare at the obsidian eyes that studied me.

His smile was all wolf, and I was pretty sure he could follow it with one hell of a bite. Galaxies swirled within his eyes, and they lost me within them as I stepped closer, peering up at him. My mouth opened as something tingled in the back of my mind. Before I could think better of it, my hands rested against his solid, muscle-covered chest, heat meeting my palms.

"See something you like, little one?"

"Did you steal the stars?" I whispered breathlessly, as my heart pounded against my ribcage.

"No, but for you, I'd steal them all," he uttered, cupping my chin. "You sleep with me tonight, little witch."

"The fuck I do, pervert!" His words yanked me out of the spell he'd been weaving over my senses. It was like pouring a bucket of melting ice over my head. "I'm not that easy. It was one time in the catacombs. Do you think it was easy for him to get me? I'm not a hooker, asshole.

Besides, I plan to marry Adrian," I said, crossing my arms over my chest, then caught myself as I remembered Adrian was now a vampire. "Or I was, but now he's dead, so that's a problem."

"I married you."

"Did not."

"Did too," he said, smiling. "I know every inch of you, and everything you like done to that gorgeous body in bed. I know how you taste on the tip of my tongue when you come on it, and how you scream when I stretch that tight pussy with my cock. I promise you. You will remember me. Maybe not today, but soon you will remember who I am, woman."

"What about the girl you left in the pit?"

"Oh, she's going to hunt my ass down and probably kick it for fucking with her. She's a spitfire and the most beautiful woman in the world."

"Dude, you're a total dick. You want to take me to your bed, but yet you love her."

"Yeah, I'm an asshole, but I'm okay with that. You promised me one week, and then if you want, you get to leave here with your coven. Now, shake on it."

I held out my hand, watching as his swallowed mine. Idiot. He had no idea that I would never agree to anything unless there was a contract involved, or I couldn't see a way out of the situation via an overlooked loophole. I smiled as his eyes narrowed.

"I'm going to need a contract with you."

"Balls."

CHAPTER THREE

I SAT AT A huge sprawling table filled with food, and every time Adam or Alden reached for it, I slapped their hands and glared at them. Ryder, the pigheaded bastard who sat across from us, watched me like *I* was the feast. The heat in his eyes alone was enough to roast me alive, and there was a visceral need within me to let him. His presence offended every sensible part of me while heating the delicate parts until I was certain I would burst into flames at any moment.

Tearing my gaze from his, I turned in time to watch Alden loading his plate full of food the fae had provided. "You know not to eat the food in Faery!" I hissed, slapping his silverware away from his hand as his eyes widened. "They can do bad things to you if you accept and eat anything they give you."

"The food can do bad things to you?" Alden asked, leaning over to whisper.

"No, the fae," I murmured behind my hand. Ryder watched me with his lips tight together, as if he were fighting a smile, or worse, laughter. Everyone seemed to be laughing at us. "It's said that if they offer you food or drink, and you consume any of it, they can keep you forever. So, stop putting food on your plate. No matter what they've done to your brain, you should remember that golden rule. You were, after all, the one who taught us, idiot. Stop being stupid!"

He shrugged and put more food on his plate, completely ignoring my warning.

"I'm hungry, and they can hear us, Synthia," Alden reached across me and grabbed a small bowl of butter. He sat back and began to slather it all over a piece of the delicious smelling bread that had just been placed on the table, along with enough roasted meats and vegetables to feed a small army.

I had to admit, the food smelled divine, and my stomach rumbled in agreement. Whatever, I wouldn't be tempted. At least one of us had to stay strong, and clearly, it wouldn't be Alden.

"Then eat it, old man. But don't you come crying to me if you turn into a brownie or worse, a redcap. Those little suckers are nasty, and I won't hesitate to pop a cap in your ass if you so much as wink at me as one."

"Pop a cap in my ass?" Chuckling, he accepted a glass filled with an amber liquid from the server, held it up to me in mock cheers, and downed the drink. Great. Now he had eaten and drank from a fae-tainted meal.

"Yeah, it means to shoot you, duh." I rolled my eyes and turned to Adam, who had a half-eaten plate of food sitting in front of him and was currently shoveling more food into his mouth. "You too? We don't even know which caste has us, and you're both throwing caution to the wind and eating and drinking whatever you want. Have you both lost your damn minds?"

"The horde," Ryder answered, and I sat back, staring across the table at him.

I'd suspected as much, but his words created a rapid beat in my chest, and my palms began to sweat. Of all the castes of fae in Faery, the horde was the most ruthless and bloodthirsty of them all.

Ryder was watching me, looking for any sign of weakness or fear. A normal person would probably be afraid of the horde. Scratch that, they should *definitely* fear the horde. But I was not a normal person. I was an enforcer, and I refused to give this asshole the satisfaction of seeing any panic on display.

"And has your *king* returned from prancing around the countryside?" My tone was flippant, and I smirked wickedly. I was daring Ryder to argue that his king wasn't out, ignoring his duties as his people flooded into our world unchecked. Someone needed to find the Horde King, stick a flower up his ass, and plant him back on his throne.

"Indeed, he has, Syn." Why did he look like the cat that had just eaten the canary? "He recently returned and took a wife soon after he ascended to the throne."

"My name is Synthia. Only people I like get to call me Syn, and I definitely don't like you."

Heat filled Ryder's eyes, and I glared at him as his attention dipped to my chest. I brought my middle finger up against my breasts, flipping him off. His mouth twitched in amusement, and his eyes rested once more on my face.

"So, Syn, what do you like to do for fun?" Taking a bite of meat, he chewed slowly and licked his lips before cutting another piece of meat and repeating the process. I sat mesmerized as I watched his mouth. He leaned forward and grinned. And just like that, the spell broke.

"I like to kill fae, especially horde fae. They're so fun to hunt." I squared my shoulders and refused to break eye contact. Two could play that game. "If your king has returned, where is he?"

I wasn't actually sure I wanted to meet him, but who could say they'd truly seen the Horde King? None of the guild elders had seen him, minus Alden. Now he would see him for the first time *with* me.

He waved his fork in a circular motion. "He's around."

"Around where?" I leaned forward and batted my thick lashes at him. In the guild, we learned seduction early so that we could use it on the fae.

"Close by." He mirrored my pose, resting his elbows on the table to study me. "Would you like to meet him?" The corner of his mouth tipped up just a bit like he was in on some great secret and would share it with me, probably for a price that I wasn't willing to pay.

"Actually, I would," I challenged through trembling lips. What the fuck was I doing? He could sift in, and I'd be a fucking goner! I had no weapons. They'd even taken away all my silverware except for my spoon because I'd tried to stab Ryder with my fork the moment he'd sat down. "Produce him."

There was a loud thunk, like the sound of an umbrella opening as wings expanded from Ryder's back. I screamed, pushing away from the table, knocking my chair to the floor to hide behind. There was a moment of silence, and then the entire room burst into uncontrollable laughter.

"Holy fairy-fucking buckets!" I shouted, peering over the chair as power erupted through the room, and Ryder's body grew.

I swallowed a girly scream and looked down, realizing I had food all over me. I lifted my head, gaping at the creature across from me, then stood on shaking legs as I stared at the enormous wings his chair seemed to accommodate surprisingly well.

"Would you like some gravy to go with the potatoes on your breasts?" Leaning forward, he looked at me as if he was starving, and I was a four-course meal. "I'd be happy to lick it off if you'd like."

"No... not an issue. I love potatoes!" I backed up, scooping a bit of the potato from my chest and flicking it to the floor. Glancing at Alden, I found him still shoveling food into his mouth. "Alden, why aren't you freaking the fuck out?" I hissed.

"Because you married the Horde King, and he's a friend now?" he answered in a dry tone before pushing more food into his mouth and chewing it.

"You guys are way messed up! This explains *so* much!" I said, staring at the wings.

"Do you want to touch them?" Ryder asked, noting where my gaze remained locked.

"Yes... *No!*" I amended quickly. "This is so fucking weird." I went to sit and missed the overturned chair, causing everyone to laugh at me again. I stood and frowned, glaring at Ryder. "I need to use the ladies' room."

"No, you don't. You are not sneaking out the window and looking for a portal."

"You can read my mind?" I sat again, only to remember the chair wasn't up right. I fixed it, sitting carefully, staring at him from a safe distance several feet away from the table.

"Hmm, wouldn't that be interesting if I could?" He shrugged as he pushed a dessert ball between his lips and chewed, studying me.

I pictured myself stabbing him a thousand times and eating the pieces of his corpse. His mouth turned up in the corners, sinfully sexy. He sat back, watching me as I crossed my arms, lifting my chin in defiance.

"You're picturing me naked, little one? I can make that fantasy your new reality."

"I am *not*!" A blush covered my cheeks as I glowered at him. Whew, at least he couldn't read my mind, because that was the last thing I was thinking.

"Now you're stripping, too? Damn, you're a dirty girl for a seventeen-year-old." His eyes were hooded, and his voice dripped with sex. "Take it all off, little one."

I blushed to my roots and shook my head vigorously. My body heated, causing my eyes to grow rounded and wide with embarrassment as hormones rushed through me. My hands lifted, covering my eyes before I spread my fingers, glaring at him because now I *was* picturing us naked. He was amazingly built in my imagination, and no matter how much I tried, I couldn't get the image out of my mind.

"Are you...? Oh, my gods, take it all." He moaned as he reached between his legs.

I jumped from the chair, launching myself at him over the table, causing dishes and food to go flying around us as we landed together on the floor.

"I am not a dirty girl!" I slapped his face, and he grinned. "I am not picturing you naked, fucking fairy! Take it back!" Ryder's hands gripped my hips where I sat above him, pressing against his lower half as my hands gripped tightly around his throat. His hips rolled, and I gaped down at him. I tried to lift off of him, but he held me in place, causing my eyes to peer down where he was hard and hung like a horse. "Is that a rock in your pocket? What *is* that?" I dropped my hand between his legs to feel what was hard in his pants against my sex. It continually grew as I touched it. My blush intensified as the realization of what I held dawned on me. "Oh, balls."

"Actually, that's a dick, one you've had many times before."

He thrust his hips forward, and I jumped up and off of him as if he were on fire. Everyone laughed at me, forcing my anger to rise with the absurdity of his words and actions.

I spun around, noting I wore enough food on me to end up as screwed as Alden and Adam without even taking a bite. Then a shiver went up my spine as comprehension sank in that I'd just tackled the Horde King, and he was *laughing* at me. He hadn't lashed out or attacked me for assaulting his person. This entire day was fucking whacked out on Scooby Snacks.

"Adam?"

"Yeah, Syn?"

"Did we drop a hit of acid again?" That was the only logical explanation. It would explain so much if this were just a bad trip. That would account for all the beautiful colors and exotic meats and smells. That would also justify Ryder's wings and why Alden was so blasé about the whole situation.

"Um..." Adam scratched his neck, turning to wince at the look on Alden's face.

"I've got to be tripping. I mean, I just tackled the Horde King and groped his rather enormous dick." I laughed nervously as I indicated its presumed size, then put my hands down so as not to embarrass myself any further. "Pretty sure that would be enough to get me dead if this scenario was real." I put my hand on my neck and pressed my fingers into my skin. "I can feel my pulse, which means I'm still alive. I told you we couldn't drop acid when we're at the guild!"

"You did acid at the guild?" Alden snapped.

"Balls."

"We were seventeen," Adam groaned, covering his mouth as he watched me. "You're not tripping, Syn. This is all really happening." He shook his head like he was having a hard time believing his own words. "You haven't said balls since Adrian died."

"He just died, duh," I snorted, stepping back as the Horde King rose to his feet. He towered over me, causing my neck to ache as I leaned back to hold his gaze, becoming lost within it. "I didn't mean to grab your penis."

"You've done a lot more than that with my *penis*, woman."

"You can lie! I know I didn't have that thing anywhere near me. I'd die!"

His husky chuckle made heat flash through me, echoing the fire that lit within his eyes. "You didn't die from my cock. That isn't what killed you, Pet. You take the entire thing and beg me for more, quite often."

"Liar." I stared at him a moment longer and yawned, feigning exhaustion. If I couldn't get to a bathroom alone, maybe I could escape from a bedroom window. "I'm tired. Can someone who isn't the Horde King show me where I will sleep tonight?"

"You sure you're ready? Because you *will* sleep with me tonight," he mused with a wolfish glint in his gaze.

My lady parts did a little flip, and I immediately shut that down. "I'm surprisingly not tired at all anymore." I shrank back, and he closed the distance between us, butting me up against the table as he placed his hands on either side of me, caging me in.

"You're sitting on my plate. Unless you're offering to be my dinner, I suggest you move back to your side of the table, *wife*. I assure you, after watching you today, there's nothing more I want to do than remind you to whom the fuck you belong."

I swallowed past the hard lump that tightened in my throat with his words. I watched as the predator side of him was exposed for me to see, and it was both exciting and terrifying at the same time.

"Are you going to move, so I don't have to touch you?"

"No," he smirked roguishly, inspecting me through heavily hooded eyes.

I leaned closer, toward his luscious mouth, watching as his eyes locked on my tongue that trailed over my lips as if he'd implanted the idea of kissing me. The moment our lips brushed over one another, and his tongue slipped out as if to delve between mine, I chuckled, ducking beneath his arms to move away.

"Like I'd kiss you? Bleh, please, you're not even my type." I smirked until a man blocked my path, his expression consumed with pain as he watched me. He alone had been the only one who hadn't laughed at what was happening to me here.

"Flower," the silver-eyed male said. I stopped mid-step, drawn by what was displayed openly in his eyes. There was a sadness to him that tugged at my heart and made me pause.

I knew that look because I'd worn it well when his kind had murdered my parents. "You're grieving and in immense pain from your loss."

He nodded slowly. "I lost someone whom I loved very much."

"You're fae. Everyone knows the fae do not love one another."

He smiled and searched my face before snorting. "Funny. Coming from you, that's really fucking ironic and almost hilarious. Excuse me, Flower." He stepped around me and left the room silently.

Tears pricked at my eyes, but I didn't understand why I'd feel bad for him or his kind. Something inside of me seemed to *think* I should. I turned on my heel, moving back around the table. Sitting, I lifted my eyes to Ryder and examined the pain flitting over his features before he muttered.

"You should leave Ristan alone," Ryder said softly.

"The fae don't love. They don't understand the emotion or what it means to care for someone. If they do, it's only an act to lure their victims in as a ploy. Which is exactly why I wouldn't have married you," I pointed out, watching his eyes narrow at my words. "You could never love me. You, of all the fae, aren't capable of loving anything because you're the evilest of them all, Horde King."

Silence met my declaration, and all eyes moved from me to Ryder. Sighing, he leaned back in his chair and tapped his index finger a few times on the table, seeming deep in thought. "I believed that too until someone worth loving knocked me on my ass and altered my way of thinking. She changed everything."

"Sounds like she wasn't all that successful if you're still trying to eat me for dinner, Fairy," I shrugged, eyeing the pie. I mean, I was already wearing my dinner. What would one piece of pie hurt?

"Hungry? You were starving earlier," Ryder asked, a brow lifted in question.

"Actually, I lost my appetite." Guess I wouldn't be eating the pie, either. Asshole.

"Good, let's go to bed."

I almost swallowed my tongue trying to think of something that would stall being alone with him, but Alden stood as well, yawning, and nodded while admitting exhaustion. Adam rose as well, leaving me with Ryder and the other fae. Everyone in the room watched me until Ryder cleared his throat, and then they all vanished at once, leaving us alone.

Ryder stood, moving around the table to where I was standing, his hand extended, and he smiled as heat ignited in his golden eyes. "Come with me, Pet."

"I really don't think that's a good idea."

"I know, but I promise not to bite, or make you dance for me."

"People do that for you?" I asked, and when he grinned, I elaborated on what I'd meant. "Dance, I mean."

"One girl did, and I lost myself with her in that moment."

"Like forgot where you were?"

"No. I knew where I was and who I was, but the way she moved, and the taste of her lips, it made me feel drunk from the fire she created within me."

"I have this bad feeling that you're talking about me. I think I should get a restraining order or something."

"Give me your hand."

"I can't sift, and you can't sift me. You'll make me heave my guts up or worse. I heard one time a fae grabbed this girl, and he tried to sift her, but only part of her actually left. Boom, she was dead instantly."

"We'll walk then," he shrugged. "Hand, now, woman."

I lifted my hand to give it to him, but the air grew thicker, and then he moved. Instead of where he'd stood, feet from me, offering his hand, Ryder was pressed against my body, and his lips touched my forehead. It felt strangely familiar and comforting. My eyes lifted to his, and he watched me, touching me with the softest fingers as they skimmed over my arms.

"You have food all over you."

"But none went through my lips or was consumed." I smiled victoriously.

"You realize that eating food from here is safe since you're the queen?"

"I don't want to be a queen. I want to live a boring life in the boring guild and kill things."

He held out his hand, and his lips twitched. "Of all the things I expected to be doing, wooing a fucking seventeen-year-old version of you wasn't one of them, Synthia. I have to admit, though, you're entertaining and utterly delicious in your innocence. I personally love it when you say *balls*. It makes mine tighten with anticipation."

"Ew, you're a pervert. You realize that, right?" I placed my hand into his, then instantly, everything changed, and we were standing in a large, beautifully decorated bedroom. "Oh, my sweet Jesus! You sifted me. You could have *killed* me!"

"You lived."

"But I could have *died*!"

"You didn't." He watched me briefly before his eyes turned toward the bed. "There's a shower in the bathroom. Use it or the bath, which you normally prefer. All of your things are in your closet. You should be set. Come to bed when you are finished."

CHAPTER FOUR

I STARED AT MY reflection, noting some subtle changes to my face. I wasn't sure what was different, or when I changed, but I didn't look like me. I looked older and exhausted. I still had my tattoos. The stars were on my shoulders, and the words written across the insides of my forearms were also there, but I was *off*. The closer I got to the mirror, the more it became clear that something was really wrong with the image.

Thoughts played out in my mind. Things like, had I been captured and turned FIZ for an extended period of time? It was plausible. Considering what the guild now knew about fae abilities, I could see something like that happening.

On the other hand, my breasts were off the hook and much larger than they had been. I kept grabbing them and testing their weight, wondering if they would stay like this once I escaped this hellish place. My stomach was flat, and I had muscles that were sleek, defined, and my ass still held the bubble shape Adrian loved to grab.

Adrian...He was a hopeless cause. He'd been turned into an undead, and I couldn't leave him here like that. He wouldn't want to be left to feed on humans like some fucking fairy bloodsucker. My chest ached with the realization, but something tingled in the back of my mind the more I tried to figure out how to free him, and the more I poked at it, the more it hurt.

Adam was more than likely in some state of denial, and lord knew what else. He wasn't FIZ. He would have been mindless, unable to speak or function. It terrified me they may have been turned into fae-induced zombies. When my mother had turned FIZ, she became a killer and tried to murder me. It wasn't unheard of to only be able to speak a few simple words when turned. I knew because of my mother.

The worst part of the entire ordeal had been the photos they'd shown me. There was no way the girl in those pictures could be Lari. I would know if my best friend were dead. I would feel it in my heart... unless the fae took that memory from me to make sure I was more compliant. But that didn't explain why Adam had looked so sad. I couldn't think about that right now. I had to get through this night with the Horde King and find a way to escape.

The Horde King was another matter altogether. He looked at me like he knew me carnally, which was insane. I was so much smarter than that. I had to be stuck in some crazy nightmare I hadn't woken from yet. I'd never agree to marry someone as condescending or vile as the King of the Horde.

Ryder was infuriating with the smooth words that dripped off his tongue like honey. I also wouldn't sleep with him because that thing in his pants wasn't right. It was like a king-sized snake, and that sucker had slithered and moved when I'd sat on him...and I'd *touched* it!

I squinted at my image in the mirror, and then bumped my forehead against it, examining my eyes. My heart pounded, and my mouth opened and closed several times before I turned, screaming as I ran naked from the room. My face slammed into something hard and unmoving, and we landed on the floor in a mass of limbs together.

"What is wrong?" Ryder looked over my shoulder to find what had spooked me.

"My eyes!" I cried, shock moving through me at what I'd seen in my reflection.

"Your eyes are beautiful." Ryder rolled me beneath him in a smooth, measured move, leaving me caged against the floor and his hard, muscular body on top of me. "And you're very naked, my pretty pet." He searched my horrified expression as sex dripped from his onyx gaze, a sinfully delicious smile curving against his generous mouth.

"I have *fairy* eyes," I whispered through trembling lips.

"Yes, you do." Slowly, he began lowering his lips toward mine.

"What are you doing?" I gasped, noting that the appendage between his legs had grown and was firmly sitting against my belly. "Oh, my word, is that your penis?"

"Penis?" His shoulders shook as he laughed.

"Yes, you know, the thing down there," I uttered hoarsely as my body responded to his magic. "Turn it off right now! Don't turn me mindless." I shivered, uncertain what was happening to me.

Whatever was occurring, it was bad, really bad. The fae had immense magical abilities to turn you senseless with need, sucking your soul out while they made you think you wanted it. I tried rolling him, but it was like trying to move an entire tree still rooted in the ground. He was firmly planted on top of me, grinning and refusing to budge while watching me struggle beneath him.

"Why are you wet down there?" I asked, feeling dampness between my thighs, along with warmth on my belly.

"That's your pussy, Synthia. If my cock were wet, you'd feel it all over your stomach."

"It is not me who is wet," I scoffed, trying to push him off me. He lifted, and I quickly grabbed on to his shoulders, pulling him back down, only to realize my mistake. My eyes rounded, and a frown tugged at my mouth.

"What's the matter, Syn?" His grin told me that he knew exactly what the problem was, and he was enjoying the fact that I was uncomfortable. *Asshole.*

"I'm naked," I groaned.

"Very." He smiled and attempted to lean back, but I pulled him down again until his chest was touching my breasts. He smiled again, rubbing his chest against mine.

"You're naked," I pointed out like an idiot.

"Again, very naked, but I fail to see that as a problem." He wiggled some more, and I glared at him, which just made him grin wider.

"This is awkward. I don't even like you, and now we're naked together, and you're a fucking fairy."

"You're a fucking fairy too." I tried to wiggle out from under him, but I just ended up giving his giant snake better access to my lady bits. "Fucking hell," he growled. "You fuck me like a possessed woman going to war for her sins, and little one, we were fucking born to sin together."

"I don't want to be a stupid fairy," I whispered as tears filled my eyes.

"You never did, but you learned to accept it and embraced your destiny. You need to remember me, Synthia. Remember us."

"But you're old, and I love Adrian. I love him, and now I have to kill him."

"No, you *loved* him. He chose to become what he is, and he is happy with his decision. You're okay with it now, too."

"I don't believe you." I watched his sinful mouth, licking my lips a moment before he brushed his against mine.

"Tell me you don't remember the feel of me, woman," he growled, claiming my mouth hungrily. His tongue delved past my lips, creating a strangled moan of need as his hips rocked against mine. The thick, velvety flesh pressed against me, just below my belly button.

I closed my eyes against the multitude of sensations his kiss created within me. I was unable to deny the taste, exoticness, the pleasure of his embrace, or the feel of him against me. Fucking fairy was turning me FIZ, and I was handing him an assist.

He didn't kiss like Adrian. There wasn't the uncertainty Adrian had. Ryder claimed my tongue with lethal precision, enticing and coaxing me into seduction. His hands held me there, trapped to do anything else other than take what he gave me. His hips adjusted, and I felt him against my opening, which caused everything inside of me to scream.

"*No!* No, please don't," I whispered through trembling lips. "Can we talk? I don't even know you. I'm not the type of girl who jumps into bed with just anyone, and I know nothing about you yet."

An aggravated growl rumbled through his chest, sending a chill down my spine. His forehead rested softly against mine, and his breathing slowed. Together, we struggled to calm the need rushing through us. Ryder's head lifted, and he peered into my eyes, searching for something before he smiled tightly and groaned. The scent of sandalwood filled my senses, and I whimpered as he pushed against my flesh to lift himself.

"You know me," he reminded softly, though I couldn't recall any memories of him for the life of me. His kiss, though. Somehow, I knew I'd tasted it before. I knew it like I knew the back of my hand; it felt familiar. Even now, I craved to have it back against my mouth, kissing me senseless as he took the choice from me.

"Maybe, but I don't remember you," I admitted softly.

Intense desire built up in his beautiful depths as his eyes roved over my naked body. I blushed, and he sat back on his haunches, pulling me up with him as he got to his feet. Once there, Ryder pulled me flush against the heat his body released while his hands cradled my hips.

Fingers dug into my flesh, biting into my hips before they released.

Slowly they trailed up my sides, creating gooseflesh that pebbled with the skilled precision this creature held in the seduction department. I sucked my bottom lip between my teeth to keep from moaning loudly as my pussy clenched with need.

Ryder stepped back, and my eyes dipped to the enormous cock nestled in thick, dark curls. They widened as it bounced with each move he made, causing my eyebrows to shoot for my hairline.

My hand moved before my brain could stop it, gripping the velvety steel member that had caught my attention. He groaned. The tip glistened with a pearlescent bead of come, and his head dropped back as I stroked it, testing the weight of it in my hand before he spoke huskily, sex dripping in his tone.

"You touch it too much, and you'll snap the thread that is keeping me from bending you over and reminding you how much you enjoy my cock."

I snatched my hand back, gasping for words and failing. Ryder sighed and dressed us, using his magic. I stared

down at the sheer negligee I now wore, then at his sweat-
pants as I watched him move away, his pants doing very
little to hide the hard cock through the soft fabric.

Adrian never had that issue, and I'd seen him in sweats
plenty of times before or after training. Or I hadn't turned
him on, which would be a hard hit to my ego, considering
I was in love with him. Ryder, though? His package was
marked *special* delivery and wide-load in flashing red letters.

"Does that thing hurt?" Shocked that I actually said it
out loud, my hand slapped over my mouth.

"I'll live. It won't be the first case of blue balls you've
given me, woman."

"Where are your wings?" He adjusted, and when they
unfurled, a shiver ran through me. "They're terrifyingly
beautiful."

"So are yours, sweet girl," he purred through a fine
layer of gravel that brushed over my flesh. I watched as
he allowed his wings to extend until they bathed me in
their shadows. "Do you want to touch them?" His eyes
narrowed as his lips turned up at the corners, forming a
seductive smile as he stepped closer, daring me to accept
the challenge he was throwing down.

"I don't have any wings," I said offhandedly as I struggled to control my breathing. Stepping closer, I shivered

violently against the power he radiated, feeling it drawing me in like I was a moth dancing against his flame. "What do they feel like?"

"Like wings and yet not. They're sensitive, but strong," he shrugged broad shoulders, causing his wings to flutter a bit, ruffling my unbound hair.

I watched him carefully, staring at them as he closed the distance between us and knelt before me. His gaze lifted, and my breathing grew rigid. Reaching out, my hand shook as I brushed my fingertips over the sharp tips. Even kneeling, he was huge, and I was highly aware of every inch of him.

Ryder's presence reminded me of standing next to a downed power line after a storm. The sheer magnitude of electricity that sizzled in the air as it slithered with a deadly current was mesmerizing.

Slowly, I stepped closer and lowered my hand to the rough, leathery part of them, and he hissed, sending heated breath fanning over my nipples. I yanked my hand back and stepped away from him abruptly as my body responded to the simple act.

He was beautiful, but it was a lethal beauty, predatory, like a lion. You knew they would eat you whole and spit out your bones, but you still wanted to get close enough to touch them.

Ryder stood, letting me take in the sheer size of him as he transformed into a taller version of himself. His ethereal brands pulsed, and I watched the hypnotic beat of gold and obsidian dancing across his arms and naked chest.

"You are the perfect killing machine, aren't you? You were exquisitely built to lure a woman in with your lethal beauty. The moment she's captured and ensnared by it, all you have to do is feed from her until she knows nothing else. I can feel it, the desire to strip myself bare and allow you to taste me. My body is literally aching from the need to let you feed from me," I whispered breathlessly.

"And yet you're still holding back?" His silky voice caressed and washed over me, awakening something within me that shed my inhibitions and wanted to follow him into carnal sin. "You're the only woman I wish to lure to me, woman."

The guild was going to move me up in rank once this was all over. No one would believe I had touched the Horde King's wings! If my plan worked, I'd have this sucker's head for a trophy soon enough. The thing was, I needed to lure him to bed, and then when he let his guard down, I'd fucking murder him.

His eyes narrowed as if he was trying to figure out what I was thinking. I did the only thing I could do. I began flirting like the other hussies in the guild. I smiled, batting my eyelashes on cue, just as they taught us.

Smiling shyly, I chewed absently on my lip as he surveyed me. His nostrils flared as if he could scent my arousal, which, unfortunately, I wasn't controlling or faking. My instructors had said I'd failed the seduction lessons, but here I was, with the Horde King, and he was staring at me like I was his feast for the Wild Hunt. My teeth released my bottom lip, causing a popping sound that drew his eyes to them.

I let him take in my body's arousal as I silently considered where I could go from here. If he assumed I wanted him, I could get him to lower his guard and move in for the kill. First things first, though, I needed a weapon. I couldn't overpower him, that much was a given, but I could out-think him since his brain was all about pussy. Lucky for us, that made the fae easy targets when they fed.

Deliberately, I let my eyes roam around the room, searching for anything I could use, and found it lacking something sharp enough to impale him. Turning back toward the bed, I noted the sword that was leaning against the wall near the headboard.

I blinked and tilted my head, slowly looking back at the beast that watched me. How could I seduce him without turning FIZ? What if I tried and failed? What if I tried and *didn't* fail? I'd be famous for taking him down.

I reached up with trembling hands and removed the robe slowly. Black onyx eyes studied me, gradually dropping to my bare breasts. Ryder didn't respond like I'd assumed he would, so it forced me to stand there awkwardly, and worse, naked. I moved closer, which he allowed, smirking as I closed the distance between us.

"Do you want me?" I rasped huskily.

"That's never been a question, woman. I have wanted you since the first moment I saw you." He smiled sadly, and I lost some of the bravado that I'd felt seconds ago. "Come here, Pet."

"I'm not a pet, you know. I'm a person with feelings."

"I'm very aware of that fact." There was sadness in his eyes that tugged at my heart. I closed the distance between us and placed my hands on his washboard abs. He felt almost human, minus the power that pulsed beneath his skin.

His hands slid around my back, pulling my body against his until breathing became hard to do. My mouth lifted, and he claimed it, gently at first, seeking permission which, considering who he was, was unexpected.

I pulled away after a moment, afraid of what I'd begun with this being. He stepped closer as I moved backward, and we danced like that until my back touched something solid and cold. His hands caged me against the wall as his mouth lowered to hover against mine.

"Are you sure this is what you want?" he asked huskily, his deep, rich timbre sending a shiver racing through me to throb in my apex.

"You terrify me, but you also excite me. I should run from you. Instead, I want to taste you on my lips."

"Is that so?" Ryder rasped, sending heat swirling into a swarm of butterflies in my belly. The man was sex incarnate, and I was in way over my head here. However, I'd never turned down a challenge yet, and I wasn't about to let this creature win this one over on me.

The guild warned us about engaging an enemy too strong to handle on your own, and yet my team was compromised, and I was alone with him. I could do this. I could take the biggest fae in their entire world down. It would send a message to every creature out there that they shouldn't be messing with guild enforcers.

"You're playing with fire, little one."

"I'm not afraid to be burned." I brought my hands up to his chest and let his power sizzle against my palms. I lifted on my toes, claiming his mouth, moaning as he picked me up, holding me between him and the wall while my fingers threaded through his hair.

It was soft as silk, and yet he was hard as steel as he slammed me against the wall, devouring me. He growled huskily as he pulled his mouth from mine, biting my lip until a cry ripped from my lungs.

"I thought you loved another?" His coy smile reminded me I had said that I love Adrian twice now.

"Love is just a lie we tell ourselves so that when we do things we shouldn't, we don't have to feel bad about it afterward. I fucked him, so I whispered the words to appease my ego after I let him have me. If you want, I can tell you I love you too, and we can pretend it's real until we finish."

"You'd tell me you love me?" he teased, moving me to the bed.

"Is that what you want?" I tried to calm the rapid beat of my heart that echoed deafeningly in my ears. I could tell this asshole anything and mean it because I intended to see him dead before the sun rose in the morning.

"No, because when you tell me you love me again, you'll damn well mean it." He set me down on the bed carefully.

Ryder's large hands pushed my knees up and apart, exposing my core to him. Galaxies of stars danced in obsidian depths before his mouth lowered, and I groaned as pleasure rocketed through me, shockingly.

My entire body hummed with need, and my hands fisted against the blankets as he made my body sing for him. His tongue slid over my flesh, and my nerves stood up and took notice since no man had ever awoken them before now.

Ryder's fingers pushed into my sex, and I shivered around them, turning to gauge the distance from us to the sword. I needed to get above him, which meant I was going to need to gain some semblance of control to get on top. The problem was, I didn't want his mouth to stop what it was doing.

That was easier said than done as his mouth clamped against my clit, and I exploded without warning. Lights burst in my vision. Cataclysmic events played out through my body, and I screamed as I came unhinged, fisting my hands in the blankets as he took me over the edge into an abyss of euphoria.

His moan was sexy. The way it vibrated against my pussy had me edging toward the cliff again. I sat up abruptly, realizing I was about to be turned into a mindless being. The motion unseated him as I ran my fingers through his hair, kissing him hard and fast while I took him to the bed.

He allowed it with a smile coated in my arousal, which I tasted as I devoured him with a kiss. I straddled his hips while my pussy rubbed against the hardness of his rigid cock that pushed against my opening invitingly.

Ryder lifted me, pushing a solid inch into my opening as I rocked against him. I lowered my mouth to his lips again, claiming mine as my hand slid across the bed. I inched slowly toward the sword that rested against the edge of the nightstand. My fingers clasped around the hilt, and I lifted it, screaming as he pushed into my body.

It was brutal, and yet my pussy clenched around his cock ravenously, taking him until I buried him deeply in my core to his thick the base. I lifted the sword and slammed it into his body; only it didn't pierce his flesh. I stared down at the red rose now smashed against his heart, and then slid my gaze to where his cock was cradled in my body. He stretched me, and it ached and burned as he held me there, watching me closely. His hands lifted my hips before slamming me back down on his hard, thick cock.

"Only one of us is getting impaled tonight, sweet imp," he chuckled, as a fire lit in his gaze and victory etched in the fine lines of his face.

I moaned, rocking against him to stop the pain that he created as he filled every inch of my body with his massive cock. His hands lifted, cupping my breasts before he trailed his thumbs over the hardness of my nipples. Fingers pinched delicate flesh, and my body clenched tighter, milking his silken cock as my stomach tightened with the need to come again.

"Do you feel me now, wife?" he asked, rolling me beneath him as his hips rocked slowly.

"I just tried to murder you, and you're worried about me *feeling* you?" I whimpered, gasping at the sensation of him seated in my body until he began moving his hips.

It was erotic and the sexiest thing I'd ever experienced, but then I exploded, and he fucked me hard. The way he pounded into my core was intense, using the arousal that coated my pussy to stretch my insides to accommodate all of him.

"Fuck, you're too tight to fuck slowly, woman," he growled, watching as he sent me careening toward the edge with precision. "You remember this, Pet? The way your greedy cunt milks me as I stretch this tight pussy? The way your pretty eyes grow heavy as I make you mine?"

"I'm not your fucking pet, asshole," I argued as my mouth opened and I screamed, coming undone. He hissed and slowed, tensing as he came over the edge with me. "Balls! You came *in* me, asshole. Get off of me!"

"Afraid I might knock you up again?"

"Again? You didn't knock me up a first time. That was just more lies. I think I'd remember giving birth and having children. Now get off of me, you ogre-sized fairy fart."

"I'm not done with you yet, little witch," he chuckled, turning me over on my stomach, entering me roughly.

My face pushed into the mattress, and I opened my mouth, screaming in pleasure as he made me orgasm again and again until I was too weak and exhausted to do anything but sleep.

CHAPTER FIVE

I STUDIED RYDER SILENTLY as he lay beside me on the bed. I ached everywhere, and I was officially confident that he'd used his fae magic on me. He'd ravished my body for hours, and I'd *begged* him for more, which meant he'd definitely manipulated me with his magic. I clutched the blankets tightly against my neck, where I'd covered myself up from his heated gaze. I could feel the memory of him in me, still drenching my pussy with his essence.

The guild should have told us how to get out of seduction gone wrong, instead of focusing only on how to lure the males into bed. I was fairly sure that was the simple part, and according to my body, it wasn't the most unpleasant experience, but the morning after sucked. It was awkward, and he watched me as if he expected me to break into hysterics, and I wasn't so sure I wouldn't disappoint him.

"Is there like some kind of fae birth control or, I don't know, a morning-after thing? Unless, of course, I can go now? The guild will have something. A supernatural... douche, maybe?" I uttered, barely audible to my own ears past the chattering of my teeth.

"I just fucked you for hours, and you think you can leave now?"

"I was hoping so, yes."

"Do you think the guild will welcome you with those pretty tri-colored violet and blue eyes?"

"I think that once I put enough distance between us, your magic will no longer work on me. I will go back to being who I was before I woke up in that meadow, and my body will stop twinging with revulsion over what I allowed you to do with me."

"Is that why it's *twinging*? I thought I just fucked your sweet pussy too hard, and it was craving more. It does want more, doesn't it?" he asked, staring down at me. "You always have been an insatiable fuck; that greedy little pussy can't get enough of me."

"You're so crude." I rolled over and put my back toward him as I sat up, wincing at the soreness between my thighs.

"Yeah? Tell me, did your teenage lover ever make you scream like that? Did your body ever tremble that hard when he made your pussy come?"

"That's none of your business," I snapped, crossing my arms over my naked breasts. I tried to keep him from seeing the hardened tips that responded to his sleepy tone, sexy-as-fuck tone.

It sent my core clenching with need, which was insane since my pussy could be described by new words this morning. Words liked fucking owned, and oh hey, wet and sore as hell or my favorite one, beat the fuck up and hungry for more fae cock. Every simple move reminded me exactly what my crazy ass had tried to do to the Horde King. In reality, all I'd managed to do was slip and take a big fat dick where it should never have gone.

"Sore?" His satisfied, smug grin was infuriating. He watched me stand, and the appendage between his legs bounced as he stretched, announcing its hardened situation. He'd grinned and asked me to fix his predicament as if that was physically possible for me this morning. I was swollen, and he was fully aware of it, and yet I *wanted* to ride him again.

"Put that thing away. It's not safe."

"Not safe for what?"

"My sanity!"

"Yeah? Because you already want to ride it for hours again? Maybe if I do this, you'll cave in to those baser needs you're fighting against?" He rocked his hips, and my mouth dropped open as my eyes glued to the massive cock that was swinging freely. "Like that?"

"Put that thing away before you poke out an eyeball or something!"

"Oh, are we upset that our vagina sorcery didn't work to take down the Horde King? Let's try again. Maybe I'll succumb to that pussy magic, little girl. You can fuck me into oblivion. I'll even let you."

"I do not have a magic pussy!"

"You're fucking wrong there, Synthia. It's magical, and I assure you, I surrender to it often, and you beg me for more."

"As if," I snorted, glaring at him from where I sat on the bed again, unwilling to let him see me limp from the ache he'd created. "You know, maybe if you say it enough, I might actually believe you. Come on, you fairy-fuck-ing-ogre-titty-licking prick, let's hear it. How much does my pussy make you come?"

My hand trailed down my body until it slipped through the wet mess of my flesh as his eyes narrowed on it, watching me. I winced, and his lips curved into a triumphant masculine grin, which was fucking sexy and made my core clench tightly.

"Not sore at all, huh?" he asked, lifting one brow point-edly as he took in the red, swollen flesh.

"Adrian's done worse," I taunted, lying through my teeth, which made his smile drop, and that brow lifted higher. "Oh, what's the matter? Get your ego bent because my *human* lover out-fucked the big, bad fae? Believe it or not, you're not God's gift to women. You're just a cocky asshole who thinks that just because he has a big dick, he can use his swagger to get a bitch all riled up."

His eyes lowered to my fingers that were drenched in arousal. I frowned, staring down before my hand moved away. "Somehow, I fucking doubt that since I'm very aware of how lacking he was when you were children, *wife*."

"Case in point, I make myself wetter than you," I said haughtily with a shrug.

"Is that a challenge? Because I like to win, Pet. You should know that every time you have challenged me, I've won. I'm not into losing, and I sure as fuck know for a fact that I make you come harder than any man you've ever been with before. I know the way you like that pussy licked and slapped to cause a sting, which prevents you from getting too worked up too quickly. I know how you like my teeth scraping over those pretty pink nipples before tugging on them gently. I know the way you like your legs pushed apart, and the perfect movement of my hips it takes to hit your pussy in that special sweet spot deep within in you that your little fucking childhood boyfriend never touched before."

Walking toward me, Ryder put his hand under my chin, lifting it until our eyes met. "I know the way your eyes light up right before your body sings for mine. The way your hands tighten against my flesh, aligned with the way your pussy clamps down on my cock while you scream my name to the gods like it's a fucking benediction. I know you because I love you, Synthia Raine. I love everything about you, and this? This, we will get through together. I will bring you back to me. You may hate me when I do, but I will never stop loving you. You're imprinted into the very marrow of my bones, and the essence of my being, woman. So, you want to forget me? Too fucking bad, little girl. You don't get to forget me, not even if remembering means you hate me. Now get dressed because I'm in the mood to help you murder Adrian."

I stared at him as my head began to ache. My hands lifted, holding pressure against my temples while he watched me.

"Synthia?"

"I'm fine."

"You're not fine. None of this is fine. This trip with you down memory lane is cute, but I need the badass goddess back, even if she doesn't want to come back to me. I need my wife because she's my partner, and I can't save this world without her. Come home to me, Syn. Come back and stand beside me." His eyes were pleading, penetrating my soul, and the pain in my head increased.

"You're insane." I dropped my hands and turned back to him. "I want to see Adam and Alden."

"Get dressed, then. Your clothes are in the closet."

"My clothes?" Confused, I spun to see if he was joking. He wasn't.

He pointed to the door on the opposite side of the room, and I turned, staring at the closet. I drifted in that direction and threw the doors open. My eyes bugged out at the extensive OPI nail polish collection. I stepped inside and walked to the shelf, picking up my favorite colors before setting them back down.

The clothes were beautiful, but way too mature for me. I thumbed through them, pulling out a pair of jeans and a tank top, then slipped on a solid black hoodie. I turned toward the door, finding Ryder there watching me as he leaned against the doorframe with his arms crossed, silently taking me in.

"Funny, you actually brought those with you when you first came here. Fitting that you'd pick them to wear as you try to leave me."

He rested his head against the door, and I noted the blanket folded neatly on the shelf, and I was drawn to it for some reason. The fabric was covered in tiny animals in pink, green, and blue. I noticed how amazingly soft it was as I caressed the top, then absently picked it up, pushing it against my face as I inhaled deeply. It smelled like innocence, and the familiar scent intensified the pain in my head.

I grabbed Ryder's arm and was swept into a vision of him with me. Ryder was holding me with three small babes around us, crawling over us as we laughed and played peek-aboo with the blanket. The little tykes clung to each of us as they grinned happily.

I shook my head, trying to dispel the images. It didn't work. Instead, golden eyes stared up at me, while a tiny finger wrapped around mine. Tears burned in my eyes, and a sob escaped my mouth as violent pain seared through my head.

"Oh, sweet girl, I fucked up." Ryder wrapped his arms around me and held me tight.

"My head hurts," I admitted in a whisper as pain pounded through me, settling behind my eyes. I leaned against him, accepting his comfort.

"I love you. If you take nothing from me when you leave me, remember that, at least," he whispered, moving to help me to stand as I almost lost my footing. "I fucking love you."

CHAPTER SIX

My vision blurred, causing me to back up from where he'd righted me before I could fall to the floor. His touch unnerved me, sending every womanly part of me into an uproar with a single caress. I yearned to rip his clothes off and fuck him until he screamed for me, and worse, I wanted him viscerally.

His eyes studied and learned, picking me apart as though he knew every layer of my soul. One hand lifted, rubbing over my naked arm while I observed the emotions playing out across his features.

"Something wrong?" he asked softly, his tone indicating he already knew I was in pain.

"What are you doing to me?" I demanded, taking a few more steps away from him, trying to escape his touch and the raw, red-hot need pulsing through me.

His presence alone made it impossible to think, but the magic oozing from his pores was immense, and my apex continually clenched painfully, begging for me to ride him. Rock-hard nipples pressed against the top I wore, alerting him to the fact that I'd gone braless. I usually wouldn't have, but these weren't my things, and I wasn't rocking someone else's bra.

"I'm not doing anything." He stood in the doorway, making it impossible to escape him. "What did you see?" He watched me expectantly.

"You, dying repeatedly," I said aloofly, shrugging. "I was okay with it."

His lips twisted into a wicked smile that pulled at my nipples and apex. It was as if he held some invisible string attached to my sexual organs that he continually tugged. I pinched my arm, using a technique the guild had taught us to redirect pain, and yet the throbbing inside my head didn't lessen. It was growing, pulsing until I felt it between my eyes. It was slipping around my head as images played out like there was a screen inside of me, old family movies turning on a reel.

"Synthia, don't fight it," he begged with tenderness in his eyes.

"You're using magic on me, aren't you?" I asked, feeling tears as they slipped free to run down my cheeks. "It hurts."

He sifted before my eyes could adjust and captured my face between his palms. He held me like I was the most delicate flower, something he cherished above all else. He rested his forehead against mine, placing his hands on the sides of my face, staring intently into my eyes.

"Tell me you don't remember this." His mouth crushed against mine, and my lips parted, granting him entry.

It was a soul-searching kiss.

The way his tongue danced with mine consumed all reason. Before I could think better of it, I was pulling him closer, devouring him with everything I had. I gave him every part of me as I relaxed in his embrace. We were both moaning with an intense need that rushed through us, opening wounds I hadn't even realized I had.

His hands released my face, slipping to my waist. He picked me up, setting me on a shelf as he continued to demand my full, undivided attention. My legs wrapped around his hips, pulling him closer, and I ripped his shirt open, groaning and out of breath as air failed to reach my lungs quickly.

He lifted my shirt, breaking the kiss long enough to pull it over my head. Ryder's mouth slammed against mine violently, pulling a gasped cry from my lungs as he dominated it, owning it like he was built to savage, and I was created to be destroyed. Hands cupped my naked breasts, brushing thumbs over my hardened nipples as I ground against the burgeoning erection I craved in his pants.

Our clothes vanished, and before I could utter a plea for mercy, he pushed his cock into my body brutally. He filled me until I screamed out against his mouth, and he swallowed it, driving into me until I met every thrust with vigor, needing to hear him come undone for me.

"Fuck, you feel like home. Ryder," I whimpered his name as if he were a cure for the ailments of the world, unable to accommodate enough of him in this position. "It aches, I need more," I moaned huskily, allowing him to lift me and push his cock into my greedy pussy, which clamped down hard in celebration of having to stretch to accept him.

My body repeatedly clenched around his large, thick cock like a vise as it sucked him off. He lifted and moved me by my hips until I was whimpering incoherently while my body sang with need.

"Fucking take my cock, sweet, greedy girl," he growled, filling me until I shuddered around him. Ryder lifted me, attempting to gaze into my eyes, but I couldn't take mine from where he fucked my body.

"More!"

Ryder laughed darkly, his lips curling into a dangerous smile. He was massive against my opening, an inhuman creature that was destroying my pussy until it stretched painfully to take what he demanded.

"You see that greedy pussy sucking me off? You feel me. I know you do. Your body knows mine, and I know yours," he growled, lifting me to the tip of his impressive cock before he slammed me home on it once again. "Yeah," he chuckled, watching as I shook with the force of multiple orgasms.

"I know how to take you to the edge and leave you there, how to bring you over that edge instantly, without mercy. I know how to hold you there, stuck on my cock while you come apart for me, and me alone, little girl. I fucking own this pussy. Not because I own you, but because I know how to make it sing for me. How to make it scream in pleasure until you're nothing but a shivering, shaking, trembling fucking mess of nerves that can do nothing else but come for me."

Everything exploded at once. My eyes filled with colors that splashed into my vision, and my body hummed with a mixture of bliss and fear. I sensed the internal combination of nerves firing through my core to my belly. It was echoing to my brain that he was holding me locked in an orgasm that wouldn't end.

Anytime I started coming down from one orgasm, he'd move slowly, building speed until he lifted me again, slamming me home on his cock to start it all over. He didn't tire, didn't stop until I was moaning endlessly. I rested my head against his chest, watching him fucking destroy me for any other man alive.

Ryder's hands held my ass, cradling it as he fucked me. It was one endless orgasm after the next, and everything inside me began firing until my vision went black. Lips brushed against mine, opening my mouth and demanding entrance. His kiss consumed me, forcing my mind to replay images that weren't mine to take.

The beast was fucking destroying me, stretching me until I'd never be the same again. It burned with how full I was in order to accept his cock, and yet still, it grew longer and wider. He placed me on the bed, grabbing my hair, and forced me to look between my thighs, where he ruined me.

"If you were a fucking witch, could you do that?" he asked, and I opened my mouth to scream, but his thick, roguish laughter stopped me cold. "Look at that greedy fucking cunt and tell me it isn't mine. Tell me, Synthia, could you do that if you weren't created for me? You want more, don't you? You crave it, even if you don't understand why. You know me, Pet. You walked down the fucking aisle and took me as your mate. You said yes, even though I didn't deserve you. You gave me children and life. I was drowning in responsibility, and you brought me back from wanting to destroy it all. You are my fucking world, and it won't turn without you in it. I need you to come back to me." His expression was pleading as he tilted my head back down so that I could continue watching him fuck me without mercy. And damn, I wanted more. I wanted everything he could give me.

He was immensely built, and my body took him easily as it begged for more still. I took everything he demanded I accept and fuck yes, I craved more. I wanted all of him. I was a never-ending orgasm that floated on the gentle waves washing ashore, even as they became violent swells that relentlessly pummeled the beach.

The sound of my flesh sucking against his cock was intensely erotic. He released my hair, and I fell back, rocking my ass as I fucked him in return while he watched. I cupped my breasts, pinching my nipples, and he growled huskily in approval. His eyes grew languid, narrowing on what I did for him, enticing him with my hands as I touched everywhere he had, needing to replace mine with his.

"You're so fucking hot, woman. Look at you, greedy girl. This pussy is drenched for me, isn't it? That's my dirty girl," he purred, watching me fuck him while he held still, allowing me to take control.

"I don't even like you."

"Yeah, you say that a lot, and then you ride my cock like this after those words roll off that talented fucking tongue. Tell me, do I feel familiar destroying this pretty pussy? Do *we* feel familiar?"

"Because you fae-fucked me," I whimpered as he slammed into my body.

"One, I can't fae-fuck you; you're a goddamn fucking goddess. Two, I never could fae-fuck you. Your pussy made me crave it too much, but even then, I didn't need to use fae magic to fuck you because you gave it to me freely, just like you are now. Three, you're too strong to be turned into anything other than needy as fuck for my cock. Four, you fucking hate me, and you fuck me the same way, and yet you love me more than you should.

"You love me wrecking this pretty cunt, writing my name on your insides until you're helpless to deny what I give to you, Synthia. I'm willing to give you every part of me. You are mine. You're not some weak-minded being. You're a fucking goddess, so fight it. Fight it for me. I can't be the one thing that destroys you. I need you to come back to me."

"Fuck you," I growled, pushing my body against his with a need to match the pain intensifying in my head.

"I am fucking you," he chuckled wickedly, lifting my hips with his hands before he pounded into my body relentlessly, sending me careening over the edge. I fought back, bucking and rocking against his thick cock to ensure he hit me just where I needed him. "Take that cock, sweet girl. Take what you need, and then take more for me, greedy little goddess." He grew longer until it pinned me in place, unable to move past the pain and pleasure he created by stretching me to my limits.

I lifted, staring down at where my body clamped him greedily, pulsing around his cock. I was milking him, clenching and releasing the inhuman cock that sat cradled between my thighs while he watched me. Golden eyes lifted, locking with mine as pain lanced through my brain.

"You're killing me."

"No, I'm refusing to let the woman I love vanish from this world. You don't get to fucking quit on me. I did this to you, and I will fucking save you," he promised, tensing as a moan slipped from his lungs, ending on an aggressive growl that took him to the edge. I watched as he came undone, my body wringing every ounce of cum from his until he snarled like a crazed beast, peering down at where we were joined.

"You came inside me again!" I groaned.

"I come in this pussy every chance I get, woman. I want more babies with you. I want golden-eyed boys and violet-eyed daughters. I want to watch your stomach swell with our child protected within your gorgeous body. I long to see your hands following their little feet as they kick you from within. I want you home. I want you to come back to me. I need you to come back, Synthia. Take back your fucking memories. You're not weak. You're the strongest woman I know. Now snap the fuck out of it."

"I can't. I don't even know who the fuck you think I am. Your cock hurts, and everything is wrong. I'm an enforcer, and I'm stuck on your big-ass cock!" I tried to move, and yet I couldn't get away from the appendage that was literally stuck in my body. "Get your dick out of me, monster!"

"I can't," he growled, staring at where he was trapped within my body. "Relax, woman."

"I can't relax! You're stuck in my vagina! Shrink that thing already."

He rocked his hips, and I moaned, causing his eyes to lift and lock with mine. Obsidian had turned to gold, and gold sent more pain echoing through my brain until it threatened to consume me, swallowing me whole. I opened my mouth and whispered the words that entered my mind.

"Where were you?"

"What?" he asked in confusion. Ryder studied me as I blinked to clear my vision of the pain.

"When I needed you... You left... Me... To die." Everything got blurry as pain split through my head. My body jerked, and Ryder cried out, holding me as the world faded to black, and agony tore through my head.

CHAPTER SEVEN

SYNTHIA, INSIDE THE SEELIE PRISON

I STARED INTO THE darkness and then gazed back up at the opening of the pit I had jumped into. Days had passed, turning into weeks. I fought every day to keep the monsters at bay, but strength wasn't something I had much of anymore, not in this place of horrors.

I had no magic, and no matter how much I reached for it, I couldn't find it. I felt mundane. My heart echoed, beating wildly in my ears as I turned toward a sound in the cave where eyes blinked, watching me from the shadows.

The monsters gathered, waiting for me to lower my guard. Ryder was going to get his ass kicked for leaving me down here. A couple of days, I'd have understood. He was so angry and bitter that I'd failed to take what his world offered me, yet I didn't know what held me back. I was sure

it wasn't my humanity. I'd been placed with the humans to
gain that part of me, to see the world through their eyes.

For days I'd mulled it over, not because he'd said to, but
because I knew I danced away from the magic I was born
to take. Goddess, yeah, fine whatever, becoming one with
Faery? It wasn't so easy.

What if I lost myself? What if I turned into a monster
and killed the world I was created to save? Or what if I
fucked up and everyone who was counting on me died
because I couldn't live up to their expectations or the hype
of what I was supposed to be?

Killing creatures came easily, which was probably why
Danu had given me to the guild to be raised among enforcers. That part of me, yeah, I was okay with keeping.
I could pop mages like a bubble, but not on a massive
enough scale to end this fight as quickly as they seemed to
think I could.

Ryder...what if he died? Where would I fit into this
world without him by my side? I didn't. I was here because
of him; because of the people he'd made me love. Okay, so
he didn't *make* me. They were easy enough to love once
you broke through their broody, obtuse, asshole ways.

I screamed his name again as the shadows began to move.
This was insane. I was freezing, starving, and everything
ached. I'd watched him staring down at me for hours after

he'd come back, telling me I was nothing to him. That I would die in this pit, and no one would ever know or even care that I was gone.

I was heartbroken to think that Ryder would feel that way or leave me here for weeks on end. Then, I recalled my conversations with Asher about the Seelie prison he had escaped. I had a lingering sensation that it wasn't Ryder speaking to me, and that time moved differently here.

Stepping back into the shadows, I slowly turned, staring toward the endless eyes that watched me. Icy fingers slipped around my neck, and I trembled at the sensations that shot through me.

Seelie wasn't the same as Unseelie. Their sexual powers were stronger, all-consuming. The moment this one touched me, I hissed and tried to fight the lure to succumb to him. It wasn't working.

"So, so pretty and abandoned by those who loved you," he hissed past serrated fangs. "They didn't want you, but we do." His fingers pushed through the skin on the back of my neck, unable to move the instant he'd touched me.

Others crawled out of the shadows, whispering and murmuring about how beautiful I was as this monster held me. The venom of his nails that were embedded in me trapped me. His mouth lowered to mine, and I cried out as he feasted on my mouth, ripping my lip off as he stared into my eyes.

"You feel no pain, only pleasure," the creature crooned as he softly stroked the side of my face.

The pain stopped. His words changed everything. Others moved from the shadows, joining him as he devoured and toyed with my body. I did nothing to stop them because I was paralyzed, unable to move, but still able to feel. It was pleasure mixed with pain. I watched as he lowered his teeth to my naked breasts, ripping them open. Something warm and wet pushed between my thighs while hands held them open. I whimpered as blood ran down my face.

"Tomorrow, we will go slower with you, but today we are starving, my pretty new toy," he explained, and I nodded. "We have been without sustenance for so long, and you are too tasty of a treat to be savored this first time."

This was wrong, all wrong. Something entered my body, and I stared down as he laughed wickedly, watching as a hand poked through my stomach, ripping it open. His hand cradled my chin, lifting my gaze to stare into his eyes.

"You like it, it feels nice, doesn't it?" Another Seelie appeared from the shadows, stroking my hair as he held my face, forcing me to look into his eyes. "I won't feed on your flesh like the others. I will feed on your emotions, and oh, sweet girl, you are full of emotion."

"It's beginning to hurt," I whispered past the blood that filled my throat.

"That's because he's eating your insides, and you're about to bleed out. You see, we're so hungry, and you're so powerful."

I called for Ryder on a sob.

The channel we used seemed empty, and only husky laughter met my whispered pleas. I sagged against the creature that caught me. He lifted me from the monster that had been feasting on my insides. I looked back over his massive shoulder to where my legs were lying, detached from my body as we walked away.

"Ouch. I need those."

"You'll heal. Nothing dies here, and tomorrow, we will begin anew with you. You will become used to it, and eventually, you'll no longer care when they eat you. You may even come to love it, but in the end, it won't matter. You are mine now."

His name was Malachi, and he wasn't wrong. Eventually, I learned to crave death and the blissfulness it would offer to escape the reality of this hellish place. He'd stopped turning off the pain as the others ate parts of me. They feasted on my flesh, and he dined on my memories and emotions until I succumbed to blissful death, night after night.

I'd fought them, but I soon learned they enjoyed the fight and hunting down their victims to consume as they figured out that the white hallway of mazes was endlessly hopeless. There were miles of them, tunnels that twisted and turned into rooms that would trap you once you'd entered. It was an entire world of mazes with no discernible way out. But Asher had escaped.

Eventually, I started using the walls to mark the days. Weeks turned to months, and months turned into years, and I understood the cold reality of what had happened. Ryder had left me to the monsters that were endlessly tormenting me.

If I wanted out, I had to save myself. He'd ensured that I wouldn't ever return to him, and those words he'd whispered from the cliffs echoed in my mind. Did anyone else realize I was gone? Did everyone hate me enough to leave me down here to endure this fate? Hadn't Adam realized I was missing by now, or had Ryder gotten rid of him, too?

I finally broke on the worst night of the tenth year of my imprisonment. My spine had been snapped in half, and I'd lain in a pool of blood as Malachi painted over my flesh. His fingers brought sensation back, of which he was very much aware.

Another Seelie tasted me sweetly, telling me how much I would enjoy him, and for a moment, I did. I came for the monster as Malachi watched from the shadows, my body finally breaking, giving him the one thing I'd refused. I gave the Seelie a piece of myself.

They took more and more, and every night, soft touches were used while Malachi let the monsters destroy me. He ruined me, allowing them to use my body as he took the memories he wanted. His emotions fed me, and I fed him parts of my mind, which he ate gluttonously.

I didn't care that he allowed the others to mutilate my body.

I cared that he raped my soul, allowing him to take it from me, and when he did, everything about me changed. I'd seek him out just to feel something, to remember what I'd lost. I depended on Malachi to make me feel the pain that no longer touched me when Ryder failed to come back for me after fifteen years.

Eventually, Malachi had taken every memory that made me happy. They'd remained elusive in my mind, as if just beyond my reach. I'd done whatever he'd asked, craving the touch of the other Seelie to know those memories Malachi had stolen from me. I'd willingly gone to them, just to see those golden eyes that burned my soul, or what was left of my soul.

It was how I'd finally escaped them. I rode the monster that loved my flesh, knowing that Malachi wasn't there to watch me, digging through my emotions to find which ones he wanted, and which memories he would take away this time.

I'd bent over, kissing the throat of this familiar monster, knowing he loved my lips against his pulse, and with my teeth, I'd ripped his throat out. He bled so fucking gloriously from the arterial bleed that painted my face. I dragged him to the entrance, leaving his corpse there before I'd gone back for the others that had taken parts of me, including Malachi.

On the twentieth year mark, I had enough bodies of my enemies to build a ladder, and I did it by adding my own corpses into the structure. I'd made it slowly, cherishing each bone and ligament that the Seelie had so willingly donated to my cause.

I'd used my claws to reach into the earth, digging deeper and deeper, until I hit the midway point. There, I'd tunneled inward, pushing past the dirt to the magical runes that were placed around the pit. I withdrew them, one by one, day by day, until the power that kept us monsters within the pit was removed, allowing me to escape the prison my husband had left me in.

At the edge of the hole, I stared down into the abyss at the eyeless corpses piled on the earth-covered floor. I reached for their power, but it wasn't their power I'd received. It was something entirely different. Something... *endless*.

My claws lengthened, and giant wings unfurled from my spine as I stood there, remembering why I had been created, and who I'd now become.

Revenge entered my mind, but that wasn't what I wanted. I'd gotten that from those who had harmed or tortured me.

My heart pounded in my chest while golden eyes filled my mind. Whose eyes, I couldn't remember, and yet they caused my heart to literally ache. My claws pushed into my chest, withdrawing the thing that made me ache as I recalled those wickedly beautiful eyes.

My mind replayed words on a loop, endlessly on repeat. I never could recall who'd said them, or why. I only knew that I was alone, and alone, I was fucking untouchable.

I was Sorcha, Goddess of the Fae, and I was fucking starving.

My wings spread out as my fingers painted on the wall. I wrote in my own blood, sending a reminder to whoever had placed me in that pit that I wasn't weak. I was a goddess. Whoever put me in that hole was going to pay for it with their blood.

CHAPTER EIGHT

A DREAM PULLED ME from my sleep. It had been of Ryder, standing over me, begging me to forgive him and to
come back home. I swallowed the scream that threatened
to bubble up, exposing my location to the monsters within
the prison.

Silently, I waited for the familiar twinge of pain and
fear that would rip through me. My captor and tormentor
enjoyed trying to make me think I was safe. The moment
I let my guard down, they'd attack me to remind me that I
wasn't ever safe, and never would be again.

Peering around the room, I slowly sat up, setting my bare
feet on the cold floor before stretching my arms wide. I sti-
fled a yawn and then winced at the pain between my thighs.
I was dressed in a soft, cotton nightgown, and inside one
of my memories, apparently.

I inhaled deeply, savoring the smell of Ryder that my memories had conjured. His unique blend of sandalwood and raw masculinity tickled my nose, reminding me of what I'd lost when he'd left me. My eyes swept the room, noting the intimate details the monster had plucked from my mind to replicate perfectly, and I marveled at the lengths Malachi would go to further my torture.

He was getting better at taking images from my head and making them seem real. The scent of Ryder was everywhere. Picking up a blanket, I held it to my nose, causing tears to prick my eyes. These were the memories I craved with the sight and smells that reminded me of my husband and our children.

"Enough, you bore me, monster," I whispered hoarsely, unable to hide the undertone of pain in my voice. "I'm waiting..." I continued, eyeing the door apprehensively. "You want to play? Let's play." I was undeterred by the fact that he was baiting me.

He'd done this to me a lot. To gain my memories, I had to show them to Malachi, and he used them against me, enjoying the mind games he played something fierce.

To ease the endless suffering of what could never be again, I gave in. Not because I wanted him to consume the memories, but because he never tired, and he was a master of torture. Twisting the knob, I stepped out into the empty hallway and swallowed down the sinking feeling that sat in my stomach like a boulder.

I knew this game. I would find Ryder, and we would make love. I would awaken with less memory and fewer pieces of my anatomy, a result of the monster allowing his friends to eat me while my guard was lowered.

If I wanted to feel my family, I had to allow him to use me. I did it to remember why I had to escape this place because, as Malachi took them from my mind, he was changing me into something cold and unfeeling—like him.

I craved the taste of Ryder's kiss, the heat from his gaze, and to get it, I would do some unsavory shit, even for mere seconds. Of everything I missed in the twenty years I'd been down here, what I missed most was Ryder, and the way his touch brought me to life.

There was no life down here.

There was only the endless torment and torture that I endured daily.

I couldn't grasp the magic because, in this prison, there wasn't any.

You were powerful, or you weren't.

You were stronger than the monsters, or you were not.

The Seelie had been down here long enough to learn ways around the spells that held them in this cage. I hadn't. It would take decades to become strong enough to fight back, which they taunted me endlessly about as they ripped me apart.

I started down the hallway, my bare feet dragging as I headed toward my next execution. I wasn't stupid enough to think I could escape Malachi. No, because out of all the monsters in this prison, he ruled it through power and his ability to use his magic against his victims.

This mirage of memories was terrifying with how familiar it felt. The scent of the magic and halls were spot-on. The imagery was intense and perfectly placed.

Entering the great hall, I paused, looking at the familiar faces as tears burned my eyes. How many times had he shown me this and then taken it from me? A couple hundred, or over a thousand times? The scent of freshly baked bread turned my head. Staring at the table laden with food, I walked toward it, noting more faces I recognized.

"Syn," Zahruk said carefully, and I nodded to him.

Don't talk to them.

Don't look too closely because then they fade to black, and the monsters will return.

I smiled tightly, waiting for the pain to start as he approached me. Sapphire eyes studied me, and then they narrowed as if he were about to break the memory and start the really fun stuff.

"You okay?" Zahruk tilted his head and studied my face as his brows drew together.

I nodded, reaching for the bread, bringing it up to my nose before putting it back. He held my gaze and stepped away, turning to make room for Ryder to move closer to where I stood.

Malachi had gone out of his way to replicate the details in this memory, right down to the black and gold specks in Ryder's eyes. I stepped closer, sniffing him cautiously. He seemed so real that tears broke free, trailing down my cheeks.

"You're okay," he uttered thickly, his hands resting on my shoulders, and I stiffened with his touch. I yanked one away, terrified of the razor-sharp claws that would surely slice through my flesh at any moment.

Ryder's touch felt so real that I almost didn't want to ruin the memory. The sizzle of sparks that erupted from his touch made my body clench, and yet I knew at any time, he'd rip me apart and remind me how weak I was. I shivered, basking in the feel of him and the pleasure of it that I knew wouldn't last. A soft moan bubbled in my throat, and my body heated from the memories that rushed through my mind with the touch.

His mouth lowered to my forehead, and I closed my eyes, waiting for the pain to come. I craved the touch of his lips like a drug that couldn't ravage my system fast enough. I didn't care if it rotted my teeth or ripped apart my flesh with sores as long as I could *feel* my husband.

"Do it now," I pleaded.

"Do what?" Ryder stiffened, and I looked away, closing my eyes, unable to watch the man that I loved turn into a monster that would devour me.

"Rip me apart. I'm ready. This is too painful. Do it, please," I replied, needing more bones to finish the ladder I'd started to create with corpses. Soon, I'd have enough to climb out of this hell, even if I had to do so with my rotting flesh and bones.

"You're safe," he growled, pulling back to look at me. "Pet?" he asked while searching my eyes.

His thumbs tipped my chin up, and I opened my eyes, staring into his for just one more glimpse of this memory. I knew it would take the monster a while to rebuild the image, considering how much magic he'd used this time to create the perfect replica of Ryder.

"You're back now. You're safe with me."

I smirked, and my head tilted as I pulled away from his touch.

"I tire of your fucking games, creature. Just do it! Rape me, murder me, or let your friends eat my fucking insides, whatever. Just be done with it already."

He swallowed audibly, watching me as his mouth fell open and he shook his head. I studied him meticulously, noting the way every detail was perfect, right down to the way the gold specks in his gaze burned. He reached for me, and I recoiled, hating that he felt so real, so fucking right against my flesh.

"You're home," Ryder whispered hoarsely. "You're no longer in the Seelie prison, Pet. You escaped it."

"Liar," I laughed coldly. "There is no escaping you. I won't run anymore. You understand me? You want me to run so that you can hunt me down and rip me apart as I beg and plead for mercy. Fuck you. I won't do it. End it now, Malachi!"

He stepped back, and I tilted my head the other way, studying him. He never waited when I screamed, not with the need to teach me who was in control here. Usually, he let me glimpse the memories, but this time he was allowing me to live in one much longer than any time before. Power radiated through the room, and my focus shifted to the black gossamer wings that extended from Ryder's back.

"Syn?" Adrian's voice entered the room, and I turned, glaring at him. He hesitated, and then slowly looked around me. "No stake, right? Not going to save my soul in the next few minutes?"

"Adrian," Vlad warned, and I stepped back, noting how many people were around me. Normally, each person who entered my memory was another monster the soul-eater had invited to dine on my body.

"Fuck, Syn?" Adrian moved closer to me.

"Do it," I hissed.

"Do what?" Adrian countered as his eyes narrowed on me.

"End it."

"End what?"

"Adrian, back the fuck away from her." Vlad's tone brokered no argument, and Adrian stiffened, doing as he'd been instructed. "She isn't okay right now."

I noted the weapons being drawn while everyone waited for me to make a move. Weapons? The Seelie didn't use weapons. They used their razor-sharp talons and teeth to rip me apart. My claws extended, and my eyes shifted back to Ryder.

Lifting my nose, I inhaled his scent as he watched me. I was done with these games. I wasn't going to let this monster think he'd won just because he could suck out my memories and replay them for me in vivid detail. Only he'd never been able to hold them this long, so what the fuck was happening?

"You're either getting better, or I'm dreaming," I whispered through the thickness of tears. "Just kill me, please? You promised to stop making it last too long. This is torture. I believe you. I know Ryder threw me away. Please end this. I'd rather die than feel this anymore."

"Synthia, I didn't throw you away," Ryder said thickly.

"Yes, you did! You left me with the monsters. Is this what you want? For me to play along with your sick fucking game? Will you end it quicker if I do? Let's play, asshole," I growled through quivering lips. "Please, it hurts too much when they take me. You promised that the Seelie wouldn't be allowed to eat me alive anymore if I gave you what you wanted. Please don't do this, Malachi."

"Jesus Christ, what the fuck did they do to her?" Adrian asked angrily.

"You know what you do to me, all of you."

"Fucking hell," Asher snapped, entering the hall. He took me in, and his eyes flooded with pain. "Look at me, Synthia," he demanded, and I did, hating the oozing fuck-me vibes that slithered over my flesh. "You are out of that hell, I promise. The Seelie are not here, nor can they touch you."

"Fuck you," I hissed vehemently.

"Synthia, calm down," Ryder whispered, his hands up with his palms exposed.

"I'm not playing into this game again. You want to convince me I'm here? Bleed for me, bitch."

"Kinky as that is, and add in the fact that you've already tried to ride my pony in front of your husband, I draw the line at blood play. I'd rather go back to you on my pony, but again, you're married."

"I didn't escape," I hissed as anger pulsed through me, balling my hands into fists at my sides. "I'd remember if I did, don't you think?"

"I think Malachi took your memories, and they're coming back, but they're not the same as they were. I'm guessing you think this is something the Seelie are doing to you because they were able to take those same memories from you. You may never recall all of what he took because that nasty fucker fed off of them, Synthia. However, this isn't them fucking with you. You got out of the prison on your own. You came here looking for what you lost. You came home to your husband."

My breathing grew labored as pain started between my eyes, wrapping around my head to mimic a migraine. I couldn't look away from Ryder because I didn't want him to disappear. If he did, how long would it be before Malachi could make him seem this real again? Memories lied. They distorted images and the truth to the one who held them. This one was vivid, and even his scent was on-point.

How many times had I pleaded for Ryder to save me before I'd given up? How often had I begged him to get me out of here? How many times had he laughed and told me I was right where he wanted me, slowly being deconstructed to nothing more than a memory myself?

I slapped Asher the moment he was close enough to reach for me, laughing methodically at what would surely come next, and watched his hand move to his face. His eyes widened as he held the red mark my hand left on his iridescent flesh. He'd attack me now. They never allowed me to hurt them, ever. I was beneath them. I was their food source and enjoyment, nothing else.

"Ouch, fucker. That wasn't nice, Synthia," he snapped.

"Why aren't you hurting me?" I hissed as the craving for nothingness filled me.

Memories were pain.

Pain reminded me that Ryder had left me here. He had to have known what was within the cave. He would have known I could never escape, and that I'd be ripped to pieces.

Abuse, I could handle. Being ripped apart every night, whatever, but feeling? Feeling the emotions reminded me of who I'd been, and sometimes I wanted it, and other times, I craved the emptiness I'd become.

"Because you are free of that hell! I'm not a monster pretending to be someone else. None of us are, Synthia," Asher snapped, his hand still against his cheek as he studied me.

"Prove to her it is you, Ryder," Adrian demanded, helplessly.

"He can't," Asher said, deflating as his multi-colored eyes surveyed me. "She thinks we're monsters. She assumes we're fucking with her and intend to hurt her. I'm guessing it was how they fed from her emotions. They forced her to relive her memories repeatedly until they would be completely consumed. They used to do this to the girls, forcing them to live through torture as they first began to break them. Eventually, once they stole enough of their mind, they could take things from deeper in their subconscious. She thinks this is a memory, and we're all waiting to give her pain. Isn't that right, sweet girl?"

Ryder pushed Asher away and grabbed my face between his hands, holding me with the roughness of his palms. I could taste the liquor on his breath as it fanned against my mouth. His hands dropped, and he pulled me closer, brushing his lips against mine.

"Does that feel like I want to hurt you?" he asked huskily. His gaze searched mine before his mouth crushed against my lips. I allowed it, holding him closer until I could feel the heat of his body mixing with mine, warming my insides until a moan escaped my throat. "Woman, I love you."

Malachi never let the memories go this far. He never let Ryder say those words.

I pulled back, glaring at him before I lifted my knee swiftly, hitting him in the balls. I sent him sailing through the air and crashing through the wall. I stood statue-still as I watched it crumble down on him, breathing in ragged breaths.

No one moved as I sauntered forward, alert and entirely in control. Ryder rose, brushing the dust from the broken wall off his shoulders before he spun around, staring at me.

"There's my girl. Welcome home." His lips curled into a smile, uncaring that I was about to destroy him and pulverize that grin.

"Fucking run, Fairy," I whispered, barely loud enough for him to hear the warning. Something fluttered behind me, and I turned my head slightly to the side and saw that I had wings.

That was new.

I watched as they completely unfurled, and I smirked, turning to glare at Ryder. He vanished, and I followed him through the jetstream of his movements.

He thought he could just come back and tell me he loved me? Fuck him. He'd left me there to die and be endlessly tortured for twenty fucking years of my life. I smiled coldly, studying the images that passed through the stream with me.

I landed before him, kicking him in the back and watching him roll across the ground into a crouching position before he sifted out.

"You better fucking run faster than that, asshole."

CHAPTER NINE

RYDER MATERIALIZED BESIDE THE Fairy Pools, and I landed in front of him, kicking out as he turned toward me. He jumped over my foot as it swiped out to take him down. I leaned in, intending to rip through his chest to take his heart, but he grabbed my hands.

"The fuck, Synthia?" he snarled.

"Fuck you!" I hissed, feeling the others as they appeared around us.

"It was supposed to be empty," he admitted and released my hand.

The ground trembled around us as I brought the earth up from beneath his feet, sending him sailing toward the water. I sifted in, kicking him in the stomach with an angry growl before he even broke the surface.

He sifted out, not attacking like I wanted him to, but appearing on the shore instead. Breathing heavily, I slowly walked out of the water toward him.

"I thought it was empty."

"It wasn't, not by any means."

I sifted, but he vanished a moment before I reached him. The surrounding men stared me down, their eyes narrowing on my wings and the pulsing brands that covered my shoulders, running down my arms and wrapping around my torso.

I vanished, appearing in the forest. I looked around as I slowly walked through the brush in bare feet, clothed only in the flimsy gown I woke up in. I could feel him watching, his scent filling the surrounding woods.

"You left me to die," I accused, sensing the others before they sifted into the area, observing me from a safe distance.

"I left you there to become this." He moved his hand up and down to indicate my body, and I smirked.

"Yeah, all I had to do was give up everything I am, right? Do you know what kind of monsters were down there? Soul-eaters, shredders, flesh-eaters, and my favorite, the ones that rip into your vagina to eat your ovaries, because, oh, you know, they're so fucking delectable to their kind. Thousands of monsters were down there, and my sweet, loving fairy-fucking husband abandoned me to them so

I could shed my humanity? Congratulations! It's gone, but so is your wife, asshole," I growled, looking up at the darkening skies.

I hissed and expelled a breath, watching as flames leaped on to the surrounding trees. The scent of burning timber and pine needles filled the air of the forest as I watched. My eyes closed as thunder and lightning crashed around us. The wind kicked up, wailing through the woods as trees began to uproot until Ryder finally stepped out from behind one.

"Twenty. Fucking. Years," I snapped.

"Three days," Ryder countered firmly, his eyes roving over me as I stared him down.

"Is that what you think I endured? Three days were spent attempting to crawl up the walls of that cave. Three days of you whispering how unworthy I was to be by your side. Three days of how you'd replace my insignificant ass on the throne. You know, at first, I doubted it was you.

"Then, as days turned to weeks, and weeks turned to months, and years passed...I knew you'd abandoned me just as they'd said you had. Oh, how I tried to hold on to hope, but then hope is such a fucking worthless thing down there. Hope made me fucking weak, because I hung on, thinking maybe, just maybe you'd realize your mistake.

Anger was okay, though. It was useful. It made me fight the shadows, trying to remain in the light as long as I could."

I sifted, landing right behind him, pushing my fingers through his spine to wrap my hand around his beating heart. The sickening slurp of his flesh made the monster within me roar for me to remove it, and yet I didn't want him dead. I wanted him to know how the pain felt.

"You cannot kill me," he said softly, pain etching his tone as he spoke.

"Oh, Ryder, I don't want to kill you. I want to rip you apart so that you know how it feels. Do you know what happens when they start to remove who you are? The sensation and consciousness of being fully aware that you are being deconstructed to nothing more than a soulless, cold thing?

"Let me tell how you the monsters dissected me. They took away my flesh, bit by bloody bit. Next, they devoured my organs, but only the ones I didn't need to live. Death isn't granted. To remove what you are, you have to endure the torture alive and remain conscious through it all. Next came my eyes, the gateway to the soul. Those were removed before they removed my limbs so that I couldn't escape or fight back. My tongue was next, so I couldn't scream.

"They do such naughty things to you when your parts are exposed, and you can't argue it. Such dark, delicious things that you almost fucking crave it because when they do, all those wounds they created open up, and you hold on to hope that death may come and end your suffering." I released his heart and turned him around to face me. The moment he did, I pushed my hand through his chest, gripping his heart and squeezing once again as tears ran down my face. Ryder grimaced in pain, and his haunted gaze never left mine.

"They don't let you bleed out, though." I looked at my hand in Ryder's chest, and I smiled. "Malachi had butterfly fingers and such precision that even the most painful of things became art. I learned to listen and give him what he wanted so that he stopped sharing me among his friends. I gave pieces of my soul because it was the only thing I had to barter. It was the only thing you'd left me.

"First, he took my parents and the Blood Kingdom, or most of their memories. It wasn't enough, and so he dug deeper. He took the friends and family I'd made here. He shredded my soul as he erased you from my mind, and in your place, he put monsters. I became his fucking toy just so I could remember you. Three days? No, I was down there for twenty years, and for twenty years, at the stroke of midnight, I died. I would rise the next dawn just to relive the endless torture over and over again."

"Three days passed here, and every day I was at the mouth of that pit to watch you." His eyes pleaded with me to understand, but I was done looking into those eyes to find my peace.

I laughed coldly, lifting my dead gaze to his. "Three days in, I was dragged into the shadows and torn apart into bloody fucking pieces, ripped in half, watching creatures eat my organs while I was compelled to enjoy it. I woke, fully healed, and thought it was only a nightmare, but then that same creature tore me apart again and again. I lost hope down there. I lost my humanity, and that is something you shouldn't have fucked with."

I pulled my hand out of his chest and materialized my swords. I moved to strike him down, but Zahruk's blade stopped mine before I could take Ryder's head. The Elite Guard stepped closer, watching me as I spun, intending to fight Zahruk, but the cold bite of steel against my neck halted me.

I turned, staring at Ryder as a maddening smile flitted across my lips. His sword was pressed against my throat, a silent threat of protection against me fighting Zahruk. I pushed against the blade, watching as he pulled it back, but not before the damage was done as it sliced through the side of my neck, leaving a bleeding wound.

"I can't be killed either, asshole."

"You were supposed to be down there alone. You were only supposed to be there long enough to understand that you belong to *this* world. You are magic and beautiful chaos, and yet you held back from taking what was there for you, what was rightfully yours to take. I wanted you to realize how helpless you were as a mortal."

"I did. I so fucking did, Ryder. I realized it about the time they began to torture me. You left me there, and I begged you to save me, but I couldn't reach you because that isn't how that place works. I will never beg you again."

"I fucked up. I know I fucked up."

"You didn't fuck up. You shattered me, Ryder. You wanted me to change, well, here I am. Am I everything you hoped that I would be?"

He stepped nearer to me, his brows creased, and his lips turned down.

I let him get closer, allowing him to touch my shoulders as his mouth drifted over mine. "I'm so sorry, Pet."

"Me too," I chuckled.

"I love you," he whispered.

"I fucking hate you." I stepped back, staring at him and his forlorn expression. "Don't look at me like this is my fault. You chose this. I chose to let you decide your fate, and it *was* a choice. I was trying to protect you by making you stronger, and you? You meant to leave me down there. You didn't even fucking consider the consequences before you did it," I spat, turning to look at his brothers. "All of you abandoned me there. Not one of you bothered to ask those who had been within that prison what was actually fucking in the hole in the ground. Three days passed for you, but me? I got a life sentence of torture and despair."

"This war isn't over, Pet."

"No, it's not. But then we haven't been fighting the war together now, have we? You've been fighting it while keeping me in the dark, and I have been fighting to protect you. Do you know how I gained my powers? I climbed out of that fucking prison on my own fucking bones mixed with the monsters who had tortured me. So you can fuck off!"

"We need to fight this war together, rather than on our own, woman. We're losing. I wonder why? Because you refused to gain your powers, and I can't be everywhere all at once! Yes, I fucked up," he snapped harshly, staring at me. "I can't win this war without you. I needed what you were created to be, not the scared little girl who wasn't sure this world was hers. You had your feet straddling both worlds, fighting two separate wars on two battlefronts. I expected you to reach for your powers to escape that pit, and instead, you refused. You are a fucking goddess. You are my wife, Synthia. I have moved pieces for decades to get us here, and the only thing that was holding us back was you."

"Is that so? I told Alden that I couldn't fight in their war. I was right fucking here. Do you want to know what held me back? *You.* You did, Ryder, not my humanity, not their world. You kept me from reaching for what was mine because I couldn't think of anything beyond you. What fucking place did I have in your world without you in it? What would I do without you? If I wasn't at your side, where the fuck did I belong in Faery? Without you, I didn't know because I couldn't see myself here without you. Now I do, but it just happens that I no longer fucking care where I belong as long as it isn't with you. Ironic, isn't it?"

"I love you, and I will love you until the day I die. I'm sorry for what I did, and I am sorry that you suffered. I only intended for you to be cold and alone, to know that you needed magic from this land to save yourself. You weren't supposed to feel any pain or be tortured. I'd have never let you remain down there had I known you were not alone. I need to know where you stand because our people are dying."

"I stand with the people of Faery. I am their goddess, after all."

"And us?" he asked carefully.

"There is no *us* anymore, Ryder. There is you and there is me from this point forward. You lost me when you decided to abandon me. I would never have walked away from you. I would never have left you in that pit, no matter what you had done. You left me to die, and I did, but worse, *we* did. I will stand beside you and fight this war with you, but afterward, I will leave Faery so that we do not become like the god and goddess who we now battle against to ensure its survival."

"I will not stop fighting to get you back." He squared his shoulders, willing me to see the promise in his eyes.

I snorted, watching him as his obsidian gaze slid over my brands. "You don't want to fight me, Ryder. That would be a war you would never win. I'm not the same girl you walked away from and abandoned. Death changes a person, and it isn't for the better. I'll be around. Fuck you later, Fairy."

I vanished, moving effortlessly into the slipstream as the world faded away around me. Ryder was the love of my life, but he'd left me when I leaped into that pit. I was pretty sure he'd never be able to get past the damage that had been done to me, especially since I couldn't get past it myself.

I was different, colder, and yet not. I was lost in the ebb and flow of pain that still lingered over me. I loved him, but loving someone and being able to forgive them wasn't the same thing. I didn't know if I would forgive him, or if I could love him enough to cope with what I'd endured.

I felt fractured.

Powerful, but fractured to the point that I was no longer myself. I was the Goddess of the Fae, and right now, I was pissed off.

CHAPTER TEN

I SPENT DAYS IN Faery, moving from one place to another as I learned my new powers. Along the way, I'd murdered thousands of mages and hunted them down with a renewed determination to eradicate them from this world. I hunted to forget and to find myself again.

I missed Ryder, and yet I wouldn't accept that only three days had passed here while an eternity had unfolded in the Seelie prison for me. Worse, I'd ripped the runes from the walls and released new monsters into this world. I'd done that, assuming what had died on my way out would remain dead. I'd believed that my immortality had brought me back, but I found three of the Seelie creatures here, hunting my people.

Ryder had been saving people while I was being ripped apart. I'd done things just to feel him, or to glimpse the life I'd shared with him, assuming he'd abandoned me.

He hadn't.

Ryder had thought he was giving me tough love—or his version of it. Elysian, Asher's sister, had found me a few days ago. She was checking in on me. Since she'd endured the same monsters for a much longer time than me, she confided that no one really knew how time worked in the prison or how much had passed. She'd also informed me that the moment Ryder had learned that the Seelie prison wasn't empty, he'd come for me, but I had been gone.

It didn't make it any easier for me. None of that information absolved Ryder of what he'd done. I'd gone into that hell on my own, yes, but he should have tried to get me out. Instead, he walked away, leaving me to the monsters. Ryder was the same, but I wasn't. I'd shed my humanity, but I'd removed everything else as well.

I wasn't the same girl, nor could I be. What if he didn't like this version of me? I didn't like it. In fact, I couldn't stand the coldness I felt or the memories that filled my head, even with my eyes open. I'd murdered three people while sleeping, and that had been an accident. What if I killed my husband?

Staring down over a village preparing to march toward the Horde Kingdom, I scrutinized it absently while Elysian spoke softly. She'd helped me hunt down three creatures that had endlessly tormented the fae, feeding on them without care of the damage they did.

"You do know that eventually, you'll need to talk about what happened to you down there, right?" she muttered.

"I had sex with a monster to remember my husband. I willingly allowed it to happen and repeatedly sought him out because I needed to remember Ryder. Without those memories, I didn't care about escaping, and I needed to care to get out of there."

She nodded as if she didn't blame me for doing something as atrocious as having sex with my tormentor just to glimpse my memories.

"I fucked monsters, Elysian. I slept with creatures that got off on ripping my body apart to feed from it night after night. I felt them fucking me. I felt them feeding from me, and I did nothing to stop it from happening."

"What could you have done? You had no power, no magic, and no help. My first week down there? I sucked off several Seelie princes who were related to me maternally, and I swallowed their cocks like a glorious whore just to fucking live. I did whatever the fuck I had to do to stay alive. I had no one, and Asher had no idea I was down there when I was first thrown in by our mother. I became a damn good whore and played my part while they ripped me to pieces. Down there, it isn't the same as up here, Synthia.

"You did whatever you had to do to survive. It doesn't mean you wanted to do what you did. It means you wanted to live. You got out, so now you have to figure out what you want. If you let this destroy you, they win. If I can survive over a thousand years down there, you can survive twenty."

"How do I tell my husband everything that happened and the details of what I did to survive that hell?" I asked softly. "I wasn't raped, not really. I mean, the first time I had sex with the monsters while the Seelie Prince ignored us. He was so powerful, Elysian. Malachi was absolute power down there. If he was even in the room, I succumbed to whatever was wanted of me. I would wake up with him holding me, with him touching me. Like he'd kept me alive, and yet I wasn't. He would hold me there for days, and then he would feed me to the monsters.

"He ate my soul, and I assumed he was like the others. He wasn't. He was ancient, cold, and worse, calculating. He made me into his bitch, and I let him because he kept the pain away and fed me memories of who I was, which made me remember that I needed to escape that place. I killed him, but I didn't. I think he broke me until I started rebuilding myself into something else, something...*stronger*. I don't know why he waited that long, or what his intentions were. I think he realized that I would be the one to take out the runes and free them all. I freed him, and now he is out here, feeding on my people. I released monsters into this world."

"Malachi is the firstborn son of Danu and King Oberon, or so the rumors go. He is a legendary lover and soothsayer who promises pleasure, and he delivers. He gives absolute pleasure as he feeds, but he gives pain too," she snorted as tears welled in her eyes. "He isn't all evil, but he is not all good either. You called him a soul-eater, and I knew of whom you spoke. I am the one who begged Asher to leave Malachi in that cage. If he allowed you to remain down there that long, he had his reasons. Malachi does nothing without knowing the end and the outcome before he even starts the game."

"He hurt you too?"

"He made me his... his personal plaything for centuries. Asher finally heard a rumor that I was down there, and he and the others fought Malachi to free me. I am Seelie, Synthia, and I was not immune to him. I am powerful and unaffected by our kind, but he is Oberon's son and the deadliest Seelie in the entire realm. If I wasn't immune, what chance did you have?"

"I feel like I betrayed my husband down there. I feel...dirty. Unclean, because if I behaved, Malachi let me see my memories," I admitted, ashamed that it slipped from my tongue.

"That's what he does, goddess. He takes the things you love the most and gives them back to you, but at a price. If Faery had a mascot, it would be Malachi."

"How do you know about mascots?" I asked, needing to get off the subject for a moment. I hated that I had sex with those monsters while Malachi watched. I didn't want it, that much I knew.

He made the pain go away, and I'd desired that more than the humanity, which made me remember I wasn't some slut who did what monsters wanted.

The memories he allowed me to glimpse were worth it and made me need to survive, fight, and get back to my children, even if my husband no longer wanted me.

"I fucked a mascot," she shrugged at me when I turned, gaping at her as my face hid little of the shock and horror I felt at what she said. "I heard Erie making fun of her sister for fucking Lucifer. The devil? Anyway, she mentioned tentacles that did the most erotic things, so I went to the human realm searching for the devil. I found him at a high school game, something to do with a foot and ball, but not like kicking someone in the balls? Humans are so weird, but anyway. They had a mascot that was the devil, and well, he had one rather large tentacle I rode for a bit, and he explained his job as a mascot. We took something called selfies because he said the chess team was never going to believe he bagged a hottie without them."

"Did he live long enough to share the selfies?" I inquired carefully, controlling my tone.

"Hell, yes, he was fun. The boy could eat some pussy really well too, which saved his life. Plus, he was pretty dorky. He opened the door for me and even offered me a blanket as if I could actually get cold. Men like that, this world can use some more of them. Anywho, back to Malachi," she said pointedly, her tone husky with an undertone of both sadness and lust. "He will come for you, as much as he will come for me. You see, Malachi doesn't allow his pretty toys to escape him easily."

"If he comes for me here, he will die," I whispered hoarsely. "I am not a fucking toy. I am Synthia Raine McKenna, daughter of Danu, Goddess of the Fae, and Queen of the Horde. I will rip him apart piece by fucking piece as he allowed his people to do to me. Let him come for me. It will be the last thing he ever does, Elysian."

"You're Synthia? Fuck, and here I thought you were some broken maiden who needed to be reminded of who she was. My bad, Your Majesty. Question, though, if you're the Queen of the Horde, what the fuck are you doing out here in no man's land, watching idiots run around like ants with their heads cut off?" she asked, smiling coldly.

"Slaughtering things that don't belong in my world," I muttered. "Fine," I said when she lifted her brow at the lie. Not that it was an actual lie since I was still covered in their blood. "I'm hiding because I'm hurt and pissed. He told me I was his world, and then he left me with the monsters. I've never wanted anything else or anyone else since the moment I met that infuriating fairy, and it terrifies me that I gave up a part of my soul to glimpse what I had with him.

"I didn't want to fight Malachi because I knew fighting him wouldn't free me. Even now, I'm not free of him. He changed me, and I don't think it is for the better. What if Ryder doesn't like who I have become? He is the same. I'm not."

"He wanted you to change, didn't he? You're never going to be able to go back and undo what was done, that much is a given. You can choose to become a victim, or you can decide to be a survivor. You can't be both. Yeah, he hasn't changed. He's still the same man who loves you. The question is, Synthia, can you love him enough to forgive him? Can you love him with who you are now?

"He fucked up, but you came out of it stronger. You arose from that hole a fucking badass who used her own blood to draw him love letters and wings. You ripped your fucking heart out and left it for him to find. Admittedly, maybe a little too far with that extra bonus, but I had a lady boner from it."

"Actually, I don't remember that part, only climbing out. Something happened down there, something traumatic that shut me off as I left. Whatever it was, it allowed another part of me to turn on. You said I almost fucked Asher, and honestly, he's hot, but I'm not that person. I don't sleep around, nor do I want to. I don't even remember Thanatos sewing my soul back together."

"Here's the thing, girlfriend. You were a badass, a very horny fucking badass, but it's still the same thing. You didn't have a soul, and yet you sought Ryder out because you and he have a deeper connection than any soul could reach. You'd have taken my brother, but Ryder's voice stopped you. Even without your heart and soul, you were his. I say you put him through a little hell of your own and see how you feel afterward. I mean, after all, he did leave you in the pit of monsters. He deserves some payback, right?"

I stared at her before turning my gaze back to the village, where people packed to head toward the stronghold. Ryder may have fucked up, but he was doing what he said he would do. He was saving our people, even though he wasn't responsible for them.

He'd opened the gates to his home for these beings, which really weren't worth saving. They didn't add to Faery or give to the land. They were just fae, and the only reason to save them was that he knew it would hurt me if they died.

"He's got a lot of shit to make up for."

"Well, he is immortal, so time isn't an issue, now is it?" she asked, pushing her blonde hair away from her iridescent skin. Unlike Asher, her brands were silver and blue and wrapped around her arms. "I didn't think I'd like you. I thought you probably lived this lavish lifestyle where you were pampered, but you're nothing like I expected. I listened to the people in the courtyard telling stories of what you have done and been through, and I realized a few things."

"Such as?" I asked, staring down the valley.

"You've been through hell, but you always get back up again. You've been defeated, but you don't see defeat, you see lessons. You were murdered and actually chose to save the lives of your children, which to me, seemed strange at first since my mother tried to kill us all. Synthia, you're chaos and darkness, but there's a light that burns so brightly within you that no amount of torture or pain will ever dim or touch it.

"I don't question why you were chosen as the Goddess of the Fae, not anymore. I see a mother, a warrior who will never accept defeat, and more, I see a woman who can be broken but never beaten. I'd gladly follow you into battle. You pick up other women, dust off their crowns, and remind them of who they are. You're the fucking queen, and yet you'd place your crown on another woman's head if she needed it. You're also powerful as fuck and banging hot. I mean, I don't lick the pink taco, as Asher calls it, but I'd consider licking yours. I bet it would taste like cherry ice cream."

"Uh, you had me until pink taco."

"Yeah, probably went too far on that one. I need to stop listening to the men when they talk. They're strange creatures."

"You're a beautiful mess, Elysian. Sometimes the most beautiful things are cracked and broken. They just need a little duct tape, and to be reminded of what and who they are."

"Where can I obtain this duct tape?"

I frowned, cocking my head as I shook it, and her eyes narrowed. "It was metaphorical."

"What is metaphorical?"

"It's like when you are trying to get a point across, and you use an awful reference, like pink tacos," I stated, shaking my head as laughter bubbled up.

"Maybe we should stop talking in metaphorical terms before I end up duct taping my broken pink taco?"

"Is your vagina broken?" I winced.

"No, which is exactly the point," she chuckled and winked with both eyes.

"You and I need to work on your people skills."

Her eyes brightened with laughter.

"I would like that. I've been stuck with my brothers forever, and I'm pretty sure they have no idea how to fit into this world we have found ourselves a part of now."

"I think you're going to fit in just fine. We're all fucking broken, but somehow, we always come through it stronger."

"So, what's the plan?"

"I'm going to remind Ryder who I am and let him see who I have become. And if he doesn't like it, too fucking bad. He shouldn't have left me in that prison. It's time to give him hell."

"That's my sister," Ciara said from behind me.

I turned, staring at the women who were sifting into the woods. Ciara smirked, her violet eyes filling with flames as she nodded at me. Fyra bowed her head, a mischievous

smirk lifting the corners of her lips. Icelyn clapped her
hands slowly, her ice-blue eyes dancing with hope, and
Lilith chewed her lip, crinkling her nose as the shadows
played around her.

"It's about fucking time, Synthia," Erie announced. "I
was about to admit defeat just to escape Callaghan and his
dick. I almost tripped and landed on that thing... *twice*. So,
what's the plan?"

I smiled past the tears in my eyes as my throat burned.
They didn't look at me like some broken thing, but as
the Queen of the Horde and Goddess of the Fae. That
meant everything to me. I didn't want to be pitied for what
had happened, because at the end of the day, Elysian was
right. I could lie down and die a victim, or I could rise as a
survivor.

"Let's go raise some hell, ladies. Shall we?" I asked with
a wicked smile curving my lips.

I wouldn't let my time in the Seelie prison destroy me,
because that wasn't something I could do. I wiped away
the tears and told them everything I had planned and what
I intended to do next.

CHAPTER ELEVEN

RYDER SAT ON HIS throne while I studied him from behind an invisible barrier. He wasn't paying attention to
the complaints being discussed, or the men arguing before
him. He was lost in thought, which probably had to do
with me cutting him off from the mental link we shared.

I'd shut everything off, including my emotions. He
could no longer feel me, so, to him, I was just gone. He'd
heard and felt nothing from me over the last several days,
and none of the women had told him where I was, or that
they'd been in touch with me.

The guard announced the next two men to the court,
explaining their grievances with one another, and Ryder
didn't even acknowledge them. His expression was pensive
and wasn't one that he displayed often. I sort of liked that
he was consumed with worry over what he'd done and
what he'd lost.

"This is Jamil and Kar, Your Majesty. Kar is taking issue with Jamil and his people slaughtering horses to eat, but wasting the meat afterward. Kar is from the Summer Court, where horses are prized pets and hard to come across. Jamil is from the Court of Nightmares, and says he can eat whatever he wishes to, including any children that enter his camp."

The men waited for Ryder to acknowledge them, and when he didn't, I smirked. I sent my magic seeking him, slithering over his legs to run up his thighs, slowly. He'd done this to me a thousand times, using his magical cock to take me in front of his court without them ever being the wiser.

One time he'd made me cry out in the presence of an entire assembly of high fae, and while I wasn't certain how it worked, I wanted him to feel me and know what it was like to be toyed with in public.

I needed him to know he wasn't the only one with power. I wanted to make him sweat; make him feel uncomfortable as his cock was ravished without me ever physically touching it.

Closing my eyes, I imagined my hands slowly caressing his chest as my lips brushed over his mouth. His eyes narrowed, and he turned, wide-eyed, looking at Zahruk. My magic fluttered over his body, and he searched the room as he repositioned himself on the throne. Moving the magic toward his thick, massive cock, I visualized freeing it from the restraints of his pants as my magic slid over the salty tip, mimicking the feeling of my tongue.

Ryder continued to fidget, spreading his legs slightly as if to allow better access. My magic wrapped around his cock, and I sent sensations of being licked and sucked in a slow, steady rhythm. He sucked in a breath as his brows furrowed, sweat beginning to build just below his hairline as he peered around the room, looking for the source of magic.

I didn't fuck around. I began to simulate the feeling of his long, hard cock being buried deep in my throat as waves of magic kissed the flesh at the base of his shaft. Magic stroked and pulsed around his cock repeatedly to take him over the edge as fast as I could. I leaned against the wall as my body burned with desire, actual tears running down my face as the results of the magic affecting my body.

Ryder sat back and spread his legs further apart as his hands tightened on the arms of his throne. He grunted, his teeth grinding together so hard the noise filled the throne room. Those around him began to notice his discomfort and chatter started to sweep throughout the crowd.

My head leaned against the wall while my magic contin-ued to pump his cock, and I watched as he struggled to fight what was happening to him. Even as I stood far away from him, I could see the bulge straining against the pants he wore. I imagined my hands around the thick shaft, stroking it slowly as my magic worked the tip, slamming it against the imaginary barrier, mimicking the sensation of being deep-throated.

Reaching over to my throne, he grabbed the pillow, pushing it onto his lap. He growled as he came undone for me. I swallowed as a smile covered my lips, and I swear I could taste his salty essence, which was unexpected...but *neat*. Looking more uncomfortable than before, Ryder lowered his eyes, sending his magic through the room, searching for me.

"He's useless. His queen left him, and now he does nothing but sits here staring off in the distance, pining for some worthless bitch," Jamil snorted, and I sifted, ripping the fabric of the world, appearing in the middle of the throne room. I flung my hand back, closing the tear between worlds as I sauntered toward the dais.

The sheer black dress I wore exposed every curve while subtly covering each minute detail of my body. My crown was firmly in place as my heels clicked across the floor loudly. Once I reached Jamil, my fist ripped through his stomach without hesitation, withdrawing the bloodied organ. I turned slowly, handing it to Kar, who stepped back from the worthless flesh I offered.

"I thought you wanted your horse back?" I smiled coldly as amber eyes watched me, not intervening in what I had just done. Kar shook his tawny head and continued to backpedal away from me. "What did you want, then?"

"For them to stop eating our horses," he announced, fear dripping from each word. "Not his stomach."

"He can't eat them anymore, now, can he? He seems to have lost his appetite," I snorted, peering down to where the other male lay bleeding out on the floor, "and his life, for insulting my king and his worthless whore." Dismissing them, I moved to take my place on the throne.

Zahruk stepped next to Ryder, and I narrowed my eyes in warning. Then, I grabbed the pillow in Ryder's lap and tilted my head to peer down at his rock-hard cock with a pointed look of victory.

"That was naughty, Synthia," Ryder growled as he glamoured away the evidence of his release.

"And? You used to be fucking delicious, and I needed a little taste to see if that were still true," I grinned coldly. "You're standing in my way, Zahruk, unless, of course, you're challenging me as Queen? If not, then I am still the Queen of the Horde, and my rightful place is on that throne."

"He's my brother," Zahruk warned.

"And my husband." I stared at Zahruk, studying the indecision burning in his pretty blue eyes. "I don't want Ryder dead, Zahruk. We have a war to fight, and we have to figure out a way to co-parent, now, don't we?"

Zahruk slowly stood aside, and I sat on my throne before the court, noting the smiles on the faces of the women. I could feel Ryder's glare burning my face, and I ignored him. His hand reached for mine on the arm of the chair, and I shifted my hand into my lap instead.

I straightened my back and stared forward, waiting for the next group of subjects to be announced. My heart raced from being near him, and butterflies danced in my belly. My skin sizzled with the power he oozed, and then sadness washed through me.

"Synthia," he uttered.

"Don't," I warned icily. "I am here as your Queen, not as your lover. What you did, it is unforgivable right now. I have a lot of things that I need to work through on my own before I could even consider trying to fix anything that might still be between us."

"I can wait." Muscles ticked in his jaw, and he folded his hands in his lap.

"I don't know if you should. You hurt me. You told me I was your fucking world, and then you walked away from me. I'm not the same girl, Ryder. Your Synthia, she died. I am what crawled out of that hole. You may not even like me anymore."

"You're wrong." Tilting his head, he grinned, trying to mask the pained expression he'd briefly shown. "Nothing can change who you are."

"I asked you not to do this here in the presence of the court." I turned my attention away from him, facing forward, ready to hear the next court grievance.

Ryder slowly sat back, staring out over the crowd who watched us. Men moved forward, and, one by one, he handed out judgments while I remained silent at his side. For better or worse, the horde didn't believe in divorce, and I'd agreed to be his wife, so I would remain such as long as we both lived. We had children together, and no matter what happened, we had to figure out how to coexist for their benefit.

When the last judgment was rendered, I sifted from my throne and entered our bedroom. I felt Ryder come in behind me, his power untethered, and I knew without asking that he intended to keep me here. He didn't want me out there alone, but he had no idea of the powers I now possessed. He was afraid his weak wife would get slaughtered. Well, she had been, and then she'd evolved.

"You won't like what happens if you try to hold me here. I've been a prisoner for twenty years. I won't be one ever again."

"Tell me how to fix this," he murmured softly.

"I did horrible things down there, Ryder. So, what the hell is there to fix?" I didn't sugarcoat it. I blurted it out and refused to look at the hate that played over his harsh beauty as I told him about having sex with the monsters in the pit.

"Not at first," I admitted as my throat tightened with tears. "The first several times I was taken by force, but then Malachi removed the pain and showed me my memories. He ate my soul. If I wanted to see you, I had to be with the monsters. So, I had sex with them because I needed to be reminded of who I was, and that was the only way I could access my memories. You, the children, this world—he took it all away from me. He took everything and then offered to let me see it for a price. I did what I had to do to remember us. The only thing I knew for certain was that you'd thrown me away and left me to my fate in that prison, refusing to come for me when I called out to you.

"Malachi left me the painful memories, but only the ones I endured before this world. I whored myself out to remember your face and your touch, and the sound of our children laughing. Eventually, I begged them to fuck me, to give me a taste of the memories. So, you tell me, husband, can you live with me, knowing what I did?" I pierced him with a cold, dead glare as I lifted my chin and crossed my arms over my chest in challenge.

"You did what you had to do to survive." The lines around his eyes softened, but there was uncertainty in his tone. "I don't care what happened. I only care that you're here with me now."

"I don't think you comprehend what crawled out of that hole, Ryder." I unfurled my wings, pushing my shoulders back as I glared at him. "Your wife died down there. My soul is in tatters. Thanatos may have sewn it together, but I don't feel anything except for rage and humiliation. I've spent days watching our people struggle, and I felt nothing for them. I have slaughtered thousands of mages and not felt an ounce of remorse. My humanity is gone, but even worse, I feel *nothing*.

"I don't even feel lust or need. That little display in the throne room was to give you a taste of what it feels like to be toyed with and manipulated by magic. It seems the playing field is now equal." I took a step forward and let Ryder see the truth in my words. "I have no compassion or care if this world survives. I mean, I know it needs to, but I don't much care either way."

"We'll fix it." He sighed and scrubbed his hand down his face as he walked toward me. I put my hand up, halting his progress.

"That's another thing. I don't want to be fixed. I'm not broken, I'm changed."

"This world is tied to our people. People you were born to save."

"*Why,* though? Why save some selfish pricks who can't be bothered to save themselves? Why save a world that is hell-bent on dying? Why should I accept some shit destiny because a fucking goddess decided my fate before I was even born? Why should I do anything you and your people want from me? You've treated me like an outsider. You have held me at arm's length. I am your wife, and yet you don't trust me with your secrets.

"Ironically, I didn't trust you with mine, either, which doesn't make me any better than you, but I don't care. That just proves to me that we were never working as a team. It is you against our enemies, and me against our enemies, but we are not working together to achieve a common goal. You've lied to me since the first moment I met you, and every moment since. I hid what Danu told me to do with her essence because it didn't make sense at the time. But then, the thought of losing you to this war hit me, and I couldn't live with the secrets. I still offered you a choice, Ryder. I made certain that you could decide your own path. I never planned to take that decision away from you, but you, on the other hand, designed my entire life to fit into your plans. You keep big secrets from me because you don't trust me."

"Synthia, we can work this out if you let me help you."

"Ryder, you left me in a hole, hoping I got my shit together. Well, I have my powers. I have no humanity, and I'm here. That's all I fucking got right now."

Closing the distance, Ryder placed his hands on my shoulders, pulling me into him and resting his forehead against mine.

"I know it was much longer for you, Pet, but three days was all that passed for the rest of us. Every fucking day I sat right at the top of that pit, staring down at you, making sure you were okay. I listened to you pleading for me to save you as you lay in the dirt weeping, but all I saw was that you were dirty and cold. From what I could see, you were safe. You were supposed to be fucking fine."

I pulled away from him and stepped back as cold resolve spread through me.

"Yeah, the thing about it is, I would never have begged you in the fucking dirt on my knees. I would never have lain down and given up. I'd have fucking raged at the sight of your face, which should have been evident when I died and proved who I was by getting on my knees to show you something I would never normally do."

"I can't fucking take it back, and even if I could, it wouldn't undo anything that's been done. There's a lot going on, and we got hit hard, Syn. So fucking hard that it shook our world, and you still wouldn't reach for the powers that were right fucking there for you, begging for you to grab them. If you'd have accepted them before Bilé killed our family, you'd have slaughtered that murderous prick without even trying!" Ryder paced in front of me as he ran his hands through his hair and along the back of his neck in frustration.

"You had Bilé on the ground about to ride his cock while you held his fucking heart in the palm of your hand," he gritted out through clenched teeth. "The only thing that stopped you was me, because I couldn't stand to watch you seat yourself on the bastard who took Dristan from me!"

I repeatedly blinked past the tears that flooded my eyes. "I know we got hit hard, Ryder. I was the one here fighting Bilé and the mages. I did what I thought was right, and I get that it's my fault you lost family members. I've had a *lot* of time to consider what I did wrong. I've spent years going over that night, accepting my fate because I knew you blamed me for their deaths, but I didn't kill them. I thought I was everything I was supposed to be, and you made me believe it as well. You told me my powers would come, and I trusted they would. You are as much to blame as me!"

"I know!" he shouted, gripping his hands into fists as a vein pulsed in his neck.

I opened my mouth, ready to argue, and then closed it, shaking my head.

"I can't be here right now." I turned to leave, but he grabbed me, holding my arm gently.

"I love you, woman. I have loved you since the moment you opened those pretty lips and told me where to stick it. I am sorry, Synthia. I know that I failed you. I did what I thought was right at that moment, but I was wrong. If you need space, fine, you have it. If you need time, take it. This war isn't going to wait for us to be ready, though. I will fight it for you and our children. I don't care what you did to survive because, at the end of the fucking day, you did what you needed to do, and that is all that fucking matters to me. You and our children are the only lights in my life, and you make me want to be a better fucking person.

"You lost your humanity, so fucking what. You're fae and not human. You lost parts of your soul, me too. You are my soul, Synthia. I lost you, and without you, I don't care about Faery either. That's a bad fucking combination to have two gods in one realm who don't care if the world fucking ends."

"You care." I stepped closer to him, cradling his face between my hands, brushing my lips across his gently. "You've always done what's best for this world. That is what made me fall in love with you. You are selfless, even though you don't see it. You are the glue that holds your broken family together. You are a good man in a storm." My hand rested against his chest, feeling his heart quicken with the slight touch. "I will sleep in my own room tonight," I said, pausing to step away from him. "Don't disturb me, not even if you hear me screaming for you. It's residual memories from the prison, something I'll deal with on my own. Goodnight." I grabbed a few of my things and began walking into the other room.

"You're not alone."

"Actually, I am, but it is okay. I learned how to accept it years ago. My demons come, but they don't stay long. The scariest part is, occasionally, I miss them."

CHAPTER TWELVE

SOMETHING TOUCHED ME IN my sleep, and a scream ripped from my throat, echoing through the room. Doors burst open, and I shook violently as the screaming intensified. The nightmare clung to me, repeating in my mind as I was torn apart while Malachi watched in the shadows. His blue eyes held mine, enjoying the pain and feeding from my emotions as I refused to show him my memories.

For five years, I'd clung to my memories as a lifeline while the Seelie tortured me daily until death overtook me. Butterfly fingers of precision had worked over my flesh, holding the pain away as the monsters jerked on tendons and nerves.

The moment Malachi released my hand, all the pain would hit me at once. He loved it. I begged for mercy, pleading to be killed just to escape what they did, and at the end of every night, I was given that sweet taste of death.

"You're okay," Ryder said, crawling into my bed and pulling me against him as I fought to control my body's violent tremors. The walls cracked as the castle shook slightly. "Gods, Synthia, breathe," he begged. His hands smoothed over my hair, touching my forehead while raining soft kisses on my face where tears trailed down my cheeks.

"Let me go," I whispered through a sob that clung to my throat as I tried to pull away from Ryder, only to have him hold me tighter.

"No," he growled. "You're not alone. I did this to you."

"Ryder..." I pleaded, fighting past the pain in my chest as my stomach clenched tightly.

"I don't care if you bring the fucking castle down on my head, woman. You're not alone anymore. I have you."

"You're so fucking stubborn and pigheaded, Fairy!"

"I know," he countered.

"I hate you!"

"I know," he whispered, a little quieter.

"I hate that I don't hate you," I admitted.

"I'm okay with that too."

"Gods, you are infuriating."

"I can live with that."

"Lay down, horse's ass."

He released me, lying beside me as I studied him. Once he was back against the pillows, I turned, facing away from him, sliding close enough to feel the heat of his body without actually having to touch him.

The doors closed as the guards exited, silent sentries as they'd rushed in when I'd screamed. I exhaled a shaky breath, and Ryder lifted his hand, touching my hip, quietly scooting closer. I pretended not to notice he did so.

"Talk to me," he pleaded while his fingers skimmed my hipbone.

"About what?"

"What were you dreaming about?" he asked.

"No."

"You can't keep it all inside, Synthia."

"How long have you been a god?"

"Since I was three hundred and seventy-two years old," he admitted, which surprised me.

"How did you become one?"

"I entered the temple and found a vial full of blue liquid had been placed on an altar. I sensed I was alone inside the temple, so I approached the altar and studied the bottle, feeling an immense power coming from within it. I knew it hadn't been left for me, but I couldn't resist the opportunity to grasp the power that could free my family from Alazander's hold. I think Danu had intended to create you with it, but I prevented that from happening by consuming the liquid. I drank it all and woke up days later, somehow changed.

"At first, it was little things, small insignificant changes that alerted me to what I was becoming. I hid it, hid the power I was gaining from everyone, even my brothers. The day I killed Alazander, I used the power I'd concealed, mixed with rage and fear. Afterward, when the beast entered me or awoke—whatever it did when it chose an heir to become king—I used the power to control the beast to be certain I didn't end up like my father. It was how I kept from going mad, I think. Now, will you please tell me about your nightmare?"

I sighed, realizing that Ryder would not let this go until we talked about my dream.

"For five years, they ripped me apart. I refused to give Malachi my memories. They would cut me open and tear the ligaments from my bones. They exposed nerves, and he would hold my hand like he was comforting me. Then, he'd let go, and all the pain would hit me at once. Elysian said he is absolute power, and the first Seelie Prince, born of their mother and Oberon.

"After five years, I lost hope. I couldn't do it anymore. I was unable to die, so every morning I would wake up whole, and they would tear me apart again. I didn't feel the cuts, the limbs they removed, or the damage they inflicted until Malachi let go. I think that's what made me want them, to have the pain go away. Comfort was only something Malachi could provide, and he wanted the memories that I would access during the pain."

I felt Ryder's eyes watching me, and I turned to look at him. "Malachi asked for small memories at first, feeding from them as I told him of my life. Once they were gone, he would kill me again, and I would wake up without them. I would reach for my memories to continue surviving, but they weren't there anymore.

"I would go through the same torture daily, as I fought to hold you and the memories to me. But each time, it got worse. He studied what hurt me the most, and he used it. So, I gave him more and more, until none of it remained. He left me the memories of the guild for some reason. I don't think the outside world interested him much. We went through the same routine every day, until one morning, you and this entire world just vanished from me. I knew I missed something, someone.

"Malachi told me that I could know what I lost, but what I had to do was something I'd promised never to do. The thing was, I didn't know what it was or why I should care about a promise I made to a faceless being. Not until I was coming undone for his monsters and your face was all I saw while I was with them. I knew then that it was you I missed. He changed the Seelie into your form so that he could learn what emotions were like when love was involved. So, night after night, I was with the monsters because they became you. Whatever part of my soul remained, it recognized you.

"Twenty years in, and he stopped pretending to be anything other than what he was. He would torture me to know more, but he stopped preventing the pain, and that's when I changed.

"I started using my corpses and those of other creatures I slaughtered to build a ladder to escape, but only when he let me run from him because he liked to stalk me. He enjoyed the hunt.

"One night, I fucked his monsters, and I gave him everything he wanted from me—or what I assumed he wanted. I no longer cared about what happened because it was an endless loop that I couldn't escape. He left me alone to endure my pain with one of the monsters, so I leaned over as I fucked the Seelie, and I ripped his throat out, murdering him. I escaped that night. I pulled the runes from the prison walls and climbed out of the cage using my bones as a ladder. When I reached the top, Malachi was there, watching me from the shadows. He knew I would be the one to release him. I freed them all because I assumed I'd killed them.

"But you cannot be killed in the Seelie prison. I thought I'd survived because of my immortality, which I believed the Seelie wouldn't have to protect them.

"I was insane when I escaped, ripped apart and partially gutted from the monsters fighting back. I don't know if I ever left that cage, though. I think a part of me stayed, and another part of me took its place. I know that when I crawled out of that hole, I wasn't me. It was my body, but there was only a hollow shell that craved what it was missing."

"You tried to take my heart and Asher's. You almost killed a god, Pet. You would have ended the fucking war without even trying. If I hadn't said something..."

"I would have fucked everyone and then killed them. I would have hated myself more than I do now."

"Hate yourself for what? For surviving? You don't get to hate yourself for that. It's not your fault, nor do I hold it against you. I am as much to blame for what happened to you. Not to mention, I am the reason you were created in the first place. I forced your mother to create you, Synthia. I have been planning to take this world back from the gods for eons. The monsters in those cages, well, they're older than that."

"I did things I'm not proud of during the five years, Ryder. I begged them to fucking kill me. I thought the Seelie were giving pleasure, and I begged for it. I don't even remember half of what happened in the first five years. I don't know how many of them used me or what they did when I begged them to do it. They were Seelie, in a cage that should have left them powerless, and yet they turned me into my adopted mother. I lay on that floor, pleading for them to hurt me, just like she did before they gave her their orders to kill anyone who came into that room. Malachi was powerful, and I was weak. I was almost human there, just as you wanted. So how the fuck did he have powers, and not me?"

"Because Oberon lived thousands of years ago, Synthia," he explained softly, touching my cheek to push away stray hairs that were glued to my face with the silent tears. "He lived when the first creatures were created, the ones in the temple. He is rumored to be among the victims in the pool, the one I showed you when I asked you to marry me. The lore says that he mated with one of the first fae women created.

"I'm guessing he mated with the Seelie Queen, and they had a son. If he is their child, he's been down there for over ten thousand years. Asher said it took them nearly a thousand years to learn to wield their power. Malachi had nine thousand years longer to hone his. You had twenty years. It took them a thousand years to get enough power, and for the prison to weaken before they could escape. It only took you twenty years to figure out how to escape. That is my wife, not some unfeeling creature. That's my badass wife who can't be contained."

"Why aren't you screaming at me? I did things that weren't pretty. It would be so much simpler if you would just condemn me, and we moved on from this."

"No, it would be easier for you to hate me if I condemned what you did. You didn't act out of spite or unfaithfulness. You did it to survive, to remind yourself of what you needed to do to get back to me. You came here, Synthia. You came home even without knowing it was your home. That isn't something a monster would do.

"That's what love is, right? It's unending and all-consuming. I lost you once, and then I felt that pain again when I stared at the corpse that sat at the bottom of that pit. I was willing to let you go because you were alive. I loved you enough to accept that you'd come back, but then Lucian called in a favor. He had Thanatos track down Malachi's monsters in that tunnel, and he tore them all apart. He took what they stole from you and brought it back. And then, Synthia, the enforcer, rode my cock, intending to end my life, and I fell a little more in love with you, even though you said balls—a lot."

"That was a really awkward phase, and to be honest, I only said it because it drove Alden insane."

"You wanted to kill Adrian and tried to stake him several times."

"Awkward, very awkward," I admitted.

"You were something else at seventeen, Pet."

"I'm tired." I turned over, and I scooted a little closer without touching him still. "If I kill you in my sleep, I'll never forgive myself, and it will totally be your fault."

"You can't kill me, I'm a god. Sleep, witch," he uttered.

"Goddess, I don't do that casting magic thing anymore."

"Yeah, I almost miss it. Life was so much simpler when we hated each other."

"You were pretty fucking hot when I hated you," I admitted.

"I'm not hot now?" he asked in a wounded tone.

"You're hot, but not in a villain kind of way. More like an *I own that* sort of way?"

"Hmm, I can live with that."

"Go to sleep. You're incorrigible."

"I love you."

"I—I'm tired." My tone filled with emotion, and it took a lot to hide it from him as my eyes grew heavy. His hand held my hip silently, protecting me the only way he could from the nightmares.

"So sleep. I got you. Sleep, and I'll hold your broken pieces together and keep your monsters at bay so that you can rest."

CHAPTER THIRTEEN

Ristan held his son in his arms, still unwilling to let anyone other than his mother, Alannah, hold the child. It was progress that Ristan had begun allowing anyone to assist him. Even if she was an evil bitch who pined for the throne and Ryder's crown, she was still his mother. My attention swung back to the map in front of me, and I swiped the pieces from it, muttering absently as Ryder and the Elite Guards lifted their heads in surprise.

"What are you doing, Synthia?" Ryder asked, watching me.

"It's worthless to plan anything. The mages know our moves before we do," I grumbled, reaching behind my back to itch where my wings sought to be free. "Bilé knows all our plans without being told. How? We're guarded, in a room that is heavily warded, and they still know all of our strategies and every move we make before we even march from the gates. It doesn't make sense." I reached around, scratching again where my spine burned and my wings tried to unfurl.

I was learning to accept the fact that I had wings now. I'd given up the idea of cutting them off, especially since Ryder had warned me that removing them would only hurt like hell when they grew back—and they *would* grow back. It wasn't that they weren't cool; it was that the fuckers itched because they were new, and occasionally I almost impaled people because they would spring free when I was upset or something happened to trigger an emotional response. I didn't have the luxury of time on my side to learn how to use them, either.

"So, Bilé can see us, or we still haven't flushed out all those who are here spying for him," Ryder countered.

I studied his features, allowing my gaze to slide over the beauty of his sharp bone structure. His eyes lifted to hold mine, and I realized that everyone around us was carefully observing each move we made. The entire war room was filled with dread and enough tension that it was smothering.

I wasn't sure what they expected from us. Ryder's brothers were probably waiting for us to fight physically, or to announce we would be the first couple in the history of the horde to file for divorce.

Leaning over the map, I studied its material while making mental notes, like the ink that had been used. It was invisible and made from materials within Faery, a relic that Ryder had actually disassembled and used to keep the information on the map hidden. It kept the outlines and locations of our troops secret from anyone who entered the war room, should they come into it without permission.

The elegantly carved pieces they used to signify troop formations were cut from an elder tree, ancient and old, grown from within Faery.

The blood Ryder utilized to create the markings and landmarks on the map was willingly donated by several high fae.

And, last but not least, the map material was created from the skin of his fae enemies who were locked in a separate prison.

"It's the fucking map and everything on it," I blurted, closing my eyes against the evidence that had been right in front of us the entire time. I scrubbed my hand over my face, groaning with the absurdity of it.

"What about the map?" Ryder leaned over the parchment, brushing his elbow against mine as he set his hands on either side of the map, studying it carefully. His narrowing eyes moved from it to me and back before he exhaled slowly.

"All the materials used to create this map are from Faery. The ink is created here, infused with the magic of a relic from this world. The pieces are carved from the heart of the elder tree, one as ancient and old as Faery. The map itself is from the skin of your fae enemies, which you took for betrayals against the horde. Bilé has access to our plans not because he had spies or because Eris spelled the map when she was planting chaos in the stronghold. He didn't need Eris to touch the map because he can access anything in this world.

"Our map is created from creatures and material made from inside Faery. He has access because Faery was created for him, and by being so, he can see and hear us freely—no need for spies. We need a new map that isn't from this world, and we need it yesterday. Bilé has eyes and ears on us even now, Ryder."

"So, even though we used the map against him, he knew, and he sent his men to die." Ryder's voice shook with anger, his fingers slipped through mine, and I fought the eruption of butterflies his simple touch created.

I let the heat of his touch filter through me, allowing the comfort it offered, and then I pulled away from it. Ryder was my drug. He was the intoxicating addiction that could awaken me from slumber, forcing me to be either high or low. He fucking ravaged through my system, leaving me sated and yet never permitting me to escape the addiction.

I had to heal before forgiveness could begin, and I wasn't sure I could do that while he offered comfort. I couldn't readily accept his forgiveness until I could forgive myself for what I had done.

He hadn't been there, nor had he witnessed what I'd allowed, which made it easy for him to ignore the vileness of the acts. I relived each one in my nightmares, watching my body being used for whatever the Seelie desired.

I hadn't fought hard enough to prevent it from happening. I had to find a new me. I had to live with this new version of myself and rebirth. The girl who had entered that pit had been naïve and weak, allowing herself to depend on others. I couldn't afford to make her mistakes because everything depended on me evolving or changing enough to do what was needed before I decided on my next steps.

The guilt I felt was soul-crushing. Even though I had been helpless with what had happened, it didn't stop the shame from soaking into my bones and consuming me. I couldn't shut it off; same for the pain that clenched around my heart when I looked at my husband and remorse slipped around my throat to choke me. Ryder held me, and I let him, but when the harder memories slipped into my mind, I pushed him away to protect him from the sins that consumed me.

"We won't win against Bilé like this," I admitted. "He's willing to sacrifice his entire army of mages just to strike us where it will hurt us the most. We care too much about our people to let them die, and he doesn't care how many sacrifices are made as long as he can take the land back."

"Then, we'll give it to him." I turned, staring blankly at Ryder as my mouth opened and closed, searching for words. His golden eyes studied me, watching me react to his words while I narrowed my eyes on him.

"Give Faery and its people to that monster, just like that? Walk away from this world and our destiny, to what end?"

The room erupted into loud objections, and I noted the fire burning in Ryder's eyes as he silently observed my reaction. Men argued with one another, some agreeing it was safer to abandon the world and live, while others argued that we should stay and fight.

Would Ryder willingly walk away from Faery and leave it to a monster that would slowly kill everything within it? We wouldn't be able to save the people. There were simply too many of them and not enough of us.

"There are other worlds in which the fae can live," Ryder shrugged, narrowing his eyes. His tone was aloof, uncaring, and it struck a nerve. He couldn't be serious, right?

This was our world as much as it was anyone else's. We belonged here, just like all the other fae! Walk away and give it to Bilé just to end the fight? My head cocked to the side as my ears heated with anger and the need to fight his logical explanation.

The room silenced at his words. I pondered them for a moment before shaking my head. He crossed his arms over his chest with his thumbs hiked, confidence oozing from his pores. I exhaled slowly, turning his words over in my mind.

"Anyone left behind would die," I stated, folding my arms and spearing him with a pointed glare, mimicking his posture to make a point. I could be an aloof asshole, too. My head lifted, holding his gaze without fear or trepidation, both of which most creatures expressed in his overpowering presence.

"Well, it's not your fucking problem, now is it? You don't care about our world or the people who depend on it to live."

"I'm not the dick trying to abandon it, now am I? I'm right fucking here beside you, fighting to save it with you, Ryder."

"You said you didn't care what happened to this world, so why are you fighting so hard to save it, Synthia? It's not your fucking problem, right?"

"I'm fighting because this world is as much ours as it is Bilé's. The people of Faery depend on us to continue fighting, to protect them and their children from that monstrous bastard who would see us all dead!" I snapped harshly, unfolding my arms to glare at him, clenching my hands into tight fists at my sides.

"Spit it out, woman," he urged with a smirk tipping the corners of his mouth.

"I won't lose Faery to some asshole who thinks he can murder our people and not face the consequences of his actions. He doesn't get to hurt us and get away with it. It doesn't matter what I feel. It matters what I know. He murdered my family, and for that, he will pay dearly."

No one got to hurt us without paying in blood for their crimes. We were the horde, and I wanted more than just blood for what Bilé had done to us. I wanted his soul, and I wanted him buried so deeply in the earth that he felt it every time we walked on it.

"You're wrong, Synthia. If you don't love something, you don't fight with every fiber of your being to keep it safe. You don't go to war to protect something unless it is worth fighting to protect. You don't seek revenge for those who have not earned your heart, because when you seek retribution, you fucking mean it and go after it with everything you fucking have."

"You can fight for a good cause based on what's right and wrong. Feelings don't have to dictate your actions. I can fight and not care about the end results, Ryder."

"Is that what you think? That you can fight this war without really caring about the outcome? You can't half-ass something and expect to win. You either put everything you have into keeping that which you love safe, or you fucking don't bother trying. Some things are worth fighting for, no matter the cost, and this is one of them. So, you can engage in this battle beside me and give me every-thing you have, or don't fucking bother lifting a sword. I'm right here, woman, waging war against Bilé to free this world with you. I'm fighting for us."

"Are you two assholes talking about the land or your love life? I'm confused," Spyder asked, looking between us, rubbing his chin as he glanced at the others in the room, puzzled by our back-and-forth argument.

I glanced briefly at Spyder and then back to Ryder's challenging stare, waiting for him to answer the question as tears pricked my eyes. Ryder didn't look away, he just stared at me, unmoving, and I frowned. I worried my bot-tom lip with my teeth and slowly shook my head.

"You're wrong. I love you and this land, but I don't have to want either of you to fight for your survival. You want me? You have to earn me, because you broke my trust,

Ryder. This world? I love this world, but I don't like it.
It is cold, vile, and even the flowers try to fuck you over
here. It is part of Faery, though, isn't it? The cold, deadly
world that Bilé and Danu created to rule over," I muttered
absently. "You created a new realm for those who needed
to be hidden from your father."

"That isn't known, Synthia," he warned, his tone turning hard.

"Can you do it again? Can you build a world to hide the
fae from the mages as we fight this war?"

I didn't care if I exposed his secret realm. The end of days
was here, and we were in the final hours. It wasn't time to
hide his dirty laundry. It was time to come together and
build a plan to get our people safely out.

"Take us out of the equation for a minute, Ryder. It's
not about us, not right now. At this moment, only Faery
and our people matter. Everything else can be put on hold.
It can wait until the fighting ends to be figured out. Stop
worrying about your fucking secrets and start thinking
like the fucking God of Faery. I am the Goddess of the
People, and you're the God of the Land. Regardless of our
relationship, we are in this fight together."

"Wait, what world did you create together?" Ristan
asked as he reentered the room, catching only a portion of
what was said.

He had a burp cloth over one shoulder, but his son wasn't using it. The babe was against his other shoulder, and his tiny wings spread wide as he sucked against Ristan's bronzed flesh, causing blood to drip down his arm. Little wings were visible in the blanket he'd wrapped his son in, and it tugged at my heart.

"Is he eating you?" I peered around Ristan, trying to get a better view of the babe.

"I did not create a new world," Ryder muttered. "Synthia is speaking of the one where we hid Ciara to protect her when I fought Alazander."

"Not big enough to hold the fae, then," Ristan frowned, swinging around to face me. "He's not eating me. He latches on to my flesh. I think it comforts him to bite me, and so I allow it."

"Because that isn't strange..." I touched the back of his son's bright red hair, watching as a blue line followed my fingers as I caressed his tiny head. I closed my eyes and blessed the babe with a long and fruitful life. His little fingers reached up to grab mine, and I smiled as I gazed into big beautiful eyes that looked like his mother's.

Ristan stared at me, and before I could argue otherwise, he handed me his son. I took him without a choice and cradled him close to me. Ristan exhaled slowly, as if he was releasing the weight of the world, and then darted forward, hugging me tightly.

My eyes prickled with tears as he kissed my forehead. He exhaled again, and I wasn't confident that it wasn't the first time he'd allowed himself to breathe since Olivia's death.

"Oh, demon," I whispered thickly, knowing I hadn't been there when he needed me most.

"Fucking hell, Flower." His voice was hoarse and tight in his throat, making him choke out the words as he spoke. "I'm so sorry you went through all that shit. I should have known better or done something to help you." I hugged him tighter until I felt a prick in my shoulder. "Watch out, he bites."

"Must get that from you," I chuckled, kissing his son's head. "What did you name him?" I shrank back slightly, instantly hating myself for not asking before now.

"Orion, because his mother prayed to the stars every night that he would be perfect. It also means son of fire, and he is destined to become a mighty hunter. I thought it was a fitting name due to his fiery hair. He looks just like her." Ristan's chin trembled as he fought back his emotions. "Olivia would have been over the moon and stars for him." Leaning down, he placed a kiss on the top of his son's head.

"It's the perfect name for a perfect boy," I admitted, kissing his red curls.

Blood dripped from my shoulder, and yet he didn't bite any further, just enough to hold on to me, as if he feared I would drop him. My fingers dusted his wings, and I watched as his tiny tail curled around my wrist, holding it there as he stroked it.

"You will come back from this," Ristan whispered against my ear, surprising me.

"In time, but will it be soon enough to make a difference? That's the real question."

"You're strong, Flower. You're beautiful turmoil who fights like a category-five hurricane, wreaking havoc upon the shores of land until it washes away and life is renewed. I know we let you down when you needed us the most, but you're stronger than the experiences you have endured. I don't blame you for Olivia's death. I know I came off hard when she died, but it was like a piece of my soul was just ripped away without warning and is still missing. If I can get through this without her, you can get through whatever it is that happened to you in that prison. Someday, you'll understand why it happened."

"If you tell me that everything happens for a reason, I may scream at you, demon." A tight smile covered his mouth, and he took a step back, out of my reach. "I don't know if I can ever be who I was before what took place in the prison."

"Maybe you're not supposed to be that girl anymore. Stop trying to be her and learn to be you. You're not what they forced you to become. You're who you were created to be. So what if they pushed you. Push back, Flower.

"Demon, it's not that simple."

"You're the fucking Queen of the Horde because you were strong enough to hold that power, and no woman has ever held it in check before. You have survived death and other harrowing events, and every time you get knocked down, you get up stronger. So, get back up because we need you to be with us for this fight." He held his arms out for his son, and Orion sifted, vanishing from my arms to go back to his father's without needing to be told.

The sight of Ristan holding the tiny babe in his strong arms sent warmth rushing through me with pride. We'd come so far in the little time we'd all been together. In all actuality, it had been a little over a year since I'd met Ryder, and even though it felt like lifetimes, it hadn't been that long. I'd fallen in love, become a mother, and faced war all before my twenty-third birthday, which most people hadn't really even begun living at my age. Shit, most people hadn't even decided a course in college at my age, and here I was, trying to save a world. I'd died, been reborn, and changed so much in the little time I'd been here, that I was doing pretty damn well, or so I had thought.

Tears burned my eyes, swimming in my vision as I watched him adjusting the tiny babe. Ristan lifted his eyes to lock with mine as he nodded, not needing words to tell me he was going to be okay. Maybe not today or tomorrow, but eventually, we were all going to be okay again.

"I know, but life isn't black or white. I now know what the gray is, and it isn't pretty."

"We don't fight for us. We fight for our children. They deserve a chance to live in this world without the threat of war breathing down their necks. Our kids deserve to know this world, so whatever you two need to do, I suggest you do it," Ristan all but commanded. "Mommy and Daddy can't be fighting when we need them the most. Not when we're readying our army to march into war together for our biggest fight."

"It's not that easy." I turned, leaving the room as my stomach flipped with the memories of the monsters. Sweat beaded on my brow as I passed people in the hallway, turning a corner to be alone. Everything felt off, wrong, like I was still trapped in that place of hell, yet to escape.

"Synthia," Ryder called, and I turned, walking backward without stopping.

"What?"

"I can do it. If you think it is something we need, I'll build you a fucking world to hide our people while we fight this war together."

"I don't know if it would work, Ryder."

It was bipolar, but how did you convince an entire race to hide while others fought a war? How long would they have to hide in that world, and what would the cost be to my husband if he built it with his magic? He'd already made one world, a beautiful one for us to escape into, but it was our haven, and it wasn't even close to being large enough to hide an entire race.

Ryder stalked toward me, closing the distance between us until he forced me to stop against the wall, caged between his hands. "If you need a fucking world big enough to fit our people, I'll make it. If you need space, I'll give it to you. I won't give up on us, though, Synthia. I'm an asshole. You knew that when you met me. I never hid that part of myself from you. I have never lied about how I felt for you or what you made me feel. That part of us has always been real."

He studied my face, licking his lips as if he intended to kiss me senseless, and I craved it more than the air that fed my lungs. Swallowing hard, I observed his sinful mouth before directing my attention back to his heated gaze.

"Except the part where you lied to me about what you are. You let me assume you had been taken from me at our wedding, and I lost our child to save you. Ryder, you broke my trust, but worse, you broke my fucking heart by not trusting me enough to tell me your secrets. We're supposed to be a team, you and I." I tried to move out from under his arms, but he sidestepped and blocked me. Giving up, I sighed and looked up at him. "Look, I don't know where or when it stopped being us against them and started being us against each other again, but it did. Now, if you don't mind, I need to see to the people in the courtyard, and then I need to rest. I will send word to Alden to bring in parchments, along with a new map. Meanwhile, we can begin creating a new realm, provided you can do it without hurting yourself or losing power as it is being created. I don't want it if it hurts you."

I ducked beneath his arms, taking off as if the floor were on fire. I couldn't deal with the heat in his gaze or the way my body clenched with the need for him to take away the pain and memories of Malachi and his monsters. And I sure as shit couldn't think or remember I was mad at him when his lips were close to mine.

That man was quicksand. The more you fought against it, the deeper you sank until you no longer struggled. The man was saying everything right, but actions spoke a lot more than words, and I'd yet to see them. If he really wanted me back, he'd make an effort.

Loving him was easy; it was second nature to me to love that beast. The real issue was, I didn't even like myself at the moment, and I had to work on me to fix what was broken. I wanted to see Ryder prove that he loved me and wanted me for more than just the power that rushed through my veins. I needed to know he was all-in, and that he could look past what I'd done to survive.

CHAPTER FOURTEEN

THE ENTIRE COURTYARD WAS filled with displaced fae that swarmed the grounds like an immigration camp. Thousands of fae came to the horde for sanctuary. During their arrival, bedlam had ensued, and they'd been neglected because of it. Now they were desperately low on food, clothing, and tents to stave off the wind and elements. Desperate people could easily become dangerous as the need to survive began to consume them.

"Have more food brought up from the cellars to feed the hungry," I said to the guards awaiting my orders. "Pass out rations per family, not per caste or group. Have the weavers and magic wielders glamour more blankets and be sure they are thick and warm enough to stave off the chill in the air. Hand them out to those who don't possess the ability to create their own supplies, clothing included. These fae shouldn't be cold when we invited them to come to our land to find shelter. Have the tanners bring in more tents. Those without families should be placed into larger shelters to share living arrangements, allowing families to have their own tents. Send for the woodworkers and have them bring scraps of wood they cannot use to make weapons to feed the fires.

"Strengthening the wards should be our main priority. Lucian should be called in to add more power, reinforcing the ones we have, and building any additional wards needed to protect the stronghold in the event of another attack. Spyder can do it if Lucian cannot be reached.

"Send additional guards to the larger groups of people. Several fights have occurred in the last few hours alone. That should not be allowed to happen, not with families here to observe or be caught in the middle. If anyone fights and does not heed the warning, they will be placed in the dungeon until they change their fucking attitude.

"Smile, as well. We're welcoming people who have been through hell into our home. Looking as if you'd rather murder them than help isn't reassuring anyone that they and their families made the right choice in coming to us for assistance. After you've handed out the supplies, ask about their abilities.

"We need to chart who is going to come in handy, or who needs to be at the back of the marching army before we leave here. Ale is also needed. We want them to be comfortable and feel safe, gentlemen. They're our guests, not our prisoners. Let's make sure they're aware of that fact."

"As you wish, My Queen," Johan, one of the guards, nodded as he rushed away with the others to follow the orders I'd given.

I stared after the guards, silently shaking off the tightening in my stomach as memories flashed through my mind. Closing my eyes, I pictured my children as they'd been before Destiny took them away to protect them. They were my happy, calm place that sent a wealth of warmth rushing through me to remove Malachi's icy claws from my soul. I heard the sound of gravel beneath feet, and I turned to see Ciara, Erie, Icelyn, Lilith, and Fyra file in behind me.

"At my sides, ladies," I muttered as I fought to dispel the last remaining ice from the nightmare I'd had before coming down to tend to the fae. "Let's go say hello to the people of Faery, shall we?" I winked and watched as wicked grins spread across their faces.

"So, are you sure we can't rough them up even a little bit?" Erie asked.

"Fae are friends, not food." I shivered at the idea.

"I wasn't going to eat them, ew," she cringed, scrunching up her nose in distaste.

Torches lit the paths along with small fairies as they zipped here and there through the crowds of people. Larger braziers added warmth around the edges, and large, winged creatures that resembled a cross between giant lions and birds blew the heat over the courtyard.

Ryder had added more torches throughout the grounds, which I appreciated since the moons of Faery were at a waxing crescent, and nights in this world were similar to a blackout in a big city.

Creatures milled about, using their abilities to ease other's discomforts, and it warmed me to see them being so giving to one another. It wasn't often the fae came together and helped each other out, and to witness it happening on this grand of a scale offered hope for a brighter future.

Families sat around fires, cradling their children closely, causing my heart to ache for my own children to be here, and yet it was too dangerous to bring them back unless we won the war.

Thanatos's warning echoed in my head every time I even considered their return. The reality of the situation hit home hard as widowed mothers begged at the gates for entrance.

Fathers brought motherless children, and occasionally cases of parents grieving the loss of their young ones met our ears. War was ugly, and it didn't care about the young or old, feeble or strong. It killed without mercy, driving through families and leaving carnage everywhere it touched.

Men stoked the fires while children sat huddled around them, shivering violently from the cold. The flames did little to stave off the icy fingers of spring that wrapped around Faery. Most families had fled their homes without anything other than the clothes on their backs.

I frowned as I took in one father who added what looked like charcoal to the fire. For several moments, I watched him doing everything he could to keep his children warm. I glamoured blankets, stepping closer as the father rose to defend his children from the threat he thought I imposed. Eyeing me suspiciously, he blocked the path to the tiny children.

"Who are you?" The father held his hands out as his children readily accepted the blankets, causing me to swallow down the urge to reassure him that I wouldn't harm them.

"She's the fucking queen! Chill the fuck out," Erie snorted as her hands landed on the dual swords that graced her slender hips.

"Queen of what?" he demanded. Fear slid across his features as he moved to where the firelight illuminated my face.

"The horde." I smiled and moved past him to place a blanket around his daughter's shoulders, ignoring his uneasiness at us helping him and his small family. "There you go, sweetheart. And you, you look fearless, good sir," I said to the tiny boy. I knelt in the dirt, uncaring that it dirtied the dress I wore. Quickly, before the boy could argue, I glamoured another blanket of fine wool and extended it to him. "For you, my brave little warrior," I offered, watching his eyes lower to my hand that was outstretched for him.

"They say you've ripped men's throats out, is it true?" The young boy's eyes were wide with wonder, and excitement lit his smile.

"Bailey! She is the Queen. You cannot speak unless she grants permission," his father corrected harshly.

"Can you keep a secret, Bailey?" I whispered behind my hand, loud enough his father could hear me. He moved closer to me, clutching the blanket in his tiny hands, and I grinned.

"Yes, My Queen," he crooned, nodding vigorously as his eyes sparkled with delight.

"Yes, I did rip a man's throat out, but only to gain the respect of the horde. Honestly, he tasted vile. Right now, though, I'm here to help my people. You shouldn't be cold or hungry when you are here on my lands. You are my guests, and I will not see my guests go hungry or shiver in the dirt when I can readily help them. What would you like to eat?" I asked, searching between the children's dirty faces. I waved a hand, watching as they were cleaned from the filth of being outside for a prolonged time. The little girl's mouth dropped open, and she rose, hugging me as her father hissed.

"I'm sorry! We're not used to being in the presence of royalty. We hail from the mountains." He dropped to his knees as she released my neck and hung her head in shame.

"Get up, now," I ordered, standing to stare at him. "I am not an average queen. You should never be on your knees in front of your children. You raise them by example, and we are horde, are we not? She was simply thanking me for cleaning the filth from her. She did no wrong, and nothing that should have sent you to your knees. Now," I said, clapping my hands with a sad smile on my lips, "what would you little beasties like to eat?"

"Ham. Ham and potatoes," the boy said with a dreamy look on his face as he licked his lips.

"Apples and berries with cream," the girl said, smiling as she expelled a sigh of wistfulness. Wide eyes smiled, watching me. The hope burning in them made my stomach tighten with her request for something so simple as fruit and cream.

I snapped my fingers and bowls brimming full of ham and potato soup appeared, along with fruit covered in thick, rich cream. I smiled at the father, who stared at the food with gratefulness. He watched his children digging into it with hunger as their bellies growled, and I grinned, watching them disregard the silverware I'd provided to dig into the food with their hands.

"This is so good!" the girl said around a mouthful of berries, causing me to laugh as her eyes widened, realizing she'd spit some out in her excitement.

"You should eat with them, or they may consume it all before you even get a bite." I glamoured another blanket and held it out to their father, watching him staring at my hands. "I've sent the steward and his men to grab more tents and clothing. They will be handed out shortly. Be sure you receive one, and if you don't, please ask for me personally, and I will make certain you are given one."

"I am filthy, My Queen. I am unworthy of what you have provided my children and me," he admitted uncomfortably, his hand rubbing his neck as tears swam in his eyes. "I am a simple carpenter, and not a warrior worthy of your magic or generosity."

"We are all just trying to survive. It doesn't matter what your role is today. When the enemy comes, we will all fight against them and play our parts to win this war. You cannot fight if you are starving. Here," I stated firmly, handing him a blanket.

My magic cleansed him of the dirt and grime, and I took in his ageless features. He was younger than I'd first suspected, with kind green eyes that stared down at where our hands touched as he accepted the blanket.

I moved on to the next family, and the next, as Ciara and the others joined in, helping the guards pass out blankets, tents, and food to those who couldn't glamour or conjure their own. It was time-consuming work to take care of thousands of displaced fae and creatures, and we'd been at it for hours without stopping or resting.

I smiled as Ryder and the Elite Guard joined us, handing out items and helping those who brought tents set them up. It was a sight to behold, the royalty of the horde out mucking around as they helped their people. It gave the fae within the courtyard reassurance that they were safe, which we should have done much sooner.

Silently, I gazed at Ryder, who was holding hands with a child that peered up at him as if he was the largest, scariest thing in creation, and yet he still clung to my beautiful beast's hand.

Our gazes locked across the courtyard as heat curled into my belly with an overwhelming need that shocked me. A blush filled my cheeks, and I wanted to laugh at the absurdity of it, but I let the butterflies he created within me remind me of how he still made me feel.

I sucked my lip between my teeth, toying with it as we flirted with our eyes amid the chaos that filled the castle's once beautiful courtyard. His mouth twisted into a knowing smile, and I dipped my attention to it briefly as heat filled my center, causing his nostrils to flare as one brow lifted with challenge burning in his eyes.

The child patting his leg caught my attention, and my heart clenched with the desire to see Ryder with our children. I dropped my head as pain lanced through my heart with longing for our little ones. To me, they'd been gone forever. It seemed endless with the time I'd endured in the Seelie prison, while to Ryder, only a few weeks had passed since we'd said goodbye.

I stopped in front of a large tent and peered through the opening to where a male watched me closely. Midnight eyes stared out at me. His thick, bluish-black hair was draped over his shoulders, and he oozed darkness and subtle power that was being suppressed on purpose. His skin was blemish-free, and sharp features told me he was from a higher caste of fae.

He didn't move or get up as I stepped into the large, opulent tent he'd placed in the middle of the courtyard as if he were entitled to the location. His shirt was opened to reveal sleek, chiseled muscles that were covered in tattoos. A soft smirk flitted over his full mouth, enjoying my eyes as they slowly took in every inch of him. High cheekbones gave him a regal appearance, with perfectly sculpted features that begged the eye to caress them.

"Aren't you pretty, My Lady? And plagued with nightmares, no? I can taste them within you, taunting you to dream for the pleasure of the Seelie creatures."

He stood, placing his drink beside him on a small table, and then made his way toward me. I inspected him, noting that his heavily hooded eyes were, in fact, black as a starless night, with a violet outline.

High fae?

"And who would you be, beautiful?" he asked huskily, touching my hair, wrapping it around his finger, studying it silently before his attention returned to mine.

"The Queen of the Horde," I announced, slowly tilting my head while cocking an eyebrow.

I watched the smirk drop from his sinfully full lips as he unwound his finger from my hair and took a step back, studying me through a curious, narrowed gaze.

"No fucking way," he chuckled. "She has brought down men twice my size in battle. She's rumored to be a cold one with breasts the size of the largest, ripest melons in Faery, and you look anything but cold, sweet girl." His eyes dropped to my breasts as if he wanted to add that my melons didn't match the rumors, but he refrained from doing so.

"I've done a lot of things in battle," I returned carefully, igniting my brands and watching the reflection of them in his darkened expression. "Men love to ad-lib details when they start rumors, and those that end up making women into blow-up dolls are such. I assure you, I am who I say I am. Considering that you're my guest, I would remind you to tread carefully."

He stepped back slowly, watching as my body glowed with my inner power, which I allowed to slither over him. I could hear the crowd behind me whispering in hushed tones and noted the woman with a similar complexion entering the tent to stand beside him. Where his hair was jet black, hers was blonde. Where his eyes were dark, hers were light with eerie iridescent pupils and emerald-green irises.

"And you would be?" I asked.

"Cillian, King of Nightmares," he announced, bowing low at the waist in a fluid, practiced motion.

"I was under the impression that a princess, not a king, ruled the Court of Nightmares."

"You assumed wrong," he said huskily, his eyes watching my brands as they pulsed. "My sister, Ayla, is here with me. She is the Princess of Nightmares. We are here among others of my line, which I have brought with us to protect from the monstrosities wreaking havoc upon our lands. Perhaps we could be of service. I do believe that Ayla invoked nightmares upon a small, heavily armed war party that entered my realm. I would be happy to remove it while I am here, Your Majesty."

"No war party was sent to your kingdom, Cillian. Only one with a betrothal contract for the hand of the eligible ruler, if unwed," I explained carefully.

"And who was to be my lucky bride? I have rumors that a goddess may be available to wed, soon?"

"Again, we were under the impression that a daughter ruled the kingdom, so we sent a suitor. No goddess is available, as she is very much wed to her king. You cursed the party we sent?"

"Just with nightmares," he shrugged his shoulders, forcing the light to catch and glint off the silver cuffs that adorned his muscular biceps. His pants hung low on his hips, exposing a happy trail that danced down the V-line he'd left visible. Thick tattoos covered his chest, revealing markings that belonged in another era, moving over his flesh seductively. He was created like the high fae, to lure women with his ethereal beauty.

"Zahruk is plagued with nightmares. He hurt one of my friends as a result of them," I accused, narrowing my eyes in anger.

"Is she okay? Maybe I could ease her pain."

"I didn't say my friend was a she."

"You're too pretty for the Horde King to allow keeping male friends around, Your Majesty," Cillian smirked roguishly. "Send her to me, and I will ease all that hurts."

"She's dead and way past helping now." I stared across the tent to witness a bunch of girls piling out of the furthest room within it.

"I'm sorry. I didn't realize your friend was gone."

"How would you? Remove the curse from my men or leave my home. I will not stand to have my people cursed as they leave for battle. Not when they only came to offer one of our own princes to your court to pay the tithe you owe. It was done in good faith, and to assist you in paying something we knew you were unable to pay," I hissed, watching him closely. "You're a guest here. Your welcome depends on you."

"Ayla, find the men you cursed, and remove it, now," he ordered without turning away from me.

My gaze followed his sister, noting the way her scowl locked on to me. I didn't break eye contact until she'd vanished into the crowd of people outside the tent. Slowly, I turned back to stare at the King of Nightmares.

"You can rid someone of nightmares, can you not, Cillian?"

"It depends on which type of nightmare we're talking about, as well as the level in which they're embedded into your subconscious, Your Grace. I am also not upon my land, and not as strong as I would be if we were there, but I can do my best to ease them."

"Are these all your sisters?" I indicated the girls at the back of the tent, changing the subject abruptly as my palms began to sweat. It didn't go unnoticed, and he frowned.

"Are you afraid of the upcoming war? Does it haunt you in your dreams as it nears us?" he asked, observing me carefully.

"War doesn't scare me, not with my beast at my side."

"But something is haunting you in your dreams. You fear dreaming. I can taste it in the air around you."

"Drop it," I stated firmly.

"I can ease the nightmares, or try to if you will allow me to do so. You've opened your home to my sisters and me. Let me help you."

"I said I was fine," I argued, watching the girls.

"You're not fine, and you didn't say you were. You said to drop it because speaking about your dreams manifest whatever haunts you. You're not having nightmares. You're reliving something traumatic in your dreams, Your Majesty. Are you not?"

"You just don't stop, do you?" I nearly jumped as the wind picked up and lightning crashed against the ground close to us. I closed my eyes, inhaling slowly before releasing it as I fought to calm the turmoil inside of me so the world would ease the storm brewing above the courtyard.

"My sisters," he said carefully, turning to a group of women who watched us. "Sitara, Pheme, Selene, Reyna, Astraea, and Terrwyn." They bowed their heads before lifting their rainbow-hued eyes back to me. "Ayla is the oldest and the most powerful of the line. Myself excluded, but then I am the King."

"And your parents?" I asked, studying the way he winced and peered back to his sisters as if it was an uncomfortable subject.

"I murdered the previous King and Queen of Nightmares, Your Majesty," he admitted on a sigh, his hands balling into fists at his side with either anger or pain at the declaration of the truth.

"Good," I said, watching his eyes widen. "I heard they were nasty assholes. Tell me, Cillian, are you a good king to your people, or will I have to replace you upon the throne?"

"Define good," he returned carefully, eyeing me with worry.

"Do you torture your people or abuse them needlessly? Do you mistreat them for your own enjoyment?"

"A court is only a court if the people choose to follow their king. I am good to our people, unlike my parents, who were cruel to us and our kingdom. I strive to be the king that our people deserve, even though we are still rebuilding the kingdom from the destruction of my parents, and their bleeding it dry to accommodate their lavish lifestyles."

"Good, do you need anything?"

"No, we can glamour everything we need."

"Because you are high fae," I stated, and his gaze narrowed on me. "You may fool others with your glamour, but I can see through it. One of your parents was high fae by birth, so who was it? Mommy or Daddy, Cillian?"

"Our mother was high fae, Your Grace. She was the Heir to the Light Kingdom but was abandoned in our court as an infant. My father was instructed to kill her if Tatianna never came back for her, but he fell in love with her instead. She wasn't the Queen of Nightmares, but she birthed all of my father's children. My stepmother murdered her in a fit of jealous rage and started abusing my sisters for her pleasure. It became a game of who could hurt the other more between my father and his wife, until the entire kingdom suffered for it because neither would concede defeat to the other."

"Your mother was Arianna?" I asked carefully, running my teeth over my lip as I nipped it, studying his reaction to her given name.

"Yes," he said softly. "She was the daughter of Tatianna, Queen of the Light Fae, and an unknown father. My father was told to murder her if the queen didn't return in a certain amount of time, but as I said, he fell in love with her. Tatianna never came for her or asked if her orders had been followed, so they were happy for a while."

"Well, that explains that mystery," I grumbled.

"When we heard that you'd kicked the King and Queen of the Light Fae out of Faery, we assumed the land would choose one of us as the next Heir of Light."

"It went to a Seelie Prince named Asher, who now carries the brands of the heir."

"I thought it went to the bloodline?" Cillian frowned, looking over to his sisters, who listened intently.

"No, it goes to whom the land chooses to wear the royal brands. It chose well, I think. It goes to the one that will best serve the land, not to whom is crowned by birth."

"Maybe it chose him because we weren't here?" one of the girls offered.

"Oh, but you were here when it chose him. I wouldn't take it personally. None of us ended up where we were supposed to be. This land has a mind of its own. You don't want it to choose you. Nothing good comes with the crown."

"If you change your mind about your nightmares, I will be here, Your Majesty." Cillian's eyes searched mine briefly before shifting to something over my shoulder.

I felt him without needing to turn around to see who was behind me. Still, I turned and gave Ryder a tight smile where he stood just outside the tent. He moved closer to me as he handed items to people who were waiting.

I nodded a goodbye to Cillian and joined Ryder. We worked long into the night, handing out supplies. I was sure that I would fall into sleep with exhaustion, too tired for the nightmares to reach for me, digging in their talons.

I was wrong.

The nightmares returned.

They always returned.

CHAPTER FIFTEEN

RYDER

Synthia tossed and turned, her body covered in sweat as nightmares plagued her mind. Cillian stood in the corner of the room, bathed in the shadows, studying her through it all. I growled a silent warning, and his mouth started to open as if he intended to speak. He shook his head, lifting his chin while watching the sweat bead on her brow. She was stuck in yet another terrifying dream, her power unfurling in dangerous waves as the nightmare held her in its icy claws, refusing to free her.

"You need to go inside her mind to witness what I see," Cillian whispered, barely loud enough to be heard in the room. His magic swirled across his skin within the dark obsidian brands that pulsed purple and black as they danced over his forearms and biceps.

"Synthia doesn't like people inside her head, trust me."

"I don't care what she likes, and neither will you when you see what is actually fucking happening to her."

"I shouldn't have fucking allowed you into this room," I snapped irritably, knowing she'd be pissed if she knew I'd brought him into our bedroom.

I'd heard him speaking to her, offering to rid her of the nightmares. I knew what he could do, and everything within me needed to know what she'd endured down in that pit. I could smell the sweat that clung to her neck when they came for her when she was awake.

I knew the moment she would run from me to protect me from the shit haunting her. I didn't want to be protected. I wanted to know what happened to my wife when I left her in that dark, deep hole in the ground.

"But you did, and she is not plagued with nightmares, Horde King. She's plagued by magic that isn't allowing her to break free to discover the truth of what occurred to her in that prison. She will never be free of the Seelie in that pit if you do not allow me to intervene. You brought me in to help her. Let me help her now. You've aided in protecting my family, and that is something I can never repay, but I can do this for you and your queen."

"I don't fucking know you, nor do I trust you."

"You shouldn't, but as I said, your wife will never escape this monster because she *can't*. He is powerful, and the only way to free her is to make her see what actually happened. He will never release her willingly because she brokered a deal, and that deal isn't completed unless she overcomes the fear and faces what transpired down there. She is fractured, but not in the way she assumes."

"You're saying that bastard can still get to her?" I growled, emotion tightening in my stomach at the thought of that monster feeling any of her emotions and still being able to torture her in her dreams. My gaze swung to Synthia. She bucked against the bed as though being endlessly tormented while being brutalized.

"He doesn't need to get to her. He still has hold of her in her dreams. Let me show you, please. You'll understand it once you see what I have witnessed."

"This monster permitted others to rape my wife," I hissed while swallowing past the rage that entered my mind, clouding my thoughts with what I would find if I agreed to enter Synthia's dream.

"No, he didn't. He never allowed them to touch your wife. Malachi made her think she took lovers, and that she'd given in to him because that emotion of betrayal was something new to him. Make no mistake, he is unlike anything in this world, but he has never experienced emotions or the worlds which she has seen. They fascinated him, as she does. Take my fucking hand or don't. You can allow me to help you free her from his magic, or you can wait for your wife to go mad. His hold on her is absolute, and he doesn't understand the pain he is causing her now that she is free from the pit."

I studied her drenched body while she continued to toss and turn, crying out as tears slipped from her closed lashes to add to the moisture already on her face. My hand slipped into Cillian's, and we entered her dream.

The inside of the cave reeked of musk and sex, and my throat tightened against what I might see, but I wasn't prepared to see Synthia during sex. She was riding a monster who wore my face, her body covered in a subtle sheen of sweat as her brands glowed. Her eyes never left his as she rocked her hips, leaning down to claim his lips as a bubbling laugh escaped her mouth.

"What the fuck is this?" I demanded.

"Look again," Cillian snorted.

I watched closely as the creature beneath her changed to that of a hauntingly ethereal male. His skin was alabaster in color, and magic pulsed on his skin with silver brands. Eyes the color of blue skies on a summer's day watched my wife, and I wanted to slaughter him. Was this Malachi she fucked, or was it another male?

"She thinks she is with him," Cillian explained.

"She is fucking him!"

"No, she's not even there. Synthia is over there," he said, pointing to where her body floated in a pool of ice-blue water.

The pool glowed around her, making her appear angelic above the silken water. Her eyes were closed, her hands floating above the surface as the male that I assumed was Malachi sat in the shadows, watching her, instead of the images of the sex scene.

He flicked a silver ball that hovered above her, and the cave changed into one of chaos, mixed with hundreds of creatures that surrounded her dirty, scantily covered form, ripping it apart.

"It's an illusion," I muttered, dragging my hand over my mouth as the reality of it slammed into me. "He is showing her *his* pain, in exchange for her pleasure?"

"He is learning her, studying her love for you. Malachi craves her emotions because he was never allowed to know them before he was placed in this hell, and he wasn't alone when he was imprisoned. Malachi was tossed in here powerless, devoured and mutilated by the monsters his parents had created before him. He doesn't understand her fire or her emotions at being abandoned. Feel him, Ryder. Sense what he is after."

I closed my eyes against Synthia's horrifying screams inside the illusion as the monsters ripped her apart slowly, devouring her without killing her. Malachi watched it, swallowing hard as they tore my wife into tiny pieces.

He felt it, though, it was evident in the way he flinched and swallowed past the pain until his hand lifted, and they ended her suffering. His gaze slipped back to where she floated, oblivious to what was happening to her.

There wasn't a scratch on her perfect flesh. Her body floated, untouched and unmarred by the marks that had covered the illusion until it was nothing more than a bloodied pulp.

"He made her think she lived through hell," I swallowed hard, shaking my head. "He never touched her, but that pool is allowing him to control her mind, to feed her whatever he wanted her to believe was real."

"Exactly, it's the full magic that runs through the mazes in the pit. Malachi has become the power source for the prison. She's floating in the original source of power, but only a sliver of it remains because he took it for himself. The magic you feel? It's all-consuming. It leaked into her body, and the moment it did, he grabbed hold of her with it."

"That explains why she didn't smell different when she returned to me." I studied her body, watching as he placed his hand on her forehead, pulling silver strings of energy from it and replacing the energy with parts of his own. "What the hell is he doing?"

"Taking a memory from her soul," Cillian exhaled. "Your Queen suffers because she gives him power with the fear that she betrayed you. It's in the air around us, the heavy scent of guilt and self-loathing. He doesn't know it's causing her pain, or why she refuses to awaken. Malachi doesn't want to hurt her. He's actually trying to protect her in his own way."

"And what the fuck does he need her to become?" I demanded through clenched teeth as Malachi reached for another string, replacing it with another like some puppet master.

"His key to freedom," Cillian admitted, pushing his long hair behind his pointed ears. "He is fully aware that he holds the Goddess of the Fae, but that she hasn't reached her full potential. He's helping her to grasp it because once she does, she will escape this place, and he will piggy-back out of it with her. Look there," he said, pointing to the bottle that held the glowing orbs he'd spun from her essence.

"What the hell is he doing with them?"

"He isn't even touching them, just taking them little by little until enough is missing for her to reach for her power. He is reconstructing her, removing every essential part, and rebuilding her into what she needed to become to leave here."

"He's here," I growled.

"Yes, he is. He's in her dreams. Every night." Cillian pushed his hand against my chest as I stepped forward. "You'll lose the advantage if you intervene now and Malachi senses you," he said as he shook his head, uneasy as he took in the anger pulsing through me.

"That's my wife, and he can get the fuck off my girl." I gritted my teeth, staring him down as my gut wrenched, churning at what Synthia was enduring.

I stepped out of the shadows, and Malachi turned, tilting his head as he studied me through iridescent violet eyes. There was very little that mimicked a human on him, unlike the other fae Danu had created. I stopped in front of him, releasing my magic as he watched me.

"You're not supposed to be here," Malachi chuckled before turning back to Synthia.

"That's my wife, asshole. You need to let her go." I strode across the room, intending to attack, but sensed the barrier he'd placed between us. I pounded on it, forcing his eyes to meet mine. "Fight me, asshole," I demanded.

"Why would I give her back to you? I love her, and you threw her away. Destiny led her to me so that I could help her."

"She fucking hates you." I clenched my fists at my sides, glaring daggers at him without backing down a fucking inch. My wings exploded from my back as my hands pushed against the barrier, moving it as I fought to free her from his hold. Even if the cost was my life. "Synthia is everything good in this world. You're hurting her."

"I don't hurt her. I show her pain, and she shows me love. It's a fair trade."

"You wouldn't know what she feels because the moment she awakens, she is mine again. This world we live in, it's facing a war. I need my wife and the mother of my children back. What you're doing to her is slowly killing her, making her ache in ways you'd never understand. Let my wife go now or fight me for her!"

"The triplets are yours, they're lovely. She loves them more than her own life, which makes her compassionate and… strange to me. My mother birthed monsters and freed them to slaughter me, and yet your wife plays games with her children and laughs at their mistakes. She lets them hide and then pretends to find them for their enjoyment. Synthia is unlike women I have met here, caring about others more than herself. Is that why you chose her to be your queen, Horde King?" Malachi tilted his head and blinked.

"I chose her because I love her."

"But you left her here with me. Did you not?" he countered, watching my throat bob as I fought my answer.

"I thought the prison was empty after the others had escaped. She should have been safe."

"She was safe because I ensured it. Had she been awake the entire time, she'd have gone mad, I assure you. There is no food here, and no one else is here except for me now—only corpses remain along with the nothingness of empty silence to keep me company. The others escaped or died, but the only one who had the power to remove the symbol of the gods was a goddess or a god strong enough to endure the power of the runes being disassembled. It also had to be a god who was connected to this world. She is, and so I protected her to free myself, among other things."

"She freed you. Now you need to set her free for Synthia to save this world and our children. She needs you to let her fucking go so she can be what she was born to be," I demanded, tightening my hands into fists at my sides.

"And who would keep me company within the shadows, then?"

"Not our fucking problem. You won't even have shadows unless she is made whole and helps me fight. She cannot do that with you devouring parts of her soul in her dreams. You use what little rest she gets to torture her. She fears sleep, dreading the endless torment by you and the monsters you made her think she bedded before they tore her apart.

"You want love, asshole? Go find your own. She's mine, and she will always be mine. You can't take something from someone else and expect it to be yours. She's a fucking beast on her own. She's beautifully built to weather the fiercest storms any world could throw at her, but she needs her entire soul to be whole."

"But you took her from someone else, and she chose you, knowing you took her from him, yes?" He laughed wickedly before peering down at her with a warm smile I wanted to rip off his face. "And her humanity, the thing you wished to eradicate from her?"

"That's a part of her. It's a part that I shouldn't have wanted her to shed because it is what makes her loyal and strong. I love all of her, and I will never stop fighting to bring her back."

"You accept her now just as she is? Because her emotions were conflicted as to who she was becoming, and whether you could love her if she changed. She is a calamity of emotions, which she couldn't come to terms with at first. Her memories have taught me much, and shown me everything she is, and what life could be like for us should we escape this prison. She also needed the pain to push her to do what was required because she is newly born and very young.

"You're right; she is beautiful and beautifully broken. I had to erase what she was to rebuild her to what she wanted to become. I created her where the gods couldn't intervene, and the Fates couldn't force. I made her into who she was born to become, and it could only be done through knowing cause and consequence. Knowing pain and feeling it inflicted on a level so profoundly deep that it redefines who you are."

Malachi turned from me and ran his hand through Synthia's hair as if lost in thought and trying to comfort her. I pounded on the barrier again, and his attention refocused on me.

"Deconstruction of a soul is a lengthy process, but it is also brutal. She fought me at first, but then she understood what I did. I built her into a goddess because that wasn't something she could do alone, no matter how much she reached for the power. Synthia is young, and while she's endured pain, she has not experienced true pain in the amount needed to wield the powers. Without my help, those powers would have controlled who she would have become. Had she accepted them when you wanted her to, you'd have lost her. She forwent the true formation of a goddess during her rebirth. Without the allotted time the

Fates needed, she'd have remained humanlike. So, I have fixed her, and she is now what she was born to be. Can you accept who she is now? She is not the same creature who entered this hell."

"I will accept my wife as she is, Malachi."

"Then, you are ready for her." Malachi stood to his full height that mirrored mine. "You accept her for who she is, and that is what she was waiting to receive. Synthia came back to you, Ryder. She would always go back because you are buried in her soul. She needed you to accept all of her. I am here because I hold her humanity. The piece I took is what she would have needed to lose, and it was also the parts she clung to the most. You can't eradicate one part of who she was, not without losing all of her.

"She will need to forgive herself for what she assumes happened in the prison, but I will remove the magic from her. It won't be instant because nothing with magic ever is. Your job will be to teach her how to be who she is now, allowing her to heal over time. I will unravel the dreams and allow her to see the truth of our relationship. You are a lot more levelheaded than she thought you would be regarding our bargain. If she doesn't uncover the truth herself, I will help her."

"Bargain?" I asked.

"She slept until she was ready to free us. Synthia knew if you jumped in to save her, I'd have used you against her without hesitation. She promised to teach a creature like me what love was if I could teach her to become what she needed to be for Faery. The thing is, once you begin to evolve through pain, lines start to blur, and the mind cannot decipher dreams from reality.

"That is what it took to bring the Goddess of the Fae to life. You're right, she is beautifully built to wage war, but neither of us would have left this place before it started, and she knew that. She may not remember it, but Synthia knew she had to get back to you, and she herself closed the door into the prison to prevent you from jumping into it to save her."

"She protected me," I uttered, not surprised that even in her darkest hour, that woman had thought of me instead of herself. She'd let Malachi do this to her, knowing that if anyone could bring her inner power forth, it was the firstborn Seelie Prince of King Oberon.

"Not the firstborn son, I am King Malachi in this prison, but my true mother named me Oberon."

"And who was your mother?"

"Danu," Malachi chuckled wickedly. "I am Synthia's brother, one of many."

Cillian snorted. "You watched her have sex? She's your sister."

"I never cared to look. I only wanted to feel her emotions. I am both fae and god, yet powerless in this place. What I have learned to use is only a sliver of the powers with which I was born. She knows who I am. She needs only to remember when she is ready. She will awaken soon, and when she does, the King of Nightmares will be in her room, and we will all be within her mind. I suggest you have him leave before that happens.

"You are finished here. Be careful, Ryder. You're King of the Horde and the God of Faery, but Synthia and I? We were created to rule this world. But I don't fucking want it after learning what it means by experiencing her memories. I will create my own kingdom in time, and I will live there without the mess of this world that our mother created. Good luck, because she wasn't just born wild, she was born with the power of Faery running through her veins."

Chapter Sixteen

CHAPTER SIXTEEN

SYNTHIA

I AWOKE COVERED IN a layer of sweat with Ryder holding me against him tightly. He refused to allow me to sleep alone, and it wasn't as if I wanted him to, anyway. I pushed him away, sitting up to throw my legs over the side of the bed.

Yawning, I stretched before rubbing the sleep from my eyes. Ryder's hand touched my shoulder, followed by his lips. He skimmed them across my back to the other shoulder, and I stood, leaving him on the bed as I padded toward the bathroom alone. I reached the door and turned, staring back at him as he watched me, taking in the anger and pain that shone from within my eyes.

"I think you should start sleeping in your room again." I turned and shut the door, heading toward the shower before he could argue.

I leaned against the counter, looking at my reflection in the mirror, and saw Ryder enter the room behind me. He stripped down to nothing but flesh without using magic, and held my eyes in the mirror, making damn sure I noted every single article as it was tossed aside. He grabbed my shoulder hard, turning me around as he removed the nightgown I wore in one solid move that left us both naked.

"Ryder," I warned carefully as nervousness rushed through me.

"Fuck you, Synthia."

"Excuse me?" I gasped, unable to figure out his game.

"You heard me," he retorted, pulling me with him into the shower before he turned on the water and held me beneath the spray. "You think you're different now, and maybe you are. You went through hell. It's expected that you would change and evolve from the experience. You think you're dirty because of what you did, but you're not. You never actually fucked those monsters, or I'd be able to smell them on you."

"You have no idea what you're talking about," I argued, hating the prick of tears in my eyes.

Ryder leaned in and buried his face in my neck, inhaling deeply as he moved down the center of my body and then back up again, smiling. "I don't smell anything but my pure, untouched wife who still carries my fucking scent. You're a fucking warrior who used what she had to survive imaginable horrors. So, I'll wash that feeling away, and I will show you that, to me, you're not less than you were before you went down that fucking hole. Afterward, you will accompany me upstairs."

"Is that so? And you think you can wash the filth from me?" I studied the way his eyes burned with naked heat banked within them, and it made my stomach flutter.

"I don't think there is anything wrong with you, not physically, Pet. A powerful creature manipulated you, and his magic played a huge role in what you endured. I need you to shake it off and stand back up with me."

"There is no difference between the two," I argued as his mouth touched my forehead, brushing over it softly as he kissed me. "I am standing, Ryder. Right in front of you, but I am no longer that woman who cowers to anyone." He moved his kisses to the side of my face and trailed down to my neck. "What are you doing?"

"I'm showing you that you're still the same woman I fell madly and irrevocably in love with. Nothing about you has changed, other than the level of your power and inner strength. There's nothing here that is different." He kissed my other cheek next, moving toward my throat.

"Or here," he continued.

His mouth moved to my shoulder, and I fought the rapid beating of my heart as heat flooded through me. His touch ignited a fire that leaped to life with abundant heat, filling every cold, dead part of me violently. Worse than the need, I felt his love breaking through the ice that encased my heart, protecting me from feeling what I had done to stay alive.

Ryder chuckled, systematically continuing to check off every inch of my body until he was kneeling on the floor of the shower. His hands pushed me against the wall as his mouth brushed over my pussy, oblivious to the water rushing down my body as he kissed me between my thighs, pushing his tongue through the slick mess he had created with his kisses.

"You taste delicious, same as you always have. I crave the taste of this pussy more than the air that fills my lungs, woman," he growled, entering my body with his finger. I stiffened with the motion, dropping my head back against the wall as my hands pushed through his hair, holding myself up as he devoured me. "You feel the same, pulsing around my fingers, milking me with your tight pussy as it begs me to fill it."

He stood, lifting my hips as black eyes filled with golden stars peered into the depths of my soul. It was as if he thought he could reach in with his gaze and pull me back from the darkness that held on to me tightly.

Ryder held me poised against his cock, brushing it against the sleekness of my opening, asking permission. I wrapped my arms around his neck, pushing down onto his cock, and a scream ripped from my throat as he entered my body, hard and fast.

"Fucking hell, you feel so good around me," he growled, moving us out of the shower and back to the bedroom, placing me on the bed. He slowly moved his hips while my hands held him to me.

I closed him out, rocking my hips as I tightly held my eyes shut from the love I witnessed burning in his endless, inky depths. A love I didn't deserve anymore, and that hurt. Tears pricked at my eyes, and I did my best just to feel him as he took me toward the edge.

"Fuck that," he growled hoarsely, withdrawing to the tip of his cock, and my eyes snapped open as he denied me. "You will look at me as I fuck you, woman. You'll know damn well who is between your legs. You don't get to shut me out. Your husband is right fucking here with you, fighting for you to see that you are unchanged in the ways you fear.

"I want to see your soul light up for me. I want to see the fire burning within those pretty eyes of yours as I take you to the edge and send you crashing over it. I'm not going to let you shut me out anymore, or ever again for that matter. I love you. I have loved you from the first moment you told me to fuck off with those pretty red lips. So, keep those beautiful eyes open for me, and show me who you have become because I want her, too.

"Show me the goddess who bows to no man, who fights for those who are weak and need her strength in their darkest hours. The woman who kneels in the mud, handing out rations to creatures that stare at her in wonder," he snapped. "The woman who didn't even notice every pair of eyes gazing at her ethereal beauty, as she stood in the cold to be sure her people had been fed and were warm. I want that woman because she is the other half of who I am, and together we're unstoppable. Show me my beautiful queen, stop fucking grieving what you think you have lost, and embrace what you have become because you are even more beautiful than any other soul in this world."

"It isn't that easy, Ryder."

"It is that fucking easy. Get the fuck up, Synthia. Get up and fight with me. I need you by my side."

"You left me there!"

"Because you fucking jumped!" he shouted, pushing into my body hard. "It was supposed to be empty. Who was it that fucking jumped into the fucking thing in the first place?"

"I did! Because you blamed me for everything! You lied to me, and you kept lying to me. I can't even fucking trust you!" I snapped, rolling him over and slamming down on him as my body tightened with the need for release.

His hands lifted, squeezing my breasts painfully as he bucked his hips. He fought the war I waged at my side as he watched me coming undone around him, screaming his name as tears slipped from my eyes.

"I hate you!" I screamed.

"I hate me, too," he admitted, flipping me over as he pushed my legs apart. "I hate that you hurt and that I can't take that hurt away from you. I hate that the pain you feel could have been avoided if I hadn't been grieving for my family. I hate that you keep shit from me and that I kept my secrets from you. I hate that we're at war with each other while another one is raging around us.

"I don't hate *you*, though. You're my fucking soul and so deeply embedded within it that I can't imagine a world where you never existed or would exist without me. You are the anchor that tethers me to this world and makes me need to be a better person. We're not the gods who fucked this world, Synthia. We're the gods who will right their wrongs and make this place a world worth saving. We will erase them from our history and rewrite our own as we fix what they ruined by destroying one another.

"Come back to me, woman. We fucked up, but we fucked up together. You and me, we're the ones this world is depending on to save it. I don't want you to stand in front of me or behind me anymore. I want you at my side where you have always belonged."

"I don't care if this world burns," I growled, bucking against him.

"Yes, you do, because if it burns, we will burn with it. You won't allow that to happen because everything inside of you demands we save Faery. I know because I can feel it too. You put your soul into me, remember? I know you, and I feel everything you feel."

"I hate you," I whispered, rolling us again, letting my shimmering transparent wings expand. "I hate that you weren't there when I needed you. I hate that you lied to me, and I didn't even realize you could lie. I hate that you kept secrets from me and that I kept them from you. I hate that I would have done anything because I craved the taste of these," I whispered, claiming his lips hungrily as tears slipped from my eyes.

"I craved the feel of your hands as you held me tightly, and the sound of your voice as you told me I was your world. You're not my anchor, Ryder, you are my everything. You're the stars that light my darkest skies. You're the monster that keeps me safe and protects me when I am at my weakest points. You're the fire that ignites and burns within me. I hate you for that, for needing you so much that I willingly did horrible things just to taste you for a moment."

"I don't care what you think you did in that pit. I don't care what happened down there, or if you think you should be ashamed of something because nothing in this world or down there is what it seems," Ryder growled, lifting me until he was sitting with me in his lap as he moved his hips hurriedly. His gossamer wings unfurled to brush against mine, which sent more erotic sensations pulsing through me. "Someday, you will remember everything that happened, and it will make sense. But for now, just know that you cannot continue blaming yourself. Now fuck me, and show me why you're mine, woman."

Our wings pushed against one another, brushing with enthusiasm, creating a frenzied need within us as it enhanced my pleasure. My arms wrapped around his neck, claiming his mouth with everything I felt and all that I was. I rode him slowly even though every instinct inside of me wanted to move faster, to erase the feeling of the creatures from my flesh, replacing it with his wanton lust and warmth.

"Your greedy pussy is milking me, woman." He moved my hips rapidly with his hands and groaned. "I'm about to come so deep in that welcoming sheath that you'll feel me there forever."

"Do it," I demanded huskily, clenching tightly against him until he was moving faster, harder, deliciously abusing my core. I felt him tense, then everything within me imploded and detonated as tremors rocked through me.

We exploded together, and I felt him coming deep inside me, breaking down all the walls I had built, opening me up to him. My mind revealed the horrors I'd lived through, while my soul brushed against the familiarity of his.

I tasted Ryder's pain, felt his regret at not knowing what was inside that pit. I tasted his love as it danced against my mouth while he devoured me. He came until my insides burned with it, and when he pulled away from my mouth, his eyes were golden and filled with pride.

"I have a surprise for you," he said as he turned me onto the bed. Kissing my forehead, he leaned back and smacked my butt cheek. "Get showered and dressed."

"You know I hate surprises."

"You won't hate this one."

Twenty minutes later, I held his hand as we walked past soldiers lining the entire hallway, all members of Ryder's personal Elite Guard. Inside the tower, Lucian and his men stood beside Erie and Callaghan in the entrance, nodding to us as we passed.

The power inside the tower was smothering until I saw Destiny standing by the window, smiling sadly. She vanished, only to reappear with my three kids, who were now anything but children. They were somewhere on the cusp of being teenagers and losing their chub.

"Oh my God," I whispered brokenly. "It isn't safe for them to be here! Thanatos said to get them out of here!"

"Sometimes, Death stands shoulder to shoulder with those he protects, Synthia," Thanatos said, coming into the room behind us, forcing me to turn and stare at him. "You need to remember why you are fighting and why you are needed in Faery. You have enough gods and goddesses here to prevent one asshole from entering this tower. You have an hour. Your time starts now."

CHAPTER SEVENTEEN

OUR KIDS SMILED, STARING at us as we slowly moved toward them, uncertain how to proceed. Most children didn't accept change easily, and ours were growing rapidly. Just a year ago, I'd died to bring them into this world, and now they were standing at my shoulders.

They'd grown a lot since we'd seen them last, which for Ryder hadn't been that long ago, but for me, it was an endless amount of time that I craved to know their smiles and hear their laughter. I stepped closer, and Zander rushed into my arms as a sob exploded from my lungs. Kahleena studied me through golden eyes and frowned slightly as she moved forward without hesitation, hugging me tightly. Cade was next, his eyes filling with worry at my reaction to them.

"I missed you guys so much." Tears formed in my eyes and spilled over my cheeks as I hugged my children.

"It hasn't been that long," Zander snorted, pulling back to look at me with a boyish grin.

I brushed my hand through his thick hair, studying the changes in his face. He looked like Zahruk and had his stoic personality, but we'd already known that before we'd sent him with Destiny. I turned as Zahruk entered the room, smirking as Zander tilted his chin to him, and Zahruk returned the gesture without thought. He smirked at Cade, who nodded his head, noting the weapons on Zahruk's sides.

"Welcome home, little monsters," Zahruk chuckled and turned, watching as Ristan walked in behind him with baby Orion in his arms.

Kahleena giggled, rushing toward Ristan, and I watched as he smiled, handing his son off to her while meeting my gaze over her head. She was still petite, but it was now easy to see the beauty she would become one day, probably tomorrow, if she continued to age quickly. Her face had thinned out, and her eyes had slanted some with thick black lashes framing them. She wasn't just beautiful; she was the vision of beauty, with her white dress hugging slim curves.

"Orion, I knew you'd be ready to meet us when we returned," Kahleena cooed, and I swallowed, knowing no one had mentioned the babe's name. "You're perfect, aren't you? You're going to be my friend, and we're going to fight monsters together."

"Excuse me?" Ryder, me, and Ristan all said at the same time as Zahruk smirked like he'd ever allow that to happen.

"This war is ending, but we will help you when the next one starts," Kahleena explained softly. "It's time to forgive Daddy and fight together. You're strongest when you are combined as one power against our enemies. Uncle Dristan says to stop being stupid and fix the problems before more people end up dead."

"Uncle Dristan?" Ryder stilled, and his eyes narrowed on Kahleena.

"Thanatos brought him to us because he isn't allowed to remain in the Underworld. He talks too much." She shrugged and focused her attention on Orion.

We all turned to Thanatos, who scratched the back of his neck while staring at us. "Dristan doesn't ever shut up about the books down there. He also slept with one soul, and then banged another one soon after getting to the Underworld. Little honey with the green eyes was going to roast him on a spit, so I sent him where he could have endless knowledge and prance around the gardens."

"Does that mean he won't be reborn?" I asked carefully.

"It means he will be reborn sooner than the others," Thanatos admitted sheepishly.

"He is ready to be reborn," Kahleena giggled as she played with Orion. "He said we'd meet again someday, but he was chasing women around the gardens, and I got bored." She shrugged and kissed Orion's chubby cheeks.

I swallowed hard, frowning at her as she kissed Orion's horns, and he made cooing noises up at her. His tail wrapped around her arm as Zander slowly stepped closer, running his finger down Orion's nose as he studied the little dangle baby.

"He made us read so many books," Cade groaned, moving closer to Zahruk while studying his swords. "That one is wicked cool."

Wicked cool?

"Hey, can we come in?" Ciara asked, and I turned, taking in the faces of the women who all had crowded the doorway.

"Of course," I said, moving to stand beside Ryder as the children rushed toward Remy, who held little Fury.

"Good surprise, Fairy," I whispered softly, letting him wrap his arms around me as he held me close.

"I needed to be reminded of everything at stake, too. We have to do this together because, without you, I would let it all die, and they deserve more from us."

"I think I had to endure the prison to become what they needed me to be, what you needed me to be. I'm glad you didn't go down there too, and that you didn't try to save me. I'm not mad at you, Ryder. I'm mad at myself."

"I know," he said, kissing the side of my head as we watched the children moving about, playing with the babies.

"Five minutes," Thanatos announced, and I nodded.

My eyes moved to Ristan, who watched me with Ryder. A sad smile played across his lips as he nodded, noting the way we stood together. Ristan, out of everyone else here, knew what it meant to see the future, and the damaging effects it could create, not to mention the mental strain it left behind. He stepped closer to Orion as he started to cry, but Kahleena rocked him in her arms, slowly turning toward Ristan.

"You won't be sad forever, Uncle Ristan," Kahleena informed with a pensive smile. "Your real destiny has yet to begin. Olivia's journey was nearing its end when she met you. She knew that her time in this world was over, and she accepted it; you need to as well."

"Kahleena, the world doesn't work like that." He studied the curve of her mouth as she grinned, keeping her secrets. "Pain just doesn't lessen because you lose a love that wasn't meant to last," he informed.

"Oh, the pain will hurt for a while, but you will heal. And you can't argue with the Fates of the world or the path chosen for you." She nodded her head, sending her platinum curls tumbling over her shoulder. "As I said, you will like your destiny, for it will give you everything you have ever wanted, and so much more."

"If you're talking about love, I don't ever plan on falling in love again."

"Not right now, because pain sucks. You might not want a new love, but love completes us. Also, you can't argue with fate. It happens to us all. Look at me. Mommy and Daddy aren't going to like who I end up with, but I will love him. There's always a plan for us before we are ever created. Sometimes you have to trust the journey before you reach your destination, and occasionally bad things happen to ensure we get to where we are supposed to go. That is why you and Aunt Olivia were together. Destiny and fate forced you to combine, and that journey gave us sweet baby Orion. Every so often, that which we crave is only ours long enough to complete a purpose, and then they're gone, and that hurts us the most."

"You're like what, ten? You know nothing about love," he argued defensively, unwilling to broach the subject, which admittedly, was a little too soon to be having.

"I understand enough. Like you, I also see the future. I know things that will happen if the parts and pieces are placed perfectly, like my future, for example. It is foretold, and so shall it be. My parents won't accept him, not at first. They'll fight who was chosen for me, and he will not bow to them. I will be the one to fix it, and I will love him."

"You're never dating," Ryder snorted as all the men in the room agreed.

"I'm going to date, Daddy. Mostly, I am going to kick his butt around before I let him kiss me. You don't need to worry. I am very strong and will only grow more powerful as time passes. He's a little broken, but the best ones always are. Besides, you and Mommy will be busy chasing babies you make while I heal my future mate. Unfortunately, he's going to do some very bad things to get me, and you need to trust me to make it work out." Her shoulders lifted and dropped in a shrug as if it wasn't a big deal.

"Uh, no. We will never be too busy to protect you," I argued, watching her smile as if I didn't know what I was talking about. "Kahleena, we will always find you."

"If I am not in this world, that will be difficult, Mother."

"Okay, I'm going to have to agree with your father. You're never dating."

"Oh, but I am. I will love him more than I could ever love another creature. He will be my beast, and I will adore him. You'll understand eventually. There's also the matter of the King of Nightmares, who you should be kind to, as he is going to be needed more around here."

"They're not welcome here," Zahruk growled, folding his arms over his chest. He met her pretty golden eyes with an angry glare, raising a brow to emphasize his declaration. He frowned as she batted her lashes, and his arms dropped at his sides in defeat.

Yup, we were fucked.

She knew how to turn warriors to putty in her hands already.

"Yes, they are. The Court of Nightmares is entwined with our destinies. Without them, we would know pain and horror, and that is not something we can endure once this war is over. We must flourish, replanting the seeds that are sown and reaped. Also, Uncle Zahruk, be kind to the woman who is fated to be your destiny, you'll meet her soon."

"That isn't happening, little girl." Zahruk looked perplexed, his dark brows rising in silent challenge. Kahleena smirked, tilting her head. "I'm not marrying anyone. Wives are too much work. I need efficient, not needy."

"You say that now, but fate marked you with that one, Uncle Zahruk," Kahleena said, shrugging her petite shoulders. "It's sealed in fate and wrapped in your destiny, so deal with it. You can't fight destiny or taunt it. You can try to escape it, or seduce it, but it will unravel you eventually. It won't let you go until you finally decide to embrace it, and then it will crown you, and you'll know true happiness. Face it, you've been marked, and stop glaring at me. I'm a child. I just know things."

"Not from drinking, though, right?" Ryder asked, and everyone turned to stare at him as laughter bubbled up around us. "Fine, I watched your stupid *Game of Thrones* shit, too. Had to see if anyone would have caught your interest," he admitted, smirking at me.

"Way too many family members were ending up together in that one," I snickered, watching him nod at my reply.

"It's time," Thanatos interjected. "Any longer and the mages will feel the presence of your kids."

"Children," Destiny called out, and everyone turned to look at her with angry glares. Kahleena's predictions had called her out on the spot. "What? Someone has to maintain the power of Faery, and I can't help who is destined to be together. Life isn't black and white. You assholes need color. So much fucking color."

Destiny walked to Ristan and looked down at Orion, who was sleeping soundly in his arms. "I know you are hurting, and I understand it is very soon after Olivia has passed, but you chose a mate that wasn't yours by fate. Olivia was yours by choice, and sometimes choice is intercepted because it is only meant to be for a short time. That doesn't mean your future isn't still playing out. Orion was meant to be born, and so he was. He was preordained to have his own destiny within Faery. See the theme here?"

She turned and pointed her finger across the room. "Zahruk, if you'd stop stroking your sword for a fucking moment, you'd see how many women are clamoring around you with besotted eyes and wet thighs." Spyder snickered, and she smirked at him evilly. "Oh, my shadowy Spyder, not even you are immune or beyond my reach. Stop pining for Lena, she's in love with Lucian and always has been from the first moment he touched his lips against hers. All of you, stop fucking whining like sulking children.

"Anything worth having and keeping is worth fighting to get. Life is made between the patches of happiness, grief, and sorrow, all of which remind you of what you have and what you will lose if you choose not to embrace your destiny because, as they say, I'm a fucking bitch. Now, my darlings, we must go. Hug your parents."

"Wow, next time at least pull our hair first before you fuck us, Destiny," I stated, and Ryder chuckled, holding me tightly before he let me go to hug the children that rushed toward us. "I love you guys." I knelt to hug them only to stand back up and frown. "You're so big now."

"Kahleena has boobs!" Zander stated offhandedly, and I forgot to control my response as my eyes widened, and I looked at Destiny in shock.

"They're no longer allowed to bathe in the garden pools naked. I guess some growing was expected, but they're not normal, even for gods," she said, shrugging as a frown marred her delicate features. "Not without bathing suits."

"I do not have boobs!" Kahleena stomped her foot and glowered at Zander.

"Do too," Cade groaned as he shook his head.

"Take it back before I wallop your big fat head!" she growled, and I threw my head back laughing. "Mother!"

"Oh, my word," I laughed harder. "Boobs are a normal part of life," I snorted, bending over as tears ran from my eyes from the uncontrollable laughter that rocked through me.

"Did I miss them?" Adam asked, calling out as he appeared in the doorway. He rushed into the room and then paused abruptly as he took in their sizes before recovering from the shock. "They were barely older than toddlers when they left!"

"And now they're arguing over boobs." I frowned, noting that Kahleena was growing up rather quickly, creating an ache in my chest that clenched tightly with sadness at having missed it all.

"What?" Adam demanded, wincing as he stared at me.

Cade snorted with Zander as they both nodded, and Kahleena stomped her foot as her small fists balled at her sides in frustration. "I don't have boobs! I can still do what the boys can do! It isn't fair."

"Jesus, I just had a flashback to us in the showers at the guild," Adam groaned. I nodded my head, doubling over to laugh again at his face of mock horror. "Yeah, funny for you, not for Adrian and me. We had to walk out of the showers with our hands in front of our laps. Asshole," he muttered crossly.

Something crashed against the tower, and Destiny rushed forward, grabbing the kids and vanishing without a word. I stared at where they'd been standing and lifted my gaze to Ryder's.

"Shall we?" I asked with a wicked smirk on my lips.

"After you, wife."

CHAPTER EIGHTEEN

OUTSIDE, THERE WAS A commotion that came from the extended courtyard. Slowly, we made our way to where all the excitement was unfolding. We were surrounded by gods, goddesses, and the entire Elite Guard, who circled us like bodyguards.

We didn't need anyone's protection, not when we were together. Still, they all flanked us in a show of solidarity. I got it, but it irked my pride to be surrounded by men who thought Ryder and I needed to be safeguarded. Although, I had to admit that I was enjoying the sheer amount of eye-candy strutting around me.

The crowd parted, allowing us to reach the center of the courtyard where two men were fighting with their bare fists over a sad-looking loaf of bread. We didn't disrupt them, just stood witness to their stupidity as the entire camp surrounded us to watch our response.

Everyone had been warned of what would happen should any fights break out, and these men had willingly broken the law. When one withdrew a dagger, Ryder intervened, tossing the man to the ground with magic as his power exploded throughout the area.

"Your Majesty," one said, bowing his dark head.

"We're fighting for our survival, and you're fighting over bread?" Ryder demanded in a lethal tone, his power suffocating those close enough to feel it oozing from him. "Get up and fight me if you must fight someone."

The entire courtyard went silent as Ryder issued the challenge. Both men fell to their knees before their king. Ryder glamoured a sword and placed it against the largest male's neck. He didn't hurt him, but the silent threat was louder than any amount of violence could have echoed throughout the grounds.

"Fight or die, Grigori, which do you choose?" Ryder glared at the male as his dark, murky eyes lifted to lock with Ryder's, anger filling them.

"I choose to fight at your side against our enemies, My King."

"Good choice," Ryder snorted, removing the sword.

The moment Ryder lowered the blade, Grigori rushed him, but Ryder was faster. His hand lifted, and Grigori turned to a fine mist of blood with a single motion, coating both of us in crimson.

I snorted at the stickiness of the blood, turning to gaze at Ryder. He spun in a circle, frowning as he studied the others who gaped at us as we stood, bathed in the blood of the largest male who had thought to challenge his king.

"Does anyone else want to indulge in treachery tonight?" Ryder asked, lifting a dark brow as he faced the horde, staring them down.

My eyes slipped to the King of Nightmares, who watched us silently, noting that we had yet to glamour away the blood dripping from our bodies. No one stepped forward or uttered a single word as Ryder stood proudly, allowing his intense power to pulse threateningly through the closed courtyard in silent challenge.

"No? Does no one else want to oppose me? The next asshole that fights over food will deal with me, do you understand? There are piles of food for you to feast on, and enough mead to get this entire courtyard drunk twice over. I will not have you fighting amongst yourselves when all of Faery is under fire from our fucking enemies. They're trying to break you, and you're allowing them to do so. Eat, fuck, and get drunk. Do not fight in my home. You are guests here, but if you cannot abide by the rules we have placed upon you, you can leave or die. The choice is yours."

"So, what? You'll throw us out?" another male snorted. "Or will you send your bitch to fight us?" He smiled coldly, and I returned it, walking toward him slowly, swaying my hips as Ryder followed close enough to me that his power had my nipples achingly hard with need.

"Well, his *bitch* does like to slaughter people." I grinned as I brushed my finger down the man's cheek.

He howled, bending over as his body turned to mush and boiled on the ground, leaving only a pile of bones and gore. I stepped back, allowing Ryder to envelop me in his arms. His lips brushed against my throat as he growled huskily, staring at the horde, who gawked at us in horror.

"Messy, but I like it," he chuckled, nipping my ear. "You just made my cock hard, woman."

"Good, because I plan on riding it," I murmured, staring out over the horde who hung on every word we spoke. "Does anyone else want to speak out of turn, or insult their king or queen? If not, I have a cock to ride, and a war to plan. So, if you intend to piss us off, can you do so now?"

The King of Nightmares smirked, staring right at us, and didn't flinch as my gaze held his. Kahleena said he was needed here, and that bothered me. It worried me that she was being forced to see the future, and yet she didn't seem concerned by it the least bit. I hadn't missed Ryder's nod to Cillian as we'd entered the courtyard, either, which had snapped my attention toward him.

"Should we feed our people together, Pet?" Ryder asked, and spun to him with surprise shining in my eyes.

"*Our* powers?"

"Together, woman. You and me, right fucking now," he smirked, and I stepped away from him, allowing my wings to unfurl as he did the same.

"You and me? You do know I am still mad at you, right?"

"You're my wife. Nothing is easy with you. That's why you're mine. I am man enough to know when to back off and when to press you. I know your faults, and I love every fucking one of them. I love you. Do you hear me? I fucking love you, woman, and I don't give a fuck who knows it," he stated, uncaring that the entire courtyard was hanging on every word he spoke and every action we showed. "Shall we?" He swallowed hard as I settled in front of him, pushing my hands against his as our fingers threaded together.

Our power erupted as our brands ignited. Silver and gold hues glowed through the courtyard until a stifling pulse of heady, sultry magic slithered over the entire assembly, causing gasps of shock and moans of pleasure to erupt.

I stepped closer to Ryder, lifting my mouth to his while feeding the entire horde and every caste present with magic, powering them to fuel their hunger for war as Ryder's lips lowered to mine, claiming me hungrily.

His growl tickled against my lips as my body heated from his touch. He chuckled and pulled away, resting his forehead against mine. Black eyes sparkled with the stars of my world as I peered into them, being swallowed whole into the galaxies that consumed me. His hand lifted, cupping my cheek as together, we exuded raw, penetrating power through the masses and listened as they groaned and came from the intensity of it.

I didn't need a guide to figure out what he'd just done here. Ryder had just declared us the unofficial High King and High Queen of Faery, and he'd shown them in a way that left no question of our absolute powers combined.

He didn't pull away from me, didn't see if anyone else noticed what he was doing because at this moment, there was Ryder, and there was me, and fuck everyone else. We were working together again, and it was everything right in the world.

I moved forward, and he smirked, watching me as my body slammed against his, and we vanished from the courtyard. We appeared in our bedroom, shredding each other's clothes that we sent flying to the floor. Before we were completely naked, Ryder glamoured us clean, then lifted me and slammed me home on his cock.

"Faster," I demanded.

He laughed darkly, pushing me against the wall as his power kissed across my flesh. The sensations carried me over the edge without warning until I was screaming his name, echoing it as he sent my body off the cliff, flying high on ecstasy.

"You dirty little bitch, you like it rough," he growled.

"Did you just call me a dirty little bitch? *Asshole* move! Should I be looking for a spying goddess again? Besides, I like it any way you give it to me. Now shut up and keep fucking me," I demanded.

"Fine, my good dirty little bitch?" Ryder laughed huskily. I glared at him before the smirk spread over my lips as he smiled, revealing white teeth. "Hey, I'm not against calling you dirty names and pulling that hair, woman. Not after how turned on you got while we gave Eris a show."

Ryder's hands lowered and spread my legs wider apart as he assaulted my core. His cock grew until I was whimpering. He studied my reaction, fucking me with wild abandonment until he shouted, grinding his teeth together as he exploded inside my body.

"I see you, Synthia. The real you. I love you more because of who you are," he uttered breathlessly as sweat covered our bodies. "I was wrong to assume you had to change to be mine. You're perfectly imperfect, and I love that about you the most."

"Ryder," I moaned, allowing my shields to lower for him as my heart clenched tightly with his words.

"I love your heart and how you wear it on your sleeve without caring who knows it's there. It doesn't make you weak. It makes you brave. You're a fucking battle queen, and the woman I love more than the air that fills my lungs and these lands. I will spend the rest of my life loving you. But I won't let you leave me, not without fighting for us."

"I'm yours," I whispered as he collected me in his arms and moved us toward the bed. "I was yours from the first moment your lips touched mine, and my entire world felt as if I'd stepped onto a tilt-a-whirl ride as you kissed me. You are my home, Ryder. Not the guild, not Faery, you. If this world dies, and the other vanishes with it, I don't care as long as you are mine. Do you understand me?"

"I do. I think you just told me that you love me and that you forgive me for being an arrogant, selfish prick." He lifted my chin and kissed me softly, pulling me into his arms tightly. We stayed like that for a few moments, then Ryder sighed, apparently deep in thought. "Kahleena said she's going to find a mate."

"Eventually," I chuckled, leaning back to look into his panicked eyes.

"Not fucking happening."

"Ryder, one day, Kahleena will be a woman. She will have needs, and eventually, she will give us grandbabies."

"Are you listening to the words rolling off your tongue, Synthia? Kahleena isn't having sex, ever! She's not even one year old yet—technically!"

"Uh, so you plan to send her to a nunnery?"

"No, but she isn't having sexual relations with any male, ever. End of discussion."

"Oh, boy," I laughed wickedly as he narrowed his eyes on me with disbelief that I was willing to allow our daughter to do something as crazy as having sex. "Yeah, come get it, Fairy," I challenged, sifting to the Fairy Pools naked, taunting him as he sifted in behind me.

"Are you planning on running from me again?" He lowered his body and moved through the water to where I waited for him.

I smirked, noticing the tiny fairies that lit the surrounding skies, creating a glowing hue of light that added to the moon's illumination. This world was exquisitely beautiful, created to lure its victims in. It was the same as my husband, filled with secrets and lethally seductive. That was part of the allure, though.

"No, I'm planning on fucking you in the first place you made me yours. I want us. I do. I want to fight the monsters that are trying to take this world from us, and I want to do that together. I'm tired of losing, Ryder. I'm tired of being at odds and watching everything we have worked toward fall apart because we can't seem to get our act together.

"So, this is our new beginning. We start here again, but this time we do it right, with a clean slate. No more lies and no more secrets. It's us now, the good parts, the ugly parts, and the scary ones. I want to face them all head-on with you at my side. I don't care what happened in the past, because we're not moving backward. We're moving toward our future and the future of this world and our children's lives. Forever starts now, okay?"

"I like the sound of that, but for the record, forever would never be long enough with you." Ryder dunked beneath the water and came up directly in front of me, grinning. "I have no intention of being gentle with you this time, fair warning."

"Good, because you know damn well that while I may like you gentle sometimes, I prefer you rough and untamed when you claim me, my proud beast. This time, no one better fuck this moment up by attacking us while we're here."

"I don't know about that; it did lead to you becoming my wife. When you got sick after we left here that first time, I felt fear for the first time since Alazander was alive. I felt this need to keep you as if I knew you were mine, but I couldn't admit it even to myself. The thought of you being mine...I was certain I didn't deserve someone so perfect or so beautiful. Then you accepted me, faults and all. You knew my past was ugly, and you didn't care. I'd planned to chain your pretty ass to my bed, but you stayed with me willingly."

"That wasn't fun for me, asshole."

"For you, maybe, but for me? Watching you take me on with fire burning in your eyes as you faced me in the hallway of my mansion? That was fucking hot, Pet. My dick was hard as I fought you. I wanted to push you up against that wall and fuck you until you understood it was a claiming mark of my kind.

"You threatened me, threatened to bring me down, and the only thing that went through my mind was how beautiful those pretty eyes were when you came undone for me. I reveled in the way your lips parted as the orgasm rushed through you, crying out my name as I plundered and destroyed your pink flesh until it knew me, and only me."

"Your brother stabbed me," I countered, reminding him that the road to where we were now standing hadn't been perfect. But the love we shared was our own fucked up version of perfect.

"You survived. But at that moment, I thought I was losing you, and that terrified me. I knew I was fucked beyond all reason with my desire for you. The thought of losing you made me ache in a way I'd never felt before. Why the fuck do you think I arranged another contract? That was the moment I knew I never wanted to lose you or let you go."

"You were engaged to be married," I frowned.

"I'd never have gone through with it. I knew the moment I set my eyes on you that I had to have you. You weren't the kind of woman that you kept on the side. Synthia, you're the kind of woman wars have been fought for, and men have been assassinated for lusting over."

"You made me think you needed to be fed with sex," I accused.

"What man wouldn't want a pretty girl feeding him? Besides, the beast did need to feed, as he was fae, and you were delicious." He smiled devilishly, and I shook my head.

"You gave me to Adam to wed."

"Because you're you," he whispered as his lips brushed against mine. "Had Faery suffered for my choice to be a selfish prick, you'd have hated me. You chose to do what was right. Had you kissed me in that room, I'd have snapped what little control I'd held on myself to take you with me. Not that it mattered. Your pretty little belly held my babes within it. Fate stepped in and ensured we would end up together."

"You're my happily fucked up ever after, Ryder," I whispered thickly as he smiled, capturing my gaze in the starlight of his.

"And you are mine. I want to make lots of babies with you and watch the world grow around us. I want the love you give me, the love I didn't understand until you were dying to bring our babes into the world. The bad stuff, the good, I'd do it all over again if it meant we ended up right here. I'm an asshole, but you accept me for who I am. You're the most stubborn woman I have ever met. Most of the time, I don't know if I want to strangle or fuck you, or do both at the same time, because you're also the most infuriating creature this world has ever produced."

"You plan on wooing me with words or that thick cock, Fairy?" I stroked my hand down the length of his shaft and licked my lips.

"I plan on doing both, witch. Now, show me how a queen feeds her king when he's ravished with a hunger for her pussy."

"You say the sweetest shit. I hope you're fucking famished," I laughed huskily as I wrapped my legs around his waist, and he took us deeper into the glowing water.

"I love you, Pet."

"I love you, too, Fairy, always and forevermore, My King," I declared without hesitation.

CHAPTER NINETEEN

I STUDIED THE NEW map that was spread out over the table in the war room, watching silently as Ryder pointed out strategic locations to place troops. It was insane how many soldiers Bilé was willing to lose just as a show of force when he made his moves.

He didn't care about the mages or their lives, which was very apparent in the way he sacrificed them to do little damage. Bilé only cared about inflicting suffering and pain upon Faery. And Danu actually thought we could reason with him? He was insane. It also made me wonder if she wasn't more attached to Bilé than she'd led us to believe.

"No," I interrupted the men, my hand moving over the map, pointing to the mountains. "That isn't wise. They'll expect us to take the cliffs above them. If we plant the Dragon King's army here," I pointed to a spot in the rough terrain of the forest, "and the Winter Court army here," I pointed to the meadow that sat in front of the forest. "The horde should be in the ravine. The Shadow Court can hide the presence of the others.

"Once the mages take the cliffs, Icelyn and her army can create enough ice to force them over the edge as the shadows move the mages toward the cliffs without the mages realizing what's happening until it is too late. Those who make it through the ice will be eaten by the dragons before they join us in the battle below. That will force the entire mage army to jump to where we are, or chance being eaten by dragons while the Winter Court holds them in place with ice. They'll be wounded, easy to kill for those of us on the ground.

"We can no longer plan our attack strategically by taking the strongest point for the battle. We have to think outside the box now because the enemy has learned our moves from the old map. They know how we think. They're not stupid. They have a god running their battle plans. It's time we started formulating our attack on the low ground and bringing them to us. Let them think they've taken the high ground. Ryder and I can be in either location. If anything goes wrong, we can be at your sides in seconds to help."

Ryder studied the map and smirked, lifting sparkling black eyes to me as his head shook. "Our queen is right.

They're going to expect us to be on those cliffs because it is the highest ground available. They know we always take the high ground because it is the most strategic placement of troops. They've had months to learn how we plan our battles and how we think. That's something we can use against them. It's very doable, but everyone would need to be placed correctly, with no missteps, or we lose the advantage. They're marching toward the mountains as we speak, so we'd need to move fast."

"Send the babes and the women to the guild," I uttered, frowning. "They can't march into that ravine with us, and we can't leave them here alone. They will be defenseless if the entire army heads into battle."

Someone shouted. "Soldiers approaching from the east through the woods!" I closed my eyes with a deep breath.

The alarms began chiming, and Ryder held out his hand, glamouring our armor on over our clothing. The entire room sifted to the battlements, peering out over the fire-lit courtyard. Guards rushed around, helping to move the children into the castle while men grabbed weapons and prepared to defend the stronghold.

"The flags," I said breathlessly. "It's the fallen kingdoms, Ryder. It's the Blood, Light, and Dark Kingdom armies."

"We don't know that," he pointed out, forcing me to frown at his words. "We cannot just accept it by their flags anymore. The mages flew those very flags when they attacked us before."

Ryder wasn't wrong, though, and I hated that he made sense. The mages weren't above pretending to be fallen kingdoms. He was smart and correct to assume it was a ruse to force us to lower our guards. But as they got closer, I could see the condition of those heading toward us. My stomach clenched as his hand tightened on mine. He could sense my unease at having to wait and see who exactly was marching toward our gates.

"They're wounded," I whispered, scenting the blood in the air with every step they took closer to us. "Send the healers out to the courtyard, along with guards, until we can be certain it isn't a ruse to get inside. Call Adam and Liam to the battlements, have them see if they can identify any of the people out there to show proof they are who they claim to be. Even if they do end up being from the lost courts, they need to be tested before they enter the stronghold, as our king has explained. Have the women waiting inside to help the healers; once we are certain it is safe, have them assist the injured."

"You were born for this role, woman," Ryder whispered against my ear, wrapping his arms around my waist as he pulled me closer against him. "You heard your queen. Do as she commands. When my wife speaks, you fucking listen. Now move!" The guards jumped into action, and I smirked, noting the tone he'd used when they'd waited for him to confirm my orders.

Lips brushed my neck as he growled huskily, unable to get enough of touching me. I wasn't complaining, because I couldn't get enough of his touch, either. Ryder wiped away the memories of hell from my mind, kissing every inch of me to show me he loved every part of me, flaws, and all. When the nightmares came, he held me through them, replacing them with his touch or stories of this world and his childhood, which he'd never told me of before.

We were closer now than we'd ever been, and I had begun to wonder if jumping into that pit of despair hadn't been in my destiny all along. Things I'd taken for granted were now cherished.

The world around me seemed more real, as if I weren't just sliding into a position, but fitting into a role I was born to play. I loved Ryder more fiercely than I had before, and I knew everything I'd done in the prison had been to remember him because he was my anchor.

I'd allowed myself to be used brutally just to catch his scent or see one of the memories Malachi had stolen. If Ryder had been there, I knew without a doubt that I'd have done anything they wanted me to, and it lessened the fact that he hadn't come in after me. I'd have ripped my own heart out to protect him, and we both knew it.

"I was born to be your queen, and you, my king," I admitted. The air beside us was displaced as Liam and Adam sifted in along with Lucian and his men close on their heels.

"I couldn't have wished or dreamed up a kinkier or sexier queen."

"Glad you noticed my finer qualities, lately."

"Woman, behave before we end up back in the bedroom, and you are spread out on our bed, naked and chained to the frame."

"Taunt me all you want, but last night you were the one chained, and I was in control. Tit for tat, Fairy," I uttered huskily.

"Are you two planning on talking to us, or do you just want to fuck in front of the entire horde again?" Adam asked with a boyish grin on his lips, studying the way we held each other tightly. "Glad to see Mommy and Daddy getting along, finally." Adam pointed down to the field. "Those are my soldiers. The General and Second-in-Command are my brothers. I thought they were lost to us. Sòlas is the one on the midnight-colored horse in the front."

"That is also our father's General leading the Blood Warriors." Liam exhaled, turning to look at me before his gaze dipped to where Ryder's arms were still wrapped around my waist. He smiled sadly, nodding at me. "Glad to see you guys getting along. It's about fucking time."

"Something to say?" Ryder asked pointedly when Liam's eyes held his for a moment too long, as if he had something to get off his chest.

"She's the only sister I have left, be gentle with her, Ryder. Family isn't forever in the midst of war, so I'm glad that you're making her happy again. I didn't relish the idea of fighting you to knock sense into that thick skull of yours until you figured out what you had right in front of you. She's a rarity, which you know. Synthia has a mind for war and a heart that is larger than the entirety of Faery. She's the type of girl you go to war to keep and the kind who will wage war to keep you at all costs. She's a forever girl, and I'm glad you figured that shit out now."

"Liam," I smirked as he shrugged.

"No, we lost our family, Synthia. You're all I have left as family, and while you don't grieve our parents as I do, I'd still choose you to be my sister."

"I love you, too, but the next time you spank one of your feeders, make sure my children aren't watching, okay?" I chuckled at the look of sheer horror that played out over his face, lighting his brilliant azure eyes. "Yeah, they heard it. They're also aware of all the jumping on the bed happening with you and your *friends*."

"Kids are way smarter than we give them credit," he grumped unhappily. "We need to go down there and render aid. Our people have traveled far to reach us. Synthia, we need a triage center in the courtyard, and then we will need to test them to be certain they are ours. Those we can vouch for can bypass security to be placed in the camp after having touched iron."

"Okay, Mira, go fetch the healers. All of them. Keely, please send word to the kitchen staff to prepare hearty stews. Make sure it is something heavy with bread to fill bellies of the injured, and that they prepare a broth for those who are unable to eat. Mireda, let the feeders know that their services will be needed to heal wounded high fae, maybe even some women. Have extra tents sent down to the camps and ask those below to help set them up for the refugees coming into the stronghold. Let's move, ladies. They depend on us now."

"Yes, My Queen," they said, bowing as I smiled at Ryder.

"Let them in the gates and test them with iron to be certain they're fae. Have the Elite Guard ready to defend, should the need arise. For now, we trust no one." Ryder kissed the top of my head, turning to Lucian. "I'm going to need you to be ready to end them if they're not fae."

"Good. After the morning we had searching for Lucifer, I need to murder something," he growled.

"I just need to murder a pussy," Spyder snapped crossly as he watched the wagons being pulled behind sickly looking horses.

My eyes swung to where Spyder stood, covered in entrails and body parts. "Like, fuck that shit up, or murder a pussy while fucking it? We're in the middle of a war. We need you to be more specific on which type of murder opportunity you need us to provide for you, Spyder." I studied the hurt in his eyes that flashed briefly before he could conceal it.

"Destroying a female's cervix. I don't get off on fucking dead chicks," Spyder snorted, clearly frustrated at whatever had happened in Spokane.

"You could fuck Eris, asshole. She's more than willing to let that Spyder get all up inside her," Lucian smirked, and power rippled from him as he prepared to assist Ryder.

"That bitch is evil. I wouldn't touch her with your dick," Spyder snarled, folding his arms over his chest with a death glare aimed at Lucian.

"You broke her heart, asshole. Of course, she's fucking evil." Lucian lifted a brow at Spyder as he shook his dark head. "This isn't the time or place for that conversation."

"Gentlemen, if we're finished talking about murdering pussy, there are wounded men and women at our gates," I smirked, watching their dark eyes slide to where I stood. "But after we help them, feel free to argue more. It's pretty amusing."

"Glad you think so," Spyder snorted, frowning as he vanished, only to reappear at the gates where the guards were preparing to open them.

"Ryder, after you," Lucian chuckled, winking at me.

"Lucian, I honestly don't care if Spyder murders a gang of pussies. Just make sure the gang is willing. He's welcome to the feeder lounge. They're skilled in all things perverted."

"You have gangs of pussy here?"

"We're fae. You want it. We got it." I grinned at Lucian. "I have it on good authority that we have a group of succubi down there at the moment with a hankering for sucking cock and playing amongst one another as the men watch."

"How the fuck do you know that?" Ryder's head whipped toward me, and his eyes narrowed.

"Because I'm the Queen, and it is my job to make sure our men are being pleasured and fed properly. Happy cocks fight better than those that are neglected and blue-balled."

"Synthia..."

"Don't Synthia me, Fairy. It is my job to be sure that everyone in this stronghold is happy, and that includes you. Unless, of course, you'd rather I hold out with that thing I do with my tongue?"

"Pet," he warned.

"No, please continue that thought. What do you do with your tongue?" Asher asked, pushing through the throngs of people on the battlement to reach where we stood.

"Seelie," Ryder warned.

"Ryder. Now that everyone knows everyone's names, please continue!" Asher scrubbed his hand down his face when I just continued smirking.

"You know every male here wants her to finish that statement because we're all wondering what she does with her tongue now," Lucian grinned, studying me through midnight eyes alight with laughter.

"I'm not," Liam snorted, rolling his eyes heavenward. "She's my sister."

"Everyone but him, and I feel you, dude, to my fucking core with that sister shit," Asher grunted, shaking his head regarded his current situation.

"Go help the wounded." I waved my hand toward the gates. "You're all incorrigible." Everyone vanished except for Ryder.

"You and me, we're doing that tongue thing tonight," he smirked, kissing my lips softly before he sifted to the ground to join the others.

I watched them moving toward the gates as the guards opened them, and the wounded started to trickle through. Exhaling, I smiled sadly at the slow movement and gait in which they entered. More wounded on the verge of war was a problem.

We were preparing to hide the weak, children, and women, and we'd just opened the gates to even more who wouldn't be able to fight. Ryder nodded in my direction, and I sifted down, helping the injured that were tested as they passed into the courtyard. We were doing as much as we could to make everyone feel safe and comfortable.

CHAPTER TWENTY

I WATCHED THE FIRES burning in the camps below as Ryder spoke to Blane and Ciara. They were arguing about the use of dragons on the cliffs that will be placed directly in the path of danger. It wasn't that Ciara feared war; she feared the loss of her husband and family. We were all afraid of what could happen to our loved ones.

We knew when we started disclosing our plan and strategy to the others that some of our decisions would be met with concern from a few of the wives. We had expected it. Turning toward Ciara, I watched the tears filling in her eyes as she argued the merit of the Dragon Guard staying here, at the stronghold, to protect the babes. I grimaced, deciding to enter the conversation finally.

"The women and babes are being moved to the guild, with Erie and Vlad, who will be protecting them," I stated firmly, flinching from the anger in her eyes at the mention of my old home. "You wanted to be a part of this war, Ciara. It's time we fight back. Our enemies are watching and very aware of every move we make now. This fortress will more than likely be emptied and burned enough to make them believe that we have abandoned this position. Everything we have done to this point has been reported to Bilé. If we plan to make a move, those spying on us need to report our movements back to the army marching toward us now.

"This castle will be empty one way or another. I will not march off to war without knowing that your children are safe and protected in the event that none of us get out of this alive. The stronghold will more than likely be infiltrated the moment we leave, and that would invite more losses that we're not willing to endure. I won't leave them here to die by the hands of the mages or the vengeful god who is waiting for us to fuck up."

"You would send our children to the human world?" she sputtered angrily.

"I would, Ciara. I would send them to the one place I built myself. To the fortified guild that is self-sustainable, to protect those we have brought into its warded barriers. I wasn't just building it to protect hunters. I was building it to protect any fae who needed a safe place to hide in the event of an emergency.

"Beneath the guild is a portal that enters the harem, and on either side of it is a trap made to hold even the gods, should they intend to wish harm to the hunters of the guild. Callaghan, Erie, and Vlad are within the guild, as are Devlin and Lena. Seventeen members of the Elite Guard have been selected to go as well. They will protect our people, who will be hidden within the catacombs that were converted into bedrooms. Each room is protected with runes and wards that Erie set in place after Bilé attacked the tower.

"I built the sanctuary to protect my own children from the gods, but it hadn't been finished in time before we had to hide them. Vlad and Devlin will protect Fury and Phoenix. Finn and Fiona are being moved too, as will the orphans. The guild has nine alarms between the top floor and the catacombs, in the event that one or more of the hunters are pretending to be loyal, but have other intentions.

"I created that sanctuary with a monster, and only he, Ryder, and I know how to penetrate the lower levels. His memories were taken the moment he'd finished creating the perfect sanctuary to hide my kids. I would not send your children there unless there was a better option, but we don't have one. Bilé can enter structures and areas within Faery. Without Lucian and Spyder standing over the babes, we cannot protect them well enough to leave them here and feel comfortable about that decision. Let us hide your children where they will be safe, so that we may end this fight and bring them home along with our own children."

"And me, where will I be? In the guild, too?" Ciara asked as she narrowed her eyes in challenge.

"On the battlefield with me, where you belong," Ryder said, sitting in a chair and folding his hands together as he looked up at her. "I have protected you since the moment you were born, failing you every time Alazander sent me out as his tool to slaughter creatures. I have placed you out of the reach of my enemies. The thought of you being harmed by those who hate us because of Alazander, well, that terrified me. Losing Dristan made me realize that I have been pushing anyone away that I didn't think was up to fighting at my side.

"I have hidden you, and yet I ensured you were trained for war because it's in your blood just as it is in mine. This time, we're all fighting to survive, and it's everyone or no one. I can't expend the power to build two worlds, and those who cannot fight will enter the world I have created, but it is incomplete. That means it is unstable. We cannot fight without knowing our families are safe, and as Synthia reminded me, neither can the lesser beings."

"I will be at your side, Ryder. I trust Synthia's decision to send our children to the man who raised her. I just don't trust the new people, and I created those little monsters from scratch." She slipped as her hand into Blane's and smiled. "And this man, he is my world, even if he's an asshole most days."

"That's a little sassy, woman, even for you. We have tonight, remember that. I'm not opposed to placing that ass over my knee and reminding you who is in charge." Blane leaned over and kissed Ciara while grabbing her ass. Ryder growled and pointed to the door as I snickered.

"Let's go, Dragon," Ciara laughed as she pulled Blane toward the hall.

"We're planning war, not sex. You're my sister. I don't need to hear about you getting your ass spanked," Ryder growled again as he scrubbed his hand over his face.

"You can spank mine after dinner," I teased as heated eyes turned to me. "We're running late, and it's the last dinner everyone we will have together with their children." I didn't conceal the pain that laced my words, knowing that ours wouldn't be in attendance.

Ryder stood, holding out his hand as my dress turned into the silvery-blue gown he loved to put on me lately, claiming it highlighted my wings nicely. Our wings unfurled simultaneously, and the moment my hand touched his, raw electrical power filled the room.

"Shall we, My Queen?"

"We shall, My King," I smirked, watching Ciara and Blane flirting with their eyes in the hallway. "You two, no babies until this is over, understood? We can't be out fighting barefoot and pregnant. Someone would end up reporting us to the Fae Children Protection Agency or some shit."

"Fae Children Protection Agency?" Ryder asked curiously.

"Yeah, apparently we got some evil fuckers in the palace. We need to regulate that as a law, one that protects the babes born and abandoned by human mothers. If we had a division like that in place before this happened, we'd only be fighting a god. Instead, we are fighting Bilé and his entire raggedy band of orphans who are butt hurt because they weren't accepted when mommy abandoned them because they weren't human enough to be in that world, and not fae enough to be in Faery.

"I'd like for us not to go to war again anytime soon, so expect changes in Faery once we have won. I want the children of this world protected. I also want those with fae blood pumping through their veins to know that they are wanted by the horde, without having to prove they are murderous pricks. I would like to provide a safe place for everyone, where war and treachery don't run thick as thieves throughout it."

"So, who is going to run this organization?" Ryder asked.

"I will," Ciara snorted. "I will run a place like that with you, Synthia. I will help you protect the children of this world from ever enduring what I did as a child."

"You impregnate Ciara and keep her busy, and I'll do the same with Synthia," Ryder chuckled to Blane, pulling me close as he pressed his forehead against mine. "I love that you want to protect everyone, but you have no idea how many creatures abandon their young."

"I do, actually. I can hear them whispering for help inside my head. This war will leave thousands of children orphans. You and me, Ryder? We are officially about to become the High King and Queen of Faery if everything goes as planned, and that means it will fall to us to protect those who need us. Someone has to step up and take care of those children, and that is us. We have the power to build palaces and create worlds. How can we not help the children of those we asked to fight beside us, those who fall during battle?"

"Okay, but you need to put that fucking bleeding heart away before you end up asking the redcaps to move in with us, Pet," he chuckled, pulling me closer as he claimed my lips. "I draw the line at those messy fucks. They drip blood everywhere and think it's normal."

"Agreed, and they try looking up my skirts every chance they get."

"They're dead," he said with a serious look in his eyes.

"You tend to try to get beneath my skirts, too," I snorted.

"That pussy is mine, Pet. I licked it, and I lick it a lot to be sure everyone knows it is mine."

"Ryder, your sister is right..." I paused, looking around the room. Moaning started from the closet, and I closed my eyes. "I think they personally plan to repopulate the world with dragons." At Ciara's loud scream, I grabbed Ryder's hand and pulled him with me out of the room, laughing. "We should go."

"Make it fast, Dragon! Family dinner, asshole," Ryder called over his shoulder as Blane growled loudly from the closet.

"How did they even fit in there?" I asked.

"I don't want to know."

"Is there another one we can fit into?"

"Let's find out," he laughed, pulling me in the opposite direction from the dinner I'd planned for him.

"No." I pulled him back to me, and our wings brushed against each other as he cocooned my body within his. "I don't want five minutes in the closet before dinner. I want forever. I want to walk into that dinner knowing that the moment it is finished, I'll be riding your cock until sunrise, heading to war by your side at dawn. This evening is for family, but tonight, you will make love to me slowly until I beg you to start fucking destroying me, like every time we try to take it slow."

"You're not a 'take it slow' kind of woman, Synthia Raine."

"Yeah, I'm aware. I'm also married to sex incarnate. He fucks like he fights, and I like experiencing both from him. Be a good boy, and I'll let you fuck whatever part of my body that you want tonight," I promised, and his eyes heated as he watched me.

"Careful, because you're about to be riding a horse come morning, and that ass has been taunting me for the last year that you haven't been able to take all of me. I don't intend to use magic this time, either."

"I'm not weak anymore, Ryder. I can take you any way I want you; remember that," I ran my hand down his chest and stepped out of his wings as he smirked wickedly.

"That ass is mine, woman," he warned in a thick timbre.

"Only if you earn it," I taunted, swaying my hips and smirking as a deep growl escaped his chest.

CHAPTER TWENTY ONE

WE ENTERED THE DINING hall, stopping at the staircase to gaze out over the crowd of people surrounding the tables. It was a large, boisterous bunch tonight, but tomorrow some of us would ride off to war together, while others were hidden and protected. Some would leave to hide within the guild, ensuring that no matter what, they'd survive this fight.

It was the only thing we could do. I'd rebuilt the guild with this war in mind. It was why I'd spent countless hours there with Lucian, Lena, and even Erie, making sure that gods and whatever Lucian was couldn't breach the defenses. And considering he was massive, and one of the strongest creatures I'd encountered in my entire lifetime, that was definitely in the guild's best interest regarding the defense system.

"We could just leave. No one would notice," Ryder offered, slipping his fingers through mine. "Come on, let's go."

Smiling, I stared down at our hands, but it wasn't his hand that held mine. It was Malachi's. I looked up at the creature watching me through ancient eyes, not speaking as he took in my response to his presence in my home.

Sweat beaded on my brow as nausea swirled violently through me. He smiled tightly as silver and electric-blue tri-colored eyes studied my reaction to his touch.

The noise in the room dimmed until everything faded away to nothingness. Malachi turned away, staring at the people who laughed and celebrated around us.

"It's time, Synthia."

"Time for what?" I whispered through trembling lips. His words sent panic rushing through me. What if I hadn't escaped after all? What if he'd woven the perfect illusion, and I'd been living it, blissfully unaware?

"It's time I let you go. You promised to show me what it was like to be outside of the Seelie prison if I promised to make you into what this world needed. You are ready to face the war, and I know what it means to feel emotions. You helped me, and your husband wants me to let you go now. You were willing to change for him, and I admit that didn't sit well with me once I realized the entirety of your soul was created by your love and your humanity. I will remove the tether of the magic that withholds the truth now, and you will regain the true memories of what really happened in the prison. That was the deal you made."

"I don't understand," I admitted as a shiver of fear sliced through my stomach to wrap around my spine.

"Pain forces us to change, and enough trauma makes our minds break. To get you to where you needed to be, I broke you. I broke the parts of you that had to be broken so that you could hold the magic the world was trying to give you. You taught me this," he stated, pointing out at the people around us who continued blissfully unaware of the monster in their midst.

No, not everyone was unaware. Lucian and Spyder were both on their feet, watching Malachi, but hadn't moved from where they stood.

"I want this, I think. I want this family thing you have. But in time, once I am prepared to give it enough of myself. Until then, sweet Synthia, I bid you goodbye. We will meet again very soon. I am *certain* of it. Our destinies were intertwined by fate, and I feel that is why I was left in that pit. I was waiting for you to be created, so that I could help you, thereby helping Faery. You told me you felt compelled in the direction, and that something pulled you to the pit. I think you were ready to change, and that's why you found me when you did. I was the only creature who could help you become you, sweet sister."

"I don't understand what is happening," I cried as my body trembled with the magic rushing through it.

"Not yet, but you will soon. I free you of the deal we made, and I wish you well, sister," he leaned over, brushing a kiss over my cheek before he vanished.

I stared at my hand, and Ryder lifted my chin, forcing me to look into his eyes, flecked brightly with the constellations. Memories from the cave slammed into my head, and I whimpered, fighting the pain it created. The pain turned into a throbbing sensation between my eyes, settling behind my eyelids, becoming violet colors that shot through my head. Pulling my hand from Ryder's, I clapped them over my ears, blinkingly rapidly to dispel the images of Malachi as he watched me approaching him.

He was ethereal and hauntingly beautiful. Monsters had reached for me, and Malachi had growled in warning, sending them all scurrying back into the shadows with the simplest noise. The cave was ice-cold and filled with a dim glow provided by tiny crystals that seemed to reflect light into its depths, illuminating a pool of turquoise waters.

"You're not supposed to be here, and yet you are. Curious. How did you enter my home, little one?" Malachi asked, stepping closer as magic slithered around me, choking my

airway. He smirked, but it wasn't cruel. It was... inquisitive. "I'm sorry. It isn't often that I find myself in the company of something so beautiful and delicate."

"I have to get out of here, now," I whispered, and then turned as something scurried from the shadows.

"There is no escaping this place," he laughed soundlessly, and yet it echoed in my head like nails on a chalkboard.

One minute he was across the room, and the next, he stood in front of me. Thick, dark wings extended from his spine as magic pulsed from the walls of the cave. The crystals ignited, and his head lowered toward mine, forcing my hand to lift and cover my mouth. Malachi pulled back, gazing at my hand protecting my lips from his.

"You refuse my kiss?"

"I am married and very much in love with my husband," I explained.

"Nobody here has ever been loved," he argued, frowning as his brows pulled together, confused by my words. "What is the emotion you feel?"

"Pain, for no one ever loving you," I admitted, sensing the truth of his words like a weight of bricks stacked on my chest. It was smothering. He meant it, and somehow it bothered me. I felt his turmoil. His pain was all exposed and jagged edges without him even knowing it.

"You feel pain for me?" he laughed outright. *The sheer volume of it caused my ears to bleed, and my hands clapped against them as I dropped to my knees, peering up at him.*

He knelt before me, tilting his head as his gaze narrowed on me. He removed my hands from my ears, and the laughter abated, silencing the pain. His nostrils flared, and he growled, exposing blunt, white teeth as he leaned over, licking the blood from where it poured from my ear.

"Who are you?" he demanded viciously.

"Synthia, Queen of the Horde, Daughter of Danu, and Goddess of the Fae."

"Danu...oh," he whispered, clasping his hand against mine, drawing his finger over my palm. *"You carry my bloodline, little one. My mother was also Danu, Goddess of Faery."*

My heart hammered wildly while I swallowed past the anger that slammed into me. My gaze followed his finger while he drew the picture of the tree representing Faery.

Lifting my eyes to hold his, I spoke softly.

"She put you here, didn't she? Danu put you in this place because you weren't what she wanted to create. She threw you away, just as Ryder has thrown me away. We weren't enough, were we? Our pieces didn't fit into their puzzles, and we're not what they wanted us to be. You're not a monster. You're a child who has been thrown away because your

mother didn't think you were good enough to love. That is her fault, not yours. We are only what we were made to be. Sometimes the things created aren't always what the gods wanted, and so they throw things like us away."

"You have no idea of the things you speak," he snapped.

"But I do, because you were imperfect, and Danu locked you inside this prison because of it. She then created others in your image, fixing the parts she thought were flawed. I'm here because of the part of myself that I cannot eradicate. I am not what they wanted, because I cannot become what is needed. I am imperfect, flawed by my humanity, which I wasn't born to house. I am here because I am in their way and failed to save my family because I don't know how to change to be what they need me to become."

"Danu can teach you," he snorted, pulling me up into a standing position with him, "if you survive the monsters within the caves."

"Danu is dead," I replied icily.

"Impossible, she is a goddess."

"She gave her life for mine to save this world." He paused, staring at me through angry silver eyes lined with turquoise. "It wasn't my choice, but then I think she was done fighting for us."

"Our mother gave her life for you and ignored her other children?" he scoffed as smothering power filled the cave. "Why are you so special?"

"Because it's my destiny is to save Faery," I admitted, unable to hide the frustration in my tone.

"Faery is never-ending."

"It is when the God of Death wants it to end. Bilé marches his armies across the land, slaughtering innocent people even now. He hates that Danu abandoned him, and so he makes the fae pay for it." Pain pushed against my chest, and I peered down where his hand touched me.

"You're weak," he chuckled.

"And you're alone, and no one is coming for us."

"You could get us out of here, but there would be a heavy price to pay."

I studied him for a moment before stepping away from his hand. "Which would be?"

"I want to know what it's like to feel. You are filled with emotions, but I want the ones you get when you think of him, the one who left you down here."

"Ryder. You want to know what it feels like to love? Kick yourself in the balls and save yourself the trouble of having your heart ripped out. Love hurts, and it has the power to destroy you in the worst way possible. You don't want that. No one should ever want that kind of pain."

Malachi smirked, watching me, crossing his massively pulsing arms over his bare chest. He was built for war, and worse, pleasure. Everything about him screamed sex, and my eyes burned with the intensity of it. It was like looking at an angel, even knowing that looking too long would cause blood to leak from your eyes.

"The little ones, you love them more than you love yourself," he announced with curiosity filling his tone. "They're your children. You're a mother? Mothers do not love what comes from their womb. No one here has known the love of a mother, ever. I want to know that emotion."

"You have major mommy issues? Great, that makes two of us."

"How can you love them?"

"Because I created them inside of me and felt them growing in my womb. Mothers are supposed to love their young—except for our mother," I smirked. "I love them because they are a part of me, and even if they turned into a bunch of little anti-heroes and weren't perfect, I'd still love them. I am their mother, and all children are beautifully imperfect. That's what a mother is supposed to do: love them no matter what they are or who they become. Our mother, Danu, she wasn't what a mother should have been, not until the end, and even then, her motives were selfish."

"You have to evolve, and I have to learn what you feel. Help me to know those emotions, and I will help you become what you are intended to be."

"At what cost?" I countered, tilting my head while studying the look of fear in his beautiful eyes.

He feared my answer, and that screamed more about his intentions than he could ever describe. He craved what he had never known. He'd been down here since the creation of Faery, and yet none of the beings down here had ever known love. He just wanted to know what emotions were, and how terribly sad was that?

"I won't word-play you and say it will be pleasant. To fix you, I have to rip you apart and put you back together again. I will allow you to know the pain I endured, and also the pleasure they forced upon me like a newly born creature. But this I promise you: through the worst of it, I'll shelter you, and then briefly allow you to taste what true pain is.

"I will show you what I have endured while you show me what it is like to know the love you hold for this man and your children. I want to know what it is like to feel something other than nothingness. In order to rebuild you, I must deconstruct you slowly. Neither of us will leave here until you are reborn as the true Goddess of the Fae. Only she can free us from this prison because she built it."

"Danu built this place, and I have stepped into her role. I understand. You want to take parts of me away, but you will replace them? You will put me back together as I am now?"

"Yes, every piece."

"How can I trust that you will keep your word?"

"You can't, but if you don't, neither of us will leave here, and anyone who comes after you will remain here with us. You are the only one who can escape this prison and live through it. Only Death can come, but even he would be endangered here, as too many of us crave his scythe."

"So, if we don't do this, we both stay here... forever?" I clarified, studying his eyes. The thing was, I felt this creature within my soul. I felt the familial bond fae shared with one another, but it was much more than that. It was amplified, pulsing through me as I stared into his eyes. I could actually feel the bond we shared clicking into place as he smiled, nodding, feeling it too as wonder played across my face.

"I've been here since before the world was fully created. When Mother brought me here, the tree was the only thing within this world. Now, I can feel it has expanded and grown to house many worlds within it, still unexplored. I do not wish to keep your memories, only feel them, as I have never known anything but lust, hunger, and hatred that burdens every creature in the prison."

"You think my life has been a walk in the park?"

"I can feel the love and sense of happiness you have known. I see the devotion in your aura for those you call family. It intrigues me and excites the darkness of this prison with your purity. I have been ripped apart until the only thing I have known is the need to survive, but I have never tasted purity, nor love.

"I have only slaughtered creatures that entered my tomb, and make no mistake, that is where you are. Mother built my tomb perfectly, never letting me feel the beauty of her world or know the feel of the sun on my face. I have only known this coldness and bitterness, and the hatred and fear of those who have been tossed in to feed me through the countless years I have been down here."

"Then let's begin, shall we, brother?" I said, placing my hand into his. He stared at our clasped hands before peering back up at me. "Tick-tock, I have a war to win."

I blinked and swallowed, staring at Ryder as my mouth opened and closed, trying to find the words that I needed to say until something slammed against the walls of the stronghold, causing the castle to shake.

"Ryder," I hissed. "I didn't do it."

"Do what?" he asked, watching as everyone stood from the tables and began vanishing.

"Malachi showed me what happened in the prison. I didn't sleep with any of the monsters. I didn't cheat on you." The weight that had been on my chest lessened, and I exhaled.

"I know, but right now, there's a bigger issue. Get the women to the guild, Synthia. Now," he ordered and started to sift, but I pulled him back. "There's no time, woman!"

"Kiss me, my beast." I stepped on tiptoes as our wings unfurled. "I love you. I will always love you. Go kill those who seek to harm us, and I'll be back as soon as I have secured our people in the fortress I erected for them."

"You owe me a raincheck on that ass, woman."

"Really? I just told you I loved you, and you talk about wanting to tap my ass?" I snorted.

"It's a really nice ass that's been taunting me for a very long time. Now go. Ass-play later, sassy witch."

"Fucking Fairy," I laughed, moving to get the women and children to safety as Ryder glamoured on his armor, heading toward the noise in the courtyard.

CHAPTER TWENTY TWO

I STOOD IN THE catacombs at the guild, watching women and babes as they moved into the underground safe rooms. It was utter chaos as Alden and Adrian did their best to situate everyone without interfering. Alden handed a blanket to a woman and her child, and I noted his graying hair and the wrinkles on his face that were more defined today.

He had aged since Lena's mother had been murdered, and I'd neglected to notice it before now. Every once in a while, his steel-gray eyes would move to Lena, and he'd pinch his forehead together in worry. He walked toward me and leaned against the wall, smirking at my narrowed glance.

"You do know that Lena's okay now. Right, old man?" I asked offhandedly, and he snorted.

"She lost everyone, how the fuck is any of that okay?"

"Because she's good in a storm. Some of us are just born to play in the rain, while others drown. Some people aren't made to endure trials, and when they fall, they stay down. We rise because it is the only thing we know. A few of us had amazing teachers who taught us always to get back up, others life forged into warriors because being a victim wasn't something they could accept. You're aging, Alden."

"That's what being human means, kid. We age, we grow old, and eventually, we die. I'm okay with that because I have lived an amazing life. Dying is just another part of the journey. I thought we'd already had this talk?"

"I'm about to go off to war, and knowing that it might take years to win it, well, what if you're not here anymore when I get back?"

"You think I won't still be around haunting this place long after I'm gone?" Alden chuckled, and I leaned my head against his arm. "I miss my sister and my family. I'm not afraid to die, Synthia Raine McKenna. If I die tomorrow, I live within you, Adam, and Adrian. I didn't have kids for a reason. I had too many to handle as it was, and some of you needed me more than others. I almost settled down to have a family, but then you came to stay here with me." Alden moved his arm around my shoulder and hugged me close, smiling down at me. "You were this tiny little girl who had been traumatized at such a tender and impressionable age. You needed me more than I needed my lineage to go on, and now here we are. You carry my name, Synthia, and you will carry it throughout time with your immortality. I will always go on through you."

"You don't regret it?" I asked, peering into his eyes.

"Raising you? Shit, kid. I raised a goddess." He squeezed me tighter and chuckled. "How many people can say that? Regret isn't something I have in my life. I'm proud of my kids, and they're all my kids. I raised them from the time they could walk and talk. I taught them to fight, how to harness magic, and I watched them grow into beings I'm proud to call mine. That's what life is, you know? You do the best you can, and you hope everything turns out alright. Sometimes you get lucky, but even when they're not perfect, you're still proud of them because they struggle and strive to be so in your eyes."

"That's a really lame argument. I died, Adrian died, and Adam is struggling with grief. He currently has a zombie stashed in a closet somewhere in his house, which I can't seem to locate. He'll probably be eaten by said zombie trying to get into her panties."

"But you're all still here, you shithead."

I snorted, punching him in the arm. "I love you, old man."

"None of that shit, girl. You're coming back, and I won't be dead when you do. You're going to handle this situation as you always have. You're going to face overwhelming odds, and you're going to kick their asses because you don't even know what failure means. You've never accepted defeat as a scenario, and now isn't the time to change that."

"I have to come back, someone has to keep this place in line," I laughed, moving away from him as I started walking backward, smiling at the pride shining in his eyes. "It's not *goodbye*, old man, it's just *see you later*." I turned, strolling toward Adrian, who stood with Erie as she leaned against the wall.

"No stakes, right?" Adrian asked, holding up his hands in mock surrender.

"I won't save you this week. Next week, though, I might have time to do that," I snorted, smirking at the laugher dancing in his eyes.

"Only if you kiss me first, and that husband of yours is watching us. The best part of my decade was him being unable to do shit about you kissing me."

"You're lucky he didn't end your existence, dick."

"Yeah, I know. How often do I get to fuck with Ryder, though? You know he hates me," Adrian said, rolling turquoise eyes toward the ceiling.

"Yeah, he does," I agreed.

"You were supposed to tell me he didn't."

"I'd be lying," I smirked as he groaned, shaking his dark head.

"Sometimes, it's okay to lie to me, Synthia." Adrian's grin disappeared, and he shook his head as a new group of kids entered the catacombs. "This is a mess. You forgot to mention you were bringing orphans."

"They're not orphans anymore. They're guild recruits. They can go upstairs, and you will train them. They have no family left, and they're perfect. They can be taught to wield magic for defense and have a partner from another race to balance them out. What better creatures to hunt fae than the fae? We have the resources to train them, and the best guild elder to manage them and their needs. Start them on their studies, and when they're old enough, begin training them to fight. Those who don't work out can come back to me, and I'll find places for them in Faery."

"Fuck me, Syn, there's an army of them."

"Exactly, and without parents, they won't last in Faery. They will be safer here, and if the time comes that they wish to re-enter Faery, if there is a Faery left standing, they'll be allowed to do so. I couldn't leave them in the stronghold alone, and we have plenty of space for them here."

"Why are you really here, Syn?" Adrian asked, forcing me to pause and looked at him. I opened my mouth to speak, and he shook his head. "No, don't fucking lie to me. Your man is defending the stronghold, and you're here talking about orphans. We don't do goodbyes. You know that. Go home and fuck some shit up. Bring those bastards to their knees. I got this; you know I do. Lucian, Spyder, and Erie set the wards up in the catacombs. Not even *the* God himself could get in here, and yet here you are, wasting time making sure you tell everyone goodbye."

"I have not said goodbye once," I argued as emotion wrapped around my chest, gripping my throat until I gave up arguing.

"No, but that's exactly what you're doing. You're telling everyone goodbye because you don't plan on making it out of this alive. Fuck that, and fuck you for thinking you can die on us. You go to war, and you go with your head held high. You fucking bring them to their knees just as we were taught and trained to do. That's what my girl does. She fucking brings men to their knees, and she gives no mercy to her enemies. Stop saying everything you think you have to say, because the only way this ends, well, that's with you coming back here and dusting off those pretty little pink nails and telling us you won. Go home to your husband and fight beside him."

"I love you too, asshole." I hugged Adrian and told myself that I wouldn't cry even as tears pricked my eyes.

"Ah, my angel-eyed girl. I never stopped loving you; it just changed into something deeper, and a lot less dirty."

"Don't tell Ryder that; who will I use to make him jealous?" I scoffed as I hugged him tightly before stepping away. "I'm going home. You have the children of the horde here, so no enforcers get into the catacombs, Adrian. Fort Knox this bitch, and don't let anyone know what is down here. Keep them protected for me, and we'll be back to collect them soon."

"You got it," he said, nodding toward Erie, who smirked wide as her brows wiggled.

"You think anyone is getting inside here? I brought my sisters, and no one fucks with War when the Raven Guard is unleashed. Also, Fred is outside surrounding the guild and murdering anything that tries to get in, minus the few enforcers they injured, who I guess lived here? Oops. My bad," Erie snorted. "Alden assigned a male to the demons to make sure it didn't happen again. We got this; you go kick some ass. Take this," she stated, handing me a locket. "If shit gets bad, say my name, and I'm there."

"Thanks, Erie."

"I'm Mórrígan."

"Thanks…"

"I'm totally just fucking with you. We are one and always have been. Batshit crazy, but who wouldn't be with all our memories scattered between lifetimes? Erie is just who I have become, and personally, I like me. I'm cool and fun."

"Thank you for protecting our families, and for this," I said, holding up the locket. I turned, scanning the room for Alden, and found him watching me with a frown on his face. "See you guys soon."

CHAPTER TWENTY THREE

I SIFTED ONTO THE battlements where I'd felt Ryder, watching as the army was made ready to ride. He turned, staring at me, his heated eyes lowering to my swaying hips as I slowly walked toward him. The entire stronghold was bathed in darkness. No fires were lit within the courtyard, and the few torches that sat burning on the fortress walls did little to offer light.

Fyra and Remy flanked us on both towers. Remy, the larger of the two dragons, growled, then inhaled deeply with a loud rumbling noise before sending flames rushing through the morning sky to light my way to my husband. Just as his flames ended, I heard what sounded like choked laughter.

"Did everything go okay?" Ryder asked softly.

"Alden is getting old on me, and he doesn't care."

"He knows what he wants, Pet. You can't demand he change into something if he isn't willing. It just pisses you off because eventually, he will die. That isn't your choice to make, though, which is what upsets you the most."

"You're too smart to be this pretty," I stated, standing on my tiptoes to kiss his hungry lips. "Seems like a crime that you got to be both."

"Woman, I'm barely keeping my shit together without bending your perky ass over the edge of this battlement and fucking you right here. Now turn around and smile so that our people see that we're taking this seriously, and not up here making a new prince or princess while they work."

"I want more," I announced, exhaling as his arms wrapped around me. "I want your pretty babies, Fairy. I want all the fucking babes."

"Careful, My Queen, I enjoy making babies with you. I'm also not opposed to changing the harem into a nursery for all those pretty babies you're planning."

"Yeah, you see, it is also fun to make those babies, but only one of us has to get fat to cook them."

"I don't have the parts, and you do," he chuckled huskily against my ear, kissing my neck softly.

"That's true, and not the least bit fair since you should at least have to experience some of it."

The wind howled around the stronghold, and I frowned, noting that packhorses were being loaded with supplies, and below us, items from the castle were being ruined and tossed aside to make it look as if we'd deserted it.

"Why are they destroying everything?" I questioned carefully.

"The attack on the stronghold breached the north side of the battlement. It provided us a good excuse to make the castle appear to be abandoned due to damage. We're just going to help it along so that the god watching our every move will think it was damaged enough that we had to flee," he informed, hugging me tightly. "When we leave here, there will be nothing left. Our children's things were in the first load to go to the guild yesterday, and Alden placed them in his apartment. Your items we salvaged from your childhood home are with him too. I have nothing I care to keep, nothing but you."

"Dristan's things?"

"Dristan is dead; he doesn't need things. I have every memory of him and every one of my other brothers, as well as Ciara, within my heart. I will carry them with me until the end of time. Their things are just that...things. Before the stronghold was attacked, you said you didn't do it. Elaborate."

"I made a deal with Malachi, one that helped us escape the prison together. I remember now. Not everything that happened, but I do know what didn't happen. I didn't break my vow to you. I kept it, Ryder."

"I know you did," he stated huskily. "If you hadn't, I'd have smelled other men on you. You are mine and only mine. This body has only known me, and even if you had, I wouldn't have cared. I wouldn't have liked it, but I'd have understood why you did what you did to survive. I could smell magic on you, but what you said and felt, it was real. I have my wife back, so everything else is fucking irrelevant."

"You knew I didn't break my vows?" I asked softly, staring into onyx eyes that smiled at me, his lips mirroring the happiness even while marching to war. Ryder was created for war, and he thrived in the face of it.

"I suspected, but you said you died, which could have explained not being able to smell another male on you. Cillian helped me find Malachi within your dreams, Synthia. I couldn't stop the nightmares alone, and the scent of something powerful leaked from you when Malachi was present in your mind as you slept. His magic wasn't like yours. So, I asked the King of Nightmares to help me figure out how to save you. What I found was someone powerful trying to protect you, even from me."

"Malachi is Oberon, the first King of Faery. His mother was also Danu, so I'm pretty much elated that he didn't try to have sex with me. I also don't think my pain was real; I think it was his."

"I think Malachi is very powerful, and that he protected you from yourself. He said there were no other creatures within the prison that could hurt you. I think he wanted you to know him, to know what he endured. I also think that he killed most of the creatures within that prison because they tried to leave him, and not that many escaped from it as you assumed."

"Maybe... Who attacked us?" I countered, not wishing to discuss the torture I'd felt in detail right now. I didn't want to break the peace we had, which would soon end as we rode out through Faery to fight Bilé and his army.

"Mages, but we handled it. I think they were testing us, seeing if we were really leaving the stronghold to head to war. They didn't intend to live long enough to inflict damage. Three of them had white eyes, and I'm pretty sure Bilé was seeing through them and noting everything we did down to the minute details of the horses being saddled. He's no longer able to follow us from the map we are using. You are to thank for that, for seeing what no one else could."

"It was just a map."

"It was what we'd planned our wars from since my father held the throne, Synthia. No one would have ever suspected the map, or that he could access its information because it had been created within Faery." Ryder chuckled, holding me tighter as we peered out over the meadow that bordered the forest we would soon pass through.

"It just made sense, seeing as there were no eyes within the war room. No spies, no one strong enough to withstand the magic of yours we used to track every message and every person leaving or coming from the stronghold."

I turned, watching Zahruk as he approached, packed to the teeth with weapons in the white robe he wore. He nodded at me while moving the rest of the way to stop beside us.

"We're ready," he informed softly, his eyes slowly surveying the war force below that was already mounting to ride into the rolling valleys of Faery. "When you're finished, the dragons will set the stronghold on fire."

Zahruk's words caused my stomach to lurch, and my hand lifted, covering the sob that fought to explode from my lips. Tears pricked my eyes as I leaned my head against Ryder's chest. This was our home, and to defeat the mages, we were walking away from it. It burned and ached something fierce to know that we had to concede sacrifices to make headway in this war.

"Zahruk, call the Elite Guard up for a moment, please." Ryder pulled me even tighter against him and whispered against my ear, "It's just a place, Pet. My home is with you and our family. Right now, that's wherever we end up together. We knew that we'd never make it out of this fight unscathed. I won't lose this war to some god who is pissed off over a lost love, and willing to destroy the entire world as a result."

"I know, but this is your home, Ryder. I've lost every home I have ever known. I know it's just rocks and what-ever the hell else you used to build it. I just hate giving an inch to this sadistic prick, knowing that we can't even kill the bastard."

"We're going to finish this together as a family. We will either survive this together or die fighting. Our children are protected. The next generation is safe from Bilé's reach. Now, we go show him why you don't fuck with the fae or those who live within Faery."

"For Faery," I whispered, and he shook his head.

"You let all of them hear you, Synthia. For Faery!" he shouted, and cries went up for victory through the soldiers. "Come, wife. We ride to slaughter the fucking mages." He glamoured on my armor, similar to that of the Elite Guard but with a silver cloak and a crown created of obsidian that matched the one he wore. "No more whispering. Today we let them hear our rage and our battle cries."

Ryder smiled down the line of his brothers as he held me tightly in front of him. Ristan stood beside me on the right, while Zahruk held the left with Ciara beside him. Savlian, ever silent, stood in line next. Beside him, Sinjinn, Aohdan, Asrian, Cailean, Lachlan, Adam, Liam, and Asher and his brethren, along with Elysian, stared out over the warriors that waited below.

"For Dristan," Ryder said, lighting a candle that sat on the edge of the battlement.

"For Eliran," Aohdan announced, lighting his.

"Olivia," Ristan whispered thickly as Ryder placed his hand on his shoulder, tightening it in silent reassurance.

"For Darynda." Zahruk lit his candle and turned to watch Sinjinn do the same for Sevrin before they both sifted away.

Adam stepped forward and lit candles in honor of his fallen family, and I joined Liam as we did the same for our parents.

Others began to move around us as more candles were placed on the battlements by those who had lost brothers or sisters, mothers or fathers, or worse, children. My eyes moved through the meadows, watching it illuminate from the candles Ryder had told his men to hand out for a blessing to the dead. They were a silent promise to bring those who had been needlessly murdered some peace and to avenge their deaths.

There were so many candles lit throughout the meadow that it glowed as if the moon had been snatched from the sky and placed into the flowering grass. Swallowing hard, I leaned my head against Ryder and shook it as the sense of helplessness at not having been able to prevent the deaths of our family and friends sank in.

"Don't do that," Ryder whispered. "You can't change what happened. You can only make sure the war ends and doesn't continue to reach others. Death is a part of Faery, just not as much as it is within the human realm. Do not grieve the dead, for they are free. We don't fight for the dead. We fight for the living and to avenge those we lost. That means more than revenge. Fighting for the living gives us an edge because when you're fighting to live, you fight with everything you have in your arsenal. Come, wife. We ride."

We sifted to the head of the army of troops, which had grown considerably over the past few days. The remainder of the High Courts' forces had finally reached us, along with the lesser fae, who had run from the forest, back toward the safety of the horde.

Ryder walked behind me as I made my way to the large warhorse he'd chosen for me. Once I was secured on the saddle, he mounted his own enormous warhorse and glamoured armor onto each of the horses.

I promised myself I wouldn't look back to watch as the stronghold was burned, but it was fucking dragons. Turning in my saddle, I watched as Remy and Fyra took to the sky. Ryder checked faces and spoke to guards before he lifted his hand and dropped it, signaling the dragons as their fire consumed the castle. The horde shouted war cries as the drums began to beat while the fortress was bathed in the fire of the dragons.

Adjusting on my mount, I shifted my eyes to Ryder. His jaw ticked, and the muscles in his neck flexed as his home burned. Flames reflected in his eyes, and something akin to sadness shone from within them. I cleared my throat as the horde grew silent.

"This is our home!" Ryder shouted, and I swallowed hard. "They will never take it from us! Brothers and sisters, today we march to war! We march on those who think we can be conquered. We will never concede and never die! For Faery!" The army repeated the last of his words after they'd escaped his lungs as a roar. "For those the enemy has needlessly taken from us! For the Blood Kingdom, the Light Kingdom, and the Dark Kingdom! For those who depend on us to fight today, we are all horde! We are the monsters that slither into their home in the shadows and bathe in their blood. We are the ones they fear because we have no fear. We ride together, we fight together, and if we fall, we will fall together!"

Tears slipped from my eyes as my throat clenched. It wasn't sadness; it was utmost pride in the beast I'd married. He was my world and my best friend. Tonight, as we walked away from our home together, and toward an unknown future, there was nowhere else I'd have wanted to be, and no one else I would want to ride beside.

"My Queen," he said softly, noting the tears.

"My King, I am proud to be your Queen at this moment, and every moment after this one. Now, let's go kill every last one of those motherfuckers for coming into our home and making a mess."

"You heard my Queen. Let's go kill some fucking mages, shall we?" he chuckled. "Careful, Pet. If you make my dick hard, I'll fuck you on my horse while I ride it into battle."

"You wouldn't," I laughed until he continued to stare at me through heated eyes. "Is that even possible?"

"Anywhere, anytime, Synthia," he smirked roguishly. "With you, nothing is untouchable."

"You guys know that we can hear you, right?" Ciara asked.

"They know. They're just trying to provide some Porn Fae-Per-View. I wonder if that shit comes with rewind or instant playback," Ristan chuckled.

"We would need some popcorn," Spyder teased.

"Maybe not on horseback." I grinned at Ryder, who shook his head. "Let's go take back our world and fuck some shit up, so we can find our happily fucked up ever after, my beast."

CHAPTER TWENTY FOUR

CAMPFIRES COVERED THE VALLEY in which we'd settled after days of endless riding to separate us from the stronghold. As far as the eye could see, men and women prepared meals over campfires. They sat amongst one another, drinking spirits as they reminisced about their homes and what they wanted to do after the war ended. The reality was that a lot of them would die before this was over. That left me numb and cold, which no fire could erase.

"Are you hungry, woman?" Ryder stood behind me, kissing my neck as we watched the camp from the hill we'd climbed to survey the area for any sign of threat as our people ate and celebrated life.

"I'm worried that we're going to lose a lot of our people in this battle. It's a war that we shouldn't even be fighting. Who wouldn't want to be a part of the horde? It may be the wildest and meanest caste of the fae, but this right here," I said, pointing down to all the different types of fae that were gathered together, willing to fight for Faery. "Their camaraderie during times of sorrow and worry makes it all worth it. This is what the mage warriors rejected being a part of, and it will be their downfall in the end."

"Being of the horde isn't that easy, Synthia. It's expecting treachery all the time. Secrets are kept and only told when there's no other choice. The horde doesn't love or judge, but they do slaughter the weakest to prevent them from joining our forces. The mage recruits were afraid of being tested if they came to us requesting to become a part of the horde. Many of them would have been slaughtered, and they were very aware that it could happen."

"How could their troops know they might have been killed? They're strong enough to wage this war, and yes, they may have a god leading them, but they are powerful in their own right. They could have stood together as they do now, creating their own caste. When they die, I feel it too, Ryder. They are fae like us."

"We're not fae, Synthia."

"We may no longer be fae, but it is and will always be who we started out as. It's part of who we are, even if it isn't what we are now," I whispered.

"How did a creature like me end up with a beautiful goddess like you?" Ryder hugged me from behind and kissed my neck.

"You forced Danu to create your perfect mate."

"I did do that, but there was no guarantee that you'd ever love me. That just meant you were mine to claim," he growled as his lips skimmed lower down my throat. "And I know you love me as much as I love you because I feel this debilitating pain at the thought of losing you. I know that if you died, I'd want to die too," he uttered hoarsely.

I opened my mouth to reply, but fog on the far side of the camp caught my eye. My vision cleared the shadows that seemed unnatural, and I swallowed down a scream. Using magic, I peered through the dense mist and found the culprit.

"Right side of the camp," I stated urgently.

"Not the answer I was expecting," he chuckled.

"Mages!" I screamed, causing my voice to come out in an amplified warning to all within the camp.

"To arms, sound the drums!" he shouted, echoing his voice through the valley.

Grabbing Ryder's hand, I sifted toward the mages, pushing power against their forces as they slipped out of the shadow of the forest bordering our camp. Ryder was beside me, holding his hands up as we combined our powers to create a shield against the machine that was dusting the field with fog—iron fog.

The camp came to life swiftly. Soldiers picked up their weapons, and the sound of metal clanking together echoed through the valley as our army prepared for battle. I exhaled, pulling the magic from the world around us as I pushed the iron molecules from the air, cleaning it before our troops broke through the line to fight.

Ryder sifted to a group of mages, materializing his obsidian armor and dual swords before he started cutting the enemy down. More mages swarmed through the woods, rushing toward him. My hands lifted and magically turned the mages to nothing more than a bloody mist that bathed us both from head to toe.

Zahruk sifted in, and as I spun around, a head slammed against me, removed from the body of the male who'd thought to sneak up behind me.

Ristan came next, his sword tearing through bodies as he howled his pain mixed with rage, jumping into the fight without a thought. I held my hand up as a mage rushed toward Ristan, slicing through the mage with my magic until his entire body slid apart. Ristan turned, his eyes gleaming as he smirked and licked his lips clean from the blood splatter.

"Where the fuck are they coming from?" Ristan asked.

"From within the woods," I said. "They must have been lying in wait, hidden in the forest."

I was struggling to contain my power, holding it to me instead of freeing it to pulverize the mages. I couldn't use up too much of it because the moment I did, I would be depleted and unable to answer the call of Ryder's power with my own.

"No, there are too many of them," Zahruk snorted, sending his blades through men as he carried on the conversation like he was merely training warriors instead of fighting enemies. "We'd have heard them approaching."

"To your left," I called to Zahruk, watching as he swiped one blade left as the other went right. Two mages fell at his feet on either side of him without Zahruk even looking as he slaughtered them.

"On your right," he yelled back to me, and I swung blindly, copying his moves, severing a head from the neck before turning back to him. "Portal?"

"Maybe."

Zahruk shrugged in reply as he swung a few more times, hitting mages with every skillful move of his twin double-edged swords. He whistled, and more men came rushing forward, along with Cailean, who was covered in armor.

"Take a team and go around the woods. Find out where these assholes are coming from. Do not engage the enemy unless you have no other choice. Be careful," he stated, cutting a mage in half before he continued. "Stay to the shadows, we don't know where Bilé is, and he could be close."

"On it," Cailean stated. Holding up his hand, his men flanked him, and they started toward the side of the field without the tents.

I paused, listening to the clash of weapons, and the sounds of men dying all around me. The pain from their deaths wasn't debilitating, but it was there. It wasn't excruciating enough to indicate we were losing.

A loud growl sounded above us, and I peered up, seeing three dragons fly toward the woods, breathing fire to create a path straight through it. The forest blazed, and mages fell out of the cover the trees provided, consumed by flames.

I felt the iron of large bolts before they shot in the direction of the dragons. I slammed my hands down, forcing the bolts that flew toward Blane, Remy, and Fyra back down onto the mages who shot them.

The largest dragon, Blane, spun his head and bellowed out a warning to the smaller two. I turned slowly, staring out over the camp before moving my eyes back to the dragons, sending more of my magic into the air to help them.

Vines exploded from the ground, racing through the forest, destroying the large ballistae launching the iron bolts into the air. I didn't stop there. I closed my eyes, becoming the vines while reaching for the mages that rushed toward a portal.

It took concentration to wrap the foliage around their legs, pulling them into the earth until they were buried so deep that oxygen couldn't fill their lungs.

Trees bowed, slamming down on the mages until they were bloodied heaps upon the ground. Fire pushed through the forest, and I controlled the air, fanning the flames until they consumed bodies of the dead and rushed toward the living.

Hands touched me, and I ignored them, unleashing the power of Faery on those who had trespassed against it without mercy or hesitation. Everything within me wailed to avenge the world and the people who had suffered for merely being born fae.

Cailean stepped from the trees, and I pulled the magic back, sending it in the direction of the mages that were sneaking toward him. Their legs caught on fire as the heat of the dragons' flames licked their skin, melting the flesh from their bones.

My vines gripped Cailean's arms and the men with him. They pulled them through the last part of the woods, bringing them back near the camp as more flames leaped through the forest. I exhaled a shuddered sigh.

My ears rang with power until my head rolled backward, and strong arms cradled me tightly. I stared up into obsidian eyes flecked with gold as Ryder lifted me into his arms, the men flanking behind us as Ryder carried me toward the tent.

"What's wrong with her? Flower, what the fuck did you just do?" Ristan demanded.

"I don't know. She just used the power of Faery as a weapon against the mages. I felt it, though, her pull to the world. She used it to take revenge against the ones who have harmed our people."

"She's the Goddess of the Fae, not Faery."

"No shit, that doesn't change the fact she just wielded the magic of Faery like it was hers to control."

"That can't be good," Zahruk uttered as he kept pace with Ryder.

"Open the tent, now," Ryder snapped, and I smiled up at him. "She's bleeding from her nose and ears."

"We need a healer now!" Zahruk yelled.

"Now! The Queen is wounded!" Ristan snarled, and someone replied in a timid voice. "Get the fuck inside, asshole. Tend to your Queen."

"Yes, My Prince," the tiny voice whispered through chattering teeth.

"I ain't your fucking prince. This isn't a cartoon movie, asshole. Move!"

"Yes, sir."

I was placed on the pallet as hands pushed my hair away from my face. I felt numb, but there was no pain. I felt powerful and electrified by the juice running through my veins. I smiled at Ryder as he watched me, kissing my forehead before he moved to the side, allowing room for the healer.

An unfamiliar male moved forward and stared down at me. His hands lifted, and they began to shake as he checked me. After a minute, he stepped back, shaking his dark head.

"What's wrong with her?" Ryder demanded.

"Nothing. Nothing is wrong. Her vitals are strong, and there is no damage to her anywhere."

"There's fucking blood everywhere, idiot. What is wrong with my Queen?"

"What was she doing when she began to bleed?" he asked carefully, terrified of the looming beast who bellowed with worry at him.

"Magic, she pulled the magic from the world and attacked the mages with it."

"Magic she had never used?"

"No shit, asshole," Zahruk growled, impatience and concern etched on his face.

I sat up, exhaling. "I used Ryder's magic."

"What?" Ryder snapped.

"You house a sliver of my soul, and therefore, you can access my magic as I can access yours. You're the God of Faery, so I sipped a taste of it in battle and did what the fuck I had to do to protect the dragons and Cailean."

"Just like that?" he asked, and I felt his pull on my magic, and his hands clapped over his ears as he shook his head, pulling away from the magic I housed. "Gods, are the fae always that loud and complaining?"

"No, they're usually a lot louder. I'm fine. I just think I took a little too much to start. I had to think fast, and I couldn't just run off and leave you to worry about me. I made do with what I had at the moment. Cailean had mages on his heels, and they were hidden in the shadows, waiting to trap him. I couldn't let him be captured, and I felt their intent to hurt him. Then there were the iron bolts. I don't ever want to watch another dragon fall to one of those things."

"Syn?" Ciara screamed, rushing into the tent with the dragons and Cailean on her heels. "Are you okay? Blane told me what you did."

"I'm fine. I just overdid it."

"You saved our asses out there, My Queen," Blane said, kneeling before me.

"Get up, asshole. Family doesn't bow to one another. That's awkward and shit."

"Still, you protected my family today. We didn't see the bolts, and that could have been a fatal mistake," he said, pushing off the ground to stand. "They're not visible to us in dragon form. My guess is they have some type of substance coating the bolts."

"Then, the next time we fight the mages, we have to be sure the mages cannot fire those bolts," I replied as Blane nodded.

"Start packing up camp. We ride within the hour. Syn, you will ride with me until I am certain you're fine. I won't accept anything less, wife."

"I wasn't planning on arguing," I snorted.

"That would be a first. Everyone else, go pack up. I won't chance Bilé finding us here, exposed with the fire burning this close to us. It would be too easy to cut us off from escape if we needed one."

"Agreed. Everyone move." I stood and allowed Ryder to pull me close against his chest. He pinched my chin between his thumb and peered down at me.

"You scare me like that again, and I'll put you over my knee and spank that ass until you either scream or beg me to fuck you."

"The latter option is more plausible, Fairy. Our people need help packing."

"Let them pack, Pet," he chuckled, glamouring on a heavy midnight-blue riding gown with a thick, silver cloak. "You discovered this power tonight?"

"Yeah, I felt fear, and Faery reached for me. I grabbed for it, and the power came from you, Ryder. I knew it the moment I brushed my magic against yours, and it reached for me. I think we're connected a lot more than we were aware."

"If there's one thing I'm not worried about, it's being connected to my wife. The handmaidens you brought with us are outside waiting to pack up our tent. Come here, woman," he smirked, lifting me into his arms, preparing to carry me out of the tent.

"Put me down. People will think I'm wounded or worse, weak."

"Let them underestimate us. It will be a fatal mistake."

CHAPTER TWENTY FIVE

THE ENTIRE COUNTRYSIDE WAS covered in destruction. Villages had been leveled to nothing more than piles of debris and rubble. It was heart-wrenching to see homes and farms reduced to burned shells of smoldering ash. Charred and mutilated bodies littered the ground, and I struggled to keep the bile from rising in my throat due to the smell of their burning flesh.

I couldn't take my eyes off the carnage as we passed a farmhouse that was still burning. All the animals had been slaughtered, the crops destroyed. The family had tried to escape the angry god who laid waste to their home but never made it past the gate; their bodies were huddled together like an ash statue.

Ryder's hold on my waist tightened, and I leaned back, resting against him, fully aware he wasn't immune to the sight of carnage we rode through. In some places, fires still blazed. The scent of charred bodies of families that had gotten stuck in their homes filled the air, billowing up into the sky in dark, angry plumes. The smell forced us to take alternative routes when it became too putrid to endure for long periods.

We'd left the horde lands days ago, and the further we got away from it, the more forbidding the land became. Long stretches of silence began to fill the army as we passed by entire cities vacant of life.

A sprawling countryside had bodies hanging from trees or piled beneath them, as if to symbolize their sacrifice to the Tree of Life. Each tree had ancient words carved into it, with the symbol of the mother and the father engraved into their trunks.

The forests were also filled with the dead, strung up like Christmas ornaments from the highest branches. They hung by their feet, iron dripping from their bodies to paint the forest floor, releasing acrid poison as Faery objected to the iron and cried as it absorbed it unwillingly. The faces of the deceased were frozen in expressions of utter horror; even in death, they hadn't found peace. Swallowing hard, I fought against the emotions shuddering through me, causing it to rain, and making the trek into the valley even more miserable.

"We will end this," Ryder whispered thickly against my ear.

"I know, but they died for nothing, and that hurts the most. Lives don't matter to this monster. He enjoys slaughtering them needlessly. Bilé is willing to throw his entire army at us and doesn't care if they live or die. Look around. Tell me, do you think we can reason with this monster? I don't see it happening. I see him ripping this world apart because he's filled with hatred and grief, and yet Danu wants us to fucking save him? It would be like reasoning with Alazander to release his concubines and stop fucking everything around him."

"You're only seeing the tragedy," he uttered softly. "Look around it to find the beauty, and then tell me what you see."

I stared at the deceased body of a young boy as tears pricked my eyes. What were once brilliant green eyes were now glazed over in death with a thick, milky film covering them. Without my heightened senses, I wouldn't have been able to see the color of his eyes before death. He couldn't have been older than ten, the same age as my boys the last time I saw them. His soft features were framed by beautiful wavy blond hair. He would have stolen lots of hearts had his life not been ended simply for being of this world.

On a branch above him, flowers began to bloom bright-ly, covering his feet and legs until he looked almost ethereal in his cocoon. The foliage was slowly covering his body, and as I watched, blossoming flower petals in tropical colors concealed his too-skinny frame until only his face remained exposed. Faery was accepting him and all the fallen fae, healing the damage the mages had done with beauty as it consumed the dead, returning them to the land from where they'd been created.

Tearing my eyes away from the scene, I faced forward. All around us, life was blossoming. Flowers covered the meadows, and while deadly, their beauty was striking against the dark ground from which they sprung. The sun heated my skin, bathing the flowers in light to enhance their coloring while offering its heat to enrich their fragrance into the air.

High in the mountains, the path into the valley we moved toward was visible, covered in dark slate rocks with moss lining the edges, marking the trail. Tall rocks marked the entrance over the passes, wrapped in clouds further than even my inhuman eyes could see. Down the side of the mountain was water so blue, it appeared to glow with fluorescent stones beneath the smooth falls crashing down from great heights, supplying the mountain with water.

It looked more like something out of a movie, made to lure people in, entrapping them in the beauty before crushing their souls. As we moved past the forest into the clearing, I noticed an abandoned stone church, covered in vines and crumbling apart in places. At the top of the structure was a large marble sculpture of the Celtic symbol for eternity and love, outlined by the sun that shone through it. Blue roses bloomed in the meadow as we passed them, and I turned in the saddle, watching Ryder's lips lift into a blinding smile.

"I see you," I whispered, realizing he was controlling the world to show me what it could be if we won.

"I see us, Pet. I see us rebuilding everything Bilé has destroyed and making it a beautiful world for our children to rule one day after we decide to step down from our roles as leaders. I see a world that needs healing, but we have forever to achieve that goal. Death will always visit us, but we will never allow it to hold its hand against our throats or change our way of life. We decide our destinies, remember? You taught me that, and it's one of the wisest things I've ever learned.

"I used to believe we could move our destinies in our own direction, sway them, but we couldn't change them. You proved that wrong, Synthia. You changed every vision Ristan was given by Danu into something much more beautiful than anyone else could have done. Danu gave him visions for a reason, *plagued* Ristan with them, and yet most of what she showed him has been wrong."

"If you're trying to get points for wooing, you're doing an amazing job. And just think, you said you don't woo." I tilted my head slightly so that Ryder could see my sly smile.

"I don't woo," he chuckled huskily. "My wife doesn't need to be wooed. She is in love with me. If I wanted to woo her, I'd just inform her that I placed an order for an endless amount of OPI nail polish to be delivered once this war ends, and our new home is constructed. I'd tell her that I had everything she'd been in love with in our old castle hidden in the dungeons in the secret passageways with our children's obnoxious amount of human shit that she adored. I didn't like the idea of her being upset over the loss of those items.

"I'd tell you that I want your babies, so many fucking babies that I never tire of naming them. I want to watch them grow within your belly without having to worry about you being harmed and feel them kicking against your stomach when I touch them. I'd tell you that there isn't, and will never be, a more beautiful High Queen of the Fae than you, Synthia Raine McKenna. And that no other woman could ever make me prouder to call her my wife than the one who agreed to be mine forever."

"Fuck," I swallowed hard as I quickly wiped away a lone tear. "I mean, yeah, that's good. That wasn't bad at all for someone who doesn't woo."

"That's what I'd tell you if I was wooing, but I'm not. You love me, so you don't need to be wooed."

"You're an asshole," I laughed, exhaling as his arms tightened around my waist before he released me. He lifted his hand, sending the order down the line to halt the progression of the army. "Everyone woman wants to be wooed, even me."

Before us stood slate rocks large enough for the horses to pass over, but the edge was a precarious drop that steepened as you went up the mountain. Skulls lined the bottom of the hill from riders and horses that hadn't made it up the steep incline to reach the start of the pass.

"That doesn't look safe."

"There's one way into the Valley of Sorrows and one way out, Pet. The Fall of Sorrow, or at least that is what the fae call it. It is the only fall in Faery that ends the life of a fae regardless of whom or what he is. Unless they have wings, like us," he explained.

"You couldn't have mentioned it when I pointed out the valley on the map?"

"No, because no matter how horrible the climb, it is the most strategic location to assemble the army. It has one way in and one way out, meaning we'll see them coming."

"We'll be trapped. If we start to lose, there will be nowhere to run."

"This is it, Pet. This is our last stand. If we lose, there is no running. I don't plan to fucking lose, do you?"

"No, but I mean, shouldn't we have another option, though? Like, okay, this didn't work, let's regroup and try again?"

"No, this is for Faery. This is where we stand together against those who would see us dead. I don't fucking run. No one comes into my home and makes me watch my people die. We have gods and goddesses on our side, and you and me, Pet. Let's take back our world and make some pretty babies after we've won."

"I think you just want to fuck, in which case, just say 'let's fuck.' It's so much easier than me getting fat and waddling around like you shot watermelon seeds into my vagina, and I grew that thing from scratch."

"I do not shoot watermelon seeds."

"Yeah? Then why the hell did I look like I'd eaten one with the babies?"

"You were carrying triplets! And you were beautifully fat."

"Not a valid argument, let's go back to you wooing."

"Woman!"

"Fairy!" I snapped.

"You make me crazed."

"Good, now let's go kick some ass. No seeds though, my vagina is not open for fertilization."

"That sounded so sexy."

"It's smexy."

"That's not a word."

"Are we doing this, or does the entire fucking army have to sit through talk of planting seeds in the queen's vagina?" Zahruk snorted.

"Hey, I was enjoying it. He's finally mastered wooing, or until he hit that low note about seeding her womb." Ristan watched us, and I shook my head. "He's ready to graduate to Woo Master of the Horde."

"That's not an actual thing, Demon. You guys are crazy."

"But you love us, Flower," Ristan laughed, climbing off his horse, and Ryder and I followed suit. "Let's go rip these assholes' hearts out and dine on them tonight!"

"Uh, how about we rip them out, and *you* eat them? Eating hearts is a hard limit for me."

"Deal—let's do this, family!" Ristan called out as we started forward.

CHAPTER TWENTY SIX

THE CLIMB TO THE top of the mountain was nothing compared to the anxiety of pulling the horses behind us. The trail was covered in uneven slate, sliding and crunching beneath their hooves, spooking them and causing them to lose their footing. It was an endless struggle to get them down the other side as well, and some ended up going over the edge in their panicked state, which was unfortunate, but better to let them go riderless.

Everyone was on edge, fear starting to take hold as we marched into the Valley of Sorrow, knowing that this was our last stand against Bilé and the mages who had invaded our world, wanting to destroy us along and our way of life.

Once we finally reached flat ground again, I was so relieved that I almost cried, taking several large breaths and exhaling slowly to allow the anxiety to flow from me in waves.

Ryder started pointing out positions for those who would guard the mouth of the valley, somehow snapping right into king mode, as I'd termed it. He'd kept his calm all the way up the mountain, cutting harnesses to give the horses a fighting chance to survive the trail, which unfortunately didn't save most of them. Ryder had shouted encouragements to those who had begun to panic, calming them as we'd made our way across the path.

I, on the other hand, couldn't hug the cliffside tightly enough as he laughed, watching me remain as far from the ledge as possible. I had wings, but I hadn't learned to use them properly, and now didn't seem like the time to try.

Ryder continued ordering our troops to split into groups at the sides of the opening into the broad valley. Ciara and Blane stood with their heads bowed together, saying their goodbyes since they were forced to split paths. The dragons would go above and follow us into the middle, where we would prepare to fight the mages. The dragons would drive the mages over the edge with their fire and jagged, gnarly teeth, which would have me running, too.

"Ciara will need us without Blane being here to lean on," I pointed out, and the men around me snorted as if they didn't agree.

"Ciara will be fine with us," Ryder muttered, scrubbing his hand down his face.

"Snort all you want, assholes. She will need us to keep her grounded since her husband will be out of sight and his fate unknown. Blane anchors Ciara to this world now, and without the babes to keep her mind on the prize, she'll need us."

"Asrian, Sinjinn, take your wives and follow the dragons. Have Lilith cast shadows to hide the troops in the woods as you make your way into the forest to hold your positions. Once the sun sets, if you need us, use the mental link. I don't want there to be any noise, no sound to alert the mages that we're here and spread out. There will be no fires tonight, either. If we've planned correctly, we are a full day's ride ahead of the mage army, but let's play it safe."

"That might be a problem," Blane said, holding Ciara in his arms as he kissed the top of her head. "There's some pretty thick shit up there. Fyra went ahead, and she's saying it isn't normal vegetation. It's more like the flowers that filled the meadow outside of this place. She said a plant just tried to skip first base and steal home with her, so she's not happy."

"I'm gonna need you to elaborate on that, please," Zahruk smirked with fire burning in his eyes.

"Ew, no," I scoffed, slapping his arm and wincing when I hit armor.

"Hey, if she's getting busy with a plant, we need to know about it," Zahruk laughed at my scrunched up face as I imagined the plant. "I might need to bring one of those plants home with us, strictly for entertainment purposes."

"She set the plant on fire, and they're all up there trying to put it out now," Blane announced, rubbing the bridge of his nose as he pinched it between his fingers.

"You are the God of Faery. Control your plants," I chuckled at Ryder's disgruntled look. "Come on, let's see those epic powers in action, husband."

"Oh, you're naughty, Pet. Remember, you asked to see it." His eyes began to glow with golden flecks as his wings shot out of his back. He vanished without warning, and my heart leaped with worry.

The entire valley hummed with power, and my hair floated with the intensity of it. Until this moment, it hadn't hit me just how powerful Ryder really was. The plants vanished, slowly reversing in the cycle of growth to push back beneath the soil as if he'd just told them to be reborn with new life.

The wind picked up, and then the rain started to flow over the edge of the cliff above us, stopping those who had been hiking up it to follow Ryder's orders dead in their tracks as a monsoon of rain flooded their way.

The hair on my arms stood while everyone stayed still and silent, unable to put into words what his immense, terrifying powers felt like when unsheathed. Night turned to day, and day turned to night as we watched the sky unleash a flood that rushed over the edges of the cliff until both sides looked like rivers forming waterfalls. Stars shot through the night sky until once more, daylight returned. Still, everyone remained silent as his power continually slithered around us, holding us in place.

"Get on the horse, Synthia," Zahruk warned, and I smiled at him stupidly as I gave myself a little pep talk about having Ryder use that magic on me in bed sometime soon.

"Not a chance, that's my guy up there. He won't hurt us." I stared up at the cliff where Ryder was moving to the edge. His wings expanded, and he crouched down, staring at me as my wings unfurled with excitement. "That's my man."

Ryder's throaty laughter sounded in my head, and I exhaled a dreamy sigh as he jumped. He soared down toward us, flapping his wings a few times before he landed smoothly, strolling right for me.

The sinful twist of his lips sent excitement rushing through me while I gazed at the man I loved more than life. He sifted, and I leaned against him, sensing he'd moved behind me as my wings curled into my spine and his arms wrapped around me patiently, allowing me time to control my new extremities.

Ryder didn't ask as he picked me up, setting me on his horse before mounting behind me, forgoing the concealment of his wings.

The world around us started to darken as we headed into the valley without waiting to see if anyone else was ready. We had to get deep enough in and around the bend to be hidden from the mages before they entered it, driven by the power we'd allowed to ooze from our pores.

"I should spank that pretty ass, Pet. I have been reserving my powers for this fight, and yet you taunt me, and I crave to impress you just to see the smile that lights in your beautiful eyes."

"Fyra's dragon fire would have thwarted our plans. It was needed, or else I wouldn't have goaded you into using your powers. Besides, you just rocked this world with your magic. It was hot as fuck. Also, we need to try our powers out in bed, soon. Very soon," I laughed huskily.

"You keep saying shit like that, and I'll end up using them on you tonight, woman."

"Please?" I whispered, and he chuckled darkly, kissing the side of my neck before he whistled, alerting the men it was time to move out. "Tell me we got this."

"We got this, Synthia. You wouldn't be here if I weren't sure we could do this together and win. I'd have tied your perky ass up and left you someplace safe if I weren't certain we would have victory. We won't make it out of this battle unscathed, but we won't lose. For once, we're the good guys."

"Good guys don't always win, Ryder."

"That's why we brought some really bad guys with us, woman."

"Smart and pretty, exactly why I let you catch me in the hunt."

"It's coming up again." His timbre was filled with gravel that slid over everything womanly within me.

"Is that so? And who will you be hunting?" I asked.

"My wife, the only woman I want to catch and take in the meadows of the wildlands where she was created. This time, you better make it a real chase, and not give up just so you can fuck me."

"I like fucking you," I uttered huskily.

"I don't like fucking you. I like owning you and hearing the noises you make for me as you come undone, begging me for more," he chuckled huskily, rubbing his erection against me. "Too bad we need utter silence, or I'd find a place and take you right now, Synthia."

"I really think they're going to become the face of porn in Faery," Ristan snorted.

"Pretend they're not here, it helps," Zahruk offered.

"Tell that to my balls," Asher exclaimed while I buried my face against the horse's mane, pushing my ass against Ryder in the process.

"You guys are assholes. You know that, right?" Ryder grunted as he kicked his horse's hindquarter, sending it into a gallop, which made the entire army behind us do the same.

My gaze slipped to the high cliffs where Icelyn, Savlian, Lilith, and Asrian remained within sight of us. They weren't close enough to fall, but seeing them at the distance they were from us created an uneasy feeling within me. I couldn't see the dragons, and yet I knew they were there.

"I can feel the dragons," I whispered.

"So can I, Pet," Ryder replied, turning to Cailean, who moved closer on his horse. "Send word to the dragons to take human form for now. If we can sense their presence, so can Bilé. We cannot give away our advantage."

"On it," Cailean said, moving swiftly the moment Ryder finished speaking.

I rested against him, letting his silent strength comfort me as we continued to move deeper into the valley. We finally reached the last bend before the valley curved. Turning the sharp corner, we exhaled at the sight of the emptiness awaiting us.

This is what we had hoped for, to have beaten the mage army to this location. This will give us a huge advantage. There was still one more bend to go around, and what we found there would be the deciding factor on what happened next.

Lucian and Spyder moved up beside us, and we continued in silence until we made it around the last bend and found a single man standing in the middle of the field. He smiled coldly and turned to blow a war horn in the opposite direction, where an entire army stood, waiting.

"Fuck," I whispered.

"Prepare for battle!" Ryder shouted over his shoulder. "They knew we were coming. We may have just walked our entire army into a trap," he growled to me.

"Let's fucking play, shall we?" Lucian chuckled as he materialized on the ground in front of us, lifting his hands and melting the men nearest to where we stood.

The mages stepped back, eyeing Lucian and Spyder warily as they smirked at the puddles that had, moments ago, been mages intending to strike us the instant we'd come around the corner.

"That was...fun," Spyder snorted, turning to wink at me as the mages began moving backward, their eyes devoid of emotion.

CHAPTER TWENTY SEVEN

THE HIGH CLIFF WALLS we'd hoped would give us the advantage were now working against us, sealing our army in on both sides of the valley. Spread miles wide, the mages filled one side to the other, blocking us from moving forward while the steep cliffs into the valley prevented an escape. Fog covered the top of the cliff, magic clinging heavily to it, concealing our vantage point of the others we'd sent up the mountain.

Staring out over the amassing army, I noted that many of the flags they flew were from each of the royal courts in Faery. We were not just fighting the mages; we were fighting fae as well. These must be the fae that we thought were fleeing from fear. Instead, they had fled to defect, and I had fought Ryder to spare their lives.

Now, they were positioned before us, the faces of our enemies smiling coldly with sightless eyes. They stood silently in battle formation as if they were being controlled, frozen in place, waiting for us to reach them.

Swallowing hard, I exhaled a shaky breath slowly, ignoring the tremor of fear that snaked up my spine. I turned to look at Ryder, who stood staring out at the traitors, clenching his fists at his side. Had he known they would betray us? Was that the reason for his harsh judgment toward the fae that fled at the beginning of the war?

Looking at the sea of fae opposing us, it suddenly made sense as to how all the kingdoms were infiltrated and massacred from the inside. Traitors were living within every caste, working for Bilé the entire time.

The wind whipped my hair against my face while I sent a silent prayer to the heavens out of habit. Faery seemed to sense the importance of what was about to unfold and trembled threateningly as gray skies cracked with thunder above us. I inhaled the scent of fresh ozone, settling my nerves that leaped to the forefront. My mind itched with the fact that if we lost this war, we would lose everything.

The mages couldn't accept that they hadn't been welcomed into the petty High Courts by their superiors, and Bilé was offering them a seat at the table. I almost wished Dresden and Tatiana were here to face them with us; to see the creatures they'd said caused no threat to their kingdom.

Turning in my saddle, I stared back at the faces of the horde and the faithful courts of Faery, faces showing no fear as they flashed the colorful banners of their kingdoms proudly. In the far back were the remaining Shadow Warriors, Adam's army. The Blood Warriors stood beside them, shoulder to shoulder, flying my father's banner in Liam's name.

A pang clenched my heart, knowing how proud my father would be of Liam, standing against opposing odds on this field beside his peers without a trace of fear.

Asher's army now adorned the iridescent colors of the Light Court with the Seelie's new banner illustrating a snake slithering through the 'A' of anarchy. I was fairly sure he didn't actually know what it meant, but it worked for him. In fact, it was honestly the perfect representation for Asher and his kingdom.

Farmers stood proudly without fear, having been given armor, weapons, and limited training. They remained at the back of the army, prepared to defend the land they loved, to protect their families from these monsters who had invaded our home and thought to destroy us.

We were all here as equals, fighting for the same purpose. There were no kings or queens on this battlefield, only a few gods and goddesses along with the loyal fae who refused to lie down and die as Bilé had demanded.

Bilé had thousands of troops that stood protecting him as he watched us from behind his army. An aura of power slithered through his warriors, and their eyes began to clear as they seemed to come back to consciousness.

It appeared that Bilé had been siphoning power from his warriors. I narrowed my gaze on the gaunt faces that were left when he'd finished giving back their power. I felt the pull on the land, tensing as he sucked power back into his body until his eyes glowed like that of the fae.

It explained why Danu had given the fae glowing eyes when they fed. She expected me to reason with this being? My mother wanted me to save this murdering prick who wanted us all dead. It pierced at my pride and my brain why she'd want him to be saved after all the damage he had done to her creation.

I swallowed a scream of frustration as I took in the army of mages that were spread out, encompassing the entire valley as far as the eye could see. Standing silent, the mages were all covered in wicked-looking armor in silver and red.

Power rushed from them, smothering us as we dismounted and prepared to fight. Behind us, war drums began to beat in a rising crescendo that mirrored my heart as the reality of the situation struck me.

Bilé and his army had beaten us here somehow, and that meant they had the advantage. The scent of smoke filled the valley already, with the forest above still smoldering. I looked down the line at the warriors who stood shoulder to shoulder with us for this fight and sent a silent prayer to the heavens for the courage to stand among them during the defining moment of this war.

I could already feel Bilé's powers within the clearing of the valley as it bounced and echoed off the cliffs that framed all sides of us. The front line of mages observed us silently, eerily as they began to remove their helmets to reveal deformed creatures with lethal smiles and serrated teeth. Their eyes were as dark as night, as if something else was peering through them at the army in which I stood.

Adam was beside Liam, their armor securing their bodies while power rushed from their pores.

Lucian and Spyder both stepped out to the front, waiting for a sign of aggression from the mages, and yet still, they hadn't moved a hair.

Callaghan stood next to me in his beast form of Balor, surrounded by his men. He held his swords at his sides, and his Templar Knight armor shone strikingly in contrast to the other armor of the horde. His thick red cape was draped over one shoulder, and additional weapons sat ready for use in their sheaths.

Ristan and Zahruk flanked Ryder and me, both wearing the obsidian armor of the horde. Cailean, Kallum, Savlian, and Bane stood behind us, all pulling magic to them, causing the braid I'd glamoured into last night to float with the power in the air. The wind picked up, sending my braid whipping against my cheek as I searched the faces of the mages.

As I observed, some of the mage warriors began to mutate into other beings, growing until they stood up to eight feet tall. Others started to shrink, their bloodied caps exposing them for the traitorous little assholes they were. I recognized several of the faces staring back at me, and I looked at Ryder, who gritted his teeth so hard that his jaw was flexing.

The redcaps on both sides of the battle lines howled, throwing their heads back to let their screams echo through the valley where we stood, preparing to battle against one another. The redcaps on the opposing side had been right beside us until days ago.

We'd aided and sheltered their families as they were making plans against us. It explained how Bilé and his army had beaten us here. We never stood a chance at gaining the element of surprise.

Ryder's knuckles brushed mine, and I turned, noting how his mouth tightened with worry. We weren't facing off against just mages. We were squaring off with traitors of the horde, traitors from all the royal kingdoms, mages, and a disgruntled god bent on revenge.

I entwined my fingers in his, fear sliding up my spine to wrap around my throat until I thought I would choke on it.

The drums continued to pound relentlessly at the back of the horde who had betrayed us, their numbers equaling one-third of the warriors Bilé had brought with him to the battle. How he'd hidden the sheer number of troops he had from us was beyond me, but I couldn't see the end of the sea of creatures that slowly exposed which caste of fae they represented.

He'd taken half of the horde from right beneath our noses, probably as he'd made his way through Faery, murdering and slaughtering the innocent while collecting those willing to betray their king.

"There's too many," I whispered under my breath as my chest clenched with fear.

"We're not weak, Synthia," Ryder said, tightening his hold on my fingers as noise sounded from the cliff to the left of us.

Dark shadows slipped over their peaks, blinding us from seeing what was on the ledge of the cliffs. I could smell the tang of blood in the air and prayed that our plans above were unfolding as we'd hoped.

Ryder squeezed my hand twice to get my attention.

"Focus on the battle ahead of us. Clear your mind of everything you can't control, and zero in on the things you can."

"Bilé has the advantage because we were betrayed by some of our own people," I hissed, wiping the sweat away from my brow with the back of my hand.

"We knew Bilé had spies within the horde who watched us as we planned and burned down the stronghold, and that someone in the horde had betrayed us to our enemies. It wasn't only the map that fed him details. Welcome to the horde, my beautiful battle queen," he frowned, then softly smiled when he saw the swords I'd materialized.

Our armor covered us from head to toe, but the crowns on our heads told the horde who we were. All down the line, our brothers and sisters waited for a signal to move as the mages before us continued to transform into hideous creatures.

Some became sluagh, legends of the notorious horde creatures that easily reached seven feet in height and had a wingspan of twelve feet. More warriors shed their glamour to reveal goblins and hags that looked more like harpies as well as a whole multitude of other beings that had once been beside us in battle and now stood against us.

I now understood why Ryder had needed and fought to maintain a strong presence in the face of the horde. They had marched into battle with us, had been beside us at the stronghold, and vanished on our trek here because they'd never been with us.

They'd been against us the entire time, choosing to side with Bilé because they thought he was stronger and would come out on top of this war. The traitorous pricks would die on the wrong side of this fight. There will be no forgiveness or mercy for their betrayal.

Power radiated from the opposing army, and I watched as the warriors parted, allowing a single man to walk through their ranks. He smiled coldly as he got closer, and his ice-blue eyes locked with mine.

Bilé was feeding his army power, and every time he offered them a jolt, they mutated into stronger, uglier creatures. He was the symbolic meaning behind the creation of the horde, and it made me wonder how Danu had never seen or noticed it before.

"He's feeding power to his army," I pointed out, and Ryder tilted his head.

"So he is, but we've been feeding our army power the entire way here, Pet," Ryder countered as my heart pounded painfully against my chest. "They're preparing to attack."

"We're ready."

I turned to look at Ciara, who held matching lightweight swords in each hand. Beside her was Adam. His hands were encased in black shadows, concealing his weapons. Neither showed the fear that they were undoubtedly feeling at this moment. Both wore varying expressions of disgust and anger as they peered out at the traitorous front lines of Bilé's army.

Beside Adam and Ciara, Zahruk glared at our rivals as he waved the heavy, double-edged swords in his hands. He wore a white cloak with gold and black braided cords securing the loose ends, concealing his lightweight armor hidden beneath. He looked like a hero from one of the video games Adam had spent endless hours playing while screaming at the television.

Ristan stood next to Zahruk. He'd released the tight reins he regularly held on his demon, which made him taller and broader in the chest. Power radiated from him, causing his hair to float behind him as he pulled his swords from their sheaths, death dripping from his eyes as he stared Bilé down.

Cailean, Savlian, Kallum, Lucian, Layton, and Spyder stood behind us, while Bane stepped up next to me. He grinned as he began producing shadows that moved around us. A battle cry ripped from the mages, and we stood silent, watching them move toward us as Ryder smirked.

This was our final stand for Faery and the only way to save our world. If we lost this war, we would lose our home, our magic, and the people of Faery would suffer and be forced out of this world and into a foreign land they may not survive in. That couldn't happen; it wasn't going to happen. It meant we had to do whatever it took to win against the creatures who wanted to destroy us.

"Hold the line!" Ryder snapped, pulling power to him as the land around us cried out and trembled with the need to give him what it could.

I closed my eyes, breathing slowly as I directed magic into Ryder, using it as a siphon to enhance the power that entered him. He turned, smiling at me as my hand touched his armor, feeding him what I could pull from Faery without leaving the land weaken.

The mages shot blue magic orbs high into the air, and I lifted my hands, pushing against the orbs as they sought to land in the middle of the army. Sweat beaded on my brow, and I groaned from the weight of them before pushing their magic back into the air.

I slammed my hands down, watching the orbs fall into the middle of Bilé's army, exploding with a splatter of blood and body parts on the surrounding mages as others continued to drop dead from the magic they'd sent to attack us.

"First blood, woman," Ryder chuckled, pushing his magic against the mages. I watched with pride as our enemy exploded, popping into nothing more than bloody mist as Ryder produced wickedly-serrated blades that glowed with a golden hue. "For Faery! For those who have died at the hands of these traitors, and for the living!" Ryder shouted above the sounds of battle.

The twin swords I used were created from the lethal god bolts we'd been collecting and glowed blue from the magic imbued in the metal. The Sword of Lugh, another relic we had recently discovered, was strapped to my back. I was pretty sure Callaghan had noticed since he kept side-eyeing me and the sword. He could damn well wait to get his weapon back until we'd won. I pushed my front leg out, locking it as I watched Bilé's army slowly closing the distance between us.

My eyes moved to Bilé, noting the male beside him who seemed to stare directly at Ryder with hatred and murder in his expression, mixed with a sense of cocky arrogance. Straining my hearing, I listened to the words he said to Bilé and tensed as Bilé chuckled, whispering a name, one that made my heart race faster if at all possible.

Shocked, I turned to look at Ryder, who had not noticed the man beside Bilé. For a moment, Ryder stood still, then shook his head and began moving forward.

Bilé grinned as he leaned down to whisper in Alazander's ear as they watched Ryder approach. Alazander was nothing more than a ghostly image, and yet I could taste the malice for Ryder that wafted from him. Ice rushed through my veins with the realization of what I was seeing.

Alazander was dead, but Bilé, as the God of Death in Faery, could manipulate that situation. Bilé was the one charged with delivering the dead to the layers of the Otherworlds in the Tree of Life. Either Alazander had never been delivered after death, or he'd always been a part of Bilé. That would explain why Alazander had gone mad with rage and insatiable lust that some of the gods were known to possess.

The mages started rushing toward us, moving with purpose as a wall of enemies descended on us from both sides. The war drums beat harder, and we all sifted together, pushing magic in the direction of the mages, and at the same time, we moved like a well-oiled machine, sending our swords into the nearest creatures that lifted theirs against us.

The sound of metal hitting metal echoed through the valley as the coppery scent of blood filled the air. Above us, on the cliffs, I could hear swords clashing together in a fight to the death. I silently prayed we hadn't murdered that part of the horde by sending them up to where they would be easily picked off by the mages who had beaten us here.

A creature moved to attack me, and I brought my blades up, crisscrossing them as I took his head from his body and turning as it dropped to the ground, narrowly missing me. Blood from Zahruk's kill splattered my eyes, stinging like tiny vipers as I lifted my hand to wipe them clean.

All around me, warriors fought and fell in a whirlwind of chaos that left me breathless. I turned as the air whistled with a blade cutting through it. I brought my sword up, deflecting the blow of a harpy who tried again, skillfully stepping to outmaneuver me.

Every hit from her sword made my arms tremble and burn as incredible power hummed through the harpy, making her stronger and more powerful than she had any right to be. She lifted her swords, exposing her chest, and I pierced it with both blades.

I twisted them into her body before adding my weight to drag her to the ground, once more withdrawing my blades to push them into her vital organs. She screamed, shrieking in pain as the bitter scent of her blood filled my nose.

I withdrew my blades, turning to look at the brawls happening all around me, and then searched the battlefield for Ryder, finding him without blades, wielding his magic effortlessly, born to wage war as a perfect killing machine.

His thick wings pierced bodies as he drove his claws into chests, ripping them apart like they were nothing more than heated butter. My hair was splattered with blood; my armor matched it perfectly, as if it were in style. I couldn't tell the difference between the blood and my *An Affair in Times Square* nail polish as blood caked the beds of my nails.

It was almost body-to-body, and absolute chaos reigned. I peered up at the darkening cliffs, watching as shadows danced over the fog, taking control. Ice covered the cliff sides, and I watched in shock as men and women fell over the edge, rushing down it to their deaths as bodies bounced onto the earthen floor. Fire melted the ice, sending the scent of putrid flesh burning into the air as those who had refused to fall made their way to the edge, burning with dragon fire on their clothing. Relief flooded my system as

I turned, barely missing the blade that had been aimed for my heart.

A siren opened her mouth to lure me in with her song, but my sword beat her to it as I brought it up, pushing it into her mouth before lifting my foot, kicking her lifeless body from my blade as yet another creature stepped up to take her place.

All around me, our army was tiring from the trek into the valley, heavy armor slowing them down as the mages moved deftly, unhindered with cloth armor instead of metal or leather, as we wore.

Lifting my blades against my opponent, I went on the assault, pushing him back until I was shoulder to shoulder with Adam, who fought tirelessly against a seven-foot-tall monster. I lifted my blade, leaving my stomach exposed as I brought my sword down swiftly, slicing the creature's head down the middle until he staggered and fell to the ground.

The scent of copper and pungent blood sat heavy in the air while I fought to breathe past the taste of blood that clung to my tongue. Adam lifted his blade, and the creature's arms moved to take advantage of his error, and I hissed with power, watching the beast explode, covering us both in entrails. Adam's green eyes shifted to me, reflecting the glow of my body in their beautiful depths.

"You have an ear on your shoulder, Syn," he chuckled, turning to deflect a blow as another creature danced into the fray.

I looked over the masses, moving through the bodies until Zahruk came into view. He was fighting against several creatures at once as his swords whizzed with power, deflecting their blows as if he were born for battle.

I watched him moving as his muscles pushed against the armor he wore, his hands tightening on the blades before each hit, knowing where it would land before his aggressor did. I felt a touch on my shoulder, and I spun, wincing as something pushed into my stomach.

I peered down, seeing a blade twisting in my abdomen as a redcap smiled evilly. "Fucking Queen of the Fae, I told you I would never be ruled by a cunt queen with tits."

I lifted my hands, and he winced as blood dripped from his lips and then splattered against my face, his death rattle escaping past the blood oozing from his lips. His head left his body, and I peered over its headless shoulders to where Spyder stood, watching me.

He pushed the redcap aside and stepped closer to me, withdrawing the dagger from my stomach. I winced and cried out past the acid burning from the blade.

"The blade was poisoned, Syn," he stated softly, barely audible above the sound of the battle raging around us.

Spyder was dead calm, which seemed out of place, considering we were in the middle of a battlefield, literally waging war. His hand pushed against the wound as his eyes turned into glowing blue depths, igniting shadows around us. He pulled my body against his.

"This is going to hurt a bit."

I screamed as burning pain ripped through me, then it stopped just as quickly as it started.

Peering down as the shadows cleared, I stared at the exposed flesh that was no more than an angry red line now. He smiled as I lifted my head and nodded my thanks. Something moved behind him, intending to use a blade on Spyder.

The moment I screamed out a warning, the creature disintegrated into nothing more than ashes that were consumed by the shadows that pulsed around Spyder.

My eyes widened, and he winked roguishly at me, withdrawing blades created of shadows and sending them directly toward me. He pushed through where my arms had hung, and a grunt sounded behind me. I spun around slowly and silently took in the man pinned on Spyder's blades. I knew his face because I'd fed his children. I'd told him to get off the ground, and never to allow his children to see him on his knees.

"The horde is changing sides," I swallowed painfully past the narrowing in my throat.

"So they are; they think we're going to lose."

"I have to find Ryder," I whispered past the horror tightening in my chest as sweat burned my eyes.

I watched as Bilé moved silently toward Ryder, sending a ball of magic rushing toward his back as Ryder battled several creatures at once. I screamed in warning and then realized he would never hear me over the battle raging around us.

Closing my mind, I grabbed the magic being directed at Ryder and sent it sailing back at Bilé, watching as he winced and turned to look at me. The creature beside him didn't falter, continuing toward Ryder with purpose. Ryder spun around, searching me out as the monster got closer to Ryder, and I realized that Ryder couldn't see Alazander. He couldn't see the monster that had tortured him and his siblings endlessly throughout their childhood.

Spyder turned, realizing what was happening, and sent his shadows racing toward Bilé. I rushed past Spyder, sweat dripping from my body as I removed my armor to reach Ryder before Alazander did. Creatures moved closer to me as I progressed across the field, and I took them down with magic, forgoing the blades as I realized I didn't need them anymore.

I wasn't an enforcer or witch. I was a goddess, and I was not losing my beast to some monster that was hell-bent on hurting him still, even though Ryder had murdered Alazander long ago. I sifted to Ryder, screaming Alazander's name, which made those of the Elite Guard near enough to hear me turned their heads in my direction. My ears rang as Alazander slowly turned, leveling golden eyes on me as his hair floated in the air around him.

"Not today, Satan," I hissed, lifting my blades, watching in horror as they went through what should have been Alazander's body. He was incorporeal.

"So, you're the whore who is destined to save this world?" he asked, throwing his head back and laughed at me as the surrounding men watched in confusion.

"She comes with powerful friends," Thanatos's voice echoed through the valley before he materialized, pushing a glowing blue hand through Alazander's chest and withdrawing a blackened heart that oozed liquid obsidian onto the ground. "You don't belong here, Alazander. Bilé has kept you alive for too long, you've begun rotting into nothing more than the hatred that fuels him when he houses you. How the tides turn against those who trespass against the laws of the gods."

Alazander howled as I watched him, covering my mouth and nose as the tart, putrid scent of death filled the valley while he was absorbed into Thanatos's glowing hold. Blue eyes locked with mine as he tilted his dark head, studying me.

"Duck," Thanatos yelled, and I did without question as something sailed past my head. I rose, staring at Bilé, who was striding toward us with magic humming through him. "I can't intervene on this one; none of us can, Synthia," Thanatos explained, touching my shoulder as a jolt of power rushed through me.

Ryder moved to stand beside me as his wings unfurled. We were ready, or we were until Ristan and Zahruk intervened and made a move against Bilé. Ryder howled as Zahruk lifted his blade at the same time that Bilé raised his hand. He sent Zahruk sailing through the air to land on a sword, where he lay unmoving on the ground.

Chaos broke out as Ristan charged Bilé, deflecting the blows along the way until he too was sent sailing through the air to land in a pile of lifeless bodies. My throat closed, and hot tears burned my eyes as I focused on what I could control, instead of what I couldn't.

Adam screamed, and I opened my mouth as everything inside of me snapped into place. Denial echoed in my mind as I watched him fall to the ground with a blade protruding through his chest.

We were losing, and our army was in the midst of turning against us. We couldn't decipher friend from foe. We couldn't tell who we were fighting against anymore. The dragons shrieked as they flew overhead, and I turned, watching them as the huge ballistae sent iron rods sailing through the air in their direction.

My magic snapped into place, and I caught the iron missiles before they took down the dragons, sending them crashing to the ground. I lifted the machines and sent them hurtling into the mass of mages who had yet to join the battle as they operated the wicked-looking machines. They were about to release iron into the air, which would kill everyone, including their own numbers.

The dragons landed, sending men sailing into the air as their mouths clamped shut on one mage, working together to rip him in half before finding another, and another. Remy, Fyra, and Blane tore through the enemies using serrated teeth to slice through any creature stupid enough to get close to the deadly dragons breathing fire between ripping mages into bloodied corpses. It was both beautiful and terrifying as they worked systematically to cut through the numbers of creatures that were doing their best to stay out of the reach of their flames.

"You're losing," Bilé laughed, his voice echoing in my ears.

I turned, staring at him with hatred dripping from my lips as I smiled. "I'm just getting started, Bilé."

CHAPTER TWENTY EIGHT

Sᴡᴇᴀᴛ ᴄʟᴜɴɢ ᴛᴏ ᴍʏ body, my hair a mixture of blood and perspiration that burned my eyes as it dripped down my face. Bodies littered the ground as everyone continued fighting around us. I wanted to rush to the men who had fallen, but I couldn't. Ryder's wings expanded as he prepared to engage in battle while the remaining Elite Guard slipped around us, protecting our backs as we faced off against the god who sought to destroy us.

"I see you found my friend," Bilé laughed coldly.

"Nice choice of friends. I can see why you'd choose Alazander. You're both murdering pricks united by one goal: to destroy a world."

"You think you're so fucking smart? I have been running this world from inside of that creature for eons. Who do you think ordered the hit on the dragons? Danu's beloved dragons, who she promised the Mórrígan that she wouldn't touch? Who do you think forced Alazander to cook the children of the Winter Court? Me. Every time he lost control of himself, it was me driving him."

Satisfaction and pride danced across Bilé's features as he smirked. "I also didn't mind fucking the weak, mindless bitches Alazander kept imprisoned for his enjoyment. Breaking their spirits as well as their bodies was something I looked forward to on a daily basis. It filled me with a great sense of fulfillment until that was also taken from me. Another thing you have ruined, you little bitch!"

Bilé tilted his head, turning it slightly to the left, then smiled as he watched Ciara slice through a beast, only to turn and battle another at her back. "There's one of my lovelies now. No matter how many times I dissected her body, I could never find the reason for our failure. I must have cut the dragon mark from her flesh at least a dozen times, only for it to grow back just as it was before. Knowing she married that dragon makes me ache to see her lifeless corpse at the end of this battle. You see, Ciara was always meant to be what you are now; instead, she was just one more disappointment."

Shaking his head, Bilé turned his focus to me and Ryder, the sadistic grin back on his face. "Alazander gifted me with the immortality of his soul, which allowed me to create chaos simply by placing his spirit in a room with those he wished to torment. Riding within Alazander was truly a magnificent gift, but having his soul has been even more fulfilling than I could have anticipated. Can you guess who he was coming for next?"

"You're a liar! The beast would have sensed you in Alazander. He would have told Ryder when he bonded with him," I said, trying to keep Bilé talking as Ryder prepared to fight him, pulling magic from the world around us.

"No; you see, the beast never felt me because I am a god. I forced it to slumber during the times that I was present. It was unable to awaken because I didn't want it to sense me. I didn't need the beast to be stronger than the horde; Alazander did. I enjoyed using Alazander's rage to destroy the creatures Danu created. Even in death, his rage grew into revenge against Ryder and everything he held dear, which includes you. That's where our goals aligned. You killed my wife!"

"Danu sacrificed her life for me," I hissed, dancing away from him as he sought to close the distance.

"You think Danu cared about you? Ask yourself this: why didn't Atum take your life or the life of one of her other children if she truly loved any of you? That's what Atum does. He takes the ones you love when your life is forfeited.

Danu was incapable of loving anything or anyone, except me. But I am the God of Death, and not even Atum could take my life from me." Bilé laughed as he whipped his blade through the air, causing me to take a step back.

"The stag tried to kill me, having grown attached to this world and the children he created as he fucked his way through Faery producing new beings and new elements. That was his little bastard grandson I just murdered, wasn't it?" he said, pointing to where Zahruk's motionless body remained in a pool of blood.

I swallowed past the putrid scent of death, ignoring the jab he took at my heart. "So I was told, but then the stag isn't like us, is he? He is only a demi-god."

"You don't hide your feelings well at all, little bitch," he snapped, lunging with a blade, but Ryder deflected the blow effortlessly. "You think you can win this fight?" he asked as the wind picked up, whipping my hair against my face as my blades materialized.

"I think we did what you and my mother could never do. Ryder and I became one, and we are more powerful than you could have ever been," I growled, watching as Bilé's face turned skeletal and began to glow an eerie blue.

My brands pulsed to life, sending power into the air as Ryder's followed my lead. The entire area was pulsing with a raw electrical current that brought the creatures following Bilé to a stall.

My magic held them in place as Ryder's power pushed through them, ripping them apart. The dragons flew above us, linked with our minds to see the plan that we had drawn out while battling Bilé's army.

Fire shot through the mages, and I grinned, watching the smile drop from Bilé's lips. His eyes narrowed on the dragons that flew side to side, burning through his arm as they rained fire down upon them. Bilé lifted his hand, and I turned, screaming a warning as I watched them drop altitude and fly in a line for the ground.

Bilé's power grasped on to the dragons, and I shot a white ball of energy into his chest, watching as it sent him sailing backward. The dragons landed safely, turning to continue sending flames into the army that was scrambling to escape them.

The tang of coppery lifeblood hovered in the air so thickly that it coated my face in mist. Deafening blood pounded in my ears, drumming to a ferocious beat that wouldn't lessen no matter what I did. The sound of steel striking steel echoed through the valley, accompanying the cries of warriors as they met their fate.

The various screams of beasts barely registered over my wildly beating heart that refused to slow. Iron was released into the air, misting toward us, the wind picking it up, carrying it in the direction of those who fought.

I turned as Ryder watched Bilé get back to his feet. I sent the land seeking the iron, then warned the others of what was coming and to prepare for the worst if I failed. I lifted my hands, moving the earth the dragons stood upon to protect them from the iron as Faery absorbed it.

Sweat trickled down my neck relentlessly, soaking my clothes as my heart thumped against my chest. Magic filled my veins as I focused on what I could control. I lost track of time as the sounds of battle dimmed to nothing while I listened to the world that offered me its help.

It was beautiful, and everything within me reached for it, becoming one with the land as I directed it to take the hit, to consume the iron that would slaughter both armies with the poison it now agreed to eradicate. The grass on the mound I held up sizzled, turning from a beautiful fluorescent green to dying black.

I felt the world's pain. I felt it crying as it consumed the iron that would have killed us all. Thunder exploded above us, and the sky turned silver as if it were trying to mirror what the land had taken. The moment the world settled, I turned, staring at where Ryder fought Bilé mindlessly. Ryder's wings struck in perfect harmony with his blades as he fought the man who had raped his mother, brutalized his sister, and ordered the destruction of several races in Faery.

I sifted without thought. The pain from the wounds I'd received didn't register as I helped Ryder fight against the man who had helped the mages try to murder my children before they'd ever tasted life. The same man who had killed me, stole who I was, and changed who I had become: Bilé, the murdering prick who had marched across our lands, wreaking havoc on my people.

All around me, the scent of sweat, blood, and the bitter smell of pervasive fear carried aloft the clashing bodies of those who still battled. Warriors fought, falling and rising to crash against one another on the land that had just saved their lives.

Men howled in pain as they dropped to the ground, lifeless in the sea of scarlet liquid that drained into the land beneath them. Friend and foe died together, their life essence draining to bathe the greenery in their life-giving blood.

Ciara cried out, and I turned, watching as she brought up her blades, striking against the men that fought her at the same time. A blade sliced through one's head until he dropped to his knees.

Zahruk stepped forward, kicking the body to the ground, and relief washed through me that he was alive.

He sifted, coming to my side as we glamoured the weapons we'd brought, weapons that he'd spent countless hours creating for this battle.

"I'm so glad you're not dead, asshole," I whispered.

"I'd still be lying in a pool of blood if not for Eliran. He said that he made a deal with Thanatos to allow his spirit to remain in Faery until after the battle, knowing we would need his aid. I'm not sure how he healed me, but I woke with him kneeling beside me, telling me to get my lazy ass back in the battle. He's tending to Ristan now." He pointed to where Ristan was lying on the ground.

I could see Eliran's wispy blond hair as he leaned over Ristan's body. He lifted his head and smiled sadly at me, nodding once before he went back to healing Ristan with the other healers watching him.

Zahruk nudged me and smirked, nodding at our weapons. "It's time."

I moved behind Bilé as he sidestepped to keep away from me. Ryder watched us, slicing his blades endlessly to send Bilé backward. I moved forward, pushing the god bolts into Bilé's body as he screamed and dropped to the ground in pain. Zahruk pushed his blade into Bilé's chest, and we stepped back, staring down the god who was supposed to be all-powerful.

"You abandoned Faery, and it has now chosen to abandon you, Bilé," I snorted. "You need the world to live, don't you?" I observed Bilé as he snarled while the Elite Guard gathered around us, peering down at the weakening god who refused to acknowledge defeat. "That is why Danu continued to create the fae: because without them, you die."

"So does the land, Synthia. Without me, it dies too." Bilé grinned up at me triumphantly through bloody teeth.

"Unless it finds another source of magic," I said, glaring at him, knowing he hated to be taunted. "Welcome to the new world order, which doesn't need you."

Dismissing Bilé, I studied the mages who fought viciously and without any signs of slowing or tiring. Of course, they wouldn't. Bilé had pushed his power into them, and now Faery refused to give him more.

Bringing my hands up, Ryder placed his hands on my shoulders, sensing my need for our combined power. I accessed the magic of Faery through him and smiled as power ripped through the clearing.

The ground began to open up, consuming the mages and those of the horde who had turned against it like quicksand, devouring them whole.

Ciara walked toward us, and I watched in horror as she began to sink. My heart leaped to my throat, and my mouth dropped open as she vanished.

"Oh, shit," I whispered, and then sighed in relief as the land spit her back out.

"I think Faery just violated me," she said offhandedly with wide, horrified eyes. "Did you see that?"

"My bad? How do I undo..." I grimaced and shrugged an apology toward her shocked gaze. I needed to figure out to use this magical land mojo correctly.

"We saw it," Ryder snorted. "Have the healers set up the tents and tend to the wounded."

"On it," she said, wiping the blood away from her cheek. She smiled brightly as a very naked Dragon King walked up to her and pulled her tightly against him, kissing her. "Help me get the healers ready to tend the wounded, and put some fucking pants on. That thing is for my eyes only, Dragon."

I chuckled, turning to look up at Ryder, who watched Blane and Ciara moving toward the cliffs where we'd hidden the healers until the end of the fight.

Speaking of healers, I looked around, searching for Eliran, and found him walking toward us with Thanatos. My heart ached, knowing I was about to say goodbye to another trusted friend and family member.

"I told you that I could not interfere with the war, but that didn't mean I couldn't grant a favor for a new friend," Thanatos said, smiling at Eliran.

Eliran's form shimmered in and out of sight, which told me his time was limited. He looked at Ryder and then smiled sadly at me. "I knew the first time we met that you would be Ryder's equal in every way. My brother is lucky to have you, Synthia. You are a true queen to your people and a fierce protector of our family. I knew I could not abandon our family during this war, so I made a bargain with Thanatos in order for my soul to remain in Faery until after the final battle. I was able to use the remainder of my healing power to save my brothers Zahruk and Ristan and did my best to aid the healers that are working to save Adam. We will meet again one day, but until then, I will be with you in spirit and look forward to watching the births of all upcoming princes and princesses the Fates have planned for you. I'm proud to call you sister."

Eliran stepped forward and accepted Thanatos's hand, vanishing. Thanatos looked out over the battlefield, then to Ryder and me. "You did well today. But there's still one challenge left before you." Nodding toward Bilé, Thanatos frowned and then disappeared.

"Are you still considering Danu's request to bargain with Bilé?" Ryder asked without looking at me, but when he did, there was worry in his sparkling depths that caused the little joy I had to vanish.

"I don't know, Ryder. I just don't know if we can or *want* to negotiate with a terrorist who wants us all dead. This is the man who tried to murder our children and me. He is the monster who tortured you and your family as he drove around in an Alazander suit."

"What?" he asked, narrowing his eyes as his forehead creased.

"He used your father to murder the dragons. He gave the order. Danu and Bilé were at war with one another, and he used the creatures Danu created to hurt her by murdering them."

"Alazander…" his words died off as he watched me.

"Was here, but not really, I guess. He was dead, but he was here as a spirit, one Bilé chose to keep with him. He used Alazander to wage war. I don't know if Alazander was truly evil, or if he was made to become so because of the god who held him. Holding a god within you, it drives you mad rather quickly. It would explain some things, I guess. He said he forced Alazander to cook the children of the Winter Court and feed them to their parents. Nothing makes sense anymore; it's all insane. Bilé and Danu fought, and they used us, too, but worse, I think they created us for something else entirely. I don't think Danu loved me nor did anything selfless to bring me back."

"She brought you back, though. Danu gave her life for you."

"But did she really? Or did they take it because it was the only thing Danu loved?"

"Synthia, she's dead."

"I know she is, but what if she didn't plan to stay dead?"

"Only one person knows what she intended. Let's go ask him. Shall we?" he asked, holding out his hand for me to accept.

I placed my bloodied hand into Ryder's, staring at the crimson that stained them both. "Ristan?" I asked, turning to look as a gurney was passing by us.

"Flower," he said weakly, grabbing my armor as he instructed the men who were carrying him to stop. "Danu was evil. She was always evil." I stared down into swirling eyes as he watched me. "Don't believe the visions she gave me to share with you, Synthia. The revelations were from Danu; therefore, they cannot be trusted. I think she planned for them to sway our choices to what she wanted us to do."

Ristan had suffered visions of the future and what my role in this world would be. Now we understood that those predictions had come from a vengeful, selfish goddess who had played games with our lives.

I found the answer in Ristan's eyes, the reality of what had been done, and what my mother had planned. The pain she'd enjoyed inflicting on him was proof of her callousness and malice.

The fact that she could have found Ristan and protected him from Bilé in the guild, but hadn't, told me more than anything else could have. Danu had gone with us, but only when I'd given her no other choice. Ryder had been right: Bilé and Danu were at war, and we were their pawns. Our lives were nothing to them and had meant less than nothing in comparison to their end goals.

CHAPTER TWENTY
NINE

BILÉ STARED AT US through cold, cruel eyes. He had a
saccharine smile across his tight lips, watching me carefully
as I paced around his prone body. He'd been secured to
the ground with god bolts holding him in place, where he
glared up at me.

Chains covered him, intricately forged chains Zahruk
had commissioned. They were created from the same material used in the god bolts and the Sword of Lugh, which
was still strapped to my back, irking Callaghan, who stood
against a tree, glowering at the weapon.

My gaze studied the meadow of the valley, already burst-
ing with new life where it had consumed the mages and
traitors of the horde. Flowers covered the entire ground,
reaching endlessly for the living as they hungered for more

victims. Small critters had escaped their cover within the cliffs, daring a chance to devour the flesh of the dead.

The Elite Guard had already buried those who had remained loyal to us, and on their graves, Faery had cemented their tombs with large rocks that sat sentry over the dead. There was beauty here, but it was a deadly beauty that fought to consume the living.

Ryder spoke low, and yet the anger burning in his tone ignited my own as I frowned at the pathetic god who lay before us. "Danu built this world around you, didn't she? You're the Tree of Life, because in the lore, Danu is the mother, and you are the God of Death. But you don't deliver death anymore, nor do you allow life to flourish by blessing the creatures she created to feed you the souls you needed to live and grow more powerful.

"That's why you're weak. You need to be powered by the lives you take to the three levels of the realms between the living and the dead. Now, you've used up all of your magic with this war. You stopped taking those who needed to pass through you to move on to a new world. Every day since then, you have sought to pull power from Faery. It's no longer handing it out to you, is it?

"No, it isn't. Faery has abandoned you because you sought to destroy it." Ryder crouched down to whittle a piece of oak beside Bilé, sending the slivers of wood into his face as he spoke. "You were so vindictive with the need to terminate us and this world that you used up all your stored power by feeding it to the mages.

"Now, you have nothing left. Faery has judged you, and the land and everyone within it, found you wanting and lacking. When Synthia and I asked for power, the land offered it because we seek to protect it from those who had trespassed against her. Faery is a living, breathing thing, and it no longer cares about you, Bilé. Danu isn't here to create a new world for you, either, which leaves you one choice: Go back into the tree and save yourself and Faery."

"You forgot the other option. Death, and join my wife within it as this world crumbles and dies," Bilé laughed soundlessly.

"You're too selfish to do that," I stated, watching him as he turned blue eyes to lock with mine.

"No, I'm not. Danu was too selfish. I am not. I have never feared death, for I know where our kind go. I love her. We may have fought our battles against one another, but at the end of the day, she was my world, and you took her from me. If dying takes me to her, I am willing to go."

"You and Danu are both selfish pricks," I hissed, glaring at Bilé. "Look at what you have done to this world! You've devastated people for your own twisted enjoyment! You sent the horde to slaughter every fucking dragon that ever existed!" Blane growled, and I lifted my gaze to his. "Oh, you didn't hear? This asshole decided to drive an Alazander suit around, murdering entire breeds because he wanted to one-up his wife. He is the monster who traumatized and terrorized Faery."

"I did that and enjoyed every minute of it," Bilé laughed. "Just as Danu enjoyed torturing and killing the women I impregnated among the Unseelie and Seelie. When I finally made a deal with her, we decided to toss my offspring into a protected prison. I hid my best creations right in front of her, concealed amid the race she loved and adored more than any other," Bilé sneered before he chuckled.

"Because you made them," Ryder snorted, watching Bilé's forehead crease at the realization of his words. "You created the horde, not Danu. That is why they turned against us in the middle of battle. That is why they can lie because a father can speak untruths, but not the mother. You called the horde to arms, and most of them came. You are the creator of my race."

"Looks like you're not nearly as stupid as I'd once assumed." Bilé grinned and nodded like he was proud of the man Ryder had become. It was unsettling and creepy.

"You're also the father to every child still alive that was born in the royal line. Alazander murdered his own sons because had he not, Danu would have seen the difference between them and us, alerting her to the fact that we were all your children." Ryder glowered down at Bilé as those around us sucked in a breath at the Ryder's revelation.

"It doesn't matter now. None of it does, which is why I will destroy this world. It wasn't Danu in that cave who led you to that potion you drank, my son. It was me, making you strong enough to endure creating a life with the little whore now standing beside you. You were supposed to knock her up and murder her once she'd birthed your babes so that we could bring Danu back to life. Why do you think Danu stepped in, protecting Synthia's life? It wasn't out of love. It was out of necessity for the end goal."

"What was the end goal?" I asked, and Bilé smiled as his head shook. "Why was my life spared?"

"You know why," Malachi whispered beside me, his nose touching my ear as he smiled against it. "It's why Destiny led you to me, Synthia. You have always known your fate and why you were created. You just couldn't believe that she could be so evil."

I turned, staring at my brother before looking around at the others. They all watched Bilé without noting Malachi was here. Swallowing hard, I closed my eyes to the reality of the situation. I think I'd always known I was created to be more than just a mate, or for this world.

"You know, Synthia. You've already figured out what you have to do. Do it. Bilé will never stop. He's driven by hatred and blinding rage, and will never quit trying to kill you and this land. His life means nothing to him, but you know that already. Don't let them win. You know what depends on this victory. I have made you strong enough to accept this destiny, now fulfill it, sister."

I looked away from Malachi as I shook my head. I wasn't done living yet. My children needed their mother, one they'd been denied because of the prick before me.

"You have to go back into the tree!" I shouted, staring at Bilé.

"No, I will not. I will never go back."

"He won't. Sister, you know what you have to do, so do it." Malachi watched me carefully, his eyes dropping to the necklace I wore that Danu had given me before my wedding. My fingers lifted the locket of her essence, and I frowned.

"Please, Danu built this world around you. She built it *for* you. She told me to reason with you, that you could change!" I pleaded with Bilé.

"I won't, nor will I ever stop trying to take everything you love away from you. I will always be there to ruin your life, as you have ruined mine. You took Danu from me, which wasn't in our plans. You were supposed to be easy to handle, but she should have known better. Anything she creates is poisonous. Had she told me she had donated an egg to that worthless fucking Blood King, I'd have killed you myself before you'd ever sucked air into your lungs. I will destroy you, and I will never stop pursuing you and your children."

"You can change," I pleaded as my heart pounded, echoing in my ears.

"The thing is, I don't want to change. I like hunting you, and your children will be even more fun, especially after I murder your husband. Kahleena will be an especially sweet treat as I will seek to punish her in a way that my son has failed to do with you."

I stared down at Bilé, seeing the truth of his words shining in his eyes. Ryder stood, kicking him in the face before he turned toward the men, issuing orders to those who waited behind him.

"I love you, Fairy." I watched as obsidian eyes lifted to lock with mine.

"I love you too, Pet," he replied, studying me as he shook his head, frustrated with the fact we weren't going to win.

We'd won the war, but we would never be able to convince Bilé to go back into the Tree of Life, returning as the power source of Faery. We'd won the war, but we would still lose everything since the world had been built around the Tree of Life.

Ryder moved to one of the tables that had been set up in the meadow. Sitting down, he lifted a glass to his lips as I stepped forward, materializing the sword Zahruk had made for me.

He'd named it the god killer. I lifted the blade high in the air, then thrust it down with all my might against Bilé's neck, watching as the sword severed Bilé's head from his shoulders with one swift blow.

Faery howled as I dropped the sword. Everyone turned to watch as I pressed the vial of glowing blue liquid against my lips. I started tipping my head back to drink the full bottle of essence needed to become what I was created to be, then Malachi seized it out of my hand. I cried out, staring at him with wide, horrified eyes as he tipped it back, draining the vial as blood pounded in my ears.

"*No!* No, you can't do this! You don't know what you've done!" I cried as tears filled my eyes. "Malachi!"

He smiled sadly as he reached for me, cupping my cheek in his hand as everyone watched in horror as the world began to rumble around us. He placed his head against my forehead as the wind howled, and Faery trembled violently.

"I do know what I have done. I just stole your destiny."

"It was my destiny to become the Tree of Life! Not yours. *I* have lived, and *I* have loved. *I* have known family and tasted passion in my lover's arms. You have never known anything but pain. This isn't fair! You deserve to live, too!" I screamed in frustration as tears trailed down my cheeks even as he swiped them away with his thumb.

"Sweetest sister, you're wrong. You showed me what it was to be loved and to know love. Synthia, you showed me how to be selfless and to give freely. You taught me what sacrificing for love was all about, and what lengths family would go to in order to protect one another. I can do this for you, my only family.

"I am free of that prison, sister. I am free to feel the sun shining on my face, and to know the world and learn it while I am growing within Faery above ground. I can't be a part of Faery any other way without destroying it, but this I can do, and I can become it for you. I knew the moment you walked into that prison that you were sent there by a greater force than either of us understood. I choose this so that I may learn this world and our people. This isn't goodbye. It's only goodbye for now. I'll be right here whenever you need me. This is my fate. As one wise, brave woman once told her soon-to-be husband, we choose our own destinies, not some preordained bullshit."

"You shouldn't have done this." I clung to him, hugging him fiercely.

"I did this for you. You are not done living yet." Malachi stepped back and took my hand in his, smiling. "Your children need you, as does your husband. Look at him, watching you. He loves you. He needs you, and so does this world, sister. Faery needed me in a different way. Life is about doing what is right. This is right for me and you, and while you won't admit it yet, you will live for both of us."

I sobbed as Malachi knelt on the grass, smiling up at me as the ground began to shake. His body contorted, and an eerie greenish-blue glow surrounded him as the land absorbed his body. Ryder stepped closer to me as roots pushed up from the earth, forming a beautiful, tall tree that stood before us. It glowed as branches extended into long, flowing limbs covered in leaves and blooming flowers of every color imaginable. I stared in awe of its beauty as one blossom floated down to my palm, and my tears fell upon it.

I turned, staring at Ryder, who tilted his head and narrowed his eyes as reality struck him at what I had intended to do. "I was never supposed to be yours. Only long enough to create our children. Danu, she didn't sacrifice her life for mine. Not as we assumed."

"Synthia's right. My sister would never have done that because she was a selfish cow who only thought of herself," Destiny admitted, and we turned to stare at her.

"Where is my daughter?" I demanded, rounding on Destiny. "I know what Danu intended to do. Where is my baby?"

"I couldn't go through with it," Destiny whispered as tears filled her eyes. "I have broken my oath to Danu. I was supposed to protect the children and keep them in the City of the Gods, giving Kahleena Danu's essence so that she could become Danu. But your daughter... she's beautiful and pure. She is everything Danu wasn't, and if I had gone through with Danu's plans, she'd have ruined Kahleena and her destiny. Bilé was to choose from the boys, to find a new host to house him so that the other gods wouldn't sense him when he left this world. The boy that wasn't chosen would have been killed.

"Instead, I sent you to your brother because he alone could make you into what you needed to be to stop her plans. I protected Malachi and fed him power so that he could be strong enough to survive that hell Danu sentenced him to. She abandoned her children, the ones of her own womb. I took care of them because I couldn't create my own, so her orphans became mine. I have protected you and led you down every path to reach this place in time. That is what destiny is, Synthia. I left nothing up to chance, not even who you would create your children with. I left the essence of the gods where Ryder could find it because you would need a reason to want this destiny."

"You could have said something!" I snapped.

"What the hell would be the fun in that?" she asked, folding her arms over her chest.

I stared at her, shaking my head as Ryder began to growl.

"Because that wouldn't be some Game of Thrones type shit, now would it?" Savlian snorted with disgust, wrinkling his nose.

"We're gods. We don't stick to the same boundaries as you and your kind. Have you never looked at mythology and saw a family tree with branches circling back to fathers and daughters creating life? I said that they weren't sane, didn't I? You all had a destiny, and Danu had more designs for each creature and everyone she touched, including..." Destiny turned, staring at me.

"Me? I'm aware of her plans for me. Danu created me to become the power source of Faery. I was to replace Bilé as the Tree of Life so they could leave this world without Atum ever knowing they'd abandoned another world. That's why I was destined to save Faery. How fucking selfless of her—but wait, she isn't selfless. Not for anyone but her husband. You see, I put it together. Atum took Danu's life instead of mine because she never loved anything but herself and Bilé. But he couldn't sense Bilé to take his life because he was here, in Faery, hidden in an entire world that radiated his power and essence.

"That is why Faery couldn't accept life, and the dead couldn't find peace. Even after we healed the tree, it wasn't enough. The host wasn't there anymore, but Danu knew she needed Kahleena and the boys, so she helped us save them by adding her power to the tree to make it accept them. She expected me to become the tree, and for her and her husband to enter my children's bodies once they were dead. Hosts with matching DNA are the perfect vessels. Now, where the fuck are my children?"

I stared at her, hating that she'd known about Danu's plan from the start. Yes, she'd helped us, but Danu had intended to use my children as vessels. Apparently, she hadn't even trusted her own husband with that knowledge, and had allowed him to slaughter countless innocent people in his grief. How much more evil could you be?

"You killed a god today, Synthia, Daughter of Danu. You were warned," Atum said, appearing beside Destiny.

My head snapped to where he stood, and I fought not to roll my eyes. "I am no longer the daughter of that monster. I did kill a god, one who took the soul of an angel. Ask her," I said, nodding to where Olivia sat beside Ristan, her soul shining with that of an angel.

Atum glared at Olivia, and slowly turned his soulless eyes back to me. "That's an angel inside Faery. A very dead angel, Synthia!"

"Bilé murdered her, and then he trespassed against her God, which is *the* God. Tell me, Atum, aren't there laws against that?" I crossed my arms as anger entered his eyes, and his hands balled into fists tightly at his sides. "Thought so. So, you see, I prevented that from happening today. The only way to free Olivia's soul was to end Bilé's life, unless you knew of another way, Atum? But you weren't willing to step in, not until I messed up. I felt your presence today. I know you watched us, waiting for me to cross a line."

"You are just like your mother."

"Danu isn't my mother. I fired her from that position." I watched Atum carefully. "She intended to leave this world and create a new one for Bilé, one within the human world. Tell me, do you think they'd have fucked that world up, too? They're not much for world-building. In fact, every world they created was allowed to cause hell within other worlds. They're both gone now and cannot come back. I did us all a favor. I stopped a goddess from coming back, one you sentenced to death. An angry god that could not be reasoned with is dead, one who willingly broke the laws that you uphold."

"And you expect to get away with his death without consequences? You're still breeding, aren't you?" Atum smirked, and I frowned. "Oh, you didn't know yet? Congratulations, though it might be a little premature to assume you can keep it."

"No," I stated, holding my stomach with my bloodied hands protectively as my heart pounded in my throat.

Power erupted into the meadow, and Atum frowned, turning to look at the cause. "I expect Synthia to get away with Bilé's death without consequences, Atum. After all, she followed the rules," Lucian announced as he and his men strolled up as if they owned the place.

"I agree, she kept to your fucking rules, and unless you want a Spyder all up inside ya, she gets a pass. Bilé intended to do exactly as Synthia said, and we will be there to back up her statement. That also means we will have to venture on up into your pristine little city. It has been a while since we've been up there. I wonder if Nyx and Eris would like to join us when we visit you. I bet they would. It's been a very long time since we were all there together. Sounds like a party." He rubbed his hands together, smiling at Atum coldly.

I studied Atum's pale complexion as he stared Spyder down. "Your children will be returned shortly, and as for you, Destiny, you broke an oath and will be punished accordingly."

"I'm aware, Atum, but I'm also aware that Danu broke the laws, and that oath was promised with the intention of her doing so. I didn't go through with her plans because of that reason. So, you will grant me leniency. Either that, or we can go to trial, and the last trial lasted almost five thousand years. You know that everyone fears me. Even Fate fears Destiny, Atum."

"Careful, the last woman who asked for leniency still remains in my bed, and you are about to replace her with such a request."

"I will bring the children back, and we will see where I end up, won't we?" she flirted with Atum, and I grimaced.

"You two can go," Spyder snorted. "Before you make poor Synthia throw up. She's too innocent for your trashy asses."

We watched Destiny and Atum vanish before I turned back to look at Ryder, who watched me carefully. "I wouldn't have allowed this world to die, and Bilé couldn't live. He wouldn't have ever stopped hunting us, nor would he have kept our children out of it. He was evil, and he enjoyed inflicting pain on others. I saw it in his eyes, Ryder. I couldn't live knowing that he could hurt our children."

"I know, Synthia. That is the only reason I haven't put you over my knee and spanked your ass."

Taking a deep breath, I sighed and hugged Ryder. The adrenaline in my body was beginning to wear off, and exhaustion was slowly overtaking me. Ryder kissed my forehead as we stared out at all the people in the valley.

"We need to find a location to build a palace because there's too many wounded here. We should also put a few things to a vote with the high fae courts while they're all present." I nodded, and Ryder continued to hold me.

CHAPTER THIRTY

I sat beside Adam, leaning my head against him, watching Ryder argue with Zahruk about how to make each king and queen equal as we cast votes on subjects Ryder wanted out of the way before we started healing Faery.

All around us, tents were erected, and men and women who hadn't been wounded prepared meals for the creatures in need. The King of Nightmares and his sisters helped tend to the injured with the healers, bringing peaceful dreams to those dying as they passed from this world to the next.

"Are they arguing over a way to make everyone at the table equal?" Adam asked, snickering as his eyes lit with laugher.

"I think so, which is insane since, you know, I'm much cooler than you," I smirked as he laughed, and I punched him in the arm, and listened to him groan as the wound in his chest ached. "When are we going to talk about the problem in your closet?"

"Actually, I need your help to handle that soon. You didn't, by chance, leave penis-shaped pillows all over my throne room, did you?"

"Blasphemy, would *I* do that?" I feigned being wounded by the accusation, unable to keep the smile from my lips.

"You would. I know you, asshole." He stood, smirking as I fell over, still crusted in the blood of the battle, too exhausted to care about how I looked. "Make a fucking round table, and don't let your wife leave dick-shaped pillows all over my castle anymore, or naked pictures of women and other shit," he said over his shoulder, glaring at me as he walked toward Ryder and Zahruk.

"I left naked men too, ya know, in case you're into that type of thing."

"You did what?" Ristan asked, taking Adam's seat as he winced, holding his stomach where a bandage was placed over the wound he'd sustained.

"No idea, he thinks I broke into his castle and left pictures of naked men in his throne room, along with dick-shaped pillows." I shrugged as a smile played across Ristan's mouth.

"So, I have taught you well, Flower," he said, snorting as I leaned my head against him. Magic rushed over me, and

I looked down at the silver dress he'd glamoured on to me while also removing all the blood from my body.

"Is it easier to breathe?" I asked, chewing my lip as I studied him.

"You mean since I got to say goodbye? A little, although you killing Bilé didn't make it any better, but I'm glad you did end his life. What made you finish it?"

"He said he'd never leave my children alone, and that wasn't something I could let happen."

"Olivia told me to find a mother for Orion so that he grows up happy. Can you fucking believe that?"

"That Olivia, the selfless angel, would want you to be happy? Absolutely, because she loved you so much that she'd want nothing less than your happiness. She truly loved you, Demon. Loving someone else doesn't mean that you will forget her, and moving on doesn't mean that, either. You loved Olivia, and that was real. That love stays with you forever."

"Grief doesn't come with some time limit, or rules for how it plays out," he snorted, exhaling the pain.

"Grief is a place you visit. It isn't a place you can stay because it is dark and there's just too much pain there. When Larissa died, I wanted to die with her, and that was weak. I loved her. She was like my sister and my best friend. I couldn't stay in that way of thinking. If I had, I'd never have returned from it. We wouldn't be here right now, and I wouldn't have had Ryder's beautiful babies or known his love."

"So, you think I should move on and get over her?" he snapped in a harsh tone, and pain swept over his features as he grimaced angrily.

I let out the breath I was holding and placed my hand on his arm, shaking my head.

"I think you should give yourself some time to heal, and when you're ready, you'll find someone, and it won't be just because you think Orion needs a mother. There are plenty of women in your life now that love that little dangle as their own, even if he does bite." I grinned and leaned my head against Ristan's shoulder. "You can both lean on all of us for a while. We're a family, and families help each other. There's enough love in this family, and enough of us to fill the empty frames that you and Olivia hadn't gotten around to finishing. And when you're ready, you will find love again, and we'll all be here to witness that, as well."

Ristan and I sat there in silence, watching Ryder and Adam discussing the table dimensions while Zahruk argued with Savlian and Cailean over who had the most kills. Ristan grinned at their playful banter and squeezed my hand.

It seemed surreal that we'd won, and the reality of it hadn't fully sunken in yet. The twisted things that had been revealed left me numb to the pain I knew I should feel. I was thankful that Malachi had stepped in but felt guilty that he had. We had made it through mostly unscathed, and as we watched our family, we started laughing until I had tears streaming down my face.

"We didn't fucking die, Flower," he laughed.

"How the hell did we *not* die?"

"I have no idea. Maybe it was because we're actually the bad guys? They normally win, right? Holy shit, we're the bad guys!" he howled with laughter until eyes started to turn toward us. We covered our mouths, laughing at the absurdity of winning. "We kicked a god's ass, and you removed his head! And you told Atum off like he was a damn inconvenience!" He slapped my leg, and I laughed harder.

"Did that actually happen? This is so weird," I swallowed as he grew serious, nodding slowly. "We did, Demon. We're going to be okay now."

"Yeah, we will be okay. We are going to be just fine. Thank you for trusting me regarding your mother and second-guessing her intentions this time. When I look back on the visions she fed me, I can see it clearly now. She pushed us to find you, driving parts and pieces together until every twisted component of her plan played out. She didn't count on you fighting back or being you, though. She didn't take love into consideration, and I think that is what has won us this war in the end. You loved Ryder, even though he was a beast that didn't understand it at the time. You have taught us all the meaning of love, and better than that, you taught us *how* to love. That isn't a small thing to do considering who we are. I'm just sorry that, in the end, Danu turned out to be the murderous bitch I told you she was."

"No one wants to think their parents are capable of that type of behavior, but Bilé, the things he said? It triggered questions in my mind. Like why wouldn't the gods take me from Danu if she loved me? That's what they do. Erie said the same thing when you demanded I bring back Olivia. Not that I could; I mean, as an angel, she didn't belong to Faery, so I had no way to call her soul back. But I recall Erie telling you to pick one of my children to sacrifice if I had been able to use my gift to bring Olivia back. Then she said the gods would take whoever I loved the most, no matter which I chose to sacrifice, and Bilé said basically the same thing today.

"The gods took what Danu loved the most: herself. She always reminded me to put lotion on Kahleena, for her skin, of course. Out of everything she did, that bugged me. Kahleena is immortal, so why would her skin regimen bother Danu? Because she planned to kill my daughter's beautiful soul while filling it with her own poisonous soul," I whispered thickly, hating that I hadn't seen through her facade from the very beginning.

"She's the mother of the year, what else would she do?" Ristan joked.

"Plus, she could enter the guild even though she told me that she couldn't. Lucian could and Erie can also, so it didn't make sense that Danu said she couldn't. She entered it, but only in the catacombs, and that was an illusion spell. No. No, she didn't want us to find you when Bilé held you in the catacombs. She just didn't care, but she made me think she did. She was evil. I just failed to see it."

"You can't change it now. It's in the past. We're not moving in that direction, Flower. We won the war, and Bilé is dead. That's our future now. We have our own world no longer controlled by angry gods who seek to manipulate us," he pointed out, wrapping his arms around me.

I stared at the table Ryder had glamoured beneath the large Tree of Life and lifted a brow. "So, they decided on the round table?" I laughed, raising my hand over my mouth as golden eyes peered over at me.

"Look at Adam," Ristan snorted, smiling wide as it reached his eyes for the first time since Olivia had been murdered. Tears burned in mine as I leaned against him. "He had Ryder build a round table, and he's proud of it. Knights of the Round Table. It's actually kind of brilliant."

"We're going to be okay now," I stated, hugging him before we stood from the bench and made our way toward Ryder and Adam.

"In time, we'll all heal," Ristan agreed. "We just need to figure shit out and fix this place back to what it was before that asshole walked through it, destroying everything he touched as he marched his army here. A round table, huh?" he asked Ryder as we approached.

"No one sits higher, or in a place above another. It's fucking round, and that works. I'd like the kings and their queens to join us. All of them, even the lesser courts." Ryder scrubbed a hand down his face, and I smiled at the look in his eyes as pride lit in mine. He would be the man to fix Faery, and I'd be at his side as he did.

"Everyone sit, please," I smiled as Ryder pulled out my chair, settling in beside me. He reached under the table and grabbed my hand, giving it a slight squeeze. "You guys, too." He stared at the lesser courts that looked wary of his decree. "You're part of this world, and that means your voices count. I'm not asking. I'm telling you to sit your asses down and help us decide the fate of Faery. It needs us now more than ever; all of us."

I watched as Sinjinn, Icelyn, Lilith, Asrian, Ciara, Blane, and the other courts of the lesser fae took their seats at the giant round table Ryder and Adam had created. Adam sat beside me, while Asher sat next to him, bumping elbows before they both stood and allowed Liam to sit between them. Cillian sat at the opposite end, staring at Asher with a frown, noting the brands on his arms.

"Okay, first of all, we clear the fucking board." Ryder stared at Blane, then slowly made eye contact with everyone around the table. "The past stays in the past, and we move into the future together. I know there's been talk about it, but I need to know how you all feel about a High King and Queen of Faery."

"I think they are needed because previously, there hasn't been anyone to enforce the laws of Faery," Adam said, and Blane eyed him thoughtfully.

"What are we, five?" Blane asked, and Adam lifted a brow.

"I'm ten, dick," Adam countered, and everyone laughed.

"He's older than me," I offered before Blane looked at me and then glanced at Adam.

"Focus, please. We have a lot of things to cover, and we can't begin to rebuild until we have a few issues resolved." Ryder tightened his hold on my hand and looked around the table, studying the faces. "All in favor of Synthia and I being the High King and Queen, say, aye."

"Nay," I smiled, letting him see the love shining in my eyes. Ayes erupted around the table, and I frowned. "Balls."

"That means a new King of the Horde will need to be crowned. Armies will need to be formed for the horde and all your kingdoms. We need to replenish the number of warriors that were lost during the battle. In the meantime, we will divide our reserves until all the armies have been reinforced with enough numbers to guard their respective palaces. We will all help to heal Faery now that the threat to its survival has been removed."

The discussion went on for hours before everything that needed to be decided had been chosen by each court. Ryder and each of the kings agreed to establish laws together, as a governing group in which every caste would abide. In one single day, we'd won the war, saved Faery, created a new power source, and established a new way to oversee all the courts in Faery. It was exhausting.

I stood beside the Tree of Life, placing my hand against it as I spoke within my mind.

"Thank you, Malachi."

"You're welcome, sister."

I smiled, running my fingers against the glowing bark as tiny fairies danced in his leaves as they began to accept him, already forming the pool at the base for the water source. I turned, staring at the wide valleys, and grinned impishly.

"Leaving so soon?" Malachi asked.

"I have a palace to build."

"So, you will go home, but you will return?"

"I'm not leaving you, not ever," I announced inside my head. *"I'm going to build my palace around you and always protect you from harm."*

"Because I'm family?" Tears burned my eyes as my throat tightened at his question—and the hope I heard buried within it.

"Because you are my family now and because you saved me from the fate that you chose for yourself. You're my brother, and I can never repay you for what you have done for me," I swallowed thickly as my other hand touched my belly, where I felt the life within it growing.

"You've been alone enough, and I wish to honor your sacrifice, Malachi. You deserve that from me. Without you, I'd have never become me. I'd have never accepted what I had to do or known that accepting one world didn't mean abandoning the other. I also want my children to know you, to

learn our history from you, because who better to teach them than the one person who has been here since the beginning of Faery?"

"Malachi is in there, isn't he?" Ryder asked, approaching the tree slowly as his eyes lowered to my belly, where my hand rested.

"Yes, and I want to live right here."

Ryder paused, staring at the cliffs before his gaze came back to lock with mine. "Right here, in the Valley of Sorrow?"

"Look at it, Ryder. There's only one way to reach us, and that is up a steep mountain that cannot hold an entire army. Not wide enough for them to attack us or for the number of troops to matter anyway, because we'd stop them at the gates. There's one way in and one way out. High cliffs for the villages, along with miles of meadows behind where the palace will be built," I pointed out. "Strategically, it's perfect. There's an entire mountain any enemy would have to climb, and the Tree of Life is right here. I say we build around it, make it the center of the palace so that everyone sees it and can access it. The fairies can still feed it and build a water source, but it would be safe from anyone who wants to harm it. Malachi gave his life for me. I want to honor him. We will rename it the

Valley of Life since it holds the Tree of Life, and it is the place in which Faery is now reborn."

"Okay."

I tilted my head and narrowed my eyes. "Did you just agree with me?" I asked in shock.

"He saved me from worshipping my wife in the form of a tree, Synthia. I owe him for his sacrifice. Plus, this is a very strategic location, as you said. There's one way in and out, and that works for me. Our people will be safe, and our children will be safe. That's all that matters now. We don't have enemies, but there's always something else coming at us. It's the way this world was created, but when it comes, we'll be ready for it. Now it's time to rest. Tomorrow we will build our palace in the Valley of Life so that we can be crowned before the armies who fought beside us in this war. Tonight, though, I will hold my wife, who carries my child already growing within her, snug in my arms."

"I told you those watermelon seeds were bad," I huffed past a radiant smile as I moved into his arms. Lifting on my toes, he met me halfway to claim my lips. "We're going to have a baby," I smiled, holding his face between my hands. "I wouldn't choose any other life than the one I have at your side, my beast."

"I love you, too. I still intend to try for a child, though."

"I'm pregnant already. Didn't you catch that?" I asked, noting the heat burning in his eyes. "Oh, why didn't you just say you wanted to get lucky?"

"What's the fun in that?" he countered, kissing my forehead as he peered over my head, staring at the tree. "Destiny led you to him so that he could save you. She knew it was the only way for you to become strong enough to face Bilé."

"I'm glad she was on our side."

"Me too. Now, what were you and Ristan laughing about earlier that had you in tears?" he asked, and I laughed through the tears of happiness.

"We lived," I whispered, sucking my bottom lip between my teeth. "It's our happily ever after fucked up after, and we lived to have the chance at our forever, Ryder. Together, we make a powerful force."

"That's because you're Synthia, and I'm Ryder, and nothing stands a chance against us now. Now, let's go get some sleep. You fought hard today. You've earned it."

CHAPTER THIRTY ONE

RYDER CREATED AN ENCHANTED home for the horde with his magic. The palace itself was breathtakingly beautiful. High pillars that brushed against the clouds of the valley, a strikingly powerful statement seen from the front gates of the courtyard. To the naked eye, it looked as if it had been crafted from glass, and yet it was impenetrable steel. The entire mouth of the valley was filled with high, reinforced walls encircling a vast courtyard that held magic pools of the clearest blue water that fed the Tree of Life, protected within the palace walls.

The entrance into the valley had been transformed into a wide opening guarded by matching statues of huge, foreboding dragons. Behind each dragon stood a god and goddess, their swords raised in silent warning. Ryder really did love to dramatize the size of my breasts, which had me wondering if he hadn't been the one to start the blow-up doll rumors.

Along the cliffs were detailed murals of the battle we'd endured and survived, noting the names of all those we'd lost, marking the turning point for the war. The memorial had been Ryder's idea, and out of everything I loved of the new kingdom, the murals reminded us of what we'd lost. I loved it more because it was a reminder of what could happen, even from the smallest threat.

Ryder had created Fairy Pools of our own, with rivers that rushed through the sprawling valley that sat behind the palace. Rivers ran through the new towns where displaced families were settling and beginning to recover from the destruction that had ravaged Faery.

An orphanage had been built, one that widowed women had agreed to run, caring for the children left without parents. I'd watched as Ryder lifted the palace from the ground, placing the foundation into the earth. Below the steel frame, he'd placed magic, creating a glow that rose into the walls and lit them in a fluorescent shade of aquamarine.

He also built a bridge from the entrance of the valley up into the enormous palace, appearing to float in mid-air, protecting the town behind it if someone invaded. On the cliffs, he'd placed more homes and trees to replenish the ones destroyed during the battle.

Ancient elder trees and saplings alike now covered the whole valley, replacing the charred oaks that had once been proud protectors before Fyra set them ablaze after being violated by the plant life. Flowers blossomed all around us, adding splashes of color where we needed it. They were still the flowers of Faery, beautiful and deadly, but they seemed less willing to touch the people of the valley now, without the anger of the previous god and goddess adding to the land.

The air was filled with life, and the scent of freshly baked bread and stew collided with desserts and other goods being cooked for the celebration we were holding tonight. Ryder and I were going to be crowned High King and High Queen of Faery before our people. It was a deliciously alluring combination, causing my growing belly to rumble with hunger.

My gaze lifted to the high, spiraling spear that topped the palace, sending light into the sky. It served as a beacon of peace and a reminder to all kingdoms of what can be accomplished together. You could see the light from anywhere in Faery, no matter how far away you were. All you had to do was look to the skies of Faery to find our shining light. Ristan had poked fun about us being like Batman, but the truth was, our people needed to see us and know we were here for them, lighting their way to recovery.

Inside the courtyard sat the Tree of Life. It was a huge, climbing tree that had taken on a life of its own. Lights shined from within, illuminating bright blue holes that allowed the tiny fairies to move through the trunk easily. Celtic markings of the warrior who had sacrificed his life for mine marked the bark surrounding the tree. My hand strayed to them often, drawing my fingers over the writing along with his name, Malachi, that the fairies had added. It gave me hope that he wasn't ever alone. Knowing him, he was lounging within, talking to fairies and learning the ways of the world.

I'd spent hours beside the tree, resting against it as I spoke with Malachi, letting him know that we were here with him, even though he'd stopped responding after the first day. Ryder explained that he was in transition, but eventually, like Bilé, he'd become strong enough to separate himself from the tree for short periods of time.

"Hiding from me?" Ryder asked as he entered the gardens.

"I was hiding, but not from you." I stood, greeting him with a smile and a kiss as his hands settled around my waist. "There are millions of people inside."

"They've come to watch the crowing of the first High King and Queen of Faery, then the signing of the treaty between kingdoms. Who wouldn't come to see your beauty, wife?" he chuckled, pulling me closer against his body. "You look gorgeous today, woman. I almost want to hide out here with you and fuck you in the flowers."

"Is that an option?" I countered with an evil grin tilting the corners of my lips.

Ryder smiled, brushing his lips across my forehead before he pulled back, staring into my eyes. "No, absolutely not," he laughed at my disgruntled look. "We've earned this position, but I don't want to be High King without you by my side. If you don't want to be High Queen of Faery, tell me now, and we'll walk away from it."

"I would be honored to rule Faery by your side, but I don't want us to be crowned inside the confines of the palace, where only a select few can be present. I want to be crowned in front of all our people. I want everyone wishing to attend to be able to see it, too. Right now, it's just royals in that palace, and we're not those people. We are the symbol of hope now, and not just to the kings and queens, but to all of Faery. If we're to show them that we are their king and queen, let us do it the right way, where all our people can bear witness. Our being crowned means more to our people than anyone else."

"You thought we'd do it any other way?" I narrowed my eyes on him, watching the golden flecks catch fire with his smile. "I know you, woman. I know how that pretty mind of yours thinks. I had the coronation moved into the courtyard that looks over the town so that everyone can watch, no matter their rank."

"You're way too smart," I laughed, and we both paused to look at one another. Ryder's eyes narrowed on me. "Kiss me, Fairy."

He pulled me against him, releasing my hands to cradle my face between his. Tilting my head back, he lowered his mouth to mine, claiming me in a toe-curling kiss that left me breathless. My hands lifted, wrapping around his neck as I deepened the kiss until I no longer cared if air filled my lungs. He growled huskily, pulling back to stare into my eyes with liquid gold burning in his.

"You kiss me like that again, and we'll be late to our own party, Pet," he warned, and I smirked, moving to do just that. "Saucy woman, I love the way you look when you're pregnant with my babe growing within you," he laughed, staring down at me, placing his hand on my stomach. His wings unfurled, and mine moved to match his as power erupted around us.

Pausing at a new presence, we turned to see Destiny appear, walking into the clearing with our children—only they were no longer children. They'd grown into adults while they'd been in the City of the Gods, looking to be in their early twenties. My throat tightened, and I fought back the tears as I took in the changes.

My heart ached to have missed out on their childhood, but I had no doubts that sending them away had been the right decision. Cade and Zander grinned when they saw us, and my heart skipped a beat.

My boys were now men, roguishly handsome men. Well-defined muscles covered their arms and chest, as well as the brands of the fae that marked their breed. Born fae and demi-god, my sons looked like they could be members of the Elite Guard already. *Ladies, beware*.

Swallowing, I tried to make words escape my mouth as Kahleena stepped around Cade and Zander, walking forward with a bright smile for us.

She had long, platinum curls that hung in delicate waves over her bare shoulders. Golden brands matched the color of her eyes, pulsing with power over bronzed skin that was a striking contrast to the simple white dress that covered her curves. She wore delicate platinum bands on her biceps, adorned with infinity symbols, and a thin necklace with a dragon in flight around her neck. A smile flitted over her mouth, and she moved into action, rushing toward Ryder, who opened his arms as she leaped into them.

"Daddy," she sobbed, and my tears broke free, rolling down my cheeks as I wiped at them. "We've missed you!"

"I missed you too, little monster," he chuckled, holding her away from him as he looked her over. "You're not little anymore, are you, daughter?"

My hands covered my mouth as my head shook. Destiny watched me, clearing her throat from the emotion choking her words.

"Atum couldn't just give them back to you. He had to be assured your daughter was still Kahleena and not Danu. He holds your mother's essence now, to be sure she doesn't succeed in her plan to return to the living."

"Do not call that monster my mother. Madisyn was my mother. She would have given her life for mine even though she wasn't blood-related. Danu was a monster, one who cared about no one but herself, not even you, Destiny. A mother sacrifices everything for her child, and that evil bitch wouldn't have willingly sacrificed anything for me. She made sacrifices for Bilé, but in the end, those were made for her own selfish reasons, not to save this world. She planned to murder my daughter so her selfish ass could return. Her own granddaughter," I swallowed past the rage coursing through my veins. "So no, she is not my mother."

"She wasn't always bad, Synthia. Danu lost the ability to see the beauty in what she created, and the love that was right in front of her. Her curse was always to create, and yet never know the love for those she created. Not all of us are designed to be good, just as not all of us are made to be evil."

A hand slipped into mine, and I stared at the dainty fingers before bringing them up to my lips to kiss them. Hands that only months ago had been chubby, tiny fingers were now slender, delicate, and beautiful.

"Mother," Kahleena whispered, hugging me tightly.

She was taller than I was, but not by much. Her build was petite, and yet she was curved in all the right places that the dress she wore did little to conceal. I mentally had to shake myself from wanting to cover her up and hide her from any eyes that would look upon her with anything but childish beauty. Kahleena wasn't a child any longer. She was a stunningly beautiful woman.

"You're so beautiful," I whispered as my hands cupped her cheeks. "You have your father's eyes." Embers of gold ignited, and she nodded as she laughed past the tears in her eyes, scrunching up her tiny nose.

"Hey, Dad," Cade said, holding a hand out to his father, and then wincing as Ryder pulled him close, slapping him on the back before he held him at arm's length. "I heard you guys kicked some major ass down here and caused some ripples from taking out a god?"

"What else would you expect?" Zander asked, studying me carefully. "We knew you would win because you're not the type to lose. Plus, you had some powerful allies standing beside you," he shrugged, grinning, and I couldn't help but notice the dimple in his cheek as he smiled. "Aren't you two supposed to be getting crowned High King and Queen of Faery right now?"

"Now that the three of you are here, we're ready." I squeezed Kahleena's hand and smiled happy tears at my sons. I turned to look at Destiny, who watched as the kids hugged Ryder and me, a sad smile turning up the corners of her mouth. "What is it?" I asked, observing her carefully.

"Fate has intervened with your children. I couldn't fully protect them from Fate. Each one carries her mark, but what it entails, no one knows. I did what I could, and kept your daughter protected from my sister, but Fate needs only whisper to inflict herself upon someone."

"Our fates are not bad, Destiny," Kahleena announced with a secretive grin on her lips. "Everything works out in the end, and who doesn't love an adventure into the unknown?"

"You've seen the future?" Destiny asked cautiously. The fear marring her tone was genuine, and it caused me to pause because out of everything she'd done, Destiny had protected my children. She'd prevented anyone from harming them, minus Fate.

"Yes, we all live," Kahleena said, scrunching her nose up. "Now, our people are waiting for their new king and queen to be crowned; let's not keep them waiting any longer. It's time you accept your fates, which always ended with Destiny crowning you, Mother."

CHAPTER THIRTY TWO

THE CROWD WAS SPREAD out so far that there was no end to it in sight. Everyone had been invited to the ceremony, and that concerned the Elite Guard. It was their worst nightmare, or so Zahruk grumbled beneath his breath as he studied the assembly for any threat. He kept moving his gaze to Ryder, who held my hand as we both smiled conspiratorially back at him.

Kahleena, Cade, and Zander stood beside us, and the kings and queens of Faery took their places behind us proudly. After the crowning ceremony, we would all be signing a treaty that would ensure peace between king-doms, no matter how tiny they were. We all wanted the same thing: for Faery to be healed from the damage done by Bilé and the mages. We wanted all people to prosper and grow without fear of persecution.

Before us stood a large stone platform with white marble pillars on all four sides. Flowering vines spiraled up the pillars and across the latticework, creating a spectacular archway. In the center of the platform was a small, raised altar. A druid stepped forward and placed two pillows on the altar, motioning for Ryder and me to kneel.

Kahleena reached for my hand and gave me a squeeze before slipping around us with Cade and Zander to join Ristan and Zahruk at the front of the crowd to watch our coronation.

I accepted Ryder's hand, and we slowly knelt before the druid, who watched us with a proud smile on his lips. Unlike the druids that Erie was hunting, these druids presently inside our world were mostly fae by blood. They had long ago left the human world to follow Danu into Faery at her behest. Luckily for the druid, Zahruk had looked into his past using his abilities, and found him to be an honorable man, not a traitorous bastard.

Zahruk had used his power on me once when I'd first met him to expose my childhood trauma. I knew it wasn't a pleasant experience to have your entire life play out like a movie on a screen.

The druid smiled at us before he turned to the people. "Today marks the end of the war and the walls between kingdoms of the Lesser Fae and the High Fae. There will be no more barriers between us or subjection over those with less fae blood than those of the high fae." The crowd cheered, and the druid raised his hands to quiet the audience.

"Today, we crown a High King and Queen of Faery who will uphold this law that every caste of fae be equal and that peace shall reign from every corner of Faery. If anyone disagrees or feels these two are not worthy of the title, speak now before the anointment oil is placed upon the king…" the druid paused as he looked at me, and I lifted a brow in challenge, "and queen you have chosen as representatives to rule over all the royal courts of Faery, as well as their subjects."

If that asshole thought he wasn't going to include me in his speech, he was wrong. I may have tits and a swollen belly, but I was a goddess, and I fought hard to get here.

The entire assembly of creatures went silent as the druid searched the crowd, waiting to see if there would be any objections. After a moment, the druid nodded his head and smiled. In his hand, he lifted a blue vial of anointing oil for the audience to see, made of a combination of lavender, sage, and ambergris.

Men moved behind us, and Adam touched my shoulder, calming my nerves with the familiarity of his touch before slipping a silver robe, symbolizing the queen, over my shoulders. Cailean stepped over to Ryder and adorned his shoulders with a gold robe, representing the king.

We were both handed a pair of gloves that we slipped on, turning to one another as the druid placed an orb in each of our left hands, and a scepter in each of our rights. Adam and Cailean moved back, turning on their heels to move to where the others waited behind us.

"Do you promise to defend Faery when needed?" the druid asked.

"We do," Ryder and I replied together, answering his questions as one person to symbolize we were united.

"Do you promise to act justly and calmly to those who rule within your kingdom?"

"We do."

"Do you promise to protect the people of this world, and always to do what is needed of you as High King and Queen of Faery?" he continued.

"We do."

Stepping forward, the druid dipped his finger in the oil. He placed his finger on Ryder's forehead, drawing a symbol for unity and prosperity, then moving to his cheeks before running a line over his chin, murmuring an ancient prayer to the gods, asking for blessings over his reign. Turning to me, the druid repeated the process as my heart thumped loudly in my chest until I was confident everyone at the assembly could hear it.

The druid reached over to the podium on his left and removed a large golden crown, intricately decorated with diamonds and black obsidian. He then placed the crown on Ryder's head. The druid moved to the podium on his right and removed a matching crown in silver, putting it on my head.

"Rise," the druid said firmly as he stepped back and smiled. To the crowd, he turned and shouted. "I give you the High King and High Queen of Faery, long may they reign!"

"Long may they reign!" everyone present echoed the chant, shouting it repeatedly, hugging one another in celebration as my eyes swam with tears.

The crowd continued to chant with the druid as he handed the anointing oil to Ryder, then moved away from us. Ryder grabbed my hand, lifting me against him as he claimed my lips, much to the crowd's amusement.

"Long may she reign," he growled proudly as his hands cradled my face.

"Long may he reign, and long live the High King of Faery. The King who claimed my heart, and wrote his name on my soul," I whispered, smiling proudly.

Ryder kissed me again, then stood at the front of the platform, motioning for everyone to quiet down. The Elite Guard took their place beside us on the platform as the chanting stopped and the crowd went silent.

"I have an important announcement to make, and then there is the matter of performing our first duty as High King and Queen of Fairy." Ryder looked back at me and extended his hand, requesting me to join him in making the announcement.

"Now that I am High King, The Horde Kingdom requires a new king." Members of the horde stomped their feet and shouted in agreement as Ryder lifted his hands to quiet the crowd again. "After much thought and consideration, the High Queen and I have chosen Zahruk, second-born son of Alazander, as the new King of the Horde."

Shocked, Zahruk turned, looked at his other brothers, who grinned, then narrowed his eyes and shook his head at Ryder. "Pick someone else, asshole," he whispered beneath his breath and took a step backward as Ryder smiled wickedly.

"There's no one better to take my place, and no one I trust more to be able to hold the horde without housing a beast. You are the grandson of a god. You already hold a beast within you, one who can take any form needed. Kneel, Zahruk."

We hadn't let anyone else in on the secret of their parentage, but then no one else needed to know that Ryder and his siblings' birthfather was a psychotic god who had enjoyed torture. We'd vowed that once we were crowned, those who had betrayed Faery would fade away into history, their names no longer mentioned among the fae.

Danu and Bilé had tried to murder the fae, and neither deserved to be a part of the world we were creating with hope and strength of a united kingdom.

"Ryder," Zahruk frowned, still shaking his head.

"You are my Second-in-Command," Ryder countered firmly. "You're my brother, and you've earned this title. You've never failed me or argued about what needed to be done for the kingdom. You're the right man to be king. The beast and I have merged into one, and since Danu isn't coming back, a new beast will not be created. You are powerful enough to lead the horde, and they, as well as every member of the Elite Guard, respect you."

"Then, who is going to watch your ass?" Zahruk snapped angrily.

"Cailean will, and Lachlan will become the Ambassador. Ristan is here as well. Everyone is right where they need to be. Now, fucking kneel, so I can declare in front of the entire world that you are my choice as King of the Horde, brother."

"You're a dick," he snorted. "You could have told me about your plans before today."

"You'd have argued it, and there's no one I trust more with my crown than you." Ryder placed his hand on Zahruk's shoulder and grinned mischievously.

"Either one of your sons could control the horde." Zahruk pointed to Cade and Zander, searching for a way out.

"Zahruk, kneel. My sons will never lead the horde unless they do so through your choice. The horde was never passed down through blood. It was decided by Danu and passed to the one who was powerful enough to hold the beast, but that cannot happen anymore with Danu gone."

"See what happens when you stab the girl who becomes the High Queen, Zahruk. She votes against you," I whispered, smiling as angry sapphire eyes locked with mine. "Now kneel, because no matter what, you're the right person to take the throne."

Begrudgingly, Zahruk kneeled before Ryder and me, bowing his head. Ryder glamoured a gold and white robe on Zahruk that matched the battle armor that he had worn during the war. He also glamoured white gloves on

Zahruk's hands, then placed the orb in one and the scepter in the other.

"Do you promise to always act in the best interest of the horde and to defend them with honor and without mercy against those who would seek to harm the kingdom?" Ryder asked.

"I do," Zahruk growled.

"Do you promise to act justly and rationally toward those who reside within your kingdom?"

"I do."

Ryder removed the cap from the anointing oil and handed the vial to me. I smiled wickedly at Zahruk as I poured some oil in the palm of my hand, and his eyes widened, no doubt worried about the amount of oil he thought I might use. I winked at Zahruk and dipped my finger in the oil, repeating the pattern and prayer said by the druid.

Ristan presented a black velvet box to Ryder, removing the lid to reveal a simple gold crown, perfect for the new Horde King. Placing the crown on Zahruk's head, Ryder leaned down and whispered, "You're going to be a great king, brother."

I raised my hands to the heavens, and a breeze began blowing the flowers in the fields, picking up the budding blossoms and tossing them throughout the air like confetti. "Rise," I commanded Zahruk. Laughing, I stuck my tongue between my teeth as the flowers stuck on the oil to his face.

Ryder and I each placed a hand on Zahruk's shoulders, and Ryder addressed the crowd. "The High King and Queen of Faery present the new King of the Horde, Zahruk, second-born son of Alazander, and brother to the High King. Long may he reign!"

"Long may he reign!" The crowd repeated the chant, and the horde stomped their feet, clapping each other on the backs.

"Hail to the King," I laughed at his angry glare as he wiped away the flower petals from his face.

Flowers still rained down on the crowd, and I smiled playfully when I noticed Zahruk shaking his head at the colorful display, secretly wishing he were anywhere else but here.

"Seriously? You just couldn't help yourself, could you? You can quit with the flowers already." Growling, Zahruk stepped around me to exit the platform, and I grabbed his arm, halting him.

"You know, if you don't like the flowers, then you really aren't going to like the pretty pink pony we picked to parade your pompous ass from the platform. I have it on good authority it is a slight to refuse a gift from the High

King and Queen." I tried to keep my facial expressions neutral, but Ryder roared with laughter, clapping Zahruk on the shoulders.

"Oh, I can't wait to see this! As a gift to the new King of the Horde, the High Queen and I will memorialize this momentous occasion with a beautifully colorful mural to be placed prominently in the Horde Kingdom. Now, where's this pretty pink pony?" Ryder laughed along with all those around us while Zahruk looked stunned, then horrified, blinking twice before growling.

"Never gonna fucking happen, bro. I'm out." Zahruk sifted, and the laughter continued as we made our way down the stairs and into the crowd. It felt terrific to laugh for a change.

Chapter Thirty-Three

A feast was set out before the assembly, and we were seated at a large table with our honored guests, all the visiting kings and queens, which were technically family, and Asher, who watched us with a weird look in his eyes. It was as if he was trying to figure out things he shouldn't have been focused on at the moment.

"So, I'm the Light King, and I have an entire kingdom that depends on me now?" he asked.

"Yes," Ryder confirmed.

"Fuck." He tipped his goblet of wine back and polished it off before signaling the server for a refill.

"Language, there are children present," I muttered and then winced.

My children weren't little anymore. They'd grown into actual adults, flirting with people inside the feast. I watched women approaching Zander and dug my fingernails into the palm of my hand to prevent myself from ripping them away from my baby.

Cade was talking to Ristan, bouncing Orion on his hip while nodding at whatever Ristan was saying. Kahleena...She'd simply vanished, and my heart raced rapidly when I couldn't find her in the ballroom. I turned to Ryder, smiling as his eyes lit up with pride as he admired me wearing the crown and robe.

"I love you," he whispered.

"I love you, and I will love you until the world ends. Forever would never be enough, Fairy."

"Look at this place." He motioned his hand to indicate the entirety of the room and our guests. I turned to stare at Ristan, who laughed at something Cade said. Babes cooed and babbled as they learned to speak while everyone smiled and consumed entirely too much food and alcohol. Alden argued about something with Vlad, and Vlad threw his head back, laughing at whatever had been said.

Adam sat staring absently at his plate as he moved the food around with his fork, and I frowned, knowing that we'd be handling the issue in the closet sooner rather than later. That situation would need to be resolved before he could finally begin healing.

Adrian was talking to Liam, showing him his daggers while Zander glared at Zahruk, who had refused to train him until tomorrow. Cillian, the King of Nightmares, sat between his sisters, rubbing the bridge of his nose as they all spoke around him, and I smiled as his eyes held mine briefly before he nodded. Scanning the room, I searched for Kahleena again and still didn't find her.

"Where's Kahleena?" I asked.

"Probably exploring the palace," Ryder acknowledged.

My stomach tightened and I stood, moving from the room as everything inside of me screamed in silent warning. I made it inside the queen's black and white room and paused, noticing something shiny on the floor.

Sensing the men behind me, I bent down, picking up Kahleena's broken necklace as my stomach dropped to the floor with fear. Someone had removed the necklace that contained a magic tracker hidden inside.

"Prepare the Elite Guard and find her, now!" I demanded, watching as the men moved into action. "She just got home!" I snapped at Ryder.

"We will find her, Synthia."

"Find her, now, Ryder. She's my baby!" I hissed as anger pulsed through me. "She's been here less than a day, and I have already lost her! I'm a horrible mother."

"You are not a horrible mother," Zander said pointedly as he watched me. "I know you're unaware of what transpired in the City of the Gods, but we were there long enough that things—happened. Kahleena is a grown adult, and she isn't just your daughter anymore. She's a powerful seer. If she hadn't wanted to be taken, she wouldn't have been. She wants him, so she made herself available to him when he showed up to take her."

"Who is he?" Ryder asked.

"I don't know. Kahleena never told us. She only said that her fate and his are tied together. She knew it couldn't be prevented, and that if we had intervened, some of us would have died." Zander shrugged with a pinched look on his face. "You shouldn't fear for her. She is your daughter, after all. She has the blood of the horde and the gods running through her veins. She has trained alongside us and is a total badass. She can handle whoever it is, and when she's ready, she'll come back or send us word if she's in trouble."

"Send the dragons! They couldn't have gotten too far," I said, turning to Blane, who nodded in agreement. My hands pushed through my hair as I inhaled slowly, releasing it as I considered our next move.

"You won't find her, not unless she wants to be found," Cade murmured softly, realizing that it was hopeless.

"I just got her back!" I cried. "I just got you all back."

"She's your daughter, Mother. Sometimes you have to believe that fate is in play and that everything will be okay. If Kahleena wanted you to rescue her, she'd show you where she was." Cade exhaled and moved to hug me. "Kahleena is just like you. She is physically strong, overly stubborn, and very strong-willed. If she gets in over her head, she'll tell Zander and me, and we will tell you."

"You can hear her?" Ryder asked, and Zander turned, smirking at him. "Then tell her to turn her ass around and come home this minute, because I forbid her from dating, or thinking she can save the prick who just took her from our home! She's a child!"

"No, he's right," I whispered as I looked around the room.

Everyone was here and ready to find our daughter. Adam had glamoured on his armor, as had Liam.

Vlad and Adrian had donned weapons, while Alden studied me, waiting for the word to leap into action.

Ciara and Blane held their children, while Remy and Fyra stood behind them, itching to be given the order to soar over the skies and find Kahleena.

Ristan watched me, his armor over his body rippling with the need to bring my little girl home safely.

Asher and the Seelie stood silent, ready to be dispatched, while Zahruk paced, his hands palming his weapons as the Princess of the Court of Nightmares watched him curiously. Everyone was prepared to do whatever it took to bring her home—everyone but me.

"Send riders out through the valley. Make it look as if we are searching for her. Blane, Remy, and Fyra, take to the skies and watch the shadows. We need to make it look real, but the boys are right. Kahleena made it easy for him to reach her, and until we know who he is, we don't make a move that could endanger her life. She believes he won't hurt her, and we have to assume she knows what she is doing."

"You want us to do *nothing*?" Ryder snapped.

"Nothing *yet*," I answered, sucking my bottom lip between my teeth as I looked into his eyes for strength.

"She's our daughter, and she's not even two yet!"

"Um, we're a tad older than that now," Cade said, frowning as he looked at Zander.

"I want the spies we employed last week out searching the entirety of Faery to learn what they can about the one who took Kahleena. Someone in this world knows who he is because he just walked into our home and took the Princess of the High Court of Faery from right beneath our noses. It's personal to him. If we move too soon, we could force him to act out in anger or fear. I won't chance Kahleena's life like that. We could do more damage if we rush out to save her. Send the spies and the shadows to find her. Once we have more information, we will go get our daughter back safely."

CHAPTER THIRTY THREE

A FEAST WAS SET out before the assembly, and we were seated at a large table with our honored guests, all the visiting kings and queens, which were technically family, and Asher, who watched us with a weird look in his eyes. It was as if he was trying to figure out things he shouldn't have been focused on at the moment.

"So, I'm the Light King, and I have an entire kingdom that depends on me now?" he asked.

"Yes," Ryder confirmed.

"Fuck." He tipped his goblet of wine back and polished it off before signaling the server for a refill.

"Language, there are children present," I muttered and then winced.

My children weren't little anymore. They'd grown into actual adults, flirting with people inside the feast. I watched women approaching Zander and dug my fingernails into the palm of my hand to prevent myself from ripping them away from my baby.

Cade was talking to Ristan, bouncing Orion on his hip while nodding at whatever Ristan was saying. Kahleena...She'd simply vanished, and my heart raced rapidly when I couldn't find her in the ballroom. I turned to Ryder, smiling as his eyes lit up with pride as he admired me wearing the crown and robe.

"I love you," he whispered.

"I love you, and I will love you until the world ends. Forever would never be enough, Fairy."

"Look at this place." He motioned his hand to indicate the entirety of the room and our guests. I turned to stare at Ristan, who laughed at something Cade said. Babes cooed and babbled as they learned to speak while everyone smiled and consumed entirely too much food and alcohol. Alden argued about something with Vlad, and Vlad threw his head back, laughing at whatever had been said.

Adam sat staring absently at his plate as he moved the food around with his fork, and I frowned, knowing that we'd be handling the issue in the closet sooner rather than later. That situation would need to be resolved before he could finally begin healing.

Adrian was talking to Liam, showing him his daggers while Zander glared at Zahruk, who had refused to train him until tomorrow. Cillian, the King of Nightmares, sat between his sisters, rubbing the bridge of his nose as they all spoke around him, and I smiled as his eyes held mine briefly before he nodded. Scanning the room, I searched for Kahleena again and still didn't find her.

"Where's Kahleena?" I asked.

"Probably exploring the palace," Ryder acknowledged.

My stomach tightened and I stood, moving from the room as everything inside of me screamed in silent warning. I made it inside the queen's black and white room and paused, noticing something shiny on the floor.

Sensing the men behind me, I bent down, picking up Kahleena's broken necklace as my stomach dropped to the floor with fear. Someone had removed the necklace that contained a magic tracker hidden inside.

"Prepare the Elite Guard and find her, now!" I demanded, watching as the men moved into action. "She just got home!" I snapped at Ryder.

"We will find her, Synthia."

"Find her, now, Ryder. She's my baby!" I hissed as anger pulsed through me. "She's been here less than a day, and I have already lost her! I'm a horrible mother."

"You are not a horrible mother," Zander said pointedly as he watched me. "I know you're unaware of what transpired in the City of the Gods, but we were there long enough that things—happened. Kahleena is a grown adult, and she isn't just your daughter anymore. She's a powerful seer. If she hadn't wanted to be taken, she wouldn't have been. She wants him, so she made herself available to him when he showed up to take her."

"Who is he?" Ryder asked.

"I don't know. Kahleena never told us. She only said that her fate and his are tied together. She knew it couldn't be prevented, and that if we had intervened, some of us would have died." Zander shrugged with a pinched look on his face. "You shouldn't fear for her. She is your daughter, after all. She has the blood of the horde and the gods running through her veins. She has trained alongside us and is a total badass. She can handle whoever it is, and when she's ready, she'll come back or send us word if she's in trouble."

"Send the dragons! They couldn't have gotten too far," I said, turning to Blane, who nodded in agreement. My hands pushed through my hair as I inhaled slowly, releasing it as I considered our next move.

"You won't find her, not unless she wants to be found," Cade murmured softly, realizing that it was hopeless.

"I just got her back!" I cried. "I just got you all back."

"She's your daughter, Mother. Sometimes you have to believe that fate is in play and that everything will be okay. If Kahleena wanted you to rescue her, she'd show you where she was." Cade exhaled and moved to hug me. "Kahleena is just like you. She is physically strong, overly stubborn, and very strong-willed. If she gets in over her head, she'll tell Zander and me, and we will tell you."

"You can hear her?" Ryder asked, and Zander turned, smirking at him. "Then tell her to turn her ass around and come home this minute, because I forbid her from dating, or thinking she can save the prick who just took her from our home! She's a child!"

"No, he's right," I whispered as I looked around the room.

Everyone was here and ready to find our daughter. Adam had glamoured on his armor, as had Liam.

Vlad and Adrian had donned weapons, while Alden studied me, waiting for the word to leap into action.

Ciara and Blane held their children, while Remy and Fyra stood behind them, itching to be given the order to soar over the skies and find Kahleena.

Ristan watched me, his armor over his body rippling with the need to bring my little girl home safely.

Asher and the Seelie stood silent, ready to be dispatched, while Zahruk paced, his hands palming his weapons as the Princess of the Court of Nightmares watched him curiously. Everyone was prepared to do whatever it took to bring her home—everyone but me.

"Send riders out through the valley. Make it look as if we are searching for her. Blane, Remy, and Fyra, take to the skies and watch the shadows. We need to make it look real, but the boys are right. Kahleena made it easy for him to reach her, and until we know who he is, we don't make a move that could endanger her life. She believes he won't hurt her, and we have to assume she knows what she is doing."

"You want us to do *nothing*?" Ryder snapped.

"Nothing *yet*," I answered, sucking my bottom lip between my teeth as I looked into his eyes for strength.

"She's our daughter, and she's not even two yet!"

"Um, we're a tad older than that now," Cade said, frowning as he looked at Zander.

"I want the spies we employed last week out searching the entirety of Faery to learn what they can about the one who took Kahleena. Someone in this world knows who he is because he just walked into our home and took the

Princess of the High Court of Faery from right beneath our noses. It's personal to him. If we move too soon, we could force him to act out in anger or fear. I won't chance Kahleena's life like that. We could do more damage if we rush out to save her. Send the spies and the shadows to find her. Once we have more information, we will go get our daughter back safely."

CHAPTER THIRTY FOUR

TWO MONTHS LATER

LIFE HAD A WAY of reminding you that you held little control over the flow of it. The world wasn't yours, and it didn't owe you anything. You had to fight for what you wanted, and what you got out of life was what you'd put into it. I'd lost friends, family, and I knew I hadn't seen the last of death. From death came new life, and that was something that kept us moving forward.

Alden had gone back to the guild with Adrian at my request to begin healing the Pacific Northwest from the demons that were wreaking havoc. The hunters were finally ready to move forward and start hunting those who preyed upon the weak, and I was unwilling to leave Faery with Kahleena missing.

Scouts were out scouring the world for any sign of her, but in the month that she'd been missing, there had been no trace of her. I would remain here until she was brought back because I had to believe she would alert her brothers if she feared for her life.

It was daunting to have so much power and be unable to find my daughter. Ryder spent countless hours scouring the mountains around the palace for any sign of her or anyone hiding within them.

My gaze slipped to the glowing tree that illuminated the entire courtyard as arms wrapped around me and settled on my growing belly. Inhaling Ryder's enticing scent, I smiled while I studied the tiny fairies that had begun gathering around the Tree of Life, fueling it with their power as water rushed around its base, fed by the Fairy Pools.

"We will find her, Synthia."

"Eventually, when she wants to be found," I replied softly, placing my hands over his as the babe moved. "I have to believe she is okay, or I'll go mad. I prefer this pregnancy to go easy, and that he is born without turmoil surrounding him."

"Our unborn son will be fine. His momma is a warrior," Ryder growled, kissing my neck.

"Look at what we've built. It's the most beautiful thing in the world." We looked out over the meadows that separated the palace from the towns below. The sound of the flowing rivers filtered up to our balcony and helped to ease my worries.

"Not even close. The most beautiful thing in this world is right here in my arms, pregnant with my son growing within her belly."

"Shush it, Fairy." I laughed as his lips brushed against my bare shoulder.

Below us was the courtyard filled with elder tree sprouts that had seeded and begun to flourish. Malachi's tree form glowed, casting a deep blue iridescent hue that spread out over the land, feeding it renewed power, directly from the source to the entire world of Faery.

Tiny fairies danced in the night air, fluttering through the glowing energy until they hummed with the wild, rapid beat of their wings. It was ironic that a world that feared Malachi and left him in a pit now depended on him for its existence.

A small river had been formed to feed the trees and flowers that covered as far as the eye could see, and from the towering cliffs, a waterfall had been created to supply water into the river. I knew Ryder had built the waterfall for me since it mirrored the one I dove from during the Wild Hunt.

Twin statues marked the entrance to the gates of the courtyard, and beyond it, the sprawling meadows had begun to cover in greenery as we made our mark on the land, creating our own kingdom. Our perfect home.

The sides of the cliff had been pushed back, giving us enough space to create villages behind the palace that filled the sides of them, going deep into them to protect those who followed us here and had chosen to stay.

"Zahruk refuses to allow us to make him a stronghold. I think he fears the mural we promised to create for him," Ryder informed, chuckling as his breath fanned my neck. Grinning, I leaned my head back against his chest and sighed.

"Ristan and Zahruk have both offered to look for Kahleena, and they've been told to stand down. While they have listened to the order, they won't leave here until she is returned safely."

"Zahruk left this morning on a scouting mission. I don't think he is following your orders as well as you assume he is."

"I didn't think he would. Even as King of the Horde, he is loyal to us. She is family, and that is everything to him and us." I smiled, holding Ryder's hands against my belly as the babe kicked, causing him to chuckle.

"I have made a match for Zahruk, and he refused again."

I turned in Ryder's arms and studied his sinfully perfect features as he dropped his gaze to mine. I lifted on my toes, claiming his mouth softly before pulling away. He looked exhausted, but then everyone was these days.

It had been weeks since we'd taken our thrones, and the work was endless as we created a new way of life in Faery while worrying over Kahleena's safety. I was also concerned about Adam, who seemed more agitated as time moved on since I was unable to go to the Dark Kingdom to help him with his current problem.

Liam had refused to leave, demanding we do more to find Kahleena, but without any clues, or even knowing where to begin, searching for her was an endless guessing game. Then there was the fact that if we did find Kahleena and her captor felt cornered or threatened, he may end her life before we could get her back.

"Maybe it's time to stop pushing Zahruk to choose a bride, and let the bride choose him, Ryder. He is a king now, and women will try for his hand more than they have in the past. He will find his mate, but we cannot force it. Cailean needs a bride soon, too. He's sleeping his way through the entire court. Lachlan, as well, needs to find someone. These are the men you can still control. Zahruk, well, he will find someone once he forgives himself for what he did to Darynda. Until then, he won't be ready."

"I have forfeited the Wild Hunt to Zahruk," he said huskily. "You escaped it this time because, by the time it comes, you will be heavy with my son growing within you. That excites me more than any Wild Hunt could ever achieve."

"Your flattery will get you everywhere, Fairy."

"I was hoping so," he chuckled.

He lifted me, heading toward the bedroom that was large enough to hold an assembly. Placing me on the bed, he removed his shirt and his pants before he settled beside me, running his fingers over my abdomen.

"I couldn't have asked for a better ending than this, woman."

"It's happy," I snorted. "It's my happy fucked up ever after that I always wanted. You are my forever, Ryder. No matter what we did to get here or the horrors we have endured, I would do it all over again, knowing that I'd get to spend eternity with the man I love."

"Indeed, I would endure my entire life over knowing that all the pain and all the suffering would lead me to you and that you'd look so fucking sexy, heavy with my child growing within you."

"Ristan needs to stop helping you woo me," I whispered thickly as he leaned over to kiss me.

"I never listened to anything he said, other than using dirty as shit words to make you wet, which seems to be a great way to get you excited."

"Mother!"

"Kahleena?" I whispered through trembling lips, and Ryder stiffened beside me as I sat up.

"I was wrong! I was very wrong," she cried hysterically.

"Where are you?"

"I don't know, but he is going to kill *me. I have to get out of here!"*

"Show me," I demanded, but the vision was pitch-black as if she were in a dark ravine or some type of cell. "I can't see anything," I cried.

Dark, masculine laughter filled my head, and the vision blurred as a male with large wings and silver eyes filled my mind. *"You will never find your daughter. Kahleena is mine."* His lips curved into a sinful smile, filled with smug victory as I tried to see around him. *"Try me, goddess. I do not fear you. I look forward to meeting you soon."*

Everything faded, and Kahleena's connection severed as I exhaled a shuddered breath. "Call the Elite Guards. He's going to kill her, Ryder."

"To arms," he screamed, leaning over to kiss me as feet padded through the hallway leading to our bedroom. "I love you, Pet," he said, leaning over once more to place a kiss to my brow.

"I love you, too. I'm coming with you," I demanded, but he shook his head. "Ryder, this is our daughter."

"Yes, and you carry our son. You must stay here and defend the palace. I will find our daughter." He headed for the door, then turned, chuckling with an edge to it. "And we thought it would be boring after the war."

"Yeah, we probably jinxed ourselves with that one," I admitted as I glamoured on a dress and stood up slowly, holding my baby-bump as he kicked. "We didn't even make it two months before something happened," I groaned.

"You were worried about our life becoming boring. I told you it wouldn't be. This is us, and this is Faery. I will get Kahleena back, I promise. You need to let me find her, and when I return, I expect a hero's welcome home."

I rose and moved to the balcony as he left the room, slipping out through the courtyard as the men mounted their horses to find our missing princess. My heart leaped to my throat as Ryder mounted his warhorse once more, dressed in his new golden armor and helmet, topped with his crown. His cloak looked like liquid gold with an emblem of twin dragons on the back that matched the guards around him. Cade and Zander were outfitted like the guards and rode directly behind their father.

Turning in his saddle, Ryder looked back at me once more, then nodded as they slowly started out of the courtyard. I swallowed against the nausea that struggled to be freed from my throat. Kahleena would come home. How could she not, with a father willing to wage war against enemies unseen to protect her?

I watched Ryder and the boys until the lights of their torches turned into dim lights that I could hardly make out in the distance. The handmaidens stood silently behind me, waiting for orders. I turned slowly, staring at Meriel.

"Prepare the team to head to the guild. Inform the hunters that we have a new enemy. I want them scouring every inch of that world for my daughter. Inform Alden that, until told otherwise, finding Kahleena is his priority."

"You don't think she is here inside Faery?" one of the handmaidens asked.

"It's my daughter, and I won't take chances guessing in which world she is being held captive. I'd rather search them both and find her, than to only search Faery, and find out she is not here."

"As you wish, My Queen."

I turned back to the darkened night and said a silent prayer that everything would turn out alright, but this was our new reality. I would find my daughter. Even if that meant I had to rip worlds apart to discover her location to find out who was responsible.

I had my husband, My High King. I'd lived the best life I could while following the rules I'd always upheld. I'd come too far, endured too much to not be able to bring my baby home. Failure wasn't an option.

We might have been where my story ended, but hers was just starting. I would make sure it was the best beginning she could have because, in her short life, she'd been hidden from the world, and now it was time to let the world see her inner beauty shine, and show everyone how brightly she burned.

END

And They Lived Happily Messed Up Ever Freaking After

The End

I'll see you in Faery soon
Until Next Time

ABOUT THE AUTHOR

Amelia Hutchins is a *WSJ* and *USA Today Bestselling* author of the Monsters, The Fae Chronicles, and Nine Realm series. She is an admitted coffee addict who drinks magical potions of caffeine and turns them into magical worlds. She writes alpha-hole males and the alpha women who knock them on their arses, hard. Amelia doesn't write romance. She writes fast-paced books that go hard against traditional standards. Sometimes a story isn't about the romance; it's about rising to a challenge, breaking through them like wrecking balls, and shaking up entire worlds to discover who they really are. If you'd like to check out more of her work, or just hang out in an amazing tribe of people who enjoy rough men, and sharp women, join her at Author Amelia Hutchins Group on Facebook.

Stalker Links

Instagram: here

Facebook group: here

Facebook Author Page: here

Printed in Great Britain
by Amazon